Celtic Mysteries

Celtic Mysteries

Classic Ghost Stories for
Today's Readers

Edited by Kevin Carolan

Hodder & Stoughton
LONDON SYDNEY AUCKLAND

British Library Cataloguing in Publication Data
A record for this book is available from the British Library

ISBN 0 340 74567 3

Typeset by Avon Dataset Ltd, Bidford-on-Avon, Warks

Printed and bound in Great Britain by
The Guernsey Press Co. Ltd, Channel Isles

Hodder & Stoughton Ltd
A Division of Hodder Headline PLC
338 Euston Road
London NW1 3BH

To my father, Patrick Russell Sparkes-Carolan,
for first telling me stories of old Ireland

Contents

Acknowledgments

Every effort has been made to trace the owners of the copyright material in this book. It is the Editor's belief that the necessary permissions from publishers, authors, and authorised agents have been obtained. In the case of any question arising as to the use of any material, the Editor will be pleased to make the necessary corrections in future editions of the book.

The Editor gratefully acknowledges permission to reprint copyright material as follows:

A. M. Heath & Co Ltd on behalf of the Estate of the late Arthur Machen for 'The Novel of the Black Seal' copyright © 1947 by Arthur Machen

Sir Rupert Hart-Davis for 'Mrs Lunt' by Sir Hugh Walpole

Mrs Sonia Rolt for 'The House of Vengeance' by L.T.C. Rolt, currently in print in the classic edition of Rolt's stories *Sleep No More*, Sutton Publishing 1996 copyright © Sonia Rolt 1996

Mr D. Sealy for 'Teig O'Kane and the Corpse' by Douglas Hyde

Introduction

Wales, Ireland, Scotland, and Cornwall. Great places to go on holiday and relax in summer. If we came back to explore the Celtic lands in the long nights of winter we might get a very different impression: bleak moors; hostile mountains; rough, treacherous seas. In summer when we laze on the beach in the sun or trek through the peaceful countryside, we don't tend to notice the evidence of the past, such as the ruined churches and ancient stone circles which lie all around us. This raw landscape together with the testimony of history was the soil from which emerged some of the greatest ghost stories ever told.

For over two thousand years, until Columbus discovered America, the British Isles were the end of the known world, a cluster of islands sticking out into the vast immensity of the Atlantic Ocean. As such it was the last refuge of tribal peoples who fled famine or warfare on the continent of Europe; once here there was nowhere else to go. This was the reason behind the arrival of the Celtic peoples about 500 BC, and the Anglo-Saxon invasion a thousand years later. The latter pushed the Celts from the fertile soil of England to the rocky borders of Wales, Scotland, Cornwall (and Brittany), as well as the bleak mountains and barren bogs of Ireland.

The life of the Celtic peoples was a constant struggle with the forces of nature to extract a living from the land or the sea. Recent years have seen great interest in Celtic spirituality, a closeness to sea and air, to the rhythm of the seasons. Yet this had a darker side, as anyone caught in a mist in the Welsh mountains, or in a storm off the Scottish isles can testify. It also handed on traditions of things that are not natural. Ireland had the great fortune to be colonised neither by Romans nor by Anglo-Saxons, and therefore preserved living oral traditions dating back to the arrival of the Celts into Ireland. These tell of battle with the original inhabitants, a small, dark race called *Tuatha na Danaan*, believed to have supernatural powers. It is generally accepted that these legends are based on fact.

Contrary to popular belief, it was not the Celtic Druids who erected the great stone circles and barrows which cover the British Isles, but which are not seen elsewhere in Europe except on the tip of Brittany. Rather it was these original, dark inhabitants. (The Romans came across them in Scotland, noting their inhuman ferocity, and calling them the 'Picts' or painted ones.) This dark people was eventually wiped out. Yet it was felt that they lived on in their old stone circles, hill forts and barrows. They became known in Ireland and Scotland as the *Daoine Sidhe*, or people of the hills. The *Sidhe* were believed to be of lesser stature than ordinary men, and one derivation of the word 'leprechaun' is *luacharma'n*, or 'dwarf'. Yet forget the image of the smiling pixie – these were hostile spirits more inclined to curse than to bless. Nor should their old stones and monuments be touched, for they may have power in them yet. The Irish economy is currently booming, and Irish society is changing very rapidly. Yet it may be a mistake to ignore the older wisdom – an idea I have tried to develop in the story 'The Ghost in the Machine'.

Arthur Machen always felt the closeness of the unseen world to the world we know, growing up as he did in the shadow of the Black Mountains. As he wrote in his autobiography:

When my eyes were first opened in earliest childhood they had before them the vision of an enchanted land. As soon as I saw anything I saw *Tym Barlwm*, that mystic tumulus, the memorial of peoples that dwelt in that region before the Celts left the Land of Summer.

In the story 'The Novel of the Black Seal' included here, Machen explores the theme that this older race lives on among us in the mountain fastness of Wales.

I mentioned earlier the darkness of the 'little people'. It may be no more than coincidence that in Scots stories the devil is repeatedly described as 'the black man'. This does not mean someone of Negroid appearance, but rather a creature with the shape of a man, so dark that it almost radiates blackness. 'Wandering Willie's Tale' by Sir Walter Scott is one of the earliest ghost stories in the English language and still one of the best. It is worth noting that Major Weir, the noxious ape in the story, was actually the name of a real sorcerer who was burned for witchcraft in Edinburgh in 1681. Like 'Thrawn Janet' and 'Mary Burnett', it is told in Scots dialect.

'Thrawn Janet' was one of Stevenson's earliest stories (*thrawn* means 'twisted'), written when he and his wife were staying at a cold, bleak cottage in the Highlands. His wife Fanny later remembered him reading it to her:

> That evening is as clear in my memory as though it were yesterday – the dim light of our one candle, the shadows in the corners of the *'laong, laigh, mirk, chalmer, perishing cauld',* the driving rain on the roof close above our heads, and the gusts of wind that shook our windows. The very sound of the names – Murdock Soulis, The Hanging Shaw in the *beild* (shelter) of the Black Hill, Balweary in the vale of Dule – sent a *'cauld grue'* (cold shiver) along my bones. By the time the tale was finished my husband had fairly frightened himself, and we crept down the stairs clinging hand in hand like two scared children.

J.S. Le Fanu is one of the greatest figures in supernatural fiction.

With *Carmilla* he invented the modern vampire story some thirty years before his fellow countryman Bram Stoker wrote *Dracula*. (Stoker idolised Le Fanu, and 'The Judge's House' is based on an earlier story of Le Fanu's.) I have included two lesser-known Le Fanu stories here which emphasise his Irish roots. 'The Child that Went with the Fairies' illustrates the power of the 'little people'. Note the description of the defences of the poor peasant woman against the *Sidhe* – the ash trees, the horseshoes, the phials of holy water. Perhaps the most unique spirit of Ireland is the banshee, a weird wailing voice announcing a death to come, and normally associated with either the figure of a woman, or a dog. Le Fanu's 'The White Cat of Drumgunniol' explores the banshee theme, as does Mrs Riddell's 'Hertford O'Donnell's Warning'.

My Own Tale

R. H. Benson

I must confess that I was a little taken aback, on my last evening before leaving for England, when Monsignor Maxwell turned on me suddenly at supper, and exclaimed aloud that I had not yet contributed a story.

I protested that I had none; that I was a prosaic person; that there was some packing to be done; that my business was to write down the stories of other people; that I had my living to make and could not be liberal with my slender store; that it was a layman's function to sit at holy and learned priests' feet, not to presume to inform them on any subject under the sun.

But it was impossible to resist; it was pointed out to me that I had listened on false pretences if I had not intended to do my share, that telling a story did not hinder my printing it. And as a final argument it was declared that unless I occupied the chair that night, all present withdrew the leave that had already been given to me, to print their stories on my return to England.

There was nothing therefore to be done; and as I had already considered the possibility of the request, I did not occupy an unduly long time in pretending to remember what I had to say.

When I was seated upstairs, and the fire had been poked according to the ritual, and the matches had gone round, and buckled shoes protruded side by side with elastic-ankled boots, I began.

'This is a very unsatisfactory story,' I said, 'because it has no explanation of any kind. You will see that even theorising is

1

useless, when I have come to the end. It is simply a series of facts that I have to relate; facts that have no significance except one that is supernatural; but it is utterly out of the question even to guess at that significance

'It is unsatisfactory, too, for a second reason; and that is, that it is on such very hackneyed lines. It is simply one more instance of that very dreary class of phenomena, named haunted houses; except that there is no ghost in it. Its only claim to interest is, as I have said, the complete futility of any attempt to explain it.'

This was rather a pompous exordium, I felt; but I thought it best not to raise expectations too high; and I was therefore deliberately dull.

'Sixteen years ago from last summer, I was in Brittany. I had left school where I had laboured two hours a week at French for four years; and gone away in order to learn it in six weeks. This I accomplished very tolerably, in company with five other boys and an English tutor. Our general adventures are not relevant; but towards the end of our stay we went over one Sunday from Portrieux in order to see a French château about three miles away.

'It was a really glorious June day, hot and fresh and exhilarating; and we lunched delightfully in the woods with a funny fat little French Count and his wife who came with us from the hotel. It is impossible to imagine less uncanny circumstances or companions.

'After lunch we all went cheerfully to the house, whose chimneys we had seen among the trees.

'I knew nothing about the dates of houses; but the sort of impression I got of this house was that it was about three hundred years old; yet it may equally have been four, or two. I did not know then; and do not know now anything about it except its name, which I will not tell you; and its owner's name which I will not tell you either – and – and something else that I will tell you. We will call the owner, if you please, Comte Jean Marie the First. The house is built in two courts. The right-hand court through which we entered was then used as a farmyard; and I should think it probable that it is still so used. This court was exceedingly untidy. There was a large manure heap in the centre; and the servants' quarters to our right looked miserably cared for. There was a cart or two with shafts turned up, near the sheds that were built against the wall opposite the gate; and there was a sleepy old dog with bleared eyes that looked at us crossly from his kennel door.

'Our French friend went across to the servants' cottages with his moustache sticking out on either side of his face, and presently came back with two girls and the keys. There was no objection, he exclaimed dramatically, to our seeing the house!

'The girls went before us, and unlocked the iron gate that led to the second court; and we went through after them.

'Now, we had heard at the hotel that the family lived in Paris; but we were not prepared for the dreadful desolation of that inner court. The living part of the house was on our left; and what had once been a lawn to our right; but the house was discoloured and weather-stained; the green paint of the closed shutters and door was cracked and blistered; and the lawn resembled a wilderness; the grass was long and rank; there were rose trees trailing along the edge and across the path; and a sun dial on the lawn reminded me strangely of a drunken man petrified in the middle of a stagger. All this of course was what was to be expected in an adventure of this kind. It would do for a Christmas number.

'But it was not our business to criticise; and after a moment or two, we followed the girls who had unlocked the front door and were waiting for us to enter.

'One of them had gone before to open the shutters.

'It was not a large house, in spite of its name; and we had soon looked through the lower rooms of it. They, too, were what you would expect; the floors were beeswaxed; there were tables and chairs of a tolerable antiquity; a little damask on the walls, and so on. But what astonished us was the fact that none of the furniture was covered up, or even moved aside; and the dust lay, I should say, half-an-inch thick on every horizontal surface. I heard the Frenchman crying on his God in an undertone – as is the custom of Gauls – and finally he burst out with a question as to why the rooms were in this state.

'The girl looked at him stolidly. She was a stout, red-faced girl.

' "It is by the Count's orders," she said.

' "And does the Count not come here?" he asked.

' "No, sir."

'Then we all went upstairs. One of the girls had preceded us again and was waiting with her hand on the door to usher us in.

' "See here the room, the most splendid," she said; and threw the door open.

'It was certainly the most splendid room. It was a great bedchamber, hung with tapestry; there was some excellent chairs with carved legs; a fine gold-framed mirror tilted forward over the carved mantelpiece; and, above all, and standing out from the wall opposite the window, was a great four-poster bed, with an elaborately carved head to it, and heavy curtains hanging from the canopy.

'But what surprised us more than anything that we had yet seen, was the sight of the bed. Except for the dust that lay on it, it might have been slept in the night before. There were actually damask sheets upon it, thrown back, and two pillows – all grey with dust. These were not arranged but tumbled about, as a bed is in the morning before it is made.

'As I was looking at this, I heard a boy cry out from the washing-stand:

' "Why, it has had water in it," he said

'This did not sound exceptional for a basin, but we all crowded round to look; and it was perfectly true; there was a grey film around the interior of it; and when he had disturbed it (as a boy would) with his finger, we could see the flowered china beneath. The line came two-thirds of the way up the sides of the basin. It must have been partly filled with water a long while ago, which gradually evaporated, leaving its mark in the dust that must have collected there week after week.

'The Frenchman lost his patience at that.

' "My sacred something!" he said, "why is the room like this?"

'The same girl who had answered him before, answered him again in the same words. She was standing by the mantelpiece watching us.

' "It is the Count's orders," she said stolidly.

' "It is by the Count's orders that the bed is not made?" snapped the man.

' "Yes, sir," said the girl simply.

'Well, that did not content the Frenchman. He exhibited a couple of francs and began to question.

'This is the story that he got out of her. She told it quite simply.

'The last time that Count Jean Marie had come to the place, it had been for his honeymoon. He had come down from Paris with his bride. They had dined together downstairs, very happily and gaily; and had slept in the room in which we were at this moment. A message had been sent out for the carriage early next morning; and the couple had driven away with their trunks, leaving the servants behind. They had not returned, but a message had come from Paris that the house was to be closed. It appeared that the servants who had been left behind had had orders that nothing was to be tidied; even the bed was not to be made; the rooms were to be locked up and left as they were.

'The Frenchman had hardly been able to restrain himself as he heard this unconvincing story; though his wife shook him by the shoulders at each violent gesture that he made, and at the end he had put a torrent of questions.

' "Were they frightened then?"

' "I do not know, sir."

' "I mean the bride and bridegroom, fool!"

' "I do not know, sir."

' "Sacred name – and – and – why do you not know?"

' "I have never seen any of them, sir."

' "Not seen them! Why you said just now –"

' "Yes, sir; but I was not born then. It was thirty years ago."

'I do not think I have ever seen people so bewildered as we were. This was entirely unexpected. The Frenchman's jaw dropped; he licked his lips once or twice, and turned away. We all stood perfectly still a moment, and then we went out.'

I indulged myself with a pause, just here I was enjoying myself more than I thought I should. I had not told the story for some while; and had forgotten what a good one it was. Besides, it had the advantage of being perfectly true. Then I went on again, with a pleased consciousness of faces turned to me.

'I must tell you this,' I said, 'I was relieved to get out of the room. It is sixteen years ago now; and I may have embroidered on my own sensations; but my impression is that I had been just a little uncomfortable even before the girl's story. I don't think that I felt that there was any presence there, or anything of that kind. It was rather the opposite; it was the feeling of an extraordinary emptiness.'

'Like a Catholic cathedral in Protestant hands,' put in a voice.

'It was very like that,' I said, 'and had, too, the same kind of pathos and terror that one feels in the presence of a child's dead body. It is unnaturally empty, and yet significant; and one does not quite know what it signifies.'

I paused again.

'Well, Reverend Fathers; that is the first Act. We went back to Portrieux: we made inquiries and got no answer. All shrugged their shoulders and said they did not know.

'There were no tales of the bride's hair turning white in the night, or of any curse or ghost or noises or lights. It was just as I have told you. Then we went back to England; and the curtain came down.

'Now, generally, such curtains have no resurrection. I suppose we have all had fifty experiences of first Acts; and we do not know to this day whether the whole play is a comedy or a tragedy; or even whether the play has been written at all.'

'Do not be modern and allusive, Mr Benson,' said Monsignor Maxwell.

'I beg your pardon, Monsignor; I will not. I forgot myself. Well, here is the second Act. There are only two; and this is a much shorter one.

'Nine years later I was in Paris; staying in the Rue Picot with some Americans. A French friend of theirs was to be married to a man; and I went to the wedding at the Madeleine. It was – well, it was like all other weddings at the Madeleine. No description can be adequate to the appearance of the officiating clergyman and the altar and the bridesmaids and the French gentlemen with polished boots and butterfly ties, and the conversation, and the gaiety, and the general impression of a confectioner's shop and a milliner's and a salon and a holy church. I observed the bride and bridegroom and forgot their names for the twentieth time, and exchanged some remarks in the sacristy with a leader of society who looked like a dissipated priest; with my eyes starting out of my head in my anxiety not to commit a *solécisme* or a *barbarisme*. And then we went home again.

'On the way home we discussed the honeymoon. The pair were going down to a country house in Brittany. I inquired the name of it; and of course it was the château I had visited nine years before. It had been lent them by Count Jean Marie the Second. The gentleman resided in England, I heard, in order to escape the conscription; he was a connection of the bride's; and was about thirty years of age.

'Well, of course I was interested; and made inquiries and related my adventure. The Americans were mildly interested too, but not excited. Thirty-nine years is ancient history to that energetic nation. But two days afterwards they were excited. One of the girls came into *déjeuner*; and said that she had met the bride and bridegroom dining together in the Bois. They had seemed perfectly well, and had saluted her politely. It seemed that they had come back to Paris after one night at the château, exactly as another bride and bridegroom had done thirty-nine years before.

'Before I finish, let me sum up the situation.

'In neither case was there apparently any shocking incident; and yet something had been experienced that broke up plans and sent away immediately from a charming house and country two pairs of persons who had deliberately formed the intention of living there for a while. In both cases the persons in question had come back to Paris.

'I need hardly say that I managed to call with my friends upon the bride and bridegroom; and, at the risk of being impertinent, asked the bride point-blank why they had changed their plans and come back to town.

'She looked at me without a trace of horror in her eyes, and smiled a little.

' "It was *triste*," she said, "a little *triste*. We thought we would come away; we desired crowds." '

I paused again

' "We desired crowds," ' I repeated. 'You remember, Reverend Fathers, that I had experienced a sense of loneliness even with my friends during five minutes spent in that upstairs room. I can only suppose that if I had remained longer I should have experienced such a further degree of that sensation that I should have felt exactly as those two pairs of brides and bridegrooms felt; and have come away immediately. I might even, if I had been in authority, have given orders that nothing was to be touched except my own luggage.'

'I do not understand that,' said one Father, looking puzzled.

'Nor do I altogether,' I answered, 'but I think I perceive it to be a fact for all that. One might feel that one was an intruder; that one had meddled with something that desired to be left alone, and that one had better not meddle further in any kind of way.'

'I suppose you went down there again,' observed Monsignor Maxwell.

'I did, a fortnight afterwards. There was only one girl left; the other was married and gone away. She did not remember me; it was nine years ago; and she was a little redder in the face and a little more stolid.

'The lawn had been clipped and mown, but was beginning to grow rank again. Then I went upstairs with her. The room was comparatively clean; there was water in the basin; and clean sheets on the bed; but there was just a little film of dust lying on everything. I pretended I knew nothing and asked questions; and I was told exactly the same story as I had heard nine years before; only this time the date was only a fortnight ago.

'When she had finished, she added:

' "It happened so once before, sir: before I was born."

' "Do you understand it?" I said.

' "No, sir; the house is a little *triste*, perhaps. Do you think so, sir?"

'I said that perhaps it was. Then I gave her two francs and came away.

'That is all, Reverend Fathers.'

There was silence for a minute. Then one listener made what I consider a tactless remark.

'Bah! that does not terrify me,' he said.

' "Terrify" is certainly not the word,' remarked a second.

'I am not quite so sure about *that*,' ended Monsignor Maxwell.

The Botathen Ghost

R. S. Hawker

There was something very painful and peculiar in the position of
the clergy in the west of England throughout the seventeenth
century. The Church of those days was in a transitory state, and
her ministers, like her formularies, embodied a strange mixture
of the old belief with the new interpretation. Their wide severance
also from the great metropolis of life and manners, the city of
London (which in those times was civilised England, much as
the Paris of our own day is France), divested the Cornish clergy
in particular of all personal access to the masterminds of their
age and body. Then, too, the barrier interposed by the rude rough
roads of their country, and by their abode in wilds that were
almost inaccessible, rendered the existence of a bishop rather a
doctrine suggested to their belief than a fact revealed to the actual
vision of each in his generation. Hence it came to pass that the
Cornish clergyman, insulated within his own limited sphere,
often without even the presence of a country squire (and un-
checked by the influence of the Fourth Estate – for until the
beginning of this nineteenth century, *Flindell's Weekly Miscel-
lany*, distributed from house to house from the pannier of a mule,
was the only light of the West), became developed about middle
life into an original mind and man, sole and absolute within his
parish boundary, eccentric when compared with his brethren in
civilised regions, and yet, in German phrase, 'a whole and
seldom man' in his dominion of souls. He was 'the parson,' in
canonical phrase – that is to say, The Person, the somebody of

consequence among his own people. These men were not, however, smoothed down into a monotonous aspect of life and manners by this remote and secluded existence. They imbibed, each in his own peculiar circle, the hue of surrounding objects, and were tinged into a distinctive colouring and character by many a contrast of scenery and people. There was the 'light of other days,' the curate by the sea-shore, who professed to check the turbulence of the 'smugglers' landing' by his presence on the sands, and who 'held the lantern' for the guidance of his flock when the nights were dark, as the only proper ecclesiastical part he could take in the proceedings. He was soothed and silenced by the gift of a keg of hollands or a chest of tea. There was the merry minister of the mines, whose cure was honeycombed by the underground men. He must needs have been artist and poet in his way, for he had to enliven his people three or four times a year, by mastering the arrangements of a 'guary,' or religious mystery, which was duly performed in the topmost hollow of a green barrow or hill, of which many survive, scooped out into vast amphitheatres and surrounded by benches of turf which held two thousand spectators. Such were the historic plays, 'The Creation' and 'Noe's Flood,' which still exist in the original Celtic as well as the English text, and suggest what critics and antiquaries these Cornish curates, masters of such revels, must have been – for the native language of Cornwall did not lapse into silence until the end of the seventeenth century. Then, moreover, here and there would be one parson more learned than his kind in the mysteries of a deep and thrilling lore of peculiar fascination. He was a man so highly honoured at college for natural gifts and knowledge of learned books which nobody else could read, that when he 'took his second orders' the bishop gave him a mantle of scarlet silk to wear upon his shoulders in church, and his lordship had put such power into it that, when the parson had it rightly on, he could 'govern any ghost or evil spirit,' and even 'stop an earthquake.'

Such a powerful minister, in combat with supernatural

visitations, was one Parson Rudall, of Launceston, whose existence and exploits we gather from the local tradition of his time, from surviving letters and other memoranda, and indeed from his own 'diurnal' which fell by chance into the hands of the present writer. Indeed the legend of Parson Rudall and the Botathen Ghost will be recognised by many Cornish people as a local remembrance of their boyhood.

It appears, then, from the diary of this learned master of the grammar school – for such was his office as well as perpetual curate of the parish – 'that a pestilential disease did break forth in our town in the beginning of the year AD 1665; yea, and it likewise invaded my school, insomuch that therewithal certain of the chief scholars sickened and died.' 'Among others who yielded to the malign influence was Master John Eliot, the eldest son and the worshipful heir of Edward Eliot, Esquire, of Trebursey, a stripling of sixteen years of age, but of uncommon parts and hopeful ingenuity. At his own especial motion and earnest desire I did consent to preach his funeral sermon.' It should be remembered here that, howsoever strange and singular it may sound to us that a mere lad should formally solicit such a performance at the hands of his master, it was in consonance with the habitual usage of those times. The old services for the dead had been abolished by law, and in the stead of sacrament and ceremony, month's mind and year's mind, the sole substitute which survived was the general desire 'to partake,' as they called it, of a posthumous discourse, replete with lofty eulogy and flattering remembrance of the living and the dead. The diary proceeds:

'I fulfilled my undertaking, and preached over the coffin in the presence of a full assemblage of mourners and lachrymose friends. An ancient gentleman, who was then and there in the church, a Mr. Bligh, of Botathen, was much affected with my discourse, and he was heard to repeat to himself certain parentheses therefrom, especially a phrase from Maro Virgilius, which I had applied to the deceased youth, *"Et puer ipse fuit cantari dignus."*

'The cause wherefore this old gentleman was moved by my

applications, was this: He had a firstborn and only son – a child who, but a very few months before, had been not unworthy the character I drew of young Master Eliot, but who, by some strange accident, had of late quite fallen away from his parent's hopes, and become moody, and sullen, and distraught. When the funeral obsequies were over, I had no sooner come out of church than I was accosted by this aged parent, and he besought me incontinently, with a singular energy, that I would resort with him forthwith to his abode at Botathen that very night; nor could I have delivered myself from his importunity, had not Mr. Eliot urged his claim to enjoy my company at his own house. Hereupon I got loose, but not until I had pledged a fast assurance that I would pay him, faithfully, an early visit the next day.'

'The Place,' as it was called, of Botathen, where old Mr. Bligh resided, was a low-roofed gabled manor-house of the fifteenth century, walled and mullioned, and with clustered chimneys of dark-grey stone from the neighbouring quarries of Ventor-gan. The mansion was flanked by a pleasance or enclosure in one space, of garden and lawn, and it was surrounded by a solemn grove of stag-horned trees. It had the sombre aspect of age and of solitude, and looked the very scene of strange and supernatural events. A legend might well belong to every gloomy glade around, and there must surely be a haunted room somewhere within its walls. Hither, according to his appointment, on the morrow, Parson Rudall betook himself. Another clergyman, as it appeared, had been invited to meet him, who, very soon after his arrival, proposed a walk together in the pleasance, on the pretext of showing him, as a stranger, the walks and trees, until the dinner-bell should strike. There, with much prolixity, and with many a solemn pause, his brother minister proceeded to 'unfold the mystery.'

A singular infelicity, he declared, had befallen young Master Bligh, once the hopeful heir of his parents and of the lands of Botathen. Whereas he had been from childhood a blithe and merry boy, 'the gladness,' like Isaac of old, of his father's age, he had suddenly, and of late, become morose and silent – nay, even austere and stern – dwelling apart, always solemn, often in tears. The lad had at first repulsed all questions as to the origin of this great change, but of late he had yielded to the importune researches of his parents, and had disclosed the secret cause. It appeared that he resorted every day, by a pathway across the fields, to this very clergyman's house, who had charge of his education, and grounded him in the studies suitable to his age. In the course of his daily walk he had to pass a certain heath or down where the road wound along through tall blocks of granite with open spaces of grassy sward between. There in a certain spot, and always in one and the same place, the lad declared that he encountered, every day, a woman with a pale and troubled face, clothed in a long loose garment of frieze, with one hand always stretched forth, and the other pressed against her side. Her name, he said, was Dorothy Dinglet, for he had known her well from his childhood, and she often used to come to his parents' house; but that which troubled him was, that she had now been dead three years, and he himself had been with the neighbours at her burial; so that, as the youth alleged, with great simplicity, since he had seen her body laid in the grave, this that he saw every day must needs be her soul or ghost. 'Questioned again and again,' said the clergyman, 'he never contradicts himself; but he relates the same and the simple tale as a thing that cannot be gainsaid. Indeed, the lad's observance is keen and calm for a boy of his age. The hair of the appearance, sayeth he, is not like anything alive, but it is so soft and light that it seemeth to melt away while you look; but her eyes are set, and never blink – no, not when the sun shineth full upon her face. She maketh no steps, but seemeth to swim along the top of the grass; and her hand, which is stretched out alway, seemeth to point at something far away, out of sight. It is her continual coming, for she never faileth to meet him, and to pass on, that hath quenched his spirits; and although he never seeth her by night, yet cannot he get his natural rest.'

'Thus far the clergyman; whereupon the dinner clock did sound, and we went into the house. After dinner, when young Master Bligh had withdrawn with his tutor, under excuse of their books, the parents did forthwith beset me as to my thoughts about their son. Said I, warily, "The case is strange but by no means impossible. It is one that I will study, and fear not to handle, if the lad will be free with me, and fulfil all that I desire." The mother was overjoyed, but I perceived that old Mr. Bligh turned pale, and was downcast with some thought which, however, he did not express. Then they bade that Master Bligh should be called to meet me in the pleasance forthwith. The boy came, and he rehearsed to me his tale with an open countenance, and, withal, a pretty modesty of speech. Verily he seemed *ingenui vultus puer ingenuique pudoris*. Then I signified to him my purpose. "Tomorrow," said I, "we will go together to the place; and if, as I doubt not, the woman shall appear, it will be for me to proceed according to knowledge, and by rules laid down in my books." '

The unaltered scenery of the legend still survives, and, like the field of the forty footsteps in another history, the place is still visited by those who take interest in the supernatural tales of old. The pathway leads along a moorland waste, where large masses of rock stand up here and there from the grassy turf, and clumps of heath and gorse weave their tapestry of golden and purple garniture on every side. Amidst all these, and winding along between the rocks, is a natural footway worn by the scant, rare tread of the village traveller. Just midway, a somewhat larger stretch than usual of green sod expands, which is skirted by the path, and which is still identified as the legendary haunt of the phantom, by the name of Parson Rudall's Ghost.

But we must draw the record of the first interview between the minister and Dorothy from his own words. 'We met,' thus he writes, 'in the pleasance very early, and before any others in the house were awake; and together the lad and myself proceeded towards the field. The youth was quite composed, and carried his Bible under his arm, from whence he read to me verses, which he said he had lately picked out, to have always in his mind. These were Job vii. 14, "Thou scarest me with dreams, and terrifiest me through visions"; and Deuteronomy xxviii. 67, "In the morning thou shalt say, Would to God it were evening, and in the evening thou shalt say, Would to God it were morning; for the fear of thine heart wherewith thou shalt fear, and for the sight of thine eyes which thou shalt see."

'I was much pleased with the lad's ingenuity in these pious applications, but for mine own part I was somewhat anxious and out of cheer. For aught I knew this might be a *dæmonium meridianum*, the most stubborn spirit to govern and guide that any man can meet, and the most perilous withal. We had hardly reached the accustomed spot, when we both saw her at once gliding towards us; punctually as the ancient writers describe the motion of their "lemures, which swoon along the ground, neither marking the sand nor bending the herbage." The aspect of the woman was exactly that which had been related by the lad. There was the pale and stony face, the strange and misty hair, the eyes firm and fixed, that gazed, yet not on us, but on something that they saw far, far away; one hand and arm stretched out, and the other grasping the girdle of her waist. She floated along the field like a sail upon a stream, and glided past the spot where we stood, pausingly. But so deep was the awe that overcame me, as I stood there in the light of day, face to face with a human soul separate from her bones and flesh, that my heart and purpose both failed me. I had resolved to speak to the spectre in the appointed form of words, but I did not. I stood like one amazed and speechless, until she had passed clean out of sight. One thing remarkable came to pass. A spaniel dog, the favourite of young Master Bligh, had followed us, and lo! when the woman drew nigh, the poor creature began to yell and bark piteously, and ran backward and away, like a thing dismayed and appalled. We returned to the house, and after I had said all that I could to pacify the lad, and to soothe the aged people, I took my leave for that time, with a promise that when I had fulfilled certain business elsewhere, which I then alleged, I would return and take orders to assuage these disturbances and their cause.

'January 7, 1665 – At my own house, I find, by my books, what is expedient to be done; and then Apage, Sathanas!

'January 9, 1665 – This day I took leave of my wife and family, under pretext of engagements elsewhere, and made my secret journey to our diocesan city, wherein the good and venerable bishop then abode.

'January 10 – *Deo gratias*, in safe arrival in Exeter; craved and obtained immediate audience of his lordship; pleading it was for counsel and admonition on a weighty and pressing cause; called to the presence; made obeisance; then and by command stated my case – the Botathen perplexity – which I moved with strong and earnest instances and solemn asseverations of that which I had myself seen and heard. Demanded by his lordship, what was the succour that I had come to entreat at his hands. Replied, licence for my exorcism, that so I might, ministerially, allay this spiritual visitant, and thus render to the living and the dead release from this surprise. "But," said our bishop, "on what authority do you allege that I am entrusted with faculty so to do? Our Church, as is well known, hath abjured certain branches of her ancient power, on grounds of perversion and abuse." "Nay, my lord," I humbly answered, "under favour, the seventy-second of the canons ratified and enjoined on us, the clergy, anno Domini 1604, doth expressly provide, that 'no minister, *unless he hath* the licence of his diocesan bishop, shall essay to exorcise a spirit, evil or good.' Therefore it was," I did here mildly allege, "that I did not presume to enter on such a work without lawful privilege under your lordship's hand and seal." Hereupon did our wise and learned bishop, sitting in his chair, condescend upon the theme at some length with many gracious interpretations from ancient writers and from Holy Scriptures, and I did humbly rejoin and reply, till the upshot was that he did call in his secretary and command him to draw the aforesaid faculty, forthwith and without further delay, assigning him a form, insomuch that the matter was incontinently done; and after I had disbursed into the secretary's hands certain moneys for signitary purposes, as the manner of such officers hath always been, the bishop did himself affix his signature under the *sigillum* of his see, and deliver the document into my hands. When I knelt down to receive his benediction, he softly said, "Let it be secret, Mr. R. Weak brethren! weak brethren!" '

This interview with the bishop, and the success with which he vanquished his lordship's scruples, would seem to have confirmed Parson Rudall very strongly in his own esteem, and to have invested him with that courage which he evidently lacked at his first encounter with the ghost.

The entries proceed: 'January 11, 1665 – Therewithal did I hasten home and prepare my instruments, and cast my figures for the onset of the next day. Took out my ring of brass, and put it on the index finger of my right hand, with the *scutum Davidis* traced thereon.

'January 12, 1665 – Rode into the gateway at Botathen, armed at all points, but not with Saul's armour, and ready. There is danger from the demons, but so there is in the surrounding air every day. At early morning then, and alone – for so the usage ordains – I betook me towards the field. It was void, and I had thereby due time to prepare. First I paced and measured out my circle on the grass. Then I did mark my pentacle in the very midst, and at the intersection of the five angles I did set up and fix my crutch of *raun* (rowan). Lastly, I took my station south, at the true line of the meridian, and stood facing due north. I waited and watched for a long time. At last there was a kind of trouble in the air, a soft and rippling sound, and all at once the shape appeared, and came on towards me gradually. I opened my parchment-scroll, and read aloud the command. She paused, and seemed to waver and doubt; stood still; then I rehearsed the sentence again, sounding out every syllable like a chant. She drew near my ring, but halted at first outside, on the brink. I sounded again, and now at the third time I gave the signal in

Syriac – the speech which is used, they say, where such ones dwell and converse in thoughts that glide.

'She was at last obedient, and swam into the midst of the circle, and there stood still, suddenly. I saw, moreover, that she drew back her pointing hand. All this while I do confess that my knees shook under me, and the drops of sweat ran down my flesh like rain. But now, although face to face with the spirit, my heart grew calm, and my mind was composed. I knew that the pentacle would govern her, and the ring must bind, until I gave the word. Then I called to mind the rule laid down of old, that no angel or fiend, no spirit, good or evil, will ever speak until they have been first spoken to. NB – This is the great law of prayer. God Himself will not yield reply until man hath made vocal entreaty, once and again. So I went on to demand, as the books advise; and the phantom made answer, willingly. Questioned wherefore not at rest. Unquiet, because of a certain sin. Asked what, and by whom. Revealed it; but it is *sub sigillo*, and therefore *nefas dictu*; more anon. Enquired, what sign she could give that she was a true spirit and not a false fiend. Stated, before next Yule-tide a fearful pestilence would lay waste the land and myriads of souls would be loosened from their flesh, until, as she piteously said, "our valleys will be full." Asked again, why she so terrified the lad. Replied: "It is the law: we must seek a youth or a maiden of clean life, and under age, to receive messages and admonitions." We conversed with many more words, but it is not lawful for me to set them down. Pen and ink would degrade and defile the thoughts she uttered, and which my mind received that day. I broke the ring and she passed, but to return once more next day. At evensong, a long discourse with that ancient transgressor, Mr. B. Great horror and remorse; entire atonement and penance; whatsoever I enjoin; full acknowledgment before pardon.

'January 13, 1665 – At sunrise I was again in the field. She came in at once, and, as it seemed, with freedom. Enquired if she knew my thoughts, and what I was going to relate? Answered,

"Nay, we only know what we perceive and hear; we cannot see the heart." Then I rehearsed the penitent words of the man she had come up to denounce, and the satisfaction he would perform. Then said she, "Peace in our midst." I went through the proper forms of dismissal, and fulfilled all as it was set down and written in my memoranda; and then, with certain fixed rites, I did dismiss that troubled ghost, until she peacefully withdrew, gliding towards the west. Neither did she ever afterward appear, but was allayed until she shall come in her second flesh to the valley of Armageddon on the last day.'

These quaint and curious details from the 'diurnal' of a simple-hearted clergyman of the seventeenth century appear to betoken his personal persuasion of the truth of what he saw and said, although the statements are strongly tinged with what some may term the superstition, and others the excessive belief, of those times. It is a singular fact, however, that the canon which author-ises exorcism under episcopal licence is still a part of the ecclesi-astical law of the Anglican Church, although it might have a singular effect on the nerves of certain of our bishops if their clergy were to resort to them for the faculty which Parson Rudall obtained. The general facts stated in his diary are to this day matters of belief in that neighborhood; and it has been always accounted a strong proof of the veracity of the Parson and the Ghost, that the plague, fatal to so many thousands, did break out in London at the close of that very year. We may well excuse a triumphant entry, on a subsequent page of the 'diurnal,' with the date of July 10, 1665: 'How sorely must the infidels and heretics of this generation be dismayed when they know that this Black Death, which is now swallowing its thousands in the streets of the great city, was foretold six months agone, under the exor-cisms of a country minister, by a visible and suppliant ghost! And what pleasures and improvements do such deny themselves who scorn and avoid all opportunity of intercourse with souls separate, and the spirits, glad and sorrowful, which inhabit the unseen world!'

Mrs Lunt

Sir Hugh Walpole

I

'Do you believe in ghosts?' I asked Runciman. I had to ask him
this very platitudinous question more because he was so difficult
a man to spend an hour with rather than for any other reason.
You know his books, perhaps, or more probably you don't know
them – *The Running Man*, *The Elm Tree*, and *Crystal and
Candlelight*. He is one of those little men who are constant
enough in this age of immense over-production of books, men
who publish every autumn their novel, who arouse by that
publication in certain critics eager appreciation and praise, who
have a small and faithful public, whose circulation is very small
indeed, who, when you meet them have little to say, are often
shy and nervous, pessimistic and remote from daily life. Such
men do fine work, are made but little of in their own day, and
perhaps fifty years after their death are rediscovered by some
digging critic and become a sort of cult with a new generation.

I asked Runciman that question because, for some unknown
reason, I had invited him to dinner at my flat, and was now faced
with a long evening filled with that most tiresome of all conversa-
tions, talk that dies every two minutes and has to be revived with
terrific exertions. Being myself a critic, and having on many
occasions praised Runciman's work, he was the more nervous
and shy with me; had I abused it, he would perhaps have had
plenty to say – he was that kind of man. But my question was a

lucky one: it roused him instantly, his long, bony body became full of a new energy, his eyes stared into a rich and exciting reminiscence, he spoke without pause, and I took care not to interrupt him. He certainly told me one of the most astounding stories I have ever heard. Whether it was true or not I cannot, of course, say: these ghost stories are nearly always at second or third hand. I had, at any rate, the good fortune to secure mine from the source. Moreover, Runciman was not a liar: he was too serious for that. He himself admitted that he was not sure, at this distance of time, as to whether the thing had gained as the years passed. However, here it is as he told it.

'It was some fifteen years ago,' he said. 'I went down to Cornwall to stay with Robert Lunt. Do you remember his name? No, I suppose you do not. He wrote several novels; some of those half-and-half things that are not quite novels, not quite poems, rather mystical and picturesque, and are the very devil to do well. De la Mare's *Return* is a good example of the kind of thing. I had reviewed somewhere his last book, and reviewed it favourably, and received from him a really touching letter showing that the man was thirsting for praise, and also, I fancied, for company. He lived in Cornwall somewhere on the sea coast, and his wife had died twelve months before; he said he was quite alone there, and would I come and spend Christmas with him; he hoped I would not think this impertinent; he expected that I would be engaged already, but he could not resist the chance. Well, I wasn't engaged; far from it. If Lunt was lonely, so was I; if Lunt was a failure, so was I; I was touched, as I have said, by his letter, and I accepted his invitation. As I went down in the train to Penzance I wondered what kind of a man he would be. I had never seen any photographs of him; he was not the sort of author whose picture the newspapers publish. He must be, I fancied, about my own age – perhaps rather older. I know when we're lonely how some of us are for ever imagining that a friend will somewhere turn up, that ideal friend who will understand all one's feelings, who will give one affection without being sentimental, who will take interest in one's affairs without being impertinent – yes, the sort of friend one never finds.

'I fancy that I became quite romantic about Lunt before I reached Penzance. We would talk, he and I, about all those literary questions that seemed to me at that time so absorbing; we would perhaps often stay together and even travel abroad on those little journeys that are so swiftly melancholy when one is alone, so delightful when one has a perfect companion. I imagined him as spare and delicate and refined, with a sort of wistfulness and rather childish play of fancy. We had both, so far, failed in our careers, but perhaps together we would do great things.

'When I arrived at Penzance it was almost dark, and the snow, threatened all day by an overhanging sky, had begun gently and timorously to fall. He had told me in his letter that a fly would be at the station to take me to his house; and there I found it – a funny old weather-beaten carriage with a funny old weather-beaten driver. At this distance of time my imagination may have created many things, but I fancy that from the moment I was shut into that carriage some dim suggestion of fear and apprehension attacked me. I fancy that I had some absurd impulse to get out of the thing and take the night train back to London again – an action that would have been very unlike me, as I had always a sort of obstinate determination to carry through anything that I had begun. In any case, I was uncomfortable in that carriage; it had, I remember, a nasty, musty smell of damp straw and stale eggs, and it seemed to confine me so closely as though it were determined that, once I was in, I should never get out again. Then, it was bitterly cold; I was colder during that drive than I have ever been before or since. It was that penetrating cold that seems to pierce your very brain, so that I could not think with any clearness, but only wish again and again that I hadn't come. Of course, I could see nothing – only feel the jolt over the uneven road – and once and again we seemed to fight our way through dark paths, because I could feel the overhanging branches of the trees knock against the cab with mysterious taps, as though they were trying to give me some urgent message.

'Well, I mustn't make more of it than the facts allow, and I mustn't see into it all the significance of the events that followed. I only know that as the drive proceeded I became more and more miserable: miserable with the cold of my body, the misgivings of my imagination, the general loneliness of my case.

'At last we stopped. The old scarecrow got slowly off his box, with many heavings and sighings, came to the cab door, and, with great difficulty and irritating slowness, opened it. I got out of it, and found that the snow was now falling very heavily indeed, and that the path was lightened with its soft, mysterious glow. Before me was a humped and ungainly shadow: the house that was to receive me. I could make nothing of it in that darkness, but only stood there shivering while the old man pulled at the door-bell with a sort of frantic energy as though he were anxious to be rid of the whole job as quickly as possible and return to his own place. At last, after what seemed an endless time, the door opened, and an old man, who might have been own brother to the driver, poked out his head. The two old men talked together, and at last my bag was shouldered and I was permitted to come in out of the piercing cold.

'Now this, I know, is not imagination. I have never at any period of my life hated at first sight so vigorously any dwelling-place into which I have ever entered as I did that house. There was nothing especially disagreeable about my first vision of the hall. It was a large, dark place, lit by two dim lamps, cold and cheerlesss; but I got no particular impression of it because at once I was conducted out of it, led along a passage, and then introduced into a room which was, I saw at once, as warm and comfortable as the hall had been dark and dismal. I was, in fact, so eagerly pleased at the large and leaping fire that I moved towards it at once, not noting, at the first moment, the presence of my host, and when I did see him I could not believe that it was he. I have told you the kind of man that I had expected; but, instead of the spare, sensitive artist, I found facing me a large, burly man, over six foot, I should fancy, as broad-shouldered as he was tall, giving evidence of great muscular strength, the lower part of his face hidden by a black, pointed beard.

'But if I was astonished at the sight of him, I was doubly amazed when he spoke. His voice was thin and piping, like that of some old woman, and the little nervous gestures that he made with his hands were even more feminine than his voice. But I had to allow, perhaps, for excitement, for excited he was; he came up to me, took my hand in both of his, and held it as though he would never let it go. In the evening, when we sat over our coffee, he apologized for this. "I was so glad to to see you," he said; "I couldn't believe that really you would come; you are the first visitor of my own kind that I have had here for ever so long. I was ashamed indeed of asking you, but I had to snatch at the chance – it means so much to me."

'His eagerness, in fact, had something disturbing about it; something pathetic, too. He simply couldn't do too much for me: he led me through funny crumbling old passages, the boards creaking under us at every step, up some dark stairs, the walls hung, so far as I could see in the dim light, with faded yellow photographs of places, and showed me into my room with a deprecating agitated gesture as though he expected me at the first sight of it to turn and run. I didn't like it any more than I liked the rest of the house; but that was not my host's fault. He had done everything he possibly could for me: there was a large fire flaming in the open fire-place, there was a hot bottle, as he explained to me, in the big four-poster bed, and the old man who had opened the door to me was already taking my clothes out of my bag and putting them away. Lunt's nervousness was almost sentimental. He put both his hands on my shoulders and said, looking at me pleadingly: "If you only knew what it is for me to have you here, the talks we'll have. Well, well, I must leave you. You'll come down and join me, won't you, as soon as you can?"

'It was then, when I was left alone in my room, that I had my second impulse to flee. Four candles in tall old silver candlesticks were burning brightly, and these, with the blazing fire, gave plenty of light; and yet the room was in some way dim, as though a faint smoke pervaded it, and I remember that I went to one of the old lattice windows and threw it open for a moment as though I felt stifled. Two things quickly made me close it. One was the intense cold which, with a fluttering scamper of snow, blew into the room; the other was the quite deafening roar of the sea, which seemed to fling itself at my very face as though it wanted to knock me down. I quickly shut the window, turned round, and saw an old woman standing just inside the door. Now every story of this kind depends for its interest on its verisimilitude. Of course, to make my tale convincing I should be able to prove to you that I saw that old woman; but I can't. I can only urge upon you my rather dreary reputation of probity. You know that I'm a teetotaller, and always have been, and, most important evidence of all, I was not expecting to see an old woman; and yet I hadn't the least doubt in the world but that it was an old woman I saw. You may talk about shadows, clothes hanging on the back of the door, and the rest of it. I don't know. I've no theories about this story, I'm not a spiritualist, I don't know that I believe in anything especially, except the beauty of beautiful things. We'll put it, if you like, that I fancied that I saw an old woman, and my fancy was so strong that I can give you to this day a pretty detailed account of her appearance. She wore a black silk dress and on her breast was a large, ugly, gold brooch; she had black hair, brushed back from her forehead and parted down the middle; she wore a collar of some white stuff round her throat; her face was one of the wickedest, most malignant, and furtive that I have ever seen – very white in colour. She was shrivelled enough now, but might once have been rather beautiful. She stood there quietly, her hands at her side. I thought that she was some kind of housekeeper. "I have everything I want, thank you," I said. "What a splendid fire!" I turned for a moment towards it, and when I looked back she was gone. I thought nothing of this, of course, but drew up an old chair covered with green faded tapestry, and thought that I would read a little from some book that I had brought down with me before I went to join my host. The fact was that I was not very intent upon joining him before I must. I didn't like him. I had already made up my mind that I would find some excuse to return to London as soon as possible. I can't tell you why I didn't like him, except that I was myself very reserved and had, like many Englishmen, a great distrust of demonstrations, especially from another man. I hadn't cared for the way in which he had put his hands on my shoulders, and I felt perhaps that I wouldn't be able to live up to all his eager excitement about me.

'I sat in my chair and took up my book, but I had not been reading for more than two minutes before I was conscious of a most unpleasant smell. Now, there are all sorts of smells – healthy and otherwise – but I think the nastiest is that chilly kind of odour that comes from bad sanitation and stuffy rooms combined; you meet it sometimes at little country inns and decrepit town lodgings. This smell was so definite that I could almost locate it; it came from near the door. I got up, approached the door, and at once it was as though I were drawing near to somebody who, if you'll forgive the impoliteness, was not accustomed to taking too many baths. I drew back just as I might had an actual person been there. Then quite suddenly the smell was gone, the room was fresh, and I saw, to my surprise, that one of the windows had opened and that snow was again blowing in. I closed it and went downstairs.

'The evening that followed was odd enough. My host was not in himself an unlikeable man; he did his very utmost to please me. He had a fine culture and a wide knowledge of books and things. He became quite cheerful as the evening went on; gave me a good dinner in a funny little old dining-room hung with some admirable mezzotints. The old serving man looked after us – a funny old man, with a long white beard like a goat – and, oddly enough, it was from him that I first recaught my earlier apprehension. He had just put the dessert on the table, had arranged my plate in front of me, when I saw him give a start and look towards the door. My attention was attracted to this because his hand, as it touched the plate, suddenly trembled. My eyes followed, but I could see nothing. That he was frightened of something was perfectly clear, and then (it may, of course, very easily have been fancy) I thought that I detected once more that strange unwholesome smell.

'I forgot this again when we were both seated in front of a splendid fire in the library. Lunt had a very fine collection of books, and it was delightful to him, as it is to every book-collector, to have somebody with him who could really appreciate them. We stood looking at one book after another and talking eagerly about some of the minor early English novelists who were my especial hobby – Bage, Godwin, Henry Mackenzie, Mrs Shelley, Mat Lewis, and others – when once again he affected me most unpleasantly by putting his arm round my shoulders. I have all my life disliked intensely to be touched by certain people. I suppose we all feel like this. It is one of those inexplicable things; and I disliked this so much that I abruptly drew away.

'Instantly he was changed into a man of furious and ungovernable rage; I thought that he was going to strike me. He stood there quivering all over, the words pouring out of his mouth incoherently, as though he were mad and did not know what he was saying. He accused me of insulting him, of abusing his hospitality, of throwing his kindness back into his face, and of a thousand other ridiculous things; and I can't tell you how strange it was to hear all this coming out in that shrill piping voice as though it were from an agitated woman, and yet to see with one's eyes that big, muscular frame, those immense shoulders, and that dark bearded face.

'I said nothing. I am, physically, a coward. I dislike, above anything else in the world, any sort of quarrel. At last I brought out, "I am very sorry. I didn't mean anything. Please forgive me," and then hurriedly turned to leave the room. At once he changed again; now he was almost in tears. He implored me not to go; said it was his wretched temper, but that he was so miserable and unhappy, and had for so long now been alone and desolate that he hardly knew what he was doing. He begged me to give him another chance, and if I would only listen to his story I would perhaps be more patient with him.

'At once, so oddly is man constituted, I changed in my feelings towards him. I was very sorry for him. I saw that he was a man on the edge of his nerves, and that he really did need some help and sympathy, and would be quite distracted if he could not get it. I put my hand on his shoulder to quieten him and to show him that I bore no malice, and I felt that his great body was quivering from head to foot. We sat down again, and in an odd, rambling manner he told me his story. It amounted to very little, and the gist of it was that, rather to have some sort of companionship than from any impulse of passion, he had married some fifteen years before the daughter of a neighbouring clergyman. They had had no very happy life together, and at the last, he told me quite frankly, he had hated her. She had been mean, overbearing, and narrow-minded; it had been, he confessed, nothing but a relief to him when, just a year ago, she had suddenly died from heart failure. He had thought then that things would go better with him, but they had not; nothing had gone right with him since. He hadn't been able to work, many of his friends had ceased to come to see him, he had found it even difficult to get servants to stay with him, he was desperately lonely, he slept badly – that was why his temper was so terribly on edge. He had no one in the house with him save the old man, who was, fortunately, an excellent cook, and a boy – the old man's grandson. "Oh, I thought," I said, "that that excellent meal tonight was cooked by your housekeeper." "My housekeeper?" he answered. "There's no woman in the house." "Oh, but one came to my room," I replied, "this evening – an old lady-like looking person in a black silk dress." "You were mistaken," he answered in the oddest voice, as though he were exerting all the strength that he possessed to keep himself quiet and controlled. "I am sure that I saw her," I answered. "There couldn't be any mistake." And I described her to him. "You were mistaken," he repeated again. "Don't you see that you must have been when I tell you there is no woman in the house?" I reassured him quickly lest there should be another outbreak of rage. Then there followed the oddest kind of appeal. Urgently, as though his very life depended upon it, he begged me to stay with him for a few days. He implied, although he said nothing definitely, that he was in great trouble, that if only I would stay for a few days all would be well, that if ever in all my life I had had a chance of doing a kind action I had one now, that he couldn't expect me to stop in so dreary a place, but that he would never forget it if I did. He spoke in a voice of such urgent distress that I reassured him as I might a child, promising that I would stay and shaking hands with him on it as though it were a kind of solemn oath between us.

II

'I am sure that you would wish me to give you this incident as it occurred, and if the final catastrophe seems to come, as it were, accidentally, I can only say to you that that was how it happened. It is since the event that I have tried to put two and two together, and that they don't altogether make four is the fault that mine shares, I suppose, with every true ghost story.

'But the truth is that after that very strange episode between us I had a very good night. I slept the sleep of all justice, cosy and warm, in my four-poster, with the murmur of the sea beyond the windows to rock my slumbers. Next morning too was bright and cheerful, the sun sparkling down on the snow, and the snow sparkling back to the sun as though they were glad to see one another. I had a very pleasant morning looking at Lunt's books, talking to him, and writing one or two letters. I must say that, after all, I liked the man. His appeal to me on the night before had touched me. So few people, you see, had ever appealed to me about anything. His nervousness was there and the constant sense of apprehension, yet he seemed to be putting the best face on it, doing his utmost to set me at my ease in order to induce me to stay, I suppose, and to give him a little of that company that he so terribly needed. I dare say if I had not been so busy about the books I would not have been so happy. There was a strange eerie silence about the house if one ever stopped to listen; and once, I remember, sitting at the old bureau writing a letter, I raised my head and looked up, and caught Lunt watching as though he wondered whether I had heard or noticed anything. And so I listened, too, and it seemed to me as though someone were on the other side of the library door with their hand raised to knock; a quaint notion, with nothing to support it, but I could have sworn that if I had gone to the door and opened it suddenly someone would have been there.

'However, I was cheerful enough, and after lunch quite happy. Lunt asked me if I would like a walk, and I said I would; and we started out in the sunshine over the crunching snow towards the sea. I don't remember of what we talked; we seemed to be now quite at our ease with one another. We crossed the fields to a certain point, looked down at the sea – smooth now, like silk – and turned back. I remember that I was so cheerful that I seemed suddenly to take a happy view of all my prospects. I began to confide in Lunt, telling him of my little plans, of my hopes for the book that I was then writing, and even began rather timidly to suggest to him that perhaps we should do something together; that what we both needed was a friend of common tastes with ourselves. I know that I was talking on, that we had crossed a little village street, and were turning up the path towards the dark avenue of trees that led to his house, when suddenly the change came.

'What I first noticed was that he was not listening to me; his gaze was fixed beyond me, into the very heart of the black clump of trees that fringed the silver landscape. I looked too, and my heart bounded. There was, standing just in front of the trees, as though she were waiting for us, the old woman whom I had seen in my room the night before. I stopped. "Why, there she is!" I said. "That's the old woman of whom I was speaking – the old woman who came to my room." He caught my shoulder with his hand. "There's nothing there," he said. "Don't you see that that's shadow? What's the matter with you? Can't you see that there's nothing?" I stepped forward, and there was nothing, and I wouldn't, to this day, be able to tell you whether it was hallucination or not. I can only say that, from that moment, the afternoon appeared to become dark. As we entered into the avenue of trees, silently and hurrying as though someone were behind us, the dusk seemed to have fallen so that I could scarcely see my way. We reached the house breathless. He hastened into his study as though I were not with him, but I followed and, closing the door behind me, said, with all the force that I had at command: "Now, what is this? What is it that's troubling you? You must tell me! How can I help you if you don't?" And he replied, in so strange a voice that it was as though he had gone out of his mind: "I tell you there's nothing! Can't you believe me when I tell you there's nothing at all? I'm quite all right . . . Oh, my God! – my God! . . . don't leave me! . . . This is the very day – the very night she said . . . But I did nothing, I tell you – I did nothing – it's only her beastly malice . . ." He broke off. He still held my arm with his hand. He made strange movements, wiping his forehead as though it were damp with sweat, almost pleading with me; then suddenly angry again, then beseeching once more, as though I had refused him the one thing he wanted.

'I saw that he was truly not far from madness, and I began myself to have a sudden terror of this damp, dark house, this great, trembling man, and something more that was worse than they. But I pitied him. How could you or any man have helped it? I made him sit down in the arm-chair beside the fire, which had now dwindled to a few glimmering red coals. I let him hold me close to him with his arm and clutch my hand with his, and I repeated, as quietly as I might: "But tell me; don't be afraid, whatever it is you have done. Tell me what danger it is you fear, and then we can face it together." "Fear! fear!" he repeated; and then, with a mighty effort which I could not but admire, he summoned all his control. "I'm off my head," he said, "with loneliness and depression. My wife died a year ago on this very night. We hated one another. I couldn't be sorry when she died, and she knew it. When that last heart attack came on, between her gasps she told me that she would return, and I've always dreaded this night. That's partly why I asked you to come, to have any one here, anybody, and you've been very kind – more kind than I had any right to expect. You must think me insane going on like this, but see me through to-night and we'll have splendid times together. Don't desert me now – now, of all times!" I promised that I would not. I soothed him as best I could. We sat there, for I know not how long, through the gathering dark; we neither of us moved, the fire died out, and the room was lit with a strange dim glow that came from the snowy landscape beyond the uncurtained windows. Ridiculous, perhaps, as I look back at it. We sat there, I in a chair close to his, hand in hand, like a couple of lovers; but, in real truth, two men terrified, fearful of what was coming, and unable to do anything to meet it.

'I think that that was perhaps the strangest part of it; a sort of paralysis that crept over me. What would you or any one else have done – summoned the old man, gone down to the village inn, fetched the local doctor? I could do nothing, but see the snow-shine move like trembling water about the furniture and hear, through the urgent silence, the faint hoot of an owl from the trees in the wood.

III

'Oddly enough, I can remember nothing, try as I may, between that strange vigil and the moment when I myself, wakened out of a brief sleep, sat up in bed to see Lunt standing inside my room holding a candle. He was wearing a nightshirt, and looked huge in the candlelight, his black beard falling intensely dark on the white stuff of his shirt. He came very quietly towards my bed, the candle throwing flickering shadows about the room. When he spoke it was in a voice low and subdued, almost a whisper. "Would you come," he asked, "only for half an hour – just for half an hour?" he repeated, staring at me as though he didn't know me. "I'm unhappy without somebody – very un-happy." Then he looked over his shoulder, held the candle high above his head, and stared piercingly at every part of the room. I could see that something had happened to him, that he had taken another step into the country of Fear – a step that had withdrawn him from me and from every other human being. He whispered: "When you come, tread softly; I don't want any one to hear us." I did what I could. I got out of bed, put on my dressing-gown and slippers, and tried to persuade him to stay with me. The fire was almost dead, but I told him that we would build it up again, and that we would sit there and wait for the morning; but no, he repeated again and again: "It's better in my own room; we're safer there." "Safe from what?" I asked him, making him look at me. "Lunt, wake up! You're as though you were asleep. There's nothing to fear. We've nobody but ourselves. Stay here and let us talk, and have done with this nonsense." But he wouldn't answer; only drew me forward down the dark passage, and then turned into his room, beckoning me to follow. He got into bed and sat hunched up there, his hands holding his knees, staring at the door, and every once and again shivering with a little tremor. The only light in the room was that from the candle, now burning low, and the only sound was the purring whisper of the sea.

'It seemed to make little difference to him that I was there. He did not look at me, but only at the door, and when I spoke to him he did not answer me nor seem to hear what I had said. I sat down beside the bed and, in order to break the silence, talked on about anything, about nothing, and was dropping off, I think, into a confused doze, when I heard his voice breaking across mine. Very clearly and distinctly he said: "If I killed her, she deserved it; she was never a good wife to me, not from the first; she shouldn't have irritated me as she did – she knew what my temper was. She had a worse one than mine, though. She can't touch me; I'm as strong as she is." And it was then, as clearly as I can now remember, that his voice suddenly sank into a sort of gentle whisper, as though he were almost glad that his fears had been confirmed. He whispered: "She's there!" I cannot possibly describe to you how that whisper seemed to let Fear loose like water through my body. I could see nothing – the candle was flaming high in the last moments of its life – I could see nothing; but Lunt suddenly screamed, with a shrill cry like a tortured animal in agony: "Keep her off me, keep her away from me, keep her off – keep her off!" He caught me, his hands digging into my shoulders; then, with an awful effect of constricted muscles, as though rigor had caught and held him, his arms slowly fell away, he slipped back on to the bed as though someone were pushing him, his hands fell against the sheet, his whole body jerked with a convulsive effort, and then he rolled over. I saw nothing; only, quite distinctly, in my nostrils was that same fetid odour that I had known on the preceding evening. I rushed to the door, opened it, shouted down the long passage again and again, and soon the old man came running. I sent him for the doctor, and then could not return to the room, but stood there listening, hearing nothing save the whisper of the sea, the loud ticking of the hall clock. I flung open the window at the end of the passage; the sea rushed in with its precipitant roar; some bells chimed the hour. Then at last, beating into myself more courage, I turned back towards the room . . .'

'Well?' I asked as Runciman paused. 'He was dead, of course?'

'Dead, the doctor afterwards said, of heart failure.'

'Well?' I asked again.

'That's all.' Runciman paused. 'I don't know whether you can even call it a ghost story. My idea of the old woman may have been all hallucination. I don't even know whether his wife was like that when she was alive. She may have been large and fat. Lunt died of an evil conscience.'

'Yes,' I said.

'The only thing,' Runciman added at last, after a long pause, 'is that on Lunt's body there were marks – on his neck especially, some on his chest – as of fingers pressing in, scratches and dull blue marks. He may, in his terror, have caught at his own throat . . .'

'Yes,' I said again.

'Anyway' – Runciman shivered – 'I don't like Cornwall – beastly county. Queer things happen there – something in the air. . . .'

'So I've heard,' I answered. 'And now have a drink. We both will.'

The House of Vengeance

L. T. C. Rolt

The bus from Hereford came to a stop in the somnolent square of the little Welsh border town. The sliding door clashed open and John Hardy, shouldering his haversack, followed two plump and basket-laden farmers' wives on to the pavement. It was a perfect spring afternoon; sunlight drenched the square and as the clatter of the bus died away along the road towards Brecon the town's rudely interrupted peace was quickly restored. The cracked bell in the Victorian clock tower chimed twice. Three thirty, he would have to step it out, thought John, if he was to make the Priory Hotel at Llanvethney before darkness fell.

He was quite unfamiliar with this Welsh border country, but his friend Alan Brett had explained to him that the hotel where they had arranged to meet and to stay lay in a long and narrow valley on the other side of the Black Mountains. Alan knew these mountains like the back of his hand, and had enthused to John so often about them that he had finally persuaded his friend to join him at the Priory Hotel for a week's walking holiday so that he could become more closely acquainted with their beauties. Because Alan had assured him he was fully equipped, John had not bothered to acquire any large-scale maps of the area. But he did not anticipate any difficulty in finding his way as a preliminary glance at his one small-scale map had shown a bridle road that led out of the little town, over a high mountain pass and so down into the head of the valley in which their rendezvous was situated.

Walking briskly, he had soon cleared the outskirts of the old town – it was little larger than a village, anyway – and set his face towards the encircling hills. He had done a great deal of walking in the Cumberland Fells and the Pennines and thought that, by contrast, the prospect before him, though it was pleasing enough, looked rather tame. Surely these gentle hills could not be the wild mountains that Alan had praised so highly. He had covered about five miles, however, when the way veered sharply to his right and began to climb steeply up the flank of a deep and narrow gorge. It was when he had climbed to the head of this gorge that he realized that the hills were merely so many stepping stones to the greater heights which they had hitherto effectually concealed.

A very different prospect now greeted him. He found himself upon the edge of a huge plateau of unenclosed upland, an expanse of short, springy turf tufted here and there with uncurling bracken fronds and starred with hundreds of sheep. From this plateau there rose majestically along the southern skyline the great gables of a range of mountains. A confirmed 'mountainy' man, John found this prospect very much more to his liking and he strode out with a will along the track which he could see climbing ahead of him round the knees of the mountains in the direction of the head of the pass.

Meanwhile the range of the Brecon Beacons in the middle distance, which normally appeared blue and remote, had become darkly threatening, its outline sharply etched against a great wall of storm cloud which was rolling up the western sky behind them. Had he not been so intrigued with the new prospect and better acquainted with the vagaries of the Welsh border country, so experienced a walker could scarcely have failed to notice so obvious a threat of impending weather change.

When he had climbed to the head of the pass, he saw that the track swung away to his left to enter a narrow defile between two mountain bluffs. For a few moments John thought that the reason why it suddenly seemed to have become so dark and chilly was that the further of these two bluffs obscured the westering sun, throwing the pass into deep shadow. In fact, this dark flank of the mountain concealed from him the swiftly advancing storm wrack which had already swallowed up the sun.

It was just at this moment when he stood upon the threshold of the pass that, just as it seemed suddenly to grow dark so, as suddenly, he was seized by a wholly irrational and almost overmastering fear. John was not a timid, nor even a particularly imaginative man and in all his long experience of walking in lonely places he had experienced nothing like it. It had to do with something which awaited him on the other side of the pass. It was as if something monstrous lurked there and it required a conscious effort of will to resist the temptation to fly back to the remembered landscape he had left behind. The weather itself might have been in league with his unreasoning fears, for as he pressed stubbornly forward through the narrow defile the whole character of the evening seemed to change. It became difficult to believe in that sunlit square where he had alighted not three hours before. The sky had become totally overcast and every vestige of colour had drained out of the landscape to leave it as sombre as the sky. A sudden chill wind, driving a scud of rain before it, blew through the pass into his face as through some draughty corridor in which a distant door had been thrown open. This forced him to lower his head and when he raised it again he found himself looking down into the head of the valley.

What he saw did nothing to assuage his misgivings. He thought he had never seen a more forbidding prospect. He might, he thought, have been looking down into the dolorous pit of some vast, abandoned quarry. The tops of the mountains that enclosed the valley were already hidden beneath curtains of hurrying cloud, but so steep were their slopes that all he could see of them were a succession of desolate screes surmounted by frowning crags and precipices already dark with rain. The clouds were rapidly coming down; already coils of white vapour were beginning to spiral among the higher crags. A sudden clatter of falling stones on the scree immediately to his right made him start and he looked up in time to see what looked like a bundle of wool come bouncing out of the mist and over the crags until it slid to rest on the screes below where it lay very still. It was sometime before the stones of the scree adjusted themselves by stealthy crepitation and it became quite still once more. How typical of this appalling place, he thought, that the only evidence of life should be the death of a sheep!

He began hurriedly to extract a waterproof cape from his haversack and had hardly got it on before the storm broke in sudden and almost unbelievable fury. The rain lashed down, stinging his face as he blundered almost sightlessly down the track. So dark and lowering was the sky that at this rate, he reflected ruefully, it would very soon be pitch dark and he cursed himself as he realized that he had brought no torch. Not only had darkness fallen surprisingly early due to the sudden change in the weather, but he realized now that he had grossly under-estimated the distance involved. He guessed that Llanvethney must still be at least six miles further down the valley.

The storm had now become a positive cloudburst which no protective clothing could possibly keep out. Cold rivulets found their way down his neck and even his stout boots were soon squelching. In this wet misery he began to doubt if he could possibly succeed in reaching his destination that night. Had not Alan once mentioned a Youth Hostel somewhere between the head of the pass and the floor of the valley? If so it would make a good emergency port in the storm if only he could find it. Unfortunately he had no idea on which side of the track the Hostel lay; nor, as yet, could he see a single light in the fast gathering darkness.

At last, however, John sighted away to his left beneath the invisible mountain wall a single light shining out, and so wet and lost and wretched was he by this time that he instantly determined to make a beeline for it whether it was the Youth Hostel or not. Surely even the dourest of Welsh hill farmers would scarcely refuse him shelter on such a night. He could just distinguish a gate to the left of the track and through this he passed, plunging down a steep slope in the direction of that solitary light. As he did so he remembered too late that this was the side of the valley which had the stream at its foot and, sure enough, he soon heard above the steady roar of the rain the chuckling of a mountain torrent in sudden spate. Yet still the light lured him on so, somehow or other, he managed to slip and slide down the steep bank, to wade knee-deep through the boulder-strewn bed of the stream and to scramble on all fours up the muddy slope opposite. There were other unseen hazards to be surmounted such as old thorn hedges and sheep fences topped with strands of barbed wire before he finally found himself standing on a rough farm track, terraced along the slope, which obviously led in the direction of the light.

A few moments later John Hardy was knocking at the door of the farmhouse. The light streamed out from a curtained window to the left of the door, its fellow on the opposite side being in darkness. There was a sound from within of hobnailed boots scuffing on flagstones followed by the rattle of door-bolts being withdrawn. The next instant he found himself confronting a very strange little figure indeed, his face thrown into high relief by the light of the paraffin lamp which he held before him, peering over it into the streaming darkness. He was so dark-skinned and dark-haired that he might have been a true Romany, yet so short in stature as to be almost a dwarf. He stared disconcertingly at John with unblinking eyes that were black as sloes and seemed furtive and filled with suspicion. He spoke very rapidly in a sing-song, lilting tongue that John did not recognize. This struck him as very strange because, although he had no command of the Welsh language he had heard it spoken often enough. Also he had understood from Alan that Welsh was no longer spoken in this part of the border so that it struck him as odd that this strange little man, if he was indeed speaking some archaic form of Welsh, apparently knew no second language. However,

41

plastered as he was in red mud and with water running out of his boots, John needed no words to express his plight and so, somewhat grudgingly, the little man stepped back and motioned him to enter. He did not lead the way into the lighted room from which he had obviously emerged, but opened a low dark doorway on the opposite side of the stone-flagged central passage and, signalling the other to follow him, led the way into a typical small Welsh farm parlour, setting the lamp down on the circular central table.

John would have greatly preferred the homely warmth of the farm kitchen which, as he fondly supposed, lay on the opposite side of the passage. Seen in the dim light of a single lamp, this typical Victorian parlour looked sombre and unwelcoming to a degree and, needless to say, there was no fire in the black and highly polished grate. He also thought it curious that, in his dripping and muddy state, he should be shown straight into the 'best parlour'. There must, he concluded, be some very good reason why he was not to be allowed to share in whatever was going on across the passage. Nevertheless, he reflected philosophically, at least he had a roof over his head which was something on such a night. As soon as he had set down the lamp, his host had straightway left the room, closing the door firmly behind him as though he had other and more urgent business to attend to. Left alone, John removed his cape and his sodden boots and stockings, laying them down beside his haversack in the empty firegrate, before selecting the least uncomfortable looking of the Victorian chairs and settling down to make the best of such cold comfort. He could still hear the steady roar of the rain outside.

Chill and unwelcoming though the room was, particularly to such a damp and benighted traveller, John must have fallen asleep from sheer fatigue, for he awoke with a start, subconsciously aware that some new sound had aroused him. Glancing down at his wristwatch he saw that it was just after midnight. He sat motionless, listening. The buffeting of the storm seemed to have ceased and in its place he thought he could hear a very unusual sound indeed which seemed to come from that lighted room across the passage. It resembled, he said, a kind of monotonous chant, although it was quite unlike any form of chant he had ever heard before. It seemed to have a primitive wildness about it although he could not have explained why he thought this, except that one voice was clearly distinguishable from the others by its curious timbre which he described as a cross between a rasping chuckle and the bleating of a large goat. Although under the circumstances it was a disquieting sound to hear, he was not particularly frightened. It was what happened next that caused the hairs on the back of his neck to stir.

First of all there was the sound of what John took to be the back door being flung violently open and then slammed to again with a thunderous crash. Instantly the murmur of voices ceased as though that mysterious company held their breath in fearful suspense. For a full minute the house was wrapped in a tense, expectant silence; then there came the sound of earth-shaking footfalls pacing down the flagged hallway. It was, John recalled, as though some ancient and gigantic stone statue had suddenly been endowed with terrible life and was stalking through the house. He remembers staring at the door of the room and praying that it would not open and that this monstrous thing would pass it by. Loud and startling as a trumpet blast a great voice suddenly cried out: 'Fear not me, fear what follows me.' Then John heard the front door open and slam shut with a violence that shook the house and all fell silent once more.

It was at this juncture that, with what strikes him now as an inexplicable act of courage or foolhardiness. John opened the casement window of his room and gazed out into the night, although it was pitch dark and he does not recall what precisely he expected to see or hear. Some shadow or sound of that huge presence which had just left the house? Or some presage of that greater fear to come which it had prophesied? At first he could hear nothing except the steady, sullen drip of water from eave or downspout, but then his ears detected a curious sound in the air, seemingly coming from directly above the house. At first it was as if some great flock of migrant birds was wheeling overhead in the darkness, whistling and piping like so many lost souls. The sound gradually grew in volume, however, and as it did so it became loud with menace, an eldritch screaming very terrible to hear. Now it was as though there blew over – or out of – those sheer mountain walls that hemmed in the valley a great wind of such force that the very crevices of the crags and the stones of invisible screes became its vocal chords, screaming and yelling in a unison of violence. 'Fear what follows me', and now indeed, as he freely admits, John became terror-stricken. There was something so utterly monstrous about this sudden crescendo of tumult in the high air. It was like no storm he had ever known. It was as if the mountains themselves had transformed or perverted a natural element into some tremendous diabolical force.

John shut the window and as he stood rocking on his feet in the centre of the room he caught a glimpse of his white face in the mirror above the fireplace and scarcely recognized it as his own. He had closed the window not a moment too soon. Outside he heard the screaming reach an ultimate pitch of menace before merging into a great roaring sound as a mighty wind rushed down upon the house from the mountain. It struck with a force that made every door and window rattle; it was as though the house had been grasped and shaken by some gigantic hand. By this time John was on his knees upon the floor. The window blew in with a crash as the house was struck by a second and even more tremendous blow. Before he lost consciousness he remembered seeing the walls of the room suddenly bellying inwards and of the lamp sliding from the table with a crash, plunging all into a chaotic darkness.

John awoke to feel the sun hot upon his face. The recollection of the previous night filled his mind with a sudden panic and then the memory of that nightmare, if such it was, gradually receded. Yet still he hesitated to open his eyes. For if it was indeed a nightmare, then surely he would still be sitting in that Victorian chair in the farm parlour and not lying in the sun. On the contrary, if it had indeed been no nightmare he would be lying, miraculously unhurt, amid the ruins of the farmhouse. At length, very warily, he opened his eyes and sat up. He found himself lying on a smooth and gentle slope of close-bitten turf, his haversack, his cape and his boots and stockings upon the grass beside him. A little distance away to his left was a shapeless mound of grey stones and beside this grew a clump of nettles and an ancient yew tree, sure signs of bygone human habitation, but of any recent ruin there was no sign whatever. The near-level slope where he sat formed the mouth of a steep cwm carved by a streamlet out of the mountain at his back so that it formed a sort of natural amphitheatre from which he could look down over the valley below. There, directly beneath him, ran the swift flowing stream which he had crossed with such difficulty the previous night and there, up the opposite slope, was surely the gateway by which he had left the track over the pass which he could see running diagonally along the opposite side of the valley. He shook his head in bewilderment as one who surfaces after a dive, not knowing where reality had ended and the dream had begun.

It was a perfect spring morning. The brilliant blue sky was flecked with innocent little cotton-wool cloudlets that drifted serenely along, the smaller ones dissolving as he watched them in the gathering heat of the sun. He saw their shadows moving along the slopes opposite and noticed that above the screes and the crags a more gentle slope extended upward towards the long, level skyline of the mountain ridge, a slope green with fresh bracken fronds and thickly populated with sheep and with mountain ponies, many with small foals at heel. These higher slopes, made invisible by low cloud the previous night, now transformed the appearance of the valley. He watched a pair of buzzards soaring effortlessly on motionless, moth-like wings upon an up-current of air above the crags opposite. Although the floor of the valley to his right was treeless, immediately to his left the stream disappeared in a little brake of alders and he could see that beyond this the valley became progressively richer and well-wooded. There were glimpses of old farmsteads of pinkish grey stone or whitewash and of blue pencils of woodsmoke spiralling upwards from morning fires.

So striking was the contrast between the beauty of the scene now spread before him and his first impression of the valley when seen from the head of the pass the previous evening, that although John was no philosopher he could scarcely avoid speculating upon it. What had appeared under that darkening stormlight to be so malign now seemed to have become wholly beneficent and of a heart-lifting beauty that seemed almost paradisial. Were good and evil purely human concepts and did this little world that he surveyed include them both?

He put on his socks and boots, rolled up his cape and, shouldering his knapsack, set off down the valley. Within the first few yards he had struck a long disused track which had obviously led into the mouth of the cwm and must have been the one he had found on scrambling up the bank the night before. He judged correctly that if he followed it it would ultimately join the main track at a point lower down the valley. He had only just regained the latter and begun to stride out towards Llanvethney when he saw coming slowly towards him up the hill a Land Rover driven by a very worried looking Alan Brett. On seeing John coming towards him apparently none the worse, Alan's face relaxed into a broad grin, and 'Gosh, am I glad to see you!' he exclaimed as he drew up beside him, leaning over and opening the door on the passenger side. And as John threw his rucksack into the back and clambered in, 'Where did you tuck yourself away last night when that storm hit you?' he asked. 'I guessed you'd be at the Youth Hostel and it was when I called there just now and found you weren't there that I began to get really worried.' John made no immediate answer to his question and such reticence was so unusual that Alan looked keenly at him and judged correctly that he should forego any further cross-questioning, leaving the story to come out in his friend's own good time. So without further comment he reversed the Land Rover into a gateway and the two drove on in companionable silence down towards Llanvethney Priory.

The further they went the more beautiful the valley became, the more luxuriant the meadows and trees along its floor and the more majestic the sweep and curve of the mountains that enclosed it. The loveliness all about him loosed John's tongue and he tried haltingly to explain to his friend the extraordinary contrast between the valley as he saw it now and his first impression of it as he entered it by the high pass the night before. In reply, Alan chuckled and 'An angel satyr walks these hills,' he quoted. 'Who wrote that?' asked the other sharply. 'A chap named Francis Kilvert,' explained Alan, 'who was curate of Clyro just the other side of the Wye in the 1870s and used to do a lot of walking in these mountains. It appears, rather enigmatically, in the diary that he kept which was published just before the last war.'

'I think I understand what he meant,' replied John after a short silence.

It was not until that evening when the two friends were comfortably ensconced in deep armchairs on either side of a blazing log fire in the big drawing room of the Priory Hotel that John told his friend the whole strange story. Throughout Alan listened with the utmost attention, never speaking a word until John had finished. Then, after a moment's silence, 'If I were to show you a large-scale map of the area, do you think you could pin-point the site of this mysterious farm where you stayed – or thought you stayed?' asked Alan. 'I am sure I could,' the other replied, whereupon his friend unfolded a map, two and a half inches to the mile, and spread it before them. It did not take John long before he had marked the spot with the point of a pencil. It was too easy; here was the line of the track descending from the pass, the stream running down almost parallel with it and, beyond it, the dense contour lines which marked the steep slope of the mountain. There was only one indentation in those contour lines and that must surely indicate the steep little cwm in which he had found himself that morning.

No sooner had he marked the place than Alan exclaimed in an awed voice, 'I thought as much, Ty yr Deol!' Then in answer to his friend's look of blank incomprehension he explained, 'Ty yr Deol, that means "the house of vengeance".' He got to his feet, opened the doors of a large glass-fronted bookcase, searched for a moment and then drew out a green-backed book. 'It's our friend Francis Kilvert again who tells us all about it in his diary, volume one' – he rifled through the pages — 'page 279 – I quote:

Near Capel y Ffin at the mouth of a dingle on the mountain side stood the house of Ty yr Deol (the house of vengeance). Some crime had been perpetrated on the spot and the place was accursed. When the workmen were building the house they heard a voice which seemed to fall from the air and come down the dingle, saying, "Move the work across the green." "For why?" called back the astonished workmen. "The spot is accursed," said the voice solemnly. "For how long?" shouted the workmen. "Until the ninth generation," returned the voice. Three attempts were made to build the house. Twice the house fell. The third time the house was built. One night in winter a young man came up the mountain to court his sweetheart who lived in the Ty yr Deol, the accursed, ill-fated house. His greyhound whined at the door, hung back and refused to enter the house, and no coaxing would induce him to come in. The young man took it as a warning and returned home. That night there was a landslip or snow slip, or a sudden mass of snow melted down the dingle driving the ice and water before it. The accursed house was overwhelmed and swept away and everyone in the house perished.'

When Alan had read this the two friends sat for many minutes in silence, gazing into the flames of the fire, each busy with his own thoughts while outside dusk thickened in the valley and the room grew dark except for the flickering firelight.

The Novel of the Black Seal

Arthur Machen

I am the daughter of a civil engineer, Steven Lally by name, who was so unfortunate as to die suddenly at the outset of his career, and before he had accumulated sufficient means to support his wife and her two children.

My mother contrived to keep the small household going on resources which must have been incredibly small; we lived in a remote country village, because most of the necessaries of life were cheaper than in a town, but even so we were brought up with the severest economy. My father was a clever and well-read man, and left behind him a small but select collection of books, containing the best Greek, Latin, and English classics, and these books were the only amusement we possessed. My brother, I remember, learnt Latin out of Descartes's *Meditationes*, and I, in place of the little tales which children are usually told to read, had nothing more charming than a translation of the *Gesta Romanorum*. We grew up thus, quiet and studious children, and in course of time my brother provided for himself in the manner I have mentioned. I continued to live at home; my poor mother had become an invalid, and demanded my continual care, and about two years ago she died after many months of painful illness. My situation was a terrible one; the shabby furniture barely sufficed to pay the debts I had been forced to contract, and the books I dispatched to my brother, knowing how he would value them. I was absolutely alone; I was aware how poorly my brother was paid; and though I came up to London in the hope

50

of finding employment, with the understanding that he would defray my expenses, I swore it should only be for a month, and that if I could not in that time find some work, I would starve rather than deprive him of the few miserable pounds he had laid by for his day of trouble. I took a little room in a distant suburb, the cheapest that I could find; I lived on bread and tea, and I spent my time in vain answering of advertisements, and vainer walks to addresses I had noted. Day followed on day, and week on week, and still I was unsuccessful, till at last the term I had appointed drew to a close, and I saw before me the grim prospect of slowly dying of starvation. My landlady was good-natured in her way; she knew the slenderness of my means, and I am sure that she would not have turned me out of doors; it remained for me then to go away, and to try to die in some quiet place. It was winter then, and a thick white fog gathered in the early part of the afternoon, becoming more dense as the day wore on; it was a Sunday, I remember, and the people of the house were at chapel. At about three o'clock I crept out and walked away as quickly as I could, for I was weak from abstinence. The white mist wrapped all the streets in silence, a hard frost had gathered thick upon the bare branches of the trees, and frost crystals glittered on the wooden fences, and on the cold, cruel ground beneath my feet. I walked on, turning to right and left in utter haphazard, without caring to look up at the names of the streets, and all that I remember of my walk on that Sunday afternoon seems but the broken fragments of an evil dream. In a confused vision I stumbled on, through roads half town and half country, grey fields melting into the cloudy world of mist on one side of me, and on the other comfortable villas with a glow of firelight flickering on the walls, but all unreal; red brick walls and lighted windows, vague trees, and glimmering country, gas-lamps beginning to star the white shadows, the vanishing perspectives of the railway line beneath high embankments, the green and red of the signal lamps – all these were but momentary pictures flashed on my tired brain and senses numbed by hunger. Now and then I would hear a quick step ringing on the iron road, and men would pass me well wrapped up, walking fast for the sake of warmth, and no doubt eagerly foretasting the pleasures of a glowing hearth, with curtains tightly drawn about the frosted panes, and the welcomes of their friends; but as the early evening darkened and night approached, foot-passengers got fewer and fewer, and I passed through street after street alone. In the white silence I stumbled on, as desolate as if I trod the streets of a buried city; and as I grew more weak and exhausted, something of the horror of death was folding thickly round my heart. Suddenly, as I turned a corner, some one accosted me courteously beneath the lamp-post, and I heard a voice asking if I could kindly point the way to Avon Road. At the sudden shock of human accents I was prostrated, and my strength gave way; I fell all huddled on the sidewalk, and wept and sobbed and laughed in violent hysteria. I had gone out prepared to die, and as I stepped across the threshold that had sheltered me, I consciously bade adieu to all hopes and all remembrances; the door clanged behind me with the noise of thunder, and I felt that an iron curtain had fallen on the brief passage of my life, that henceforth I was to walk a little way in a world of gloom and shadow; I entered on the stage of the first act of death. Then came my wandering in the mist, the whiteness wrapping all things, the void streets, and muffled silence, till when that voice spoke to me it was as if I had died and life returned to me. In a few minutes I was able to compose my feelings, and as I rose I saw that I was confronted by a middle-aged gentleman of pleasing appearance, neatly and correctly dressed. He looked at me with an expression of great pity, but before I could stammer out my ignorance of the neighbourhood, for indeed I had not the slightest notion of where I had wandered, he spoke.

'My dear madam,' he said, 'you seem in some terrible distress. You cannot think how you alarmed me. But may I inquire the nature of your trouble? I assure you that you can safely confide in me.'

'You are very kind,' I replied, 'but I fear there is nothing to be done. My condition seems a hopeless one.'

'Oh, nonsense, nonsense! You are too young to talk like that. Come, let us walk down here and you must tell me your difficulty. Perhaps I may be able to help you.'

There was something very soothing and persuasive in his manner, and as we walked together I gave him an outline of my story, and told of the despair that had oppressed me almost to death.

'You were wrong to give in so completely,' he said, when I was silent. 'A month is too short a time in which to feel one's way in London. London, let me tell you, Miss Lally, does not lie open and undefended; it is a fortified place, fossed and double-moated with curious intricacies. As must always happen in large towns, the conditions of life have become hugely artificial, no mere simple palisade is run up to oppose the man or woman who would take the place by storm, but serried lines of subtle contrivances, mines, and pitfalls which it needs a strange skill to overcome. You, in your simplicity, fancied you had only to shout for these walls to sink into nothingness, but the time is gone for such startling victories as these. Take courage; you will learn the secret of success before very long.'

'Alas! sir,' I replied, 'I have no doubt your conclusions are correct, but at the present moment I seem to be in a fair way to die of starvation. You spoke of a secret; for Heaven's sake tell it me, if you have any pity for my distress.'

He laughed genially. 'There lies the strangeness of it all. Those who know the secret cannot tell it if they would; it is positively as ineffable as the central doctrine of freemasonry. But I may say this, that you yourself have penetrated at least the outer husk of the mystery,' and he laughed again.

'Pray do not jest with me,' I said. 'What have I done, *que sais-je*? I am so far ignorant that I have not the slightest idea of how my next meal is to be provided.'

'Excuse me. You ask what you have done. You have met me.

Come, we will fence no longer. I see you have self-education, the only education which is not infinitely pernicious, and I am in want of a governess for my two children. I have been a widower for some years; my name is Gregg. I offer you the post I have named, and shall we say a salary of a hundred a year?'

I could only stutter out my thanks, and slipping a card with his address, and a banknote by way of earnest, into my hand, Mr. Gregg bade me good-bye, asking me to call in a day or two.

Such was my introduction to Professor Gregg, and can you wonder that the remembrance of despair and the cold blast that had blown from the gates of death upon me made me regard him as a second father? Before the close of the week I was installed in my new duties. The professor had leased an old brick manor-house in a western suburb of London, and here, surrounded by pleasant lawns and orchards, and soothed with the murmur of ancient elms that rocked their boughs above the roof, the new chapter of my life began. Knowing as you do the nature of the professor's occupations, you will not be surprised to hear that the house teemed with books, and cabinets full of strange, and even hideous, objects filled every available nook in the vast low rooms. Gregg was a man whose one thought was for knowledge, and I too before long caught something of his enthusiasm, and strove to enter into his passion of research. In a few months I was perhaps more his secretary than the governess of the two children, and many a night I have sat at the desk in the glow of the shaded lamp while he, pacing up and down in the rich gloom of the firelight, dictated to me the substance of his *Textbook of Ethnology*. But amidst these more sober and accurate studies I always detected a something hidden, a longing and desire for some object to which he did not allude; and now and then he would break short in what he was saying and lapse into reverie, entranced, as it seemed to me, by some distant prospect of adventurous discovery. The textbook was at last finished, and we began to receive proofs from the printers, which were entrusted to me for a first reading, and then underwent the final revision of the professor. All the while his wariness of the actual business he was engaged on increased, and it was with the joyous laugh of a schoolboy when term is over that he one day handed me a copy of the book. 'There,' he said, 'I have kept my word; I promised to write it, and it is done with. Now I shall be free to live for stranger things; I confess it, Miss Lally, I covet the renown of Columbus; you will, I hope, see me play the part of an explorer.'

'Surely,' I said, 'there is little left to explore. You have been born a few hundred years too late for that.'

'I think you are wrong,' he replied; 'there are still, depend upon it, quaint, undiscovered countries and continents of strange extent. Ah, Miss Lally! believe me, we stand amidst sacraments and mysteries full of awe, and it doth not yet appear what we shall be. Life, believe me, is no simple thing, no mass of grey matter and congeries of veins and muscles to be laid naked by the surgeon's knife; man is the secret which I am about to explore, and before I can discover him I must cross over weltering seas indeed, and oceans and the mists of many thousand years. You know the myth of the lost Atlantis; what if it be true, and I am destined to be called the discoverer of that wonderful land?'

I could see excitement boiling beneath his words, and in his face was the heat of the hunter; before me stood a man who believed himself summoned to tourney with the unknown. A pang of joy possessed me when I reflected that I was to be in a way associated with him in the adventure, and I, too, burned with the lust of the chase, not pausing to consider that I knew not what we were to unshadow.

The next morning Professor Gregg took me into his inner study, where, ranged against the wall, stood a nest of pigeonholes, every drawer neatly labelled, and the results of years of toil classified in a few feet of space.

'Here,' he said, 'is my life; here are all the facts which I have gathered together with so much pains, and yet it is all nothing.

No, nothing to what I am about to attempt. Look at this'; and he took me to an old bureau, a piece fantastic and faded, which stood in a corner of the room. He unlocked the front and opened one of the drawers.

'A few scraps of paper,' he went on, pointing to the drawer, 'and a lump of black stone, rudely annotated with queer marks and scratches – that is all that drawer holds. Here, you see, is an old envelope with the dark red stamp of twenty years ago, but I have pencilled a few lines at the back; here is a sheet of manuscript, and here some cuttings from obscure local journals. And if you ask me the subject-matter of the collection, it will not seem extraordinary – a servant-girl at a farmhouse, who disappeared from her place and has never been heard of, a child supposed to have slipped down some old working on the mountains, some queer scribbling on a limestone rock, a man murdered with a blow from a strange weapon; such is the scent I have to go upon. Yes, as you say, there is a ready explanation for all this; the girl may have run away to London, or Liverpool, or New York; the child may be at the bottom of the disused shaft; and the letters on the rock may be the idle whims of some vagrant. Yes, yes, I admit all that; but I know I hold the true key. Look!' and he held out a slip of yellow paper.

'Characters found inscribed on a limestone rock on the Grey Hills', I read, and then there was a word erased, presumably the name of a county, and a date some fifteen years back. Beneath was traced a number of uncouth characters, shaped somewhat like wedges or daggers, as strange and outlandish as the Hebrew alphabet.

'Now the seal,' said Professor Gregg, and he handed me the black stone, a thing about two inches long, and something like an old-fashioned tobacco-stopper, much enlarged.

I held it up to the light, and saw to my surprise the characters on the paper repeated on the seal.

'Yes,' said the professor, 'they are the same. And the marks on the limestone rock were made fifteen years ago, with some red substance. And the characters on the seal are four thousand years old at least. Perhaps much more.'

'Is it a hoax?' I said.

'No, I anticipated that. I was not to be led to give my life to a practical joke. I have tested the matter very carefully. Only one person besides myself knows of the mere existence of that black seal. Besides, there are other reasons which I cannot enter into now.'

'But what does it all mean?' I said. 'I cannot understand to what conclusion all this leads.'

'My dear Miss Lally, that is a question I would rather leave unanswered for some little time. Perhaps I shall never be able to say what secrets are held here in solution; a few vague hints, the outlines of village tragedies, a few marks done with red earth upon a rock, and an ancient seal. A queer set of data to go upon? Half a dozen pieces of evidence, and twenty years before even so much could be got together; and who knows what mirage or *terra incognita* may be beyond all this? I look across deep waters, Miss Lally, and the land beyond may be but a haze after all. But still I believe it is not so, and a few months will show whether I am right or wrong.'

He left me, and alone I endeavoured to fathom the mystery, wondering to what goal such eccentric odds and ends of evidence could lead. I myself am not wholly devoid of imagination, and I had reason to respect the professor's solidity of intellect; yet I saw in the contents of the drawer but the materials of fantasy, and vainly tried to conceive what theory could be founded on the fragments that had been placed before me. Indeed, I could discover in what I had heard and seen but the first chapter of an extravagant romance; and yet deep in my heart I burned with curiosity, and day after day I looked eagerly in Professor Gregg's face for some hint of what was to happen.

It was one evening after dinner that the word came.

'I hope you can make your preparations without much trouble,' he said suddenly to me. 'We shall be leaving here in a week's time.'

'Really!' I said in astonishment. 'Where are we going?'

'I have taken a country house in the west of England, not far from Caermaen, a quiet little town, once a city, and the head-quarters of a Roman legion. It is very dull there, but the country is pretty, and the air is wholesome.'

I detected a glint in his eyes, and guessed that this sudden move had some relation to our conversation of a few days before.

'I shall just take a few books with me,' said Professor Gregg, 'that is all. Everything else will remain here for our return. I have got a holiday,' he went on, smiling at me, 'and I shan't be sorry to be quit for a time of my old bones and stones and rubbish. Do you know,' he went on, 'I have been grinding away at facts for thirty years; it is time for fancies.'

The days passed quickly; I could see that the professor was all quivering with suppressed excitement, and I could scarce credit the eager appetence of his glance as we left the old manor-house behind us and began our journey. We set out at midday, and it was in the dusk of the evening that we arrived at a little country station. I was tired and excited, and the drive through the lanes seems all a dream. First the deserted streets of a forgotten village, while I heard Professor Gregg's voice talking of the Augustan Legion and the clash of arms, and all the tremendous pomp that followed the eagles; then the broad river swimming to full tide with the last afterglow glimmering duskily in the yellow water, the wide meadows, the cornfields whitening, and the deep lane winding on the slope between the hills and the water. At last we began to ascend, and the air grew rarer. I looked down and saw the pure white mist tracking the outline of the river like a shroud, and a vague and shadowy country; imaginations and fantasy of swelling hills and hanging woods, and half-shaped outlines of hills beyond, and in the distance the glare of the furnace fire on the mountain, glowing by turns a pillar of shining flame and fading to a dull point of red. We were slowly mounting a carriage drive, and then there came to me the cool breath and the secret of the great wood that was above us; I seemed to wander in its deepest depths, and there was the sound of trickling water, the scent of the green leaves, and the breath of the summer night. The carriage stopped at last, and I could scarcely distinguish the form of the house, as I waited a moment at the pillared porch. The rest of the evening seemed a dream of strange things bounded by the great silence of the wood and the valley and the river.

The next morning, when I awoke and looked out of the bow window of the big, old-fashioned bedroom, I saw under a grey sky a country that was still all mystery. The long, lovely valley, with the river winding in and out below, crossed in mid-vision by a mediaeval bridge of vaulted and buttressed stone, the clear presence of the rising ground beyond, and the woods that I had only seen in shadow the night before, seemed tinged with enchantment, and the soft breath of air that sighed in at the opened pane was like no other wind. I looked across the valley, and beyond, hill followed on hill as wave on wave, and here a faint blue pillar of smoke rose still in the morning air from the chimney of an ancient grey farmhouse, there was a rugged height crowned with dark firs, and in the distance I saw the white streak of a road that climbed and vanished into some unimagined country. But the boundary of all was a great wall of mountain, vast in the west, and ending like a fortress with a steep ascent and a domed tumulus clear against the sky.

I saw Professor Gregg walking up and down the terrace path below the windows, and it was evident that he was revelling in the sense of liberty, and the thought that he had for a while bidden good-bye to task-work. When I joined him there was exultation in his voice as he pointed out the sweep of valley and the river that wound beneath the lovely hills.

'Yes,' he said, 'it is a strangely beautiful country; and to me, at least, it seems full of mystery. You have not forgotten the drawer I showed you, Miss Lally? No; and you have guessed that

I have come here not merely for the sake of the children and the fresh air?'

'I think I have guessed as much as that,' I replied; 'but you must remember I do not know the mere nature of your investigations; and as for the connection between the search and this wonderful valley, it is past my guessing.'

He smiled queerly at me. 'You must not think I am making a mystery for the sake of mystery,' he said. 'I do not speak out because, so far, there is nothing to be spoken, nothing definite, I mean, nothing that can be set down in hard black and white, as dull and sure and irreproachable as any blue-book. And then I have another reason: Many years ago a chance paragraph in a newspaper caught my attention, and focussed in an instant the vagrant thoughts and half-formed fancies of many idle and speculative hours into a certain hypothesis. I saw at once that I was treading on a thin crust; my theory was wild and fantastic in the extreme, and I would not for any consideration have written a hint of it for publication. But I thought that in the company of scientific men like myself, men who knew the course of discovery, and were aware that the gas that blazes and flares in the gin-palace was once a wild hypothesis – I thought that with such men as these I might hazard my dream – let us say Atlantis, or the philosopher's stone, or what you like – without danger of ridicule. I found I was grossly mistaken; my friends looked blankly at me and at one another, and I could see something of pity, and something also of insolent contempt, in the glances they exchanged. One of them called on me next day, and hinted that I must be suffering from overwork and brain exhaustion. "In plain terms," I said, "you think I am going mad. I think not"; and I showed him out with some little appearance of heat. Since that day I vowed that I would never whisper the nature of my theory to any living soul; to no one but yourself have I ever shown the contents of that drawer. After all, I may be following a rainbow; I may have been misled by the play of coincidence; but as I stand here in this mystic hush and silence, amidst the woods and wild hills, I am more than ever sure that I am hot on the scent. Come, it is time we went in.'

To me in all this there was something both of wonder and excitement; I knew how in his ordinary work Professor Gregg moved step by step, testing every inch of the way, and never venturing on assertion without proof that was impregnable. Yet I divined, more from his glance and the vehemence of his tone than from the spoken word, that he had in his every thought the vision of the almost incredible continually with him; and I, who was with some share of imagination no little of a sceptic, offended at a hint of the marvellous, could not help asking myself whether he were cherishing a monomania, and barring out from this one subject all the scientific method of his other life.

Yet, with this image of mystery haunting my thoughts, I surrendered wholly to the charm of the country. Above the faded house on the hillside began the great forest – a long, dark line seen from the opposing hills, stretching above the river for many a mile from north to south, and yielding in the north to even wilder country, barren and savage hills, and ragged common-land, a territory all strange and unvisited, and more unknown to Englishmen than the very heart of Africa. The space of a couple of steep fields alone separated the house from the wood, and the children were delighted to follow me up the long alleys of undergrowth, between smooth pleached walls of shining beech, to the highest point in the wood, whence one looked on one side across the river and the rise and fall of the country to the great western mountain wall, and on the other over the surge and dip of the myriad trees of the forest, over level meadows and the shining yellow sea to the faint coast beyond. I used to sit at this point on the warm sunlit turf which marked the track of the Roman Road, while the two children raced about hunting for the whinberries that grew here and there on the banks. Here, beneath the deep blue sky and the great clouds rolling, like olden galleons with sails full-bellied, from the sea to the hills, as I listened to the whispered charm of the great and ancient wood, I lived solely for delight, and only remembered strange things when we would return to the house and find Professor Gregg either shut up in the little room he had made his study, or else pacing the terrace with the look, patient and enthusiastic, of the determined seeker.

One morning, some eight or nine days after our arrival, I looked out of my window and saw the whole landscape transmuted before me. The clouds had dipped low and hidden the mountain in the west; a southern wind was driving the rain in shifting pillars up the valley, and the little brooklet that burst the hill below the house now raged, a red torrent, down the river. We were perforce obliged to keep snug within-doors; and when I had attended to my pupils, I sat down in the morning-room, where the ruins of a library still encumbered an old-fashioned bookcase. I had inspected the shelves once or twice, but their contents had failed to attract me; volumes of eighteenth-century sermons, an old book on farriery, a collection of poems by 'persons of quality,' Prideaux's *Connection*, and an odd volume of Pope, were the boundaries of the library, and there seemed little doubt that everything of interest or value had been removed. Now, however, in desperation, I began to re-examine the musty sheepskin and calf bindings, and found, much to my delight, a fine old quarto printed by the Stephani, containing the three books of Pomponius Mela, *De Situ Orbis*, and other of the ancient geographers. I knew enough of Latin to steer my way through an ordinary sentence, and I soon became absorbed in the odd mixture of fact and fancy – light shining on a little of the space of the world, and beyond, mist and shadow and awful forms. Glancing over the clear-printed pages, my attention was caught by the heading of a chapter in Solinus, and I read the words:

MIRA DE INTIMIS GENTIBUS LIBYAE, DE LAPIDE HEXECONTALITHO,

– 'The wonders of the people that inhabit the inner parts of Libya, and of the stone called Sixtystone.'

The odd title attracted me, and I read on:

Gens ista avia et secreta habitat, in montibus horrendis foeda mysteria celebrat. De hominibus nihil aliud illi praeferunt quam figuram, ab humano ritu prorsus exulant, oderunt deum lucis. Stridunt potius quam loquuntur; vox absona nec sine horrore auditur. Lapide quodam gloriantur, quem Hexecontalithon vocant; dicunt enim hunc lapidem sexaginta notas ostendere. Cujus lapidis nomen secretum ineffabile colunt: quod Ixaxar.

'This folk,' I translated to myself, 'dwells in remote and secret places, and celebrates foul mysteries on savage hills. Nothing have they in common with men save the face, and the customs of humanity are wholly strange to them; and they hate the sun. They hiss rather than speak; their voices are harsh, and not to be heard without fear. They boast of a certain stone, which they call Sixtystone; for they say that it displays sixty characters. And this stone has a secret unspeakable name; which is Ixaxar.'

I laughed at the queer inconsequence of all this, and thought it fit for 'Sinbad the Sailor,' or other of the supplementary *Nights*. When I saw Professor Gregg in the course of the day, I told him of my find in the bookcase, and the fantastic rubbish I had been reading. To my surprise he looked up at me with an expression of great interest.

'That is really very curious,' he said. 'I have never thought it worth while to look into the old geographers, and I dare say I have missed a good deal. Ah, that is the passage, is it? It seems a shame to rob you of your entertainment, but I really think I must carry off the book.'

The next day the professor called me to come to the study. I found him sitting at a table in the full light of the window, scrutinizing something very attentively with a magnifying glass.

'Ah, Miss Lally,' he began, 'I want to use your eyes. This glass is pretty good, but not like my old one that I left in town.

Would you mind examining the thing yourself, and telling me how many characters are cut on it?'

He handed me the object in his hand. I saw that it was the black seal he had shown me in London, and my heart began to beat with the thought that I was presently to know something. I took the seal, and, holding it up to the light, checked off the grotesque dagger-shaped characters one by one.

'I make sixty-two,' I said at last.

'Sixty-two? Nonsense; it's impossible, Ah, I see what you have done, you have counted that and that,' and he pointed to two marks which I had certainly taken as letters with the rest.

'Yes, yes,' Professor Gregg went on, 'but those are obviously scratches, done accidentally; I saw that at once. Yes, then that's quite right. Thank you very much, Miss Lally.'

I was going away, rather disappointed at my having been called in merely to count the number of marks on the black seal, when suddenly there flashed into my mind what I had read in the morning.

'But, Professor Gregg,' I cried, breathless, 'the seal, the seal. Why, it is the stone Hexecontalithos that Solinus writes of; it is Ixaxar.'

'Yes,' he said, 'I suppose it is. Or it may be a mere coincidence. It never does to be too sure, you know, in these matters. Coincidence killed the professor.'

I went away puzzled by what I had heard, and as much as ever at a loss to find the ruling clue in this maze of strange evidence. For three days the bad weather lasted, changing from driving rain to a dense mist, fine and dripping, and we seemed to be shut up in a white cloud that veiled all the world away from us. All the while Professor Gregg was darkling in his room, unwilling, it appeared, to dispense confidences or talk of any kind, and I heard him walking to and fro with a quick, impatient step, as if he were in some way wearied of inaction. The fourth morning was fine, and at breakfast the professor said briskly:

'We want some extra help about the house; a boy of fifteen or sixteen, you know. There are a lot of little odd jobs that take up the maids' time which a boy could do much better.'

'The girls have not complained to me in any way,' I replied. 'Indeed, Anne said there was much less work than in London, owing to there being so little dust.'

'Ah, yes, they are very good girls. But I think we shall do much better with a boy. In fact, that is what has been bothering me for the last two days.'

'Bothering you?' I said in astonishment, for as a matter of fact the professor never took the slightest interest in the affairs of the house.

'Yes,' he said, 'the weather, you know. I really couldn't go out in that Scotch mist; I don't know the country very well, and I should have lost my way. But I am going to get the boy this morning.'

'But how do you know there is such a boy as you want anywhere about?'

'Oh, I have no doubt as to that. I may have to walk a mile or two at the most, but I am sure to find just the boy I require.'

I thought the professor was joking, but, though his tone was airy enough, there was something grim and set about his features that puzzled me. He got his stick, and stood at the door looking meditatively before him, and as I passed through the hall he called to me.

'By the way, Miss Lally, there was one thing I wanted to say to you. I dare say you may have heard that some of these country lads are not over-bright; "idiotic" would be a harsh word to use, and they are usually called "naturals," or something of the kind. I hope you won't mind if the boy I am after should turn out not too keen-witted; he will be perfectly harmless, of course, and blacking boots doesn't need much mental effort.'

With that he was gone, striding up the road that led to the wood, and I remained stupefied; and then for the first time my astonishment was mingled with a sudden note of terror, arising I knew not whence, and all unexplained even to myself, and yet

I felt about my heart for an instant something of the chill of death, and that shapeless, formless dread of the unknown that is worse than death itself. I tried to find courage in the sweet air that blew up from the sea, and in the sunlight after rain, but the mystic woods seemed to darken around me; and the vision of the river coiling between the reeds, and the silver grey of the ancient bridge, fashioned in my mind symbols of vague dread, as the mind of a child fashions terror from things harmless and familiar.

Two hours later Professor Gregg returned. I met him as he came down the road, and asked quietly if he had been able to find a boy.

'Oh, yes,' he answered; 'I found one easily enough. His name is Jervase Cradock, and I expect he will make himself very useful. His father has been dead for many years, and the mother, whom I saw, seemed very glad at the prospect of a few shillings extra coming in on Saturday nights. As I expected, he is not too sharp, has fits at times, the mother said; but as he will not be trusted with the china, that doesn't much matter, does it? And he is not in any way dangerous, you know, merely a little weak.'

'When is he coming?'

'To-morrow morning at eight o'clock. Anne will show him what he has to do, and how to do it. At first he will go home every night, but perhaps it may ultimately turn out more convenient for him to sleep here, and only go home for Sundays.'

I found nothing to say to all this; Professor Gregg spoke in a quiet tone of matter-of-fact, as indeed was warranted by the circumstance; and yet I could not quell my sensation of astonishment at the whole affair. I knew that in reality no assistance was wanted in the housework, and the professor's prediction that the boy he was to engage might prove a little 'simple,' followed by so exact a fulfilment, struck me as bizarre in the extreme. The next morning I heard from the housemaid that the boy Cradock had come at eight, and that she had been trying to make him useful. 'He doesn't seem quite all there, I don't think, miss,' was her comment, and later in the day I saw him helping the old man who worked in the garden. He was a youth of about fourteen, with black hair and black eyes and an olive skin, and I saw at once from the curious vacancy of his expression that he was mentally weak. He touched his forehead awkwardly as I went by, and I heard him answering the gardener in a queer, harsh voice that caught my attention; it gave me the impression of some one speaking deep below under the earth, and there was a strange sibilance, like the hissing of the phonograph as the pointer travels over the cylinder. I heard that he seemed anxious to do what he could, and was quite docile and obedient, and Morgan the gardener, who knew his mother, assured me he was perfectly harmless. 'He's always been a bit queer,' he said, 'and no wonder, after what his mother went through before he was born. I did know his father, Thomas Cradock, well, and a very fine workman he was too, indeed. He got something wrong with his lungs owing to working in the wet woods, and never got over it, and went off quite sudden like. And they do say as how Mrs. Cradock was quite off her head; anyhow, she was found by Mr. Hillyer, Ty Coch, all crouched up on the Grey Hills, over there, crying and weeping like a lost soul. And Jervase, he was born about eight months afterwards, and, as I was saying, he was a bit queer always; and they do say when he could scarcely walk he would frighten the other children into fits with the noises he would make.'

A word in the story had stirred up some remembrance within me, and, vaguely curious, I asked the old man where the Grey Hills were.

'Up there,' he said, with the same gesture he had used before; 'you go past the "Fox and Hounds," and through the forest, by the old ruins. It's a good five mile from here, and a strange sort of a place. The poorest soil between this and Monmouth, they do say, though it's good feed for sheep. Yes, it was a sad thing for poor Mrs. Cradock.'

The old man turned to his work, and I strolled on down the path between the espaliers, gnarled and gouty with age, thinking of the story I had heard, and groping for the point in it that had some key to my memory. In an instant it came before me; I had seen the phrase 'Grey Hills' on the slip of yellowed paper that Professor Gregg had taken from the drawer in his cabinet. Again I was seized with pangs of mingled curiosity and fear; I remembered the strange characters copied from the limestone rock, and then again their identity with the inscription of the age-old seal, and the fantastic fables of the Latin geographer. I saw beyond doubt that, unless coincidence had set all the scene and disposed all these bizarre events with curious art, I was to be a spectator of things far removed from the usual and customary traffic and jostle of life. Professor Gregg I noted day by day; he was hot on his trail, growing lean with eagerness; and in the evenings, when the sun was swimming on the verge of the mountain, he would pace the terrace to and fro with his eyes on the ground, while the mist grew white in the valley, and the stillness of the evening brought far voices near, and the blue smoke rose a straight column from the diamond-shaped chimney of the grey farm-house, just as I had seen it on the first morning. I have told you I was of sceptical habit; but though I understood little or nothing, I began to dread, vainly proposing to myself the iterated dogmas of science that all life is material, and that in the system of things there is no undiscovered land, even beyond the remotest stars, where the supernatural can find a footing. Yet there struck in on this the thought that matter is as really awful and unknown as spirit, that science itself but dallies on the threshold, scarcely gaining more than a glimpse of the wonders of the inner place.

There is one day that stands up from amidst the others as a grim red beacon, betokening evil to come. I was sitting on a bench in the garden, watching the boy Cradock weeding, when I was suddenly alarmed by a harsh and choking sound, like the cry of a wild beast in anguish, and I was unspeakably shocked to see the unfortunate lad standing in full view before me, his whole body quivering and shaking at short intervals as though shocks of electricity were passing through him, his teeth grinding, foam gathering on his lips, and his face all swollen and blackened to a hideous mask of humanity. I shrieked with terror, and Professor Gregg came running; and as I pointed to Cradock, the boy with one convulsive shudder fell face forward, and lay on the wet earth, his body writhing like a wounded blind-worm, and an inconceivable babble of sounds bursting and rattling and hissing from his lips. He seemed to pour forth an infamous jargon, with words, or what seemed words, that might have belonged to a tongue dead since untold ages and buried deep beneath Nilotic mud, or in the inmost recesses of the Mexican forest. For a moment the thought passed through my mind, as my ears were still revolted with that infernal clamour, 'Surely this is the very speech of hell,' and then I cried out again and again, and ran away shuddering to my inmost soul. I had seen Professor Gregg's face as he stooped over the wretched boy and raised him, and I was appalled by the glow of exultation that shone on every lineament and feature. As I sat in my room with drawn blinds, and my eyes hidden in my hands, I heard heavy steps beneath, and I was told afterwards that Professor Gregg had carried Cradock to his study, and had locked the door. I heard voices murmur indistinctly, and I trembled to think of what might be passing within a few feet of where I sat; I longed to escape to the woods and sunshine, and yet I dreaded the sights that might confront me on the way; and at last, as I held the handle of the door nervously, I heard Professor Gregg's voice calling to me with a cheerful ring. 'It's all right now, Miss Lally,' he said. 'The poor fellow has got over it, and I have been arranging for him to sleep here after to-morrow. Perhaps I may be able to do something for him.'

'Yes,' he said later, 'it was a very painful sight, and I don't wonder you were alarmed. We may hope that good food will build him up a little, but I am afraid he will never be really cured,' and he affected the dismal and conventional air with which one speaks of hopeless illness; and yet beneath it I detected the delight that leapt up rampant within him, and fought and struggled to find utterance. It was as if one glanced down on the even surface of the sea, clear and immobile, and saw beneath raging depths and and a storm of contending billows. It was indeed to me a torturing and offensive problem that this man, who had so bounteously rescued me from the sharpness of death, and showed himself in all the relations of life full of benevolence, and pity, and kindly forethought, should so manifestly be for once on the side of the demons, and take a ghastly pleasure in the torments of an afflicted fellow creature. Apart, I struggled with the horned difficulty, and strove to find the solution; but without the hint of a clue, beset by mystery and contradiction. I saw nothing that might help me, and began to wonder whether, after all, I had not escaped from the white mist of the suburb at too dear a rate. I hinted something of my thought to the professor; I said enough to let him know that I was in the most acute perplexity, but the moment after regretted what I had done when I saw his face contort with a spasm of pain.

'My dear Miss Lally,' he said, 'you surely do not wish to leave us? No, no, you would not do it. You do not know how I rely on you; how confidently I go forward, assured that you are here to watch over my children. You, Miss Lally, are my rear-guard; for let me tell you the business in which I am engaged is not wholly devoid of peril. You have not forgotten what I said the first morning here; my lips are shut by an old and firm resolve till they can open to utter no ingenious hypothesis or vague surmise, but irrefragable fact, as certain as a demonstration in mathematics. Think over it, Miss Lally; not for a moment would I endeavour to keep you here against your own instincts, and yet I tell you frankly that I am persuaded it is here, here amidst the woods, that your duty lies.'

I was touched by the eloquence of his tone, and by the remembrance that the man, after all, had been my salvation, and I gave him my hand on a promise to serve him loyally and without question. A few days later the rector of our church – a little church, grey and severe and quaint, that hovered on the very banks of the river and watched the tides swim and return – came to see us, and Professor Gregg easily persuaded him to stay and share our dinner. Mr. Meyrick was a member of an antique family of squires, whose old manor-house stood amongst the hills some seven miles away, and thus rooted in the soil, the rector was a living store of all the old fading customs and lore of the country. His manner, genial, with a deal of retired oddity, won on Professor Gregg; and towards the cheese, when a curious Burgundy had begun its incantations, the two men glowed like the wine, and talked of philology with the enthusiasm of a burgess over the peerage. The parson was expounding the pronunciation of the Welsh *ll*, and producing sounds like the gurgle of his native brooks, when Professor Gregg struck in.

'By the way,' he said, 'that was a very odd word I met with the other day. You know my boy, poor Jervase Cradock? Well, he has got the bad habit of talking to himself, and the day before yesterday I was walking in the garden here and heard him; he was evidently quite unconscious of my presence. A lot of what he said I couldn't make out, but one word struck me distinctly. It was such an odd sound, half sibilant, half guttural, and as quaint as those double *l*'s you have been demonstrating. I do not know whether I can give you an idea of the sound; "Ishakshar" is perhaps as near as I can get. But the *k* ought to be a Greek *chi* or a Spanish *j*. Now what does it mean in Welsh?'

'In Welsh?' said the parson. 'There is no such word in Welsh, nor any word remotely resembling it. I know the book-Welsh, as they call it, and the colloquial dialects as well as any man, but there's no word like that from Anglesea to Usk. Besides, none of the Cradocks speak a word of Welsh; it's dying out about here.'

'Really. You interest me extremely, Mr. Meyrick. I confess the word didn't strike me as having the Welsh ring. But I thought it might be some local corruption.'

'No, I never heard such a word, or anything like it. Indeed,' he added, smiling whimsically, 'if it belongs to any language, I

71

should say it must be that of the fairies – the Tylwydd Têg, as we call them.'

The talk went on to the discovery of a Roman villa in the neighbourhood; and soon after I left the room, and sat down apart to wonder at the drawing together of such strange clues of evidence. As the professor had spoken of the curious word, I had caught the glint of his eye upon me; and though the pronunciation he gave was grotesque in the extreme, I recognized the name of the stone of sixty characters mentioned by Solinus, the black seal shut up in some secret drawer of the study, stamped for ever by a vanished race with signs that no man could read, signs that might, for all I knew, be the veils of awful things done long ago, and forgotten before the hills were moulded into form.

When the next morning I came down, I found Professor Gregg pacing the terrace in his eternal walk.

'Look at that bridge,' he said, when he saw me; 'observe the quaint and Gothic design, the angles between the arches, and the silvery grey of the stone in the awe of the morning light. I confess it seems to me symbolic; it should illustrate a mystical allegory of the passage from one world to another.'

'Professor Gregg,' I said quietly, 'it is time that I knew something of what has happened, and of what is to happen.'

For the moment he put me off, but I returned again with the same question in the evening, and then Professor Gregg flamed with excitement. 'Don't you understand yet?' he cried. 'But I have told you a good deal; yes, and shown you a good deal; you have heard pretty nearly all that I have heard, and seen what I have seen; or at least,' and his voice chilled as he spoke, 'enough to make a good deal clear as noonday. The servants told you, I have no doubt, that the wretched boy Cradock had another seizure the night before last; he awoke me with cries in that voice you heard in the garden, and I went to him, and God forbid you should see what I saw that night. But all this is useless; my time here is drawing to a close; I must be back in town in three weeks, as I have a course of lectures to prepare, and need all my books about me. In a very few days it will be all over, and I shall no longer hint, and no longer be liable to ridicule as a madman and a quack. No, I shall speak plainly, and I shall be heard with such emotions as perhaps no other man has ever drawn from the breasts of his fellows.'

He paused, and seemed to grow radiant with the joy of great and wonderful discovery.

'But all that is for the future, the near future certainly, but still the future,' he went on at length. 'There is something to be done yet; you will remember my telling you that my researches were not altogether devoid of peril? Yes, there is a certain amount of danger to be faced; I did not know how much when I spoke on the subject before, and to a certain extent I am still in the dark. But it will be a strange adventure, the last of all, the last demonstration in the chain.'

He was walking up and down the room as he spoke, and I could hear in his voice the contending tones of exultation and despondence, or perhaps I should say awe, the awe of a man who goes forth on unknown waters, and I thought of his allusion to Columbus on the night he had laid his book before me. The evening was a little chilly, and a fire of logs had been lighted in the study where we were; the remittent flame and the glow on the walls reminded me of the old days. I was sitting silent in an armchair by the fire, wondering over all I had heard, and still vainly speculating as to the secret springs concealed from me under all the phantasmagoria I had witnessed, when I became suddenly aware of a sensation that change of some sort had been at work in the room, and that there was something unfamiliar in its aspect. For some time I looked about me, trying in vain to localize the alteration that I knew had been made; the table by the window, the chairs, the faded settee were all as I had known them. Suddenly, as a sought-for recollection flashes into the mind, I knew what was amiss. I was facing the professor's desk, which stood on the other side of the fire, and above the desk was a grimy-looking bust of Pitt, that I had never seen there before.

And then I remembered the true position of this work of art: in the furthest corner by the door was an old cupboard, projecting into the room, and on the top of the cupboard, fifteen feet from the floor, the bust had been, and there, no doubt, it had delayed, accumulating dirt, since the early days of the century.

I was utterly amazed, and sat silent, still in a confusion of thought. There was, so far as I knew, no such thing as a stepladder in the house, for I had asked for one to make some alterations in the curtains of my room, and a tall man standing on a chair would have found it impossible to take down the bust. It had been placed, not on the edge of the cupboard, but far back against the wall; and Professor Gregg was, if anything, under the average height.

'How on earth did you manage to get down Pitt?' I said at last.

The professor looked curiously at me, and seemed to hesitate a little.

'They must have found you a step-ladder, or perhaps the gardener brought in a short ladder from outside?'

'No, I have had no ladder of any kind. Now, Miss Lally,' he went on with an awkward simulation of jest, 'there is a little puzzle for you; a problem in the manner of the inimitable Holmes; there are the facts, plain and patent: summon your acuteness to the solution of the puzzle. For Heaven's sake,' he cried with a breaking voice, 'say no more about it! I tell you, I never touched the thing,' and he went out of the room with horror manifest on his face, and his hand shook and jarred the door behind him.

I looked round the room in vague surprise, not at all realizing what had happened, making vain and idle surmises by way of explanation, and wondering at the stirring of black waters by an idle word and the trivial change of an ornament. 'This is some petty business, some whim on which I have jarred,' I reflected; 'the professor is perhaps scrupulous and superstitious over trifles, and my question may have outraged unacknowledged fears, as though one killed a spider or spilled the salt before the very eyes of a practical Scotchwoman.' I was immersed in these fond suspicions, and began to plume myself a little on my immunity from such empty fears, when the truth fell heavily as lead upon my heart, and I recognized with cold terror that some awful influence had been at work. The bust was simply inaccessible; without a ladder no one could have touched it.

I went out to the kitchen and spoke as quietly as I could to the housemaid.

'Who moved that bust from the top of the cupboard, Anne?' I said to her. 'Professor Gregg says he has not touched it. Did you find an old step-ladder in one of the outhouses?'

The girl looked at me blankly.

'I never touched it,' she said. 'I found it where it is now the other morning when I dusted the room. I remember now, it was Wednesday morning, because it was the morning after Cradock was taken bad in the night. My room is next to his, you know, miss,' the girl went on piteously, 'and it was awful to hear how he cried and called out names that I couldn't understand. It made me feel all afraid; and then master came, and I heard him speak, and he took down Cradock to the study and gave him something.'

'And you found that bust moved the next morning?'

'Yes, miss. There was a queer sort of smell in the study when I came down and opened the windows; a bad smell it was, and I wondered what it could be. Do you know, miss, I went a long time ago to the Zoo in London with my cousin Thomas Barker, one afternoon that I had off, when I was at Mrs. Prince's in Stanhope Gate, and we went into the snake-house to see the snakes, and it was just the same sort of smell; very sick it made me feel, I remember, and I got Barker to take me out. And it was just the same kind of smell in the study, as I was saying, and I was wondering what it could be from, when I see that bust with Pitt cut in it, standing on the master's desk, and I thought to myself, "Now who has done that, and how have they done it?" And when I came to dust the things, I looked at the bust, and I saw a great mark on it where the dust was gone, for I don't think it can have been touched with a duster for years and years, and it wasn't like finger-marks, but a large patch like, broad and spread out. So I passed my hand over it, without thinking what I was doing, and where that patch was it was all sticky and slimy, as if a snail had crawled over it. Very strange, isn't it, miss? and I wonder who can have done it, and how that mess was made.'

The well-meant gabble of the servant touched me to the quick; I lay down upon my bed, and bit my lip that I should not cry out loud in the sharp anguish of my terror and bewilderment. Indeed, I was almost mad with dread; I believe that if it had been daylight I should have fled hot foot, forgetting all courage and all the debt of gratitude that was due to Professor Gregg, not caring whether my fate were that I must starve slowly, so long as I might escape from the net of blind and panic fear that every day seemed to draw a little closer round me. If I knew, I thought, if I knew what there were to dread, I could guard against it; but here, in this lonely house, shut in on all sides by the olden woods and the vaulted hills, terror seems to spring inconsequent from every covert, and the flesh is aghast at the half-hearted murmurs of horrible things. All in vain I strove to summon scepticism to my aid, and endeavoured by cool common sense to buttress my belief in a world of natural order, for the air that blew in at the open window was a mystic breath, and in the darkness I felt the silence go heavy and sorrowful as a mass of requiem, and I conjured images of strange shapes gathering fast amidst the reeds, beside the wash of the river.

In the morning from the moment that I set foot in the breakfast-room, I felt that the unknown plot was drawing to a crisis; the professor's face was firm and set, and he seemed hardly to hear our voices when we spoke.

'I am going out for a rather long walk,' he said, when the meal was over. 'You mustn't be expecting me, now, or thinking anything has happened if I don't turn up to dinner. I have been getting stupid lately, and I dare say a miniature walking tour will do me good. Perhaps I may even spend the night in some little inn, if I find any place that looks clean and comfortable.'

I heard this, and knew by my experience of Professor Gregg's manner that it was no ordinary business or pleasure that impelled him. I knew not, nor even remotely guessed, where he was bound, nor had I the vaguest notion of his errand, but all the fear of the night before returned; and as he stood, smiling, on the terrace, ready to set out, I implored him to stay, and to forget all his dreams of the undiscovered continent.

'No, no, Miss Lally,' he replied, still smiling, 'it's too late now. *Vestigia nulla retrorsum*, you know, is the device of all true explorers; though I hope it won't be literally true in my case. But, indeed, you are wrong to alarm yourself so; I look upon my little expedition as quite commonplace; no more exciting than a day with the geological hammers. There is a risk, of course, but so there is on the commonest excursion. I can afford to be jaunty; I am doing nothing so hazardous as 'Arry does a hundred times over in the course of every Bank Holiday. Well, then, you must look more cheerfully; and so good-bye till to-morrow at latest.'

He walked briskly up the road, and I saw him open the gate that marks the entrance of the wood, and then he vanished in the gloom of the trees.

All the day passed heavily with a strange darkness in the air, and again I felt as if imprisoned amidst the ancient woods, shut in an olden land of mystery and dread, and as if all was long ago and forgotten by the living outside. I hoped and dreaded; and when the dinner-hour came I waited, expecting to hear the professor's step in the hall, and his voice exulting at I knew not what triumph. I composed my face to welcome him gladly, but the night descended dark, and he did not come.

In the morning, when the maid knocked at my door, I called out to her, and asked if her master had returned; and when she replied that his bedroom door stood open and empty, I felt the cold clasp of despair. Still, I fancied he might have discovered genial company, and would return for luncheon, or perhaps in the afternoon, and I took the children for a walk in the forest, and tried my best to play and laugh with them, and to shut out the thoughts of mystery and veiled terror. Hour after hour I waited, and my thoughts grew darker; again the night came and found me watching, and at last, as I was making much ado to finish my dinner, I heard steps outside and the sound of a man's voice.

The maid came in and looked oddly at me. 'Please, miss,' she began, 'Mr. Morgan, the gardener, wants to speak to you for a minute, if you didn't mind.'

'Show him in, please,' I answered, and set my lips tight.

The old man came slowly into the room, and the servant shut the door behind him.

'Sit down, Mr. Morgan,' I said; 'what is it that you want to say to me?'

'Well, miss, Mr. Gregg he gave me something for you yesterday morning, just before he went off; and he told me particular not to hand it up before eight o'clock this evening exactly, if so be as he wasn't back again home before, and if he should come home before I was just to return it to him in his own hands. So, you see, as Mr. Gregg isn't here yet, I suppose I'd better give you the parcel directly.'

He pulled out something from his pocket, and gave it to me, half rising. I took it silently, and seeing that Morgan seemed doubtful as to what he was to do next, I thanked him and bade him good night, and he went out. I was left alone in the room with the parcel in my hand – a paper parcel, neatly sealed and directed to me, with the instructions Morgan had quoted, all written in the professor's large, loose hand. I broke the seals with a choking at my heart, and found an envelope inside, addressed also, but open, and I took the letter out.

My dear Miss Lally (it began) – To quote the old logic manual, the case of your reading this note is a case of my having made a blunder of some sort, and, I am afraid, a blunder that turns these lines into a farewell. It is practically certain that neither you nor any one else will ever see me again. I have made my will with provision for this eventuality, and I hope you will consent to accept the small remembrance addressed to you, and my sincere thanks for the way in which you joined your fortunes to mine. The fate which has come upon me is desperate and terrible beyond the remotest dreams of man; but this fate you have a right to know – if you please. If you look in the left-hand drawer of my dressing-table, you will find the key of the escritoire, properly labelled. In the well of the escritoire is a large envelope sealed and addressed to your name. I advise you to throw it forthwith into the fire; you will sleep better of nights if you do so. But if you must know the history of what has happened, it is all written down for you to read.

The signature was firmly written below, and again I turned the page and read out the words one by one, aghast and white to the lips, my hands cold as ice, and sickness choking me. The dead silence of the room, and the thought of the dark woods and hills closing me in on every side, oppressed me, helpless and without capacity, and not knowing where to turn for counsel. At last I resolved that though knowledge should haunt my whole life and all the days to come, I must know the meaning of the strange terrors that had so long tormented me, rising grey, dim, and awful, like the shadows in the wood at dusk. I carefully carried out Professor Gregg's directions, and not without reluctance broke the seal of the envelope, and spread out his manuscript before me. That manuscript I always carry with me, and I see that I cannot deny your unspoken request to read it. This, then, was what I read that night, sitting at the desk, with a shaded lamp beside me.

The young lady who called herself Miss Lally then proceeded to recite

THE STATEMENT OF WILLIAM GREGG, F.R.S., ETC.

It is many years since the first glimmer of the theory which is now almost, if not quite, reduced to fact dawned on my mind. A somewhat extensive course of miscellaneous and obsolete reading had done a great deal to prepare the way, and, later, when I became somewhat of a specialist, and immersed myself in the studies known as ethnological, I was now and then startled by facts that would not square with orthodox scientific opinion, and by discoveries that seemed to hint at something still hidden for all our research. More particularly I became convinced that much of the folk-lore of the world is but an exaggerated account of events that really happened, and I was especially drawn to consider the stories of the fairies, the good folk of the Celtic races. Here, I thought I could detect the fringe of embroidery and exaggeration, the fantastic guise, the little people dressed in green and gold sporting in the flowers, and I thought I saw a distinct analogy between the name given to this race (supposed to be imaginary) and the description of their appearance and manners. Just as our remote ancestors called the dreaded beings 'fair' and 'good' precisely because they dreaded them, so they had dressed them up in charming forms, knowing the truth to be the very reverse. Literature, too, had gone early to work, and had lent a powerful hand in the transformation, so that the playful elves of Shakespeare are already far removed from the true original, and the real horror is disguised in a form of prankish mischief. But in the older tales, the stories that used to make men cross themselves as they sat around the burning logs, we tread a different stage; I saw a widely opposed spirit in certain histories of children and of men and women who vanished strangely from the earth. They would be seen by a peasant in the fields walking towards some green and rounded hillock, and seen no more on earth; and there are stories of mothers who have left a child quietly sleeping, with the cottage door rudely barred with a piece of wood, and have returned, not to find the plump and rosy little Saxon, but a thin and wizened creature, with sallow skin and black, piercing eyes, the child of another race. Then, again, there were myths darker still; the dread of witch and wizard, the lurid evil of the Sabbath, and the hint of demons who mingled with the daughters of men. And just as we have turned the terrible 'fair folk' into a company of benignant, if freakish elves, so we have hidden from us the black foulness of the witch and her companions under a popular *diablerie* of old women and broom-sticks, and a comic cat with tail on end. So the Greeks called the hideous furies benevolent ladies, and thus the northern nations have followed their example. I pursued my investigations, stealing odd hours from other and more imperative labours, and I asked myself the question: Supposing these traditions to be true, who were the demons who are reported to have attended the Sabbaths? I need not say that I laid aside what I may call the supernatural hypothesis of the Middle Ages, and came to the conclusion that fairies and devils were of one and the same race and origin; invention, no doubt, and the Gothic fancy of old days, had done much in the way of exaggeration and distortion; yet I firmly believe that beneath all this imagery there was a black background of truth. As for some of the alleged wonders, I hesitated. While I should be very loath to receive any one specific instance of modern spiritualism as containing even a grain of the genuine, yet I was not wholly prepared to deny that human flesh may now and then, once perhaps in ten million cases, be the veil of powers which seem magical to us – powers which, so far from proceeding from the heights and leading men thither, are in reality survivals from the depths of being. The amoeba and the snail have powers which we do not possess; and I thought it possible that the theory of reversion might explain many things which seem wholly inexplicable. Thus stood my position; I saw good reason to believe that much of the tradition, a vast deal of the earliest and uncorrupted tradition of the so-called fairies, represented solid fact, and I thought that the purely supernatural element in these traditions was to be accounted for on the hypothesis that a race which had fallen out of the grand march of evolution might have retained, as a survival, certain powers which would be to us wholly miraculous. Such was my theory as it stood conceived in my mind; and working with this in view, I seemed to gather confirmation from every side, from the spoils of a tumulus or a barrow, from a local paper reporting an antiquarian meeting in the country, and from general literature of all kinds. Amongst other instances, I remember being struck by the phrase 'articulate-speaking men' in Homer, as if the writer knew or had heard of men whose speech was so rude that it could hardly be termed articulate; and on my hypothesis of a race who had lagged far behind the rest, I could easily conceive that such a folk would speak a jargon but little removed from the inarticulate noises of brute beasts.

Thus I stood, satisfied that my conjecture was at all events not far removed from fact, when a chance paragraph in a small country print one day arrested my attention. It was a short account of what was to all appearance the usual sordid tragedy of the village – a young girl unaccountably missing, and evil rumour blatant and busy with her reputation. Yet I could read between the lines that all this scandal was purely hypothetical, and in all probability invented to account for what was in any other manner unaccountable. A flight to London or Liverpool, or an undiscovered body lying with a weight about its neck in the foul depths of a woodland pool, or perhaps murder – such were the theories of the wretched girl's neighbours. But as I idly scanned the paragraph, a flash of thought passed through me with the violence of an electric shock: what if the obscure and horrible race of the hills still survived, still remained haunting wild places and barren hills, and now and then repeating the evil of Gothic legend, unchanged and unchangeable as the Turanian Shelta, or the Basques of Spain? I have said that the thought came with violence; and indeed I drew in my breath sharply, and clung with both hands to my elbow-chair, in a strange confusion of horror and elation. It was as if one of my *confrères* of physical science, roaming in a quiet English wood, had been suddenly stricken aghast by the presence of the slimy and loathsome terror of the ichthyosaurus, the original of the stories of the awful worms killed by valorous knights, or had seen the sun darkened by the pterodactyl, the dragon of tradition. Yet as a resolute explorer of knowledge, the thought of such a discovery threw me into a passion of joy, and I cut out the slip from the paper and put it in a drawer in my old bureau, resolved that it should be but the first piece in a collection of the strangest significance. I sat long that evening dreaming of the conclusions I should establish, nor did cooler reflection at first dash my confidence. Yet as I began to put the case fairly, I saw that I might be building on an unstable foundation; the facts might possibly be in accordance with local opinion, and I regarded the affair with a mood of some reserve. Yet I resolved to remain perched on the look-out, and I hugged to myself the thought that I alone was watching and wakeful, while the great crowd of thinkers and searchers stood heedless and indifferent, perhaps letting the most prerogative facts pass by unnoticed.

Several years elapsed before I was enabled to add to the contents of the drawer; and the second find was in reality not a valuable one, for it was a mere repetition of the first, with only the variation of another and distant locality. Yet I gained something; for in the second case, as in the first, the tragedy took place in a desolate and lonely country, and so far my theory seemed justified. But the third piece was to me far more decisive. Again, amongst outland hills, far even from a main road of traffic, an old man was found done to death, and the instrument of execution was left beside him. Here, indeed, there were rumour and conjecture, for the deadly tool was a primitive stone axe, bound by gut to the wooden handle, and surmises the most extravagant and improbable were indulged in. Yet, as I thought with a kind of glee, the wildest conjectures went far astray; and I took the pains to enter into correspondence with the local doctor, who was called at the inquest. He, a man of some acuteness, was dumb-foundered. 'It will not do to speak of these things in country places,' he wrote to me; 'but frankly, there is some hideous mystery here. I have obtained possession of the stone axe, and have been so curious as to test its powers. I took it into the back garden of my house one Sunday afternoon when my family and the servants were all out, and there, sheltered by the poplar hedges, I made my experiments. I found the thing utterly unmanageable; whether there is some peculiar balance, some nice adjustment of weights, which require incessant practice, or whether an effectual blow can be struck only by a certain trick of the muscles, I do not know; but I can assure you that I went into the house with but a sorry opinion of my athletic capacities. It was like an inexperienced man trying "putting the hammer"; the force exerted seemed to return on oneself, and I found myself hurled backwards with violence, while the axe fell harmless to the ground. On another occasion I tried the experiment with a clever woodman of the place; but this man, who had handled his axe for forty years, could do nothing with the stone implement, and missed every stroke most ludicrously. In short, if it were not so supremely absurd, I should say that for four thousand years no one on earth could have struck an effective blow with the tool that undoubtedly was used to murder the old man.' This, as may be imagined, was to me rare news; and afterwards, when I heard the whole story, and learned that the unfortunate old man had babbled tales of what might be seen at night on a certain wild hillside, hinting at unheard-of wonders, and that he had been found cold one morning on the very hill in question, my exultation was extreme, for I felt I was leaving conjecture far behind me. But the next step was of still greater importance. I had possessed for many years an extraordinary stone seal – a piece of dull black stone, two inches long from the handle to the stamp, and the stamping end a rough hexagon an inch and a quarter in diameter. Altogether, it presented the appearance of an enlarged tobacco stopper of an old-fashioned make. It had been sent to me by an agent in the East, who informed me that it had been found near the site of the ancient Babylon. But the characters engraved on the seal were to me an intolerable puzzle. Somewhat of the cuneiform pattern, there were yet striking differences, which I detected at the first glance, and all efforts to read the inscription on the hypothesis that the rules for deciphering the arrow-headed writing would apply proved futile. A riddle such as this stung my pride, and at odd moments I would take the Black Seal out of the cabinet, and scrutinize it with so much idle perseverance that every letter was familiar to my mind, and I could have drawn the inscription from memory without the slightest error. Judge, then, of my surprise when I one day received from a correspondent in the west of England a letter and an enclosure that positively left me thunderstruck. I saw carefully traced on a large piece of paper the very characters of the Black Seal, without alteration of any kind, and above the inscription my friend had written: *Inscription found on a limestone rock on the Grey Hills, Monmouthshire. Done in some red earth, and quite recent.* I turned to the letter.

My friend wrote: 'I send you the enclosed inscription with all due reserve. A shepherd who passed by the stone a week ago swears that there was then no mark of any kind. The characters, as I have noted, are formed by drawing some red earth over the stone, and are of an average height of one inch. They look to me like a kind of cuneiform character, a good deal altered, but this, of course, is impossible. It may be either a hoax, or more probably some scribble of the gipsies, who are plentiful enough in this wild country. They have, as you are aware, many hieroglyphics which they use in communicating with one another. I happened to visit the stone in question two days ago in connection with a rather painful incident which has occurred here.'

As it may be supposed, I wrote immediately to my friend, thanking him for the copy of the inscription, and asking him in a casual manner the history of the incident he mentioned. To be brief, I heard that a woman named Cradock, who had lost her husband a day before, had set out to communicate the sad news to a cousin who lived some five miles away. She took a short cut which led by the Grey Hills. Mrs. Cradock, who was then quite a young woman, never arrived at her relative's house. Late that night a farmer, who had lost a couple of sheep, supposed to have wandered from the flock, was walking over the Grey Hills, with a lantern and his dog. His attention was attracted by a noise, which he described as a kind of wailing, mournful and pitiable to hear; and, guided by the sound, he found the unfortunate Mrs. Cradock crouched on the ground by the limestone rock, swaying her body to and fro, and lamenting and crying in so heart-rending a manner that the farmer was, as he says, at first obliged to stop his ears, or he would have run away. The woman allowed herself to be taken home, and a neighbour came to see to her necessities. All the night she never ceased her crying, mixing her lament with words of some unintelligible jargon, and when the doctor arrived he pronounced her insane. She lay on her bed for a week, now wailing, as people said, like one lost and damned for eternity, and now sunk in a heavy coma; it was thought that grief at the loss of her husband had unsettled her mind, and the medical man did not at one time expect her to live. I need not say that I was deeply interested in this story, and I made my friend write to me at intervals with all the particulars of the case. I heard then that in the course of six weeks the woman gradually recovered the use of her faculties, and some months later she gave birth to a son, christened Jervase, who unhappily proved to be of weak intellect. Such were the facts known to the village; but to me, while I whitened at the suggested thought of the hideous enormities that had doubtless been committed, all this was nothing short of conviction, and I incautiously hazarded a hint of something like the truth to some scientific friends. The moment the words had left my lips I bitterly regretted having spoken, and thus given away the great secret of my life, but with a good deal of relief mixed with indignation I found my fears altogether misplaced, for my friends ridiculed me to my face, and I was regarded as a madman; and beneath a natural anger I chuckled to myself, feeling as secure amidst these blockheads as if I had confided what I knew to the desert sands.

But now, knowing so much, I resolved I would know all, and I concentrated my efforts on the task of deciphering the inscription on the Black Seal. For many years I made this puzzle the sole object of my leisure moments, for the greater portion of my time was, of course, devoted to other duties, and it was only now and then that I could snatch a week of clear research. If I were to tell the full history of this curious investigation, this statement would be wearisome in the extreme, for it would contain simply the account of long and tedious failure. By what I knew already of ancient scripts I was well equipped for the chase, as I always termed it to myself. I had correspondents amongst all the scientific men in Europe, and, indeed, in the world, and I could not believe that in these days any character, however ancient and however perplexed, could long resist the search-light I should bring to bear upon it. Yet in point of fact, it was fully fourteen years before I succeeded. With every year my professional duties increased, and my leisure became smaller. This no doubt retarded me a good deal; and yet, when I look back on those years, I am astonished at the vast scope of my investigation of the Black Seal. I made my bureau a centre, and from all the world and from all the ages I gathered transcripts of ancient writing. Nothing, I resolved, should pass me unawares, and the faintest hint should be welcomed and followed up. But as one covert after another was tried and proved empty of result, I began in the course of years to despair, and to wonder whether the Black Seal were the sole relic of some race that had vanished from the world, and left no other trace of its existence – had perished, in fine, as Atlantis is said to have done, in some great cataclysm, its secrets perhaps drowned beneath the ocean or moulded into the heart of the hills. The thought chilled my warmth a little, and though I still persevered, it was no longer with the same certainty of faith. A chance came to the rescue. I was staying in a considerable town in the north of England, and took the opportunity of going over the very creditable museum that had for some time been established in the place. The curator was one of my correspondents; and, as we were looking through one of the mineral cases, my attention was struck by a specimen, a piece of black stone some four inches square, the appearance of which reminded me in a measure of the Black Seal. I took it up carelessly, and was turning it over in my hand, when I saw, to my astonishment, that the under side was inscribed. I said, quietly enough, to my friend the curator that the specimen interested me, and that I should be much obliged if he would allow me to take it with me to my hotel for a couple of days. He, of course, made no objection, and I hurried to my rooms and found that my first glance had not deceived me. There were two inscriptions; one in the regular cunei-form character, another in the character of the Black Seal, and I realized that my task was accomplished. I made an exact copy of the two inscriptions; and when I got to my London study, and had the seal before me, I was able seriously to grapple with the great problem. The inter-preting inscription on the museum specimen, though in itself curious enough, did not bear on my quest, but the transliteration made me master of the secret of the Black Seal. Conjecture, of course, had to enter into my calcula-tions; there was here and there uncertainty about a particular ideograph, and one sign recurring again and again on the seal baffled me for many successive nights. But at last the secret stood open before me in plain English, and I read the key of the awful transmutation of the hills. The last word was hardly written, when with fingers all trembling and unsteady I tore the scrap of paper into the minutest fragments, and saw them flame and blacken in the red hollow of the fire, and then I crushed the grey films that remained into finest powder. Never since then have I written those words; never will I write the phrases which tell how man can be reduced to the slime from which he came, and be forced to put on the flesh of the reptile and the snake. There was now but one thing remaining. I knew, but I desired to see, and I was after some time able to take a house in the neighbourhood of the Grey Hills, and not far from the cottage where Mrs. Cradock and her son Jervase resided. I need not go into a full and detailed account of the apparently inexplicable events which have occurred here, where I am writing this. I knew that I should find in Jervase Cradock something of the blood of the 'Little

People,' and I found later that he had more than once encountered his kinsmen in lonely places in that lonely land. When I was summoned one day to the garden, and found him in a seizure speaking or hissing the ghastly jargon of the Black Seal, I am afraid that exultation prevailed over pity. I heard bursting from his lips the secrets of the underworld, and the word of dread, 'Ishakshar,' signification of which I must be excused from giving.

But there is one incident I cannot pass over unnoticed. In the waste hollow of the night I awoke at the sound of those hissing syllables I knew so well; and on going to the wretched boy's room, I found him convulsed and foaming at the mouth, struggling on the bed as if he strove to escape the grasp of writhing demons. I took him down to my room and lit the lamp, while he lay twisting on the floor, calling on the power within his flesh to leave him. I saw his body swell and become distended as a bladder, while the face blackened before my eyes; and then at the crisis I did what was necessary according to the directions on the Seal, and putting all scruple on one side, I became a man of science, observant of what was passing. Yet the sight I had to witness was horrible, almost beyond the power of human conception and the most fearful fantasy. Something pushed out from the body there on the floor, and stretched forth a slimy, wavering tentacle, across the room, grasped the bust upon the cupboard, and laid it down on my desk.

When it was over, and I was left to walk up and down all the rest of the night, white and shuddering, with sweat pouring from my flesh, I vainly tried to reason within myself: I said, truly enough, that I had seen nothing really supernatural, that a snail pushing out his horns and drawing them in was but an instance on a smaller scale of what I had witnessed; and yet horror broke through all such reasonings and left me shattered and loathing myself for the share I had taken in the night's work.

There is little more to be said. I am going now to the final trial and encounter; for I have determined that there shall be nothing wanting, and I shall meet the 'Little People' face to face. I shall have the Black Seal and the knowledge of its secrets to help me, and if I unhappily do not return from my journey, there is no need to conjure up here a picture of the awfulness of my fate.

Pausing a little at the end of Professor Gregg's statement, Miss Lally continued her tale in the following words:

Such was the almost incredible story that the professor had left behind him. When I had finished reading it, it was late at night, but the next morning I took Morgan with me, and we proceeded to search the Grey Hills for some trace of the lost professor. I will not weary you with a description of the savage desolation of that tract of country, a tract of utterest loneliness, of bare green hills dotted over with grey limestone boulders, worn by the ravages of time into fantastic semblances of men and beasts. Finally, after many hours of weary searching, we found what I told you – the watch and chain, the purse, and the ring – wrapped in a piece of coarse parchment. When Morgan cut the gut that bound the parcel together, and I saw the professor's property, I burst into tears, but the sight of the dreaded characters of the Black Seal repeated on the parchment froze me to silent horror, and I think I understood for the first time the awful fate that had come upon my late employer.

I have only to add that Professor Gregg's lawyer treated my account of what had happened as a fairy-tale, and refused even to glance at the documents I laid before him. It was he who was responsible for the statement that appeared in the public press, to the effect that Professor Gregg had been drowned, and that his body must have been swept into the open sea.

Miss Lally stopped speaking, and looked at Mr. Phillipps, with a glance of some inquiry. He, for his part, was sunken in a deep reverie of thought; and when he looked up and saw the bustle of the evening gathering in the square, men and women hurrying to partake of dinner, and crowds already besetting the music-halls, all the hum and press of actual life seemed unreal and visionary, a dream in the morning after an awakening.

Wandering Willie's Tale

Sir Walter Scott

Ye maun have heard of Sir Robert Redgauntlet of that Ilk, who lived in these parts before the dear years. The country will lang mind him; and our fathers used to draw breath thick if ever they heard him named. He was out wi' the Hielandmen in Montrose's time; and again he was in the hills wi' Glencairn in the saxteen hundred and fifty-twa; and sae when King Charles the Second came in, wha was in sic favour as the Laird of Redgauntlet? He was knighted at Lonon court, wi' the King's ain sword; and being a red-hot prelatist, he came down here, rampauging like a lion, with commissions of lieutenancy (and of lunacy, for what I ken), to put down a' the Whigs and Covenanters in the country. Wild wark they made of it; for the Whigs were as dour as the Cavaliers were fierce, and it was which should first tire the other. Redgauntlet was aye for the strong hand; and his name is kend as wide in the country as Claverhouse's or Tam Dalyell's. Glen, nor dargle, nor mountain, nor cave, could hide the puir hill-folk when Redgauntlet was out with bugle and bloodhound after them, as if they had been sae mony deer. And troth when they fand them, they didna mak muckle mair ceremony than a Hielandman wi' a roebuck – It was just, 'Will ye tak the test?' – if not, 'Make ready – present – fire!' – and there lay the recusant.

Far and wide was Sir Robert hated and feared. Men thought he had a direct compact with Satan – that he was proof against steel – and that bullets happed aff his buffcoat like hailstanes from a hearth – that he had a mear that would turn a hare on the side of Carrifra-gawns in:[1] – and muckle to the same purpose, of whilk mair anon. The best blessing they wared on him was, 'Deil scowp wi' Redgauntlet!' He wasna a bad maister to his ain folk, though, and was weel aneugh liked by his tenants; and as for the lackies and troopers that raid out wi' him to the persecutions, as the Whigs caa'd those killing times, they wad hae drunken themsells blind to his health at ony time.

Now you are to ken that my gudesire lived on Redgauntlet's grund – they ca' the place Primrose-Knowe. We had lived on the grund, and under the Redgauntlets, since the riding days, and lang before. It was a pleasant bit: and I think the air is callerer and fresher there than onywhere else in the country. It's a' deserted now; and I sat on the broken door-cheek three days since, and was glad I couldna see the plight the place was in; but that's a' wide o' the mark. There dwelt my gudesire, Steenie Steenson, a rambling, rattling chiel' he had been in his young days, and could play weel on the pipes; he was famous at Hoopers and Girders – a' Cumberland couldna touch him at Jockie Lattin – and he had the finest finger for the back-lilt between Berwick and Carlisle. The like o' Steenie wasna the sort that they made Whigs o'. And so he became a Tory, as they ca' it, which we now ca' Jacobites, just out of a kind of needcessity, that he might belang to some side or other. He had nae ill-will to the Whig bodies, and liked little to see the blude rin, though, being obliged to follow Sir Robert in hunting and hosting, watching and warding, he saw muckle mischief, and maybe did some, that he couldna avoid.

Now Steenie was a kind of favourite with his master, and kend a' the folks about the Castle, and was often sent for to play the pipes when they were at their merriment. Auld Dougal MacCallum, the butler, that had followed Sir Robert through gude and ill, thick and thin, pool and stream, was specially fond of the pipes, and aye gae my gudesire his gude word wi' the

[1] A precipitous side of a mountain in Moffatdale.

Laird; for Dougal could turn his master round his finger.

Weel, round came the Revolution, and it had like to have broken the hearts baith of Dougal and his master. But the change was not a'thegether sae great as they feared, and other folk thought for. The Whigs made an unco crawing what they wad do with their auld enemies, and in special wi' Sir Robert Red-gauntlet. But there were ower mony great folks dipped in the same doings, to mak a spick and span new warld. So Parliament passed it a' ower easy; and Sir Robert, bating that he was held to hunting foxes instead of Covenanters, remained just the man he was. His revel was as loud, and his hall as weel lighted, as ever it had been, though maybe he lacked the fines of the non-conformists, that used to come to stock his larder and cellar; for it is certain he began to be keener about the rents than his tenants used to find him before, and they behoved to be prompt to the rent-day, or else the Laird wasna pleased. And he was sic an awsome body, that naebody cared to anger him; for the oaths he swore, and the rage that he used to get into, and the looks that he put on, made men sometimes think him a devil incarnate.

Weel, my gudesire was nae manager – no that he was a very great misguider – but he hadna the saving gift, and he got twa terms' rent in arrear. He got the first brash at Whitsunday put ower wi' fair word and piping; but when Martinmas came, there was a summons from the grund-officer to come wi' the rent on a day preceese, or else Steenie behoved to flit. Sair wark he had to get the siller; but he was weel-freended, and at last he got the haill scraped thegether – a thousand merks – the maist of it was from a neighbour they caa'd Laurie Lapraik – a sly tod. Laurie had walth o' gear – could hunt wi the hound and rin wi' the hare – and be a Whig or Tory, saunt or sinner, as the wind stood. He was a professor in this Revolution warld, but he liked an orra sough of this warld, and a tune on the pipes weel aneugh at a by-time, and abune a', he thought he had gude security for the siller he lent my gudesire ower the stocking at Primrose-Knowe.

Away trots my gudesire to Redgauntlet Castle, wi' a heavy

purse and a light heart, glad to be out of the Laird's danger. Weel, the first thing he learned at the Castle was, that Sir Robert had fretted himself into a fit of the gout, because he did not appear before twelve o'clock. It wasna a'thegether for the sake of the money, Dougal thought; but because he didna like to part wi' my gudesire off the grund. Dougal was glad to see Steenie, and brought him into the great oak parlour, and there sat the Laird his leesome lane, excepting that he had beside him a great, ill-favoured jackanape, that was a special pet of his; a cankered beast it was, and mony an ill-natured trick it played – ill to please it was, and easily angered – ran about the haill castle, chattering and yowling, and pinching, and biting folk, especially before ill-weather, or disturbances in the state. Sir Robert caa'd it Major Weir,[2] after the warlock that was burnt; 'and few folk liked either the name or the conditions of the creature – they thought there was something in it by ordinar – and my gudesire was not just easy in his mind when the door shut on him, and he saw himself in the room wi' naebody but the Laird, Dougal MacCallum, and the Major, a thing that hadna chanced to him before.

Sir Robert sat, or, I should say, lay, in a great armed chair, wi' his grand velvet gown, and his feet on a cradle; for he had baith gout and gravel, and his face looked as gash and ghastly as Satan's. Major Weir sat opposite to him, in a red laced coat, and the Laird's wig on his head; and aye as Sir Robert girned wi' pain, the jackanape girned too, like a sheep's-head between a pair of tangs – an illfaur'd, fearsome couple they were. The Laird's buff-coat was hung on a pin behind him, and his broad-sword and his pistols within reach; for he keepit up the auld fashion of having the weapons ready, and a horse saddled day and night, just as he used to do when he was able to loup on horseback, and away after ony of the hill-folk he could get speerings of. Some said it was for fear of the Whigs taking

---

[2] A celebrated wizard, executed at Edinburgh for sorcery and other crimes.

vengeance, but I judge it was just his auld custom – he wasna gien to fear onything. The rental-book, wi' its black cover and brass clasps, was lying beside him; and a book of sculduddry sangs was put betwixt the leaves, to keep it open at the place where it bore evidence against the Goodman of Primrose-Knowe, as behind the hand with his mails and duties. Sir Robert gave my gudesire a look, as if he would have withered his heart in his bosom. Ye maun ken he had a way of bending his brows, that men saw the visible mark of a horse-shoe in his forehead, deep-dinted, as if it had been stamped there.

'Are ye come light-handed, ye son of a toom whistle?' said Sir Robert. 'Zounds! if you are —'

My gudesire, with as gude a countenance as he could put on, made a leg, and placed the bag of money on the table wi' a dash, like a man that does something clever. The Laird drew it to him hastily: 'Is it all here, Steenie, man?'

'Your honour will find it right,' said my gudesire.

'Here, Dougal,' said the Laird, 'gie Steenie a tass of brandy downstairs, till I count the siller and write the receipt.'

But they werena weel out of the room, when Sir Robert gied a yelloch that garr'd the Castle rock. Back ran Dougal – in flew the livery-men – yell on yell gied the Laird, ilk ane mair awfu' than the ither. My gudesire knew not whether to stand or flee, but he ventured back into the parlour, where a' was gaun hirdy-girdie – naebody to say 'come in,' or 'gae out.' Terribly the Laird roared for cauld water to his feet, and wine to cool his throat; and hell, hell, hell, and its flames, was aye the word in his mouth. They brought him water, and when they plunged his swoln feet into the tub, he cried out it was burning; and folk say that it *did* bubble and sparkle like a seething caldron. He flung the cup at Dougal's head, and said he had given him blood instead of burgundy; and, sure aneugh, the lass washed clotted blood aff the carpet the neist day. The jackanape they caa'd Major Weir, it jibbered and cried as if it was mocking its master; my gudesire's head was like to turn – he forgot baith siller and receipt, and down stairs he banged; but as he ran, the shrieks came faint and fainter; there was a deep-drawn shivering groan, and word gaed through the Castle, that the Laird was dead.

Weel, away came my gudesire, wi' his finger in his mouth, and his best hope was, that Dougal had seen the money-bag, and heard the Laird speak of writing the receipt. The young Laird, now Sir John, came from Edinburgh, to see things put to rights. Sir John and his father never gree'd weel. Sir John had been bred an advocate, and after-wards sat in the last Scots Parliament and voted for the Union, having gotten, it was thought, a rug of the compensations – if his father could have come out of his grave, he would have brained him for it on his awn hearthstane. Some thought it was easier counting with the auld rough knight than the fair-spoken young ane – but mair of that anon.

Dougal MacCallum, poor body, neither grat nor graned, but gaed about the house looking like a corpse, but directing, as was his duty, a' the order of the grand funeral. Now, Dougal looked aye waur and waur when night was coming, and was aye the last to gang to his bed, whilk was in a little round just opposite the chamber of dais, whilk his master occupied while he was living, and where he now lay in state, as they caa'd it, weel-a-day! The night before the funeral, Dougal could keep his awn counsel nae langer; he cam doun with his proud spirit, and fairly asked auld Hutcheon to sit in his room with him for an hour. When they were in the round, Dougal took ae tass of brandy to himself, and gave another to Hutcheon, and wished him all health, and lang life, and said that, for himsell, he wasna lang for this world; for that, every night since Sir Robert's death, his silver call had sounded from the state-chamber, just as it used to do at nights in his lifetime, to call Dougal to help to turn him in his bed. Dougal said, that being alone with the dead on that floor of the tower, (for naebody cared to wake Sir Robert Redgauntlet like another corpse,) he had never daured to answer the call, but that now his conscience checked him for neglecting his duty; for, 'though death breaks service,' said MacCallum, 'it shall never break my service to Sir Robert; and I will answer his next whistle, so be you will stand by me, Hutcheon.'

Hutcheon had nae will to the wark, but he had stood by Dougal in battle and broil, and he wad not fail him at this pinch; so down the carles sat ower a stoup of brandy, and Hutcheon, who was something of a clerk, would have read a chapter of the Bible; but Dougal would hear naething but a blaud of Davie Lindsay, whilk was the waur preparation.

When midnight came, and the house was quiet as the grave, sure aneugh the silver whistle sounded as sharp and shrill as if Sir Robert was blowing it, and up gat the twa auld serving-men, and tottered into the room where the dead man lay. Hutcheon saw aneugh at the first glance; for there were torches in the room, which showed him the foul fiend, in his ain shape, sitting on the Laird's coffin! Over he cowped as if he had been dead. He could not tell how lang he lay in a trance at the door, but when he gathered himself, he cried on his neighbour, and getting nae answer, raised the house, when Dougal was found lying dead within twa steps of the bed where his master's coffin was placed. As for the whistle, it was gaen anes and aye; but mony a time was it heard at the top of the house on the bartizan, and amang the auld chimneys and turrets, where the howlets have their nests. Sir John hushed the matter up, and the funeral passed over without mair bogle-wark.

But when a' was over, and the Laird was beginning to settle his affairs, every tenant was called up for his arrears, and my gudesire for the full sum that stood against him in the rental-book. Weel, away he trots to the Castle, to tell his story, and there he is introduced to Sir John, sitting in his father's chair, in deep mourning, with weepers and hanging cravat, and a small walking rapier by his side, instead of the auld broadsword, that had a hundred-weight of steel about it, what with blade, chape, and basket-hilt. I have heard their communing so often tauld ower, that I almost think I was there mysell, though I couldna be born at the time.

'I wuss ye joy, sir, of the head seat, and the white loaf, and the braid lairdship. Your father was a kind man to friends and followers; muckle grace to you, Sir John, to fill his shoon – his boots, I suld say, for he seldom wore shoon, unless it were muils when he had the gout.'

'Ay, Steenie,' quoth the Laird, sighing deeply and putting his napkin to his een, 'his was a sudden call, and he will be missed in the country; no time to set his house in order – weel prepared Godward, no doubt, which is the root of the matter – but left us behind a tangled hesp to wind, Steenie. – Hem! hem! We maun go to business, Steenie; much to do, and little time to do it in.'

Here he opened the fatal volume. I have heard of a thing they call Doomsday-book – I am clear it has been a rental of back-ganging tenants.

'Stephen,' said Sir John, still in the same soft, sleekit tone of voice, 'Stephen Stevenson, or Steenson, ye are down here for a year's rent behind the hand – due at last term.'

Stephen. 'Please your honour, Sir John, I paid it to your father.'

Sir John. 'Ye took a receipt then, doubtless, Stephen; and can produce it?'

Stephen. 'Indeed, I hadna time, an it like your honour; for nae sooner had I set doun the siller, and just as his honour Sir Robert, that's gaen, drew it till him to count it, and write out the receipt, he was ta'en wi' the pains that removed him.'

'That was unlucky,' said Sir John, after a pause. 'But ye maybe paid it in the presence of somebody. I want but a *talis qualis* evidence, Stephen. I would go ower strictly to work with no poor man.'

Stephen. 'Troth, Sir John, there was naebody in the room but Dougal MacCallum the butler. But, as your honour kens, he has e'en followed his auld master.'

'Very unlucky again, Stephen,' said Sir John, without altering his voice a single note. 'The man to whom ye paid the money is dead – and the man who witnessed the payment is dead too – and the siller, which should have been to the fore, is neither seen nor heard tell of in the repositories. How am I to believe a' this?'

Stephen. 'I dinna ken, your honour; but there is a bit memorandum note of the very coins; for, God help me! I had to borrow out of twenty purses; and I am sure that ilka man there set down will take his grit oath for what purpose I borrowed the money.'

Sir John. 'I have little doubt ye *borrowed* the money, Steenie. It is the *payment* to my father that I want to have some proof of.'

Stephen. 'The siller maun be about the house, Sir John. And since your honour never got it, and his honour that was canna have ta'en it wi' him, maybe some of the family may have seen it.'

Sir John. 'We will examine the servants, Stephen; that is but reasonable.'

But lackey and lass, and page and groom, all denied stoutly that they had ever seen such a bag of money as my gudesire described. What was waur, he had unluckily not mentioned to any living soul of them his purpose of paying his rent. A quean had noticed something under his arm, but she took it for the pipes.

Sir John Redgauntlet ordered the servants out of the room, and then said to my gudesire: 'Now, Steenie, ye see you have fair play; and, as I have little doubt ye ken better where to find the siller than ony other body, I beg, in fair terms, and for your own sake, that you will end this fasherie; for, Stephen, ye maun pay or flit.'

'The Lord forgie your opinion,' said Stephen, driven almost to his wit's end – 'I am an honest man.'

'So am I, Stephen,' said his honour; 'and so are all the folks in the house, I hope. But if there be a knave amongst us, it must be he that tells the story he cannot prove.' He paused, and then added, mair sternly, 'If I understand your trick, sir, you want to take advantage of some malicious reports concerning things in this family, and particularly respecting my father's sudden death, thereby to cheat me out of the money, and perhaps take away my character, by insinuating that I have received the rent I am demanding. – Where do you suppose this money to be? – I insist upon knowing.'

My gudesire saw everything look sae muckle against him, that he grew nearly desperate – however, he shifted from one foot to another, looked to every corner of the room, and made no answer.

'Speak out, sirrah,' said the Laird, assuming a look of his father's, a very particular ane, which he had when he was angry – it seemed as if the wrinkles of his frown made that selfsame fearful shape of a horse's shoe in the middle of his brow; – 'Speak out, sir! I *will* know your thoughts; – do you suppose that I have this money?'

'Far be it frae me to say so,' said Stephen.

'Do you charge any of my people with having taken it?'

'I wad be laith to charge them that may be innocent,' said my gudesire; 'and if there be any one that is guilty, I have nae proof.'

'Somewhere the money must be, if there is a word of truth in your story,' said Sir John; 'I ask where you think it is – and demand a correct answer?'

'In hell, if you *will* have my thoughts of it,' said my gudesire, driven to extremity – 'in hell! with your father, his jackanape, and his silver whistle.'

Down the stairs he ran (for the parlour was nae place for him after such a word), and he heard the Laird swearing blood and wounds behind him, as fast as ever did Sir Robert, and roaring for the bailie and the baron-officer.

Away rode my gudesire to his chief creditor, (him they caa'd Laurie Lapraik,) to try if he could make onything out of him; but when he tauld his story, he got but the warst word in his wame – thief, beggar, and dyvour, were the saftest terms; and to the boot of these hard terms, Laurie brought up the auld story of his dipping his hand in the blood of God's saunts, just as if a tenant could have helped riding with the Laird, and that a laird like Sir Robert Redgauntlet. My gudesire was, by this time, far beyond the bounds of patience, and, while he and Laurie were at deil speed the liars, he was wanchancie aneugh to abuse Lapraik's doctrine as weel as the man, and said things that garr'd folk's flesh grue that heard them; – he wasna just himsell, and he had lived wi' a wild set in his day.

At last they parted, and my gudesire was to ride hame through the wood of Pitmurkie, that is a' fou of black firs, as they say. – I ken the wood, but the firs may be black or white for what I can tell. – At the entry of the wood there is a wild common, and on the edge of the common, a little lonely change-house, that was keepit then by an ostlerwife, they suld hae caa'd her Tibbie Faw, and there puir Steenie cried for a mutchkin of brandy, for he had had no refreshment the haill day. Tibbie was earnest wi' him to take a bite of meat, but he couldna think o't, nor would he take his foot out of the stirrup, and took off the brandy wholely at twa draughts, and named a toast at each: the first was, the memory of Sir Robert Redgauntlet, and might he never lie quiet in his grave till he had righted his poor bond-tenant; and the second was, a health to Man's Enemy, if he would but get him back the pock of siller, or tell him what came o't, for he saw the haill world was like to regard him as a thief and a cheat, and he took that waur than even the ruin of his house and hauld.

On he rode, little caring where. It was dark night turned, and the trees made it yet darker, and he let the beast take its ain road through the wood; when, all of a sudden, from tired and wearied that it was before, the nag began to spring, and flee, and stend, that my gudesire could hardly keep the saddle. – Upon the whilk, a horseman, suddenly riding up beside him, said: 'That's a mettle beast of yours, freend; will you sell him?' – So saying, he touched the horse's neck with his riding-wand, and it fell into its auld heigh-ho of a stumbling trot. 'But his spunk's soon out of him, I think,' continued the stranger, 'and that is like mony a man's courage, that thinks he wad do great things till he come to the proof.'

My gudesire scarce listened to this, but spurred his horse, with, 'Gude e'en to you, freend.'

But it's like the stranger was ane that doesna lightly yield his point; for, ride as Steenie liked, he was aye beside him at the selfsame pace. At last my gudesire, Steenie Steenson, grew half angry; and, to say the truth, half feared.

'What is it that ye want with me, freend?' he said. 'If ye be a robber, I have nae money; if ye be a leal man, wanting company, I have nae heart to mirth or speaking; and if ye want to ken the road, I scarce ken it mysell.'

'If you will tell me your grief,' said the stranger, 'I am one that, though I have been sair miscaa'd in the world, am the only hand for helping my freends.'

So my gudesire, to ease his ain heart, mair than from any hope of help, told him the story from beginning to end.

'It's a hard pinch,' said the stranger; 'but I think I can help you.'

'If you could lend the money, sir, and take a lang day – I ken nae other help on earth,' said my gudesire.

'But there may be some under the earth,' said the stranger. 'Come, I'll be frank wi' you; I could lend you the money on bond, but you would maybe scruple my terms. Now, I can tell you, that your auld Laird is disturbed in his grave by your curses, and the wailing of your family, and if ye daur venture to go to see him, he will give you the receipt.'

My gudesire's hair stood on end at this proposal, but he thought his companion might be some humoursome chield that was trying to frighten him, and might end with lending him the money. Besides, he was bauld wi' brandy, and desperate wi' distress; and he said, he had courage to go to the gate of hell, and a step farther, for that receipt. – The stranger laughed.

Weel, they rode on through the thickest of the wood, when, all of a sudden, the horse stopped at the door of a great house; and, but that he knew the place was ten miles off, my father would have thought he was at Redgauntlet Castle. They rode into the outer courtyard, through the muckle faulding yetts, and aneath the auld portcullis; and the whole front of the house was lighted, and there were pipes and fiddles, and as much dancing and deray within as used to be in Sir Robert's house at Pace and Yule, and such high seasons. They lap off, and my gudesire, as seemed to him, fastened his horse to the very ring he had tied him to that morning, when he gaed to wait on the young Sir John.

'God!' said my gudesire, 'if Sir Robert's death be but a dream.'

He knocked at the ha' door just as he was wont, and his auld acquaintance, Dougal MacCallum – just after his wont, too – came to open the door, and said: 'Piper Steenie, are ye there, lad? Sir Robert has been crying for you.'

My gudesire was like a man in a dream – he looked for the stranger, but he was gane for the time. At last he just tried to say: 'Ha! Dougal Driveower, are ye living? I thought ye had been dead.'

'Never fash yoursell wi' me,' said Dougal, 'but look to yoursell; and see ye tak naething frae onybody here, neither meat, drink, or siller, except just the receipt that is your ain.'

So saying, he led the way out through halls and trances that were weel kend to my gudesire, and into the auld oak parlour; and there was as much singing of profane sangs, and birling of red wine, and speaking blasphemy and sculduddry, as had ever been in Redgauntlet Castle when it was at the blithest.

But, Lord take us in keeping! what a set of ghastly revellers they were that sat round that table! – My gudesire kend mony that had long before gane to their place, for often had he piped to the most part in the hall of Redgauntlet. There was the fierce Middleton, and the dissolute Rothes, and the crafty Lauderdale; and Dalyell, with his bald head and a beard to his girdle; and Earlshall, with Cameron's blude on his hand; and wild Bonshaw, that tied blessed Mr Cargill's limbs till the blude sprang; and Dunbarton Douglas, the twice-turned traitor baith to country and king. There was the Bluidy Advocate MacKenyie, who, for his worldly wit and wisdom, had been to the rest as a god. And there was Claverhouse, as beautiful as when he lived, with his long, dark, curled locks, streaming down over his laced buff-coat, and his left hand always on his right spule-blade, to hide the wound that the silver bullet had made. He sat apart from them all, and looked at them with a melancholy, haughty countenance; while the rest hallooed, and sung, and laughed, that the room rang. But their smiles were fearfully contorted from time to time; and their laughter passed into such wild sounds, as made my gudesire's very nails grow blue, and chilled the marrow in his banes.

They that waited at the table were just the wicked serving-men and troopers, that had done their work and cruel bidding on earth. There was the Lang Lad of the Nethertown, that helped to take Argyle; and the Bishop's summoner, that they called the Deil's Rattle-bag; and the wicked guardsmen, in their laced coats; and the savage Highland Amorites, that shed blood like water; and many a proud serving-man, haughty of heart and bloody of hand, cringing to the rich, and making them wickeder than they would be; grinding the poor to powder, when the rich had broken them to fragments. And mony, mony mair were coming and ganging, a' as busy in their vocation as if they had been alive.

Sir Robert Redgauntlet, in the midst of a' this fearful riot, cried, wi' a voice like thunder, on Steenie Piper, to come to the board-head where he was sitting; his legs stretched out before him, and swathed up with flannel, with his holster pistols aside him, while the great broadsword rested against his chair, just as my gudesire had seen him the last time upon earth – the very cushion for the jackanape was close to him, but the creature itsell was not there – it wasna its hour, it's likely; for he heard them say as he came forward, 'Is not the Major come yet?' And another answered: 'The jackanape will be here betimes the morn.' And when my gudesire came forward, Sir Robert, or his ghaist, or the deevil in his likeness, said: 'Weel, piper, hae ye settled wi' my son for the year's rent?'

With much ado my father gat breath to say, that Sir John would not settle without his honour's receipt.

'Ye shall hae that for a tune of the pipes, Steenie,' said the appearance of Sir Robert. 'Play us up Weel hoddled, Luckie.'

Now this was a tune my gudesire learned frae a warlock, that heard it when they were worshipping Satan at their meetings; and my gudesire had sometimes played it at the ranting suppers in Redgauntlet Castle, but never very willingly; and now he grew cauld at the very name of it, and said, for excuse, he hadna his pipes wi' him.

'MacCallum, ye limb of Beelzebub,' said the fearfu' Sir Robert, 'bring Steenie the pipes that I am keeping for him!'

MacCallum brought a pair of pipes might have served the piper of Donald of the Isles. But he gave my gudesire a nudge as he offered them; and looking secretly and closely, Steenie saw that the chanter was of steel, and heated to a white heat; so he had fair warning not to trust his fingers with it. So he excused himself again, and said, he was faint and frightened, and had not wind aneugh to fill the bag.

'Then ye maun eat and drink, Steenie,' said the figure; 'for we do little else here; and it's ill speaking between a fou man and a fasting.'

Now these were the very words that the bloody Earl of Douglas said to keep the king's messenger in hand, while he cut the head off MacLellan of Bombie, at the Threave Castle; and that put Steenie mair and mair on his guard. So he spoke up like a man, and said he came neither to eat, or drink, or make minstrelsy; but simply for his ain – to ken what was come o' the money he had paid, and to get a discharge for it; and he was so stout-hearted by this time, that he charged Sir Robert for conscience-sake – (he had no power to say the holy name) – and as he hoped for peace and rest, to spread no snares for him, but just to give him his ain.

The appearance gnashed its teeth and laughed, but it took from a large pocket-book the receipt, and handed it to Steenie. 'There is your receipt, ye pitiful cur; and for the money, my dog-whelp of a son may go look for it in the Cat's Cradle.'

My gudesire uttered mony thanks, and was about to retire, when Sir Robert roared aloud: 'Stop though, thou sack-doudling son of a whore! I am not done with thee. HERE we do nothing for nothing; and you must return on this very day twelvemonth, to pay your master the homage that you owe me for my protection.'

My father's tongue was loosed of a suddenty, and he said aloud: 'I refer mysell to God's pleasure, and not to yours.'

He had no sooner uttered the word than all was dark around him; and he sunk on the earth with such a sudden shock, that he lost both breath and sense.

How lang Steenie lay there, he could not tell; but when he came to himsell, he was lying in the auld kirkyard of Redgauntlet parochine just at the door of the family aisle, and the scutcheon of the auld knight, Sir Robert, hanging over his head. There was a deep morning fog on grass and gravestane around him, and his horse was feeding quietly beside the minister's twa cows. Steenie would have thought the whole was a dream, but he had the receipt in his hand, fairly written and signed by the auld laird; only the last letters of his name were a little disorderly, written like one seized with sudden pain.

Sorely troubled in his mind, he left that dreary place, rode through the mist to Redgauntlet Castle, and with much ado he got speech of the Laird.

'Well, you dyvour bankrupt,' was the first word, 'have you brought me my rent?'

'No,' answered my gudesire, 'I have not; but I have brought your honour Sir Robert's receipt for it.'

'How, sirrah? – Sir Robert's receipt! – You told me he had not given you one.'

'Will your honour please to see if that bit line is right?' Sir John looked at every line, and at every letter, with much attention; and at last, at the date, which my gudesire had not observed: '*From my appointed place*,' he read, '*this twenty-fifth of November*.' 'What! – That is yesterday! Villain, thou must have gone to hell for this!'

'I got it from your honour's father – whether he be in heaven or hell, I know not,' said Steenie.

'I will delate you for a warlock to the Privy Council!' said Sir John. 'I will send you to your master, the devil, with the help of a tar-barrel and a torch!'

'I intend to delate mysell to the Presbytery,' said Steenie, 'and tell them all I have seen last night, whilk are things fitter for them to judge of than a borrel man like me.'

Sir John paused, composed himsell, and desired to hear the full history; and my gudesire told it him from point to point, as I have told it you – word for word, neither more nor less.

Sir John was silent again for a long time, and at last he said, very composedly: 'Steenie, this story of yours concerns the honour of many a noble family besides mine; and if it be a leasing-making, to keep yourself out of my danger, the least you can expect is to have a red-hot iron driven through your tongue, and that will be as bad as scauding your fingers with a red-hot chanter. But yet it may be true, Steenie; and if the money cast up, I shall not know what to think of it. – But where shall we find the Cat's Cradle? There are cats enough about the old house, but I think they kitten without the ceremony of bed or cradle.'

'We were best ask Hutcheon,' said my gudesire; 'he kens a' the odd corners about as weel as – another servingman that is now gane, and that I wad not like to name.'

Aweel, Hutcheon, when he was asked, told them, that a ruinous turret, lang disused, next to the clock-house, only accessible by a ladder, for the opening was on the outside, and far above the battlements, was called of old the Cat's Cradle.

'There will I go immediately,' said Sir John; and he took (with what purpose, heaven kens) one of his father's pistols from the hall-table, where they had lain since the night he died, and hastened to the battlements.

It was a dangerous place to climb, for the ladder was auld and frail, and wanted ane or twa rounds. However, up got Sir John, and entered at the turret door, where his body stopped the only little light that was in the bit turret. Something flees at him wi' a vengeance, maist dang him back ower – bang gaed the knight's pistol, and Hutcheon, that held the ladder, and my gudesire that stood beside him, hears a loud skelloch. A minute after, Sir John flings the body of the jackanape down to them, and cries that the siller is fund, and that they should come up and help him. And there was the bag of siller sure aneugh, and mony orra things besides, that had been missing for mony a day. And Sir John, when he had riped the turret weel, led my gudesire into the dining-parlour, and took him by the hand, and spoke kindly to him, and said he was sorry he should have doubted his word, and that he would hereafter be a good master to him, to make amends.

'And now, Steenie,' said Sir John, 'although this vision of yours tends, on the whole, to my father's credit, as an honest man, that he should, even after his death, desire to see justice done to a poor man like you, yet you are sensible that ill-dispositioned men might make bad constructions upon it, concerning his soul's health. So, I think, we had better lay the haill dirdum on that ill-deedie creature, Major Weir, and say naething about your dream in the wood of Pitmurkie. You had taken ower muckle brandy to be very certain about onything; and, Steenie, this receipt,' (his hand shook while he held it out,) – 'it's but a queer kind of document, and we will do best, I think, to put it quietly in the fire.'

'Od, but for as queer as it is, it's a' the voucher I have for my rent,' said my gudesire, who was afraid, it may be, of losing the benefit of Sir Robert's discharge.

'I will bear the contents to your credit in the rental-book, and give you a discharge under my own hand,' said Sir John, 'and that on the spot. And, Steenie, if you can hold your tongue about this matter, you shall sit, from this term downward, at an easier rent.'

'Mony thanks to your honour,' said Steenie, who saw easily in what corner the wind was; 'doubtless I will be conformable to all your honour's commands; only I would willingly speak wi' some powerful minister on the subject, for I do not like the sort of soumons of appointment whilk your honour's father —'

'Do not call the phantom my father!' said Sir John, interrupting him.

'Weel, then, the thing that was so like him,' said my gudesire; 'he spoke of my coming back to him this time twelvemonth, and it's a weight on my conscience.'

'Aweel, then,' said Sir John, 'if you be so much distressed in mind, you may speak to our minister of the parish; he is a douce man, regards the honour of our family, and the mair that he may look for some patronage from me.'

Wi' that, my gudesire readily agreed that the receipt should be burnt, and the Laird threw it into the chimney with his ain hand. Burn it would not for them, though; but away it flew up the lum, wi' a lang train of sparks at its tail, and a hissing noise like a squib.

My gudesire gaed down to the manse, and the minister, when he had heard the story said, it was his real opinion, that though my gudesire had gaen very far in tampering with dangerous matters, yet, as he had refused the devil's arles, (for such was the offer of meat and drink,) and had refused to do homage by piping at his bidding, he hoped, that if he held a circumspect walk hereafter, Satan could take little advantage by what was come and gane. And, indeed, my gudesire, of his ain accord, long forswore baith the pipes and the brandy – it was not even till the year was out, and the fatal day passed, that he would so much as take the fiddle, or drink usquebaugh or tippenny.

Sir John made up his story about the jackanape as he liked himsell; and some believe till this day there was no more in the matter than the filching nature of the brute. Indeed, ye'll no hinder some to threap, that it was nane o' the Auld Enemy that Dougal and my gudesire saw in the Laird's room, but only that wanchancy creature, the Major, capering on the coffin; and that, as to the blawing on the Laird's whistle that was heard after he was dead, the filthy brute could do that as weel as the Laird himself, if no better. But Heaven kens the truth, whilk first came out by the minister's wife, after Sir John and her ain gudeman were baith in the moulds. And then my gudesire, wha was failed in his limbs, but not in his judgment or memory – at least nothing to speak of – was obliged to tell the real narrative to his freends, for the credit of his good name. He might else have been charged for a warlock.

Thrawn[1] *Janet*

Robert Louis Stevenson

The Reverend Murdoch Soulis was long minister of the moorland parish of Balweary, in the vale of Dule. A severe, bleak-faced old man, dreadful to his hearers, he dwelt in the last years of his life, without relative or servant or any human company, in the small and lonely manse under the Hanging Shaw. In spite of the iron composure of his features, his eye was wild, scared, and uncertain; and when he dwelt, in private admonition, on the future of the impenitent, it seemed as if his eye pierced through the storms of time to the terrors of eternity. Many young persons, coming to prepare themselves against the season of the Holy Communion, were dreadfully affected by his talk. He had a sermon on I st Peter, v. and 8th, 'The devil as a roaring lion,' on the Sunday after every seventeenth of August, and he was accustomed to surpass himself upon that text both by the appalling nature of the matter and the terror of his bearing in the pulpit. The children were frightened into fits, and the old looked more than usually oracular, and were, all that day, full of those hints that Hamlet deprecated. The manse itself, where it stood by the water of Dule among some thick trees, with the Shaw overhanging it on the one side, and on the other many cold, moorish hill-tops rising toward the sky, had begun, at a very early period of Mr. Soulis's ministry, to be avoided in the dusk hours by all who valued themselves upon their prudence; and guidmen sitting

[1]twisted

113

at the clachan² alehouse shook their heads together at the thought of passing late by that uncanny neighbourhood. There was one spot, to be more particular, which was regarded with especial awe. The manse stood between the highroad and the water of Dule, with a gable to each; its back was towards the kirktown of Balweary, nearly half a mile away; in front of it, a bare garden, hedged with thorn, occupied the land between the river and the road. The house was two stories high, with two large rooms on each. It opened not directly on the garden, but on a causewayed path, or passage, giving on the road on the one hand, and closed on the other by the tall willows and elders that bordered on the stream. And it was this strip of causeway that enjoyed among the young parishioners of Balweary so infamous a reputation. The minister walked there often after dark, sometimes groaning aloud in the instancy of his unspoken prayers; and when he was from home, and the manse door was locked, the more daring school-boys ventured, with beating hearts, to 'follow my leader' across that legendary spot.

This atmosphere of terror, surrounding, as it did, a man of God of spotless character and orthodoxy, was a common cause of wonder and subject of inquiry among the few strangers who were led by chance or business into that unknown, outlying country. But many even of the people of the parish were ignorant of the strange events which had marked the first year of Mr. Soulis's ministrations; and among those who were better in-formed, some were naturally reticent, and others shy of that particular topic. Now and again, only, one of the older folk would warm into courage over his third tumbler, and recount the cause of the minister's strange looks and solitary life.

Fifty years syne, when Mr. Soulis cam' first into Ba'weary, he was still a young man – a callant, the folk said – fu' o' book-learnin' an' grand at the exposition, but, as was natural in sae

²small village

114

young a man, wi' nae leevin' experience in religion. The younger sort were greatly taken wi' his gifts and his gab; but auld, concerned, serious men and women were moved even to prayer for the young man, whom they took to be a self-deceiver, and the parish that was like to be sae ill-supplied. It was before the days o' the moderates – weary fa' them; but ill things are like guid – they baith come bit by bit, a pickle[3] at a time; and there were folk even then that said the Lord had left the college professors to their ain devices, an' the lads that went to study wi' them wad hae done mair an' better sittin' in a peatbog, like their forbears of the persecution, wi' a Bible under their oxter[4] an' a speerit o' prayer in their heart. There was nae doubt onyway, but that Mr. Soulis had been ower lang at the college. He was careful and troubled for mony things besides the ae thing needful. He had a feck o' books wi' him – mair than had ever been seen before in a' that presbytery; and a sair wark the carrier had wi' them, for they were a' like to have smoored in the De'il's Hag between this and Kilmackerlie. They were books o' divinity, to be sure, or so they ca'd them; but the serious were o' opinion there was little service for sae mony, when the hail o' God's Word would gang in the neuk o' a plaid. Then he wad sit half the day and half the nicht forbye, which was scant decent – writin', nae less; an' first they were feared he wad read his sermons; an' syne it proved he was writin' a book himsel', which was surely no' fittin' for ane o' his years an' sma' experience.

Onyway it behoved him to get an auld, decent wife[5] to keep the manse for him an' see to his bit denners; an' he was recommended to an auld limmer[6] – Janet M'Clour, they ca'd her – an' sae far left to himsel' as to be ower persuaded. There was mony advised him to the contrar, for Janet was mair than suspeckit by

[3] a little
[4] armpit
[5] housekeeper or woman
[6] hussy

the best folk in Ba'weary. Lang or that, she had had a wean to a dragoon; she hadna come forrit for maybe thretty year; and bairns had seen her mumblin' to hersel' up on Key's Loan in the gloamin', whilk was an unco time an' place for a Godfearin' woman. Howsoever, it was the laird himsel' that had first tauld the minister o' Janet; an' in thae days he wad hae gane a far gate to pleesure the laird. When folk tauld him that Janet was sib to the de'il, it was a' superstition by his way o' it; an' when they cast up the Bible to him an' the witch of Endor, he wad threep it doun their thrapples that thir days were a' gane by, an' the de'il was mercifully restrained.

Weel, when it got about the clachan that Janet M'Clour was to be servant at the manse, the folk were fair mad wi' her an' him thegither; an' some o' the guidwives had nae better to dae than get round her door-cheeks and chairge her wi' a' that was ken't again' her, frae the sodger's bairn to John Tamson's twa kye.[7] She was nae great speaker; folk usually let her gang her ain gate, an' she let them gang theirs, wi' neither Fair-guid-een nor Fair-guid-day; but when she buckled to, she had a tongue to deave the miller. Up she got, an' there wasna an auld story in Ba'weary but she gart somebody lowp for it that day; they couldna say ae thing but she could say twa to it; till, at the hinder end, the guidwives up an' claught haud of her, an' clawed the coats aff her back, and pu'd her doun the clachan to the water o' Dule, to see if she were a witch or no, soom or droun. The carline[8] skirled till ye could hear her at the Hangin' Shaw, an' she focht like ten; there was mony a guidwife bure the mark o' her neist day an' mony a lang day after; an' just in the hettest o' the collieshangie,[9] wha suld come up (for his sins) but the new minister!

'Women,' said he (an' he had a grand voice), 'I charge you in the Lord's name to let her go.'

[7]cows
[8]hag
[9]uproar

Janet ran to him – she was fair wud wi' terror – an' clang to him, an' prayed him, for Christ's sake, save her frae the cummers;[10] an' they, for their pairt, tauld him a' that was ken't, an' maybe mair.

'Woman,' says he to Janet, 'is this true?'

'As the Lord sees me,' says she, 'as the Lord made me, no' a word o't. Forbye the bairn,' says she, 'I've been a decent woman a' my days.'

'Will you,' says Mr. Soulis, 'in the name of God, and before me, His unworthy minister, renounce the devil and his works?'

Weel, it wad appear that when he askit that, she gave a girn that fairly frichit them that saw her, an' they could hear her teeth play dirl thegither in her chafts; but there was naething for it but the ae way or the ither; an' Janet lifted up her hand an' renounced the de'il before them a'.

'And now,' says Mr. Soulis to the guidwives, 'home with ye, one and all, and pray to God for His forgiveness.'

An' he gied Janet his arm, though she had little on her but a sark,[11] and took her up the clachan to her ain door like a leddy o' the land; an' her screighin' an' laughin' as was a scandal to be heard.

There were mony grave folk lang ower their prayers that nicht; but when the morn cam' there was sic a fear fell upon a' Ba'weary that the bairns hid theirsels, an' even the men-folk stood an' keekit frae their doors. For there was Janet comin' doun the clachan – her or her likeness, nane could tell – wi' her neck thrawn, an' her heid on ae side, like a body that has been hangit, an' a girn on her face like an unstreakit corp. By an' by they got used wi' it, an' even speered at her to ken what was wrang; but frae that day forth she couldna speak like a Christian woman, but slavered an' played click wi' her teeth like a pair o' shears; an' frae that day forth the name o' God cam' never on her lips.

[10]women
[11]smock

Whiles she wad try to say it, but it michtna be. Them that kenned best said least; but they never gied that Thing the name o' Janet M'Clour; for the auld Janet, by their way o't, was in muckle hell that day. But the minister was neither to haud nor to bind; he preached about naething but the folk's cruelty that had gi'en her a stroke of the palsy; he skelpit[12] the bairns that meddled her; an' he had her up to the manse[13] that same nicht, an' dwalled there a' his lane wi' her under the Hangin' Shaw.

Weel, time gaed by: and the idler sort commenced to think mair lichtly o' that black business. The minister was weel thocht o'; he was aye late at the writing, folk wad see his can'le doon by the Dule water after twal' at e'en; and he seemed pleased wi' himsel' an' upsitten as at first, though a' body could see that he was dwining.[14] As for Janet she cam' an' she gaed; if she didna speak muckle afore, it was reason she should speak less then; she meddled naebody; but she was an eldritch thing to see, an' nane wad hae mistrysted wi' her for Ba'weary glebe.

About the end o' July there cam' a spell o' weather, the like o't never was in that country-side; it was lown an' het an' heartless; the herds couldna win up the Black Hill, the bairns were ower weariet to play; an' yet it was gousty too, wi' claps o' het wund that rumm'led in the glens, and bits o' shouers that slockened naething. We aye thocht it büt to thun'er on the morn; but the morn cam', an' the morn's morning, an' it was aye the same uncanny weather, sair on folks and bestial. O' a' that were the waur, nane suffered like Mr. Soulis; he could neither sleep nor eat, he tauld his elders; an' when he wasna writin' at his weary book, he wad be stravaguin[15] ower a' the country-side like a man possessed, when a' body else was blithe to keep caller ben the house.

---

[12]slapped
[13]vicarage
[14]pining away
[15]wandering

Abune Hangin' Shaw, in the bield[16] o' the Black Hill, there's a bit enclosed grund wi' an iron yett;[17] an' it seems, in the auld days, that was the kirkyaird o' Ba'weary, an' consecrated by the Papists before the blessed licht shone upon the kingdom. It was a great howff,[18] o' Mr. Soulis's onyway; there he wad sit an' consider his sermons; an' indeed it's a bieldy bit. Weel, as he cam' ower the wast end o' the Black Hill, ae day, he saw first twa, an' syne fower, an' syne seeven corbie craws fleein' round an' round abune the auld kirkyaird. They flew laigh an' heavy, an' squawked to ither as they gaed; an' it was clear to Mr. Soulis that something had put them frae their ordinar. He wasna easy fleyed,[19] an' gaed straucht up to the wa's; an' what suld he find there but a man, or the appearance o' a man, sittin' in the inside upon a grave. He was of a great stature, an' black as hell, and his e'en were singular to see.[20] Mr. Soulis had heard tell o' black men, mony's the time; but there was something unco about this black man that daunted him. Het as he was, he took a kind o' cauld grue in the marrow o' his banes; but up he spak for a' that; an' says he: 'My friend, are you a stranger in this place?' The black man answered never a word; he got upon his feet, an' begoud on to hirsle[21] to the wa' on the far side; but he aye lookit at the minister; an' the minister stood an' lookit back; till a' in a meenit the black man was ower the wa' an' rinnin' for the bield o' the trees. Mr. Soulis, he hardly kenned why, ran after him; but he was fair forjeskit wi' his walk an' the het, unhalesome weather; an' rin as he likit, he got nae mair than a glisk o' the black man

[16]shelter
[17]gate
[18]haunt
[19]frightened
[20]It was a common belief in Scotland that the devil appeared as a black man. This appears in several witch trials and I think in Law's *Memorials*, that delightful storehouse of the quaint and grisly.
[21]sheepyard

amang the birks, till he won doun to the foot o' the hillside, an' there he saw him ance mair, gaun, hap-step-an'-lawp, ower Dule water to the manse.

Mr. Soulis wasna weel pleased that this fearsome gangrel[22] suld mak' sae free wi' Ba' weary manse; an' he ran the harder, an', wet shoon, ower the burn, an' up the walk; but the de'il a black man was there to see. He stepped out upon the road, but there was naebody there; he gaed a' ower the gairden, but na, nae black man. At the hinder end, an' a bit feared as was but natural, he lifted the hasp an' into the manse; and there was Janet M'Clour before his e'en, wi' her thrawn craig,[23] an' nane sae pleased to see him. An' he aye minded sinsyne, when first he set his e'en upon her, he had the same cauld and deidly grue.

'Janet,' says he, 'have you seen a black man?'

'A black man!' quo' she. 'Save us a'! Ye're no wise, minister. There's nae black man in a' Ba'weary.'

But she didna speak plain, ye maun understand; but yam-yammered, like a powney wi' the bit in its moo.

'Weel,' says he, 'Janet, if there was nae black man, I have spoken with the Accuser of the Brethren.'

An' he sat doun like ane wi' a fever, an' his teeth chittered in his heid.

'Hoots,' says she, 'think shame to yoursel', minister'; an' gied him a drap brandy that she keept aye by her.

Syne Mr. Soulis gaed into his study amang a' his books. It's a lang, laigh, mirk[24] chalmer, perishin' cauld in winter, an' no' very dry even in the top o' the simmer, for the manse stands near the burn. Sae doun he sat, and thocht of a' that had come an' gane since he was in Ba'weary, an' his hame, an' the days when he was a bairn an' ran daffin' on the braes,[25] an' that black man

[22]vagrant
[23]neck
[24]low, gloomy
[25]hillside

aye ran in his heid like the owercome of a sang. Aye the mair he thocht, the mair he thocht o' the black man. He tried the prayer, an' the words wouldna come to him; an' he tried, they say, to write at his book, but he couldna mak' nar mair o' that. There was whiles he thocht the black man was at his oxter, an' the swat stood upon him cauld as well-water; and there was ither whiles, when he cam' to himsel' like a christened bairn an' minded naething.

The upshot was that he gaed to the window an' stood glowrin' at Dule water. The trees are unco thick, an' the water lies deep an' black under the manse; an' there was Janet washin' the cla'es wi' her coats kilted. She had her back to the minister, an' he, for his pairt, hardly kenned what he was lookin' at. Syne she turned round, an' shawed her face; Mr. Soulis had the same cauld grue as twice that day afore, an' it was borne in upon him what folk said, that Janet was deid lang syne, an' this was a bogle in her clay-cauld flesh. He drew back a pickle and he scanned her narrowly. She was tramp-trampin' in the cla'es croonin' to hersel'; and eh! Gude guide us, but it was a fearsome face. Whiles she sang louder, but there was nae man born o' woman that could tell the words o' her sang; an' whiles she lookit side-lang doun, but there was naething there for her to look at. There gaed a scunner[26] through the flesh upon his banes; an' that was Heeven's advertisement. But Mr. Soulis just blamed himsel', he said, to think sae ill o' a puir, auld afflicted wife that hadna a freend forbye himsel'; an' he put up a bit prayer for him an' her, an' drank a little caller water – for his heart rose again' the meat – an' gaed up to his naked bed in the gloamin'.[27]

That was a nicht that has never been forgotten in Ba'weary, the nicht o' the seeventeenth o' August, seeventeen hun'er an' twal'. It had been het afore, as I hae said, but that nicht it was hetter than ever. The sun gaed doun amang unco-lookin' clouds;

[26]loathing
[27]twilight

it fell as mirk as the pit; no' a star, no' a breath o' wund; ye couldna see your han' afore your face, an' even the auld folk cuist the covers frae their beds an' lay pechin' for their breath. Wi' a' that he had upon his mind, it was gey an' unlikely Mr. Soulis wad get muckle sleep. He lay an' he tummeled; the gude, caller bed that he got into brunt his very banes; whiles he slept, an' whiles he waukened; whiles he heard the time o' nicht, an' whiles a tyke yowlin' up the muir, as if somebody was deid; whiles he thocht he heard bogles[28] claverin' in his lug,[29] an' whiles he saw spunkies[30] in the room. He behoved, he judged, to be sick; an' sick he was – little he jaloosed the sickness.

At the hinder end, he got a clearness in his mind, sat up in his sark on the bed-side, an' fell thinkin' ance mair o' the black man an' Janet. He couldna weel tell how – maybe it was the cauld to his feet – but it cam' in upon him wi' a spate that there was some connection between thir twa, an' that either or baith o' them were bogles. An' just at that moment, in Janet's room, which was neist to his, there cam' a stramp o' feet as if men were wars'lin', an' then a loud bang; an' then a wund gaed reishling round the fower quarters o' the house; an' then a' was ance mair as seelent as the grave.

Mr. Soulis was feared for neither man nor de'il. He got his tinder-box, an' lit a can'le, an' made three steps o't ower to Janet's door. It was on the hasp, an' he pushed it open, an' keeked bauldly in. It was a big room, as big as the minister's ain, an' plenished wi' grand, auld solid gear, for he had naething else. There was a fower-posted bed wi' auld tapestry; an' a braw cabinet o' aik, that was fu' o' the minister's divinity books, an' put there to be out o' the gate; an' a wheen duds o' Janet's lying here an' there about the floor. But nae Janet could Mr. Soulis see; nor ony sign o' a contention. In he gaed (an' there's few that wad hae followed

---

[28]spectres
[29]chimney
[30]will o' the wisps

him) an' lookit a' round, an' listened. But there was naething to be heard, neither inside the manse nor in a' Ba'weary parish, an' naething to be seen but the muckle shadows turnin' round the can'le. An' then, a' at aince, the minister's heart played dunt an' stood stock-still; an' a cauld wund blew amang the hairs o' his heid. Whaten a weary sicht was that for the puir man's e'en! For there was Janet hangin' frae a nail beside the auld aik cabinet: her heid aye lay on her shouther, her e'en were steekit, the tongue projected frae her mouth, an' her heels were twa feet clear abune the floor.

'God forgive us all!' thocht Mr. Soulis, 'poor Janet's dead.'

He cam' a step nearer to the corp; an' then his heart fair whammled in his inside. For by what cantrip[31] it wad ill beseem a man to judge, she was hangin' frae a single nail an' by a single wursted thread for darnin' hose.

It's a awfu' thing to be your lane[32] at nicht wi' siccan prodigies o' darkness; but Mr. Soulis was strong in the Lord. He turned an' gaed his ways oot o' that room, an' lockit the door ahint him; an' step by step, doun the stairs, as heavy as leed; and set doun the can'le on the table at the stairfoot. He couldna pray, he couldna think, he was dreepin' wi' caul' swat, an' naething could he hear but the dunt-dunt-duntin' o' his ain heart. He micht maybe hae stood there an hour, or maybe twa, he minded sae little; when a' o' a sudden, he heard a laigh, uncanny steer[33] upstairs; a foot gaed to an' fro in the chalmer whaur the corp was hangin'; syne the door was opened, though he minded weel that he had lockit it; an' syne there was a step upon the landin', an' it seemed to him as if the corp was lookin' ower the rail and doun upon him whaur he stood.

He took up the can'le again (for he couldna want the licht), an' as saftly as ever he could, gaed straucht out o' the manse an'

[31]spell
[32]alone
[33]commotion

to the far end o' the causeway. It was aye pit-mirk; the flame o' the can'le, when he set it on the grund, brunt steedy and clear as in a room; naething moved, but the Dule water seepin' and sabbin' doun the glen, an' yon unhaly footstep that cam' ploddin' doun the stairs inside the manse. He kenned the foot ower weel, for it was Janet's; an' at ilka step that cam' a wee thing nearer, the cauld got deeper in his vitals. He commended his soul to Him that made an' keepit him; 'and, O Lord,' said he, 'give me strength this night to war against the powers of evil.'

By this time the foot was comin' through the passage for the door; he could hear a hand skirt alang the wa', as if the fearsome thing was feelin' for its way. The saughs tossed an' maned thegither, a long sigh cam' ower the hills, the flame o' the can'le was blawn aboot; an' there stood the corp of Thrawn Janet, wi' her grogram goun an' her black mutch, wi' the heid aye upon the shouther, an' the girn still upon the face o't – leevin', ye wad hae said – deid, as Mr. Soulis weel kenned – upon the threshold o' the manse.

It's a strange thing that the soul of man should be that thirled into his perishable body; but the minister saw that, an' his heart didna break.

She didna stand there lang; she began to move again an' cam' slowly towards Mr. Soulis whaur he stood under the saughs. A' the life o' his body, a' the strength o'his speerit, were glowerin' frae his e'en. It seemed she was gaun to speak, but wanted words, an' made a sign wi' the left hand. There cam' a clap o' wund, like a cat's fuff; oot gaed the can'le, the saughs skreighed like folk; an' Mr. Soulis kenned that, live or die, this was the end o't.

'Witch, beldame,[34] devil!' he cried, 'I charge you, by the power of God, begone – if you be dead, to the grave – if you be damned, to hell.'

An' at that moment the Lord's ain hand out o' the Heevens struck the Horror whaur it stood; the auld, deid, desecrated corp

---

[34]hag

o' the witch-wife, sae lang keepit frae the grave and hirsled round by de'ils, lowed up like a brunstane spunk[35] an' fell in ashes to the grund; the thunder followed, peal on dirlin' peal, the rairin' rain upon the back o' that; and Mr. Soulis lowped through the garden hedge, an' ran, wi' skelloch upon skelloch,[36] for the clachan.

That same mornin', John Christie saw the Black Man pass the Muckle Cairn as it was chappin' six; before eicht, he gaed by the change-house at Knockdow; an' no' lang after, Sandy M'Lellan saw him gaun linkin' doun the braes frae Kilmackerlie. There's little doubt but it was him that dwalled sae lang in Janet's body; but he was awa' at last; an' sinsyne the de'il has never fashed[37] us in Ba'weary.

But it was a sair dispensation for the minister; lang, lang he lay ravin' in his bed; an' frae that hour to this, he was the man ye ken the day.

[35]blazed like tinder
[36]yell
[37]troubled

Mary Burnet

James Hogg

The following incidents are related as having occurred at a shepherd's house, not a hundred miles from St. Mary's Loch; but, as the descendants of one of the families still reside in the vicinity, I deem it requisite to use names which cannot be recognised, save by those who have heard the story.

John Allanson, the farmer's son of Inverlawn, was a handsome, roving, and incautious young man, enthusiastic, amorous, and fond of adventure, and one who could hardly be said to fear the face of either man, woman, or spirit. Among other love adventures, he fell a-courting Mary Burnet, of Kirkstyle, a most beautiful and innocent maiden, and one who had been bred up in rural simplicity. She loved him, but yet she was afraid of him; and though she had no objection to meeting with him among others, yet she carefully avoided meeting him alone, though often and earnestly urged to it. One day, the young man, finding an opportunity, at Our Lady's Chapel, after mass, urged his suit for a private meeting so ardently, and with so many vows of love and sacred esteem, that Mary was so far won as to promise, that *perhaps* she would come and meet him.

The trysting place was a little green sequestered spot, on the very verge of the lake, well known to many an angler, and to none better than the writer of this old tale; and the hour appointed, the time when the King's Elwand (now foolishly termed the Belt of Orion) set his first golden knob above the hill. Allanson came too early; and he watched the sky with such eagerness and devotion, that he thought every little star that arose in the south-east the top knob of the King's Elwand. At last the Elwand did arise in good earnest, and then the youth, with a heart palpitating with agitation, had nothing for it but to watch the heathery brow by which bonny Mary Burnet was to descend. No Mary Burnet made her appearance, even although the King's Elwand had now measured its own equivocal length five or six times up the lift.

Young Allanson now felt all the most poignant miseries of disappointment; and, as the story goes, uttered in his heart an unhallowed wish – he wished that some witch or fairy would influence his Mary to come to him in spite of her maidenly scruples. This wish was thrice repeated with all the energy of disappointed love. It was thrice repeated, and no more, when, behold, Mary appeared on the brae, with wild and eccentric motions, speeding to the appointed place. Allanson's excitement seems to have been more than he was able to bear, as he instantly became delirious with joy, and always professed that he could remember nothing of their first meeting, save that Mary remained silent, and spoke not a word, either good or bad. In a short time she fell a-sobbing and weeping, refusing to be comforted, and then, uttering a piercing shriek, sprung up, and ran from him with amazing speed.

At this part of the loch, which, as I said, is well known to many, the shore is overhung by a precipitous cliff, of no great height, but still inaccessible, either from above or below. Save in a great drought, the water comes to within a yard of the bottom of this cliff, and the intermediate space is filled with rough unshapely pieces of rock fallen from above. Along this narrow and rude space, hardly passable by the angler at noon, did Mary bound with the swiftness of a kid, although surrounded with darkness. Her lover, pursuing with all his energy, called out, 'Mary! Mary! my dear Mary, stop and speak with me. I'll conduct you home, or anywhere you please, but do not run from me. Stop, my dearest Mary – stop!'

Mary would not stop; but ran on, till, coming to a little cliff that jutted into the lake, round which there was no passage, and, perceiving that her lover would there overtake her, she uttered another shriek, and plunged into the lake. The loud sound of her fall into the still water rung in the young man's ears like the knell of death; and if before he was crazed with love, he was now as much so with despair. He saw her floating lightly away from the shore towards the deepest part of the loch; but, in a short time, she began to sink, and gradually disappeared, without uttering a throb or a cry. A good while previous to this, Allanson had flung off his bonnet, shoes, and coat, and plunged in. He swam to the place where Mary disappeared; but there was neither boil nor gurgle on the water, nor even a bell of departing breath, to mark the place where his beloved had sunk. Being strangely impressed, at that trying moment, with a determination to live or die with her, he tried to dive, in hopes either to bring her up or to die in her arms; and he thought of their being so found on the shore of the lake, with a melancholy satisfaction; but by no effort of his could he reach the bottom, nor knew he what distance he was still from it. With an exhausted frame, and a despairing heart, he was obliged again to seek the shore, and, dripping wet as he was, and half-naked, he ran to her father's house with the woeful tidings. Everything there was quiet. The old shepherd's family, of whom Mary was the youngest, and sole daughter, were all sunk in silent repose; and oh, how the distracted lover wept at the thoughts of wakening them to hear the doleful tidings! But waken them he must; so, going to the little window close by the goodman's bed, he called, in a melancholy tone, 'Andrew! Andrew Burnet, are you waking?'

'Troth, man, I think I be; or, at least, I'm half-and-half. What hast thou to say to auld Andrew Burnet at this time o' night?'

'Are you waking, I say?'

'Gudewife, am I waking? Because if I be, tell that stravaiger sae. He'll maybe tak your word for it, for mine he winna tak.'

'O Andrew, none of your humour to-night; I bring you tidings the most woeful, the most dismal, the most heart-rending, that ever were brought to an honest man's door.'

'To his window, you mean,' cried Andrew, bolting out of bed, and proceeding to the door. 'Gude sauff us, man, come in, whaever you be, and tell us your tidings face to face; and then we'll can better judge of the truth of them. If they be in concord wi' your voice, they are melancholy indeed. Have the reavers come, and are our kye driven?'

'Oh, alas! waur than that – a thousand times waur than that! Your daughter – your dear beloved and only daughter, Mary —'

'What of Mary?' cried the good-man. 'What of Mary?' cried her mother, shuddering and groaning with terror; and at the same time she kindled a light.

The sight of their neighbour, half-naked, and dripping with wet, and madness and despair in his looks, sent a chillness to their hearts, that held them in silence, and they were unable to utter a word, till he went on thus: 'Mary is gone; your darling and mine is lost, and sleeps this night in a watery grave – and I have been her destroyer!'

'Thou art mad, John Allanson,' said the old man, vehemently, 'raving mad; at least I hope so. Wicked as thou art, thou hadst not the heart to kill my dear child. O yes, you are mad – God be thankful, you are mad. I see it in your looks and demeanour. Heaven be praised, you are mad! You *are* mad; but you'll get better again. But what do I say?' continued he, as recollecting himself – 'We can soon convince our own senses. Wife, lead the way to our daughter's bed.'

With a heart throbbing with terror and dismay, old Jean Linton led the way to Mary's chamber, followed by the two men, who were eagerly gazing, one over each of her shoulders. Mary's little apartment was in the farther end of the long narrow cottage; and as soon as they entered it, they perceived a form lying on the bed, with the bedclothes drawn over its head; and on the lid of Mary's little chest, that stood at the bedside, her clothes were lying neatly folded, as they wont to be. Hope seemed to dawn on the faces of the two old people when they beheld this, but the lover's heart sunk still deeper in despair. The father called her name, but the form on the bed returned no answer; however, they all heard distinctly sobs, as of one weeping. The old man then ventured to pull down the clothes from her face; and, strange to say, there indeed lay Mary Burnet, drowned in tears, yet apparently nowise surprised at the ghastly appearance of the three naked figures. Allanson gasped for breath, for he remained still incredulous. He touched her clothes – he lifted her robes one by one – and all of them were dry, neat, and clean, and had no appearance of having sunk in the lake.

There can be no doubt that Allanson was confounded by the strange event that had befallen him, and felt like one struggling with a frightful vision, or some energy beyond the power of man to comprehend. Nevertheless the assurance that Mary was there in life, weeping although she was, put him once more beside himself with joy; and he kneeled at her bedside, beseeching permission but to kiss her hand. She, however, repulsed him with disdain, saying with great emphasis: 'You are a bad man, John Allanson, and I entreat you to go out of my sight. The sufferings that I have undergone this night have been beyond the power of flesh and blood to endure; and by some cursed agency of yours have these sufferings been brought about. I therefore pray you, in His name, whose law you have transgressed, to depart out of my sight.'

Wholly overcome by conflicting passions, by circumstances so contrary to one another, and so discordant with everything either in the works of Nature or Providence, the young man could do nothing but stand like a rigid statue, with his hands lifted up, and his visage like that of a corpse, until led away by the two old people from their daughter's apartment. Then they lighted up a fire to dry him, and began to question him with the most intense curiosity; but they could elicit nothing from him, but the most disjointed exclamations – such as, 'Lord in Heaven, what can be the meaning of this?' And at other times: 'It is all the enchantment of the devil; the evil spirits have got dominion over me!'

Finding they could make nothing of him, they began to form conjectures of their own. Jean affirmed that it had been the Mermaid of the loch that had come to him in Mary's shape, to allure him to his destruction; but Andrew Burnet, setting his bonnet to one side, and raising his left hand to a level with it, so that he might have full scope to motion and flourish, suiting his action to his words, thus began, with a face of sapience never to be excelled:

'Gudewife, it doth strike me that thou art very wide of the mark. It must have been a spirit of a great deal higher quality than a meer-maiden, who played this extraordinary prank. The meer-maiden is not a spirit, but a beastly sensitive creature, with a malicious spirit within it. Now, what influence could a cauld clatch of a creature like that, wi' a tail like a great saumont-fish, hae ower our bairn, either to make her happy or unhappy? Or where could it borrow her claes, Jean? Tell me that. Na, na, Jean Linton, depend on it, the spirit that courtit wi' poor sinfu' Jock there, has been a fairy; but whether a good ane or an ill ane, it is hard to determine.'

Andrew's disquisition was interrupted by the young man falling into a fit of trembling that was fearful to look at, and threatened soon to terminate his existence. Jean ran for the family cordial, observing by the way, that 'though he was a wicked person, he was still a fellow-creature, and might live to repent;' and influenced by this spark of genuine humanity, she made him swallow two horn-spoonfuls of strong *aquavitae*. Andrew then put a piece of scarlet thread round each wrist, and taking a strong rowan-tree staff in his hand, he conveyed his trembling and astonished guest home, giving him at parting this sage advice:

'I'll tell you what it is, Jock Allanson – ye hae run a near risk o' perdition, and, escaping that for the present, o' losing your right reason. But take an auld man's advice – never gang again

131

out by night to beguile ony honest man's daughter, lest a worse thing befall thee.'

Next morning Mary dressed herself more neatly than usual, but there was manifestly a deep melancholy settled on her lovely face, and at times the unbidden tear would start into her eye. She spoke no word, either good or bad, that ever her mother could recollect, that whole morning; but she once or twice observed her daughter gazing at her, as with an intense and melancholy interest. About nine o'clock in the morning, she took a hay-raik over her shoulder, and went down to a meadow at the east end of the loch, to coil a part of her father's hay, her father and brother engaging to join her about noon, when they came from the sheepfold. As soon as old Andrew came home, his wife and he, as was natural, instantly began to converse on the events of the preceding night; and in the course of their conversation Andrew said, 'Gudeness be about us, Jean, was not yon an awfu' speech o' our bairn's to young Jock Allanson last night?'

'Ay, it was a downsetter, gudeman, and spoken like a good Christian lass.'

'I'm no sae sure o' that, Jean Linton. My good woman, Jean Linton, I'm no sae sure o' that. Yon speech has gi'en me a great deal o' trouble o' heart; for d'ye ken, an' take my life – ay, an' take your life, Jean – nane o' us can tell whether it was in the Almighty's name or the devil's that she discharged her lover.'

'O fy, Andrew, how can ye say sae? How can ye doubt that it was in the Almighty's name?'

'Couldna she have said sae then, and that wad hae put it beyond a' doubt? And that wad hae been the natural way too; but instead of that she says, "I pray you, in the name of him whose law you have transgressed, to depart out o' my sight." I confess I'm terrified when I think about yon speech, Jean Linton. Didna she say too that "her sufferings had been beyond what flesh and blood could have endured?" What was she but flesh and blood. Didna that remark infer that she was something mair than a mortal creature? Jean Linton, Jean Linton! what will you say if it should turn out that our daughter is drowned, and that yon was the fairy we had in the house a' the night and this morning?'

'O haud your tongue, Andrew Burnet, and dinna make my heart cauld within me. We hae aye trusted in the Lord yet, and he has never forsaken us, nor will he yet gie the Wicked One power ower us or ours.'

'Ye say very weel, Jean, and we maun e'en hope for the best,' quoth old Andrew; and away he went, accompanied by his son Alexander, to assist their beloved Mary on the meadow.

No sooner had Andrew set his head over the bents, and come in view of the meadow, than he said to his son, 'I wish Jock Allanson maunna hae been east-the-loch fishing for geds the day, for I think my Mary has made very little progress in the meadow.'

'She's ower muckle ta'en up about other things this while to mind her wark,' said Alexander; 'I wadna wonder, father, if that lassie gangs a black gate yet.'

Andrew uttered a long and a deep sigh, that seemed to ruffle the very fountains of life, and, without speaking another word, walked on to the hayfield. It was three hours since Mary had left home, and she ought at least to have put up a dozen coils of hay each hour. But, in place of that, she had put up only seven altogether, and the last was unfinished. Her own hay-raik, that had an M and a B neatly cut on the head of it, was leaning on the unfinished coil, and Mary was wanting. Her brother, thinking she had hid herself from them in sport, ran from one coil to another, calling her many bad names, playfully; but after he had turned them all up, and several deep swathes besides, she was not to be found. This young man, who slept in the byre, knew nothing of the events of the foregoing night, the old people and Allanson having mutually engaged to keep them a profound secret, and he had therefore less reason than his father to be seriously alarmed. When they began to work at the hay Andrew could work none; he looked this way and that way, but in no way could he see Mary approaching; so he put on his coat and went away home, to pour his sorrows into the bosom of his wife; and, in the meantime, he desired his son to run to all the neighbouring farming-houses and cots, every one, and make inquiries if anybody had seen Mary.

When Andrew went home and informed his wife that their darling was missing, the grief and astonishment of the aged couple knew no bounds. They sat down and wept together, and declared over and over that this act of Providence was too strong for them, and too high to be understood. Jean besought her husband to kneel instantly, and pray urgently to God to restore their child to them; but he declined it, on account of the wrong frame of his mind, for he declared, that his rage against John Allanson was so extreme as to unfit him for approaching the throne of his Maker. 'But if the profligate refuses to listen to the entreaties of an injured parent,' added he, 'he shall feel the weight of an injured father's arm.'

Andrew went straight away to Inverlawn, though without the least hope of finding young Allanson at home; but, on reaching the place, to his amazement, he found the young man lying ill of a burning fever, raving incessantly of witches, spirits, and Mary Burnet. To such a height had his frenzy arrived, that when Andrew went there, it required three men to hold him in the bed. Both his parents testified their opinions openly, that their son was bewitched, or possessed of a demon, and the whole family was thrown into the greatest consternation. The good old shepherd, finding enough of grief there already, was obliged to confine his to his own bosom, and return disconsolate to his little family circle, in which there was a woeful blank that night.

His son returned also from a fruitless search. No one had seen any traces of his sister, but an old crazy woman, at a place called Oxcleuch, said that she had seen her go by in a grand chariot with young Jock Allanson, toward the Birkhill Path, and by that time they were at the Cross of Dumgree. The young man said he asked her what sort of a chariot it was, as there was never such a thing in that country as a chariot, nor yet a road for one. But she replied that he was widely mistaken, for that a great number of chariots sometimes passed that way, though never any of them returned. Those words appearing to be merely the ravings of superannuation, they were not regarded; but when no other traces of Mary could be found, old Andrew went up to consult this crazy dame once more, but he was not able to bring any such thing to her recollection. She spoke only in parables, which to him were incomprehensible.

Bonny Mary Burnet was lost. She left her father's house at nine o'clock on a Wednesday morning, 17th of September, neatly dressed in a white jerkin and green bonnet, with her hay-raik over her shoulder; and that was the last sight she was doomed ever to see of her native cottage. She seemed to have had some presentiment of this, as appeared from her demeanour that morning before she left it. Mary Burnet of Kirkstyle was lost, and great was the sensation produced over the whole country by the mysterious event. There was a long ballad extant at one period on the melancholy catastrophe, which was supposed to have been composed by the chaplain of St. Mary's; but I have only heard tell of it, without ever hearing it sung or recited. Many of the verses concluded thus:

> *But Bonny Mary Burnet*
> *We will never see again.*

The story soon got abroad, with all its horrid circumstances (and there is little doubt that it was grievously exaggerated), and there was no obloquy that was not thrown on the survivor, who certainly in some degree deserved it, for, instead of growing better, he grew ten times more wicked than he was before. In one thing the whole country agreed, that it had been the real Mary Burnet who was drowned in the loch, and that the being which was found in her bed, lying weeping and complaining of suffering, and which vanished the next day, had been a fairy, an evil spirit, or a changeling of some sort, for that it never spoke save once, and that in a mysterious manner; nor did it partake of any food with the rest of the family. Her father and mother knew not what to say or what to think, but they wandered through this weary world like people wandering in a dream. Everything that belonged to Mary Burnet was kept by her parents as the most sacred relics, and many a tear did her aged mother shed over them. Every article of her dress brought the once comely wearer to mind. Andrew often said, 'That to have lost the darling child of their old age in any way would have been a great trial, but to lose her in the way that they had done, was really mair than human frailty could endure.'

Many a weary day did he walk by the shores of the loch, looking eagerly for some vestige of her garments, and though he trembled at every appearance, yet did he continue to search on. He had a number of small bones collected, that had belonged to lambs and other minor animals, and, haply, some of them to fishes, from a fond supposition that they might once have formed joints of her toes or fingers. These he kept concealed in a little bag, in order, as he said, 'to let the doctors see them.' But no relic, besides these, could he ever discover of Mary's body.

Young Allanson recovered from his raging fever scarcely in the manner of other men, for he recovered all at once, after a few days' raving and madness. Mary Burnet, it appeared, was by him no more remembered. He grew ten times more wicked than before, and hesitated at no means of accomplishing his unhallowed purposes. The devout shepherds and cottages around detested him; and, both in their families and in the wild, when there was no ear to hear but that of Heaven, they prayed protection from his devices, as if he had been the Wicked One; and they all prophesied that he would make a bad end.

One fine day about the middle of October, when the days begin to get very short, and the nights long and dark, on a Friday morning, the next year but one after Mary Burnet was lost, a memorable day in the fairy annals, John Allanson, younger of Inverlawn, went to a great hiring fair at a village called Moffat in

Annandale, in order to hire a housemaid. His character was so notorious, that not one young woman in the district would serve in his father's house; so away he went to the fair at Moffat, to hire the prettiest and loveliest girl he could there find, with the intention of ruining her as soon as she came home, This is no supposititious accusation, for he acknowledged his plan to Mr. David Welch of Cariferan, who rode down to the market with him, and seemed to boast of it, and dwell on it with delight. But the maidens of Annandale had a guardian angel in the fair that day, of which neither he nor they were aware.

Allanson looked through the hiring-market, and through the hiring-market, and at length fixed on one young woman, which indeed was not difficult to do, for there was no such form there for elegance and beauty. Mr. Welch stood still and eyed him. He took the beauty aside. She was clothed in green, and as lovely as a new-blown rose.

'Are you to hire, pretty maiden?'

'Yes, sir.'

'Will you hire with me?'

'I care not though I do. But if I hire with you, it must be for a long term.'

'Certainly. The longer the better. What are your wages to be?'

'You know, if I hire, I must be paid in kind. I must have the first living creature that I see about Inverlawn to myself.'

'I wish it may be me, then. But what do you know about Inverlawn?'

'I think I *should* know about it.'

'Bless me! I know the face as well as I know my own, and better. But the name has somehow escaped me. Pray, may I I ask your name?'

'Hush! hush!' said she solemnly, and holding up her hand at the same time. 'Hush, hush, you had better say nothing about that here.'

'I am in utter amazement!' he exclaimed. 'What is the meaning of this? I conjure you to tell me your name!'

'It is Mary Burnet,' said she, in a soft whisper; and at the same time she let down a green veil over her face.

If Allanson's death-warrant had been announced to him at that moment, it could not have deprived him so completely of sense and motion. His visage changed into that of a corpse, his jaws fell down, and his eyes became glazed, so as apparently to throw no reflections inwardly. Mr. Welch, who had kept his eye steadily on them all the while, perceived his comrade's dilemma, and went up to him. 'Allanson? Mr. Allanson? What is the matter with you, man?' said he. 'Why, the girl has bewitched you, and turned you into a statue!'

Allanson made some sound in his throat, as if attempting to speak, but his tongue refused its office, and he only jabbered. Mr. Welch, conceiving that he was seized with some fit, or about to faint, supported him into the Johnston Arms; but he either could not, or would not grant him any explanation. Welch being, however, resolved to see the maiden in green once more, persuaded Allanson, after causing him to drink a good deal, to go out into the hiring-market again, in search of her. They ranged the market through and through, but the maiden in green was gone, and not to be found. She had vanished in the crowd the moment she divulged her name, and even though Welch had his eye fixed on her, he could not discover which way she went. Allanson appeared to be in a kind of stupor as well as terror, but when he found that she had left the market, he began to recover himself, and to look out again for the top of the market.

He soon found one more beautiful than the last. She was like a sylph, clothed in robes of pure snowy white, with green ribands. Again he pointed this new flower out to Mr. David Welch, who declared that such a perfect model of beauty he had never in his life seen. Allanson, being resolved to have this one at any wages, took her aside, and put the usual question: 'Do you wish to hire, pretty maiden?'

'Yes, sir.'

'Will you hire with me?'

'I care not though I do.'

'What, then, are your wages to be? Come – say? And be reasonable; I am determined not to part with you for a trifle.'

'My wages must be in a kind; I work on no other conditions. Pray, how are all the good people about Inverlawn?'

Allanson's breath began to cut, and a chillness to creep through his whole frame, and he answered, with a faltering tongue: 'I thank you – much in their ordinary way.'

'And your aged neighbours,' rejoined she, 'are they still alive and well?'

'I – I – I think they are,' said he, panting for breath. 'But I am at a loss to know whom I am indebted to for these kind recollections.'

'What,' said she, 'have you so soon forgot Mary Burnet of Kirkstyle?'

Allanson started as if a bullet had gone through his heart. The lovely sylph-like form glided into the crowd, and left the astounded libertine once more standing like a rigid statue, until aroused by his friend, Mr. Welch. He tried a third fair one, and got the same answers, and the same name given. Indeed, the first time ever I heard the tale, it bore that he tried *seven*, who all turned out to be Mary Burnets of Kirkstyle; but I think it unlikely that he would try so many, as he must long ere that time have been sensible that he laboured under some power of enchantment. However, when nothing else would do, he helped himself to a good proportion of strong drink. While he was thus engaged, a phenomenon of beauty and grandeur came into the fair, that caught the sole attention of all present. This was a lovely dame, riding in a gilded chariot, with two livery-men before, and two behind, clothed in green and gold; and never sure was there so splendid a meteor seen in a Moffat fair. The word instantly circulated in the market, that this was the Lady Elizabeth Douglas, eldest daughter to the Earl of Morton, who then sojourned at Auchincastle, in the vicinity of Moffat, and which lady at that time was celebrated as a great beauty all over

Scotland. She was afterwards Lady Keith; and the mention of this name in the tale, as it were by mere accident, fixes the era of it in the reign of James the Fourth, at the very time that fairies, brownies, and witches, were at the rifest in Scotland.

Every one in the market believed the lady to be the daughter of the Earl of Morton; and when she came to the Johnston Arms, a gentleman in green came out bareheaded, and received her out of the carriage. All the crowd gazed at such unparalleled beauty and grandeur, but none was half so much overcome as Allanson. He had never conceived aught half so lovely either in earth, or heaven, or fairyland; and while he stood in a burning fever of admiration, think of his astonishment, and the astonishment of the countless crowd that looked on, when this brilliant and matchless beauty beckoned him towards her! He could not believe his senses, but looked this way and that way to see how others regarded the affair; but she beckoned him a second time, with such a winning courtesy and smile, that immediately he pulled off his beaver cap and hasted up to her; and without more ado she gave him her arm, and the two walked into the hostel.

Allanson conceived that he was thus distinguished by Lady Elizabeth Douglas, the flower of the land, and so did all the people of the market; and greatly they wondered who the young farmer could be that was thus particularly favoured; for it ought to have been mentioned that he had not one personal acquaintance in the fair save Mr. David Welch of Cariferan. The first thing the lady did was to inquire kindly after his health. Allanson thanked her ladyship with all the courtesy he was master of; and being by this time persuaded that she was in love with him, he became as light as if treading on the air. She next inquired after his father and mother. Oho? thought he to himself, poor creature, she is terribly in for it! but her love shall not be thrown away upon a backward or ungrateful object. He answered her with great politeness, and at length began to talk of her noble father and young Lord William, but she cut him short by asking if he did not recognise her.

'Oh, yes! He knew who her ladyship was, and remembered that he had seen her comely face often before, although he could not, at that particular moment, recall to his memory the precise time or places of their meeting.'

She next asked for his old neighbours of Kirkstyle, and if they were still in life and health!

Allanson felt as if his heart were a piece of ice. A chillness spread over his whole frame; he sank back on a seat, and remained motionless; but the beautiful and adorable creature soothed him with kind words, till he again gathered courage to speak.

'What!' said he; 'and has it been your own lovely self who has been playing tricks on me this whole day?'

'A first love is not easily extinguished, Mr. Allanson,' said she. 'You may guess from my appearance, that I have been fortunate in life; but, for all that, my first love for you has continued the same, unaltered and unchanged, and you must forgive the little freedoms I used to-day to try your affections, and the effects my appearance would have on you.'

'It argues something for my good taste, however, that I never pitched on any face for beauty to-day but your own,' said he. 'But now that we have met once more, we shall not so easily part again. I will devote the rest of my life to you, only let me know the place of your abode.'

'It is hard by,' said she, 'only a very little space from this; and happy, happy, would I be to see you there to-night, were it proper or convenient. But my lord is at present from home and in a distant country.'

'I should not conceive that any particular hindrance to my visit,' said he.

With great apparent reluctance she at length consented to admit of his visit, and offered to leave one of her gentlemen, whom she could trust, to be his conductor; but this he positively refused. It was his desire, he said, that no eye of man should see him enter or leave her happy dwelling. She said he was a selfwilled man, but should have his own way; and after giving him such directions as would infallibly lead him to her mansion, she mounted her chariot and was driven away.

Allanson was uplifted above every sublunary concern. Seeking out his friend, David Welch, he imparted to him his extraordinary good fortune, but he did not tell him that she was not the Lady Elizabeth Douglas. Welch insisted on accompanying him on the way, and refused to turn back till he came to the very point of the road next to the lady's splendid mansion; and in spite of all that Allanson could say, Welch remained there till he saw his comrade enter the court gate, which glowed with lights as innumerable as the stars of the firmament.

Allanson had promised to his father and mother to be home on the morning after the fair to breakfast. He came not either that day or the next; and the third day the old man mounted his white pony, and rode away towards Moffat in search of his son. He called at Cariferan on his way, and made inquiries at Mr. Welch. The latter manifested some astonishment that the young man had not returned; nevertheless he assured his father of his safety, and desired him to return home; and then with reluctance confessed that the young man was engaged in an amour with the Earl of Morton's beautiful daughter; that he had gone to the castle by appointment, and that he, David Welch, had accompanied him to the gate, and seen him enter, and it was apparent that his reception had been a kind one, since he had tarried so long.

Mr. Welch, seeing the old man greatly distressed, was persuaded to accompany him on his journey, as the last who had seen his son, and seen him enter the castle. On reaching Moffat they found his steed standing at the hostel, whither it had returned on the night of the fair, before the company broke up; but the owner had not been heard of since seen in company with Lady Elizabeth Douglas. The old man set out for Auchin-castle, taking Mr. David Welch along with him; but long ere they reached the place, Mr. Welch assured him he would not find his son there, as it was nearly in a different direction that they rode on the evening of the fair. However, to the castle they went, and were admitted to the Earl, who, after hearing the old man's tale, seemed to consider him in a state of derangement. He sent for his daughter Elizabeth, and questioned her concerning her meeting with the son of the old respectable countryman – of her appointment with him on the night of the preceding Friday, and concluded by saying he hoped she had him still in safe concealment about the castle.

The lady, hearing her father talk in this manner, and seeing the serious and dejected looks of the old man, knew not what to say, and asked an explanation. But Mr. Welch put a stop to it by declaring to old Allanson that the Lady Elizabeth was not the lady with whom his son made the appointment, for he had seen her, and would engage to know her again among ten thousand; nor was that the castle towards which he had accompanied his son, nor any thing like it. 'But go with me,' continued he, 'and, though I am a stranger in this district, I think I can take you to the very place.'

They set out again; and Mr. Welch traced the road from Moffat, by which young Allanson and he had gone, until, after travelling several miles, they came to a place where a road struck off to the right at an angle. 'Now I know we are right,' said Welch; 'for here we stopped, and your son intreated me to return, which I refused, and accompanied him to yon large tree, and a little way beyond it, from whence I saw him received in at the splendid gate. We shall be in sight of the mansion in three minutes.'

They passed on to the tree, and a space beyond it; but then Mr. Welch lost the use of his speech, as he perceived that there was neither palace nor gate there, but a tremendous gulf, fifty fathoms deep, and a dark stream foaming and boiling below.

'How is this?' said old Allanson. 'There is neither mansion nor habitation of man here!'

Welch's tongue for a long time refused its office, and he stood like a statue, gazing on the altered and awful scene. 'He only, who made the spirits of men,' said he, at last, 'and all the spirits that sojourn in the earth and air, can tell how his is. We are wandering in a world of enchantment, and have been influenced by some agencies above human nature, or without its pale; for here of a certainty did I take leave of your son – and there, in that direction, and apparently either on the verge of that gulf, or the space above it, did I see him received in at the court gate of a mansion, splendid beyond all conception. How can human comprehension make anything of this?'

They went forward to the verge, Mr. Welch leading the way to the very spot on which he saw the gate opened, and there they found marks where a horse had been plunging. Its feet had been over the brink, but it seemed to have recovered itself, and deep, deep down, and far within, lay the mangled corpse of John Allanson; and in this manner, mysterious beyond all example, terminated the career of that wicked and flagitious young man. What a beautiful moral may be extracted from this fairy tale!

But among all these turnings and windings, there is no account given, you will say, of the fate of Mary Burnet; for this last appearance of hers at Moffat seems to have been altogether a phantom or illusion. Gentle and kind reader, I can give you no account of the fate of that maiden; for though the ancient fairy-tale proceeds, it seems to me to involve her fate in ten times more mystery than what we have hitherto seen of it.

The yearly return of the day on which Mary was lost, was observed as a day of mourning by her aged and disconsolate parents – a day of sorrow, of fasting, and humiliation. Seven years came and passed away, and the seventh returning day of fasting and prayer was at hand. On the evening previous to it, old Andrew was moving along the sands of the loch, still looking for some relic of his beloved Mary, when he was aware of a little shrivelled old man, who came posting towards him. The creature was not above five spans in height, and had a face scarcely like that of a human creature; but he was, nevertheless, civil in his deportment, and sensible in speech. He bade Andrew a good evening, and asked him what he was looking for. Andrew answered, that he was looking for that which he should never find.

'Pray, what is your name, ancient shepherd?' said the stranger; 'for methinks I should know something of you, and perhaps have a commission to you.'

'Alas! why should you ask after my name?' said Andrew. 'My name is now nothing to any one.'

'Had not you once a beautiful daughter, named Mary?' said the stranger.

'It is a heartrending question, man,' said Andrew; 'but *certes*, I had once a beloved daughter named Mary.'

'What became of her?' asked the stranger.

Andrew shook his head, turned round, and began to move away; it was a theme that his heart could not brook. He sauntered along the loch sands, his dim eye scanning every white pebble as he passed along. There was a hopelessness in his stooping form, his gait, his eye, his features – in every step that he took there was a hopeless apathy. The dwarf followed him, and began to expostulate with him. 'Old man, I see you are pining under some real or fancied affliction,' said he. 'But in continuing to do so, you are neither acting according to the dictates of reason nor true religion. What is man that he should fret, or the son of man that he should repine, under the chastening hand of his Maker?'

'I am far frae justifying myself,' returned Andrew, surveying his shrivelled monitor with some degree of astonishment. 'But there are some feelings that neither reason nor religion can o'ermaster; and there are some that a parent may cherish without sin.'

'I deny the position,' said the stranger, 'taken either absolutely or relatively. All repining under the Supreme decree is leavened with unrighteousness. But, subtleties aside, I ask you, as I did before, What became of your daughter?'

'Ask the Father of her spirit, and the framer of her body,' said Andrew solemnly; 'ask Him into whose hands I committed her from childhood. He alone knows what became of her, but I do not.'

'How long is it since you lost her?'

'It is seven years to-morrow!'

'Ay! you remember the time well. And you have mourned for her all that while?'

'Yes; and I will go down to the grave mourning for my only daughter, the child of my age, and of all my affection. Oh, thou unearthly-looking monitor, knowest thou aught of my darling child? for if thou dost, thou wilt know that she was not like other women. There was a simplicity and a purity about my Mary, that was hardly consistent with our frail nature.'

'Wouldst thou like to see her again?' said the dwarf.

Andrew turned round, his whole frame shaking as with a palsy, and gazed on the audacious imp. 'See her again, creature!' cried he vehemently. 'Would I like to see her again, sayest thou?'

'I said so,' said the dwarf, 'and I say further, Dost thou know this token? Look, and see if thou dost!'

Andrew took the token, and looked at it, then at the shrivelled stranger, and then at the token again; and at length he burst into tears, and wept aloud; but they were tears of joy, and his weeping seemed to have some breathings of laughter intermingled in it. And still as he kissed the token, he called out in broken and convulsive sentences: 'Yes, auld body, I *do* know it! – I *do* know it! – I *do* know it! It is indeed the same golden Edward, with three holes in it, with which I presented my Mary on her birthday, in her eighteenth year, to buy a new suit for the holidays. But when she took it she said – ay, I mind weel what my bonny woman said. "It is sae bonny and sae kenspeckle," said she, "that I think I'll keep it for the sake of the giver." O dear, dear! Blessed little creature, tell me how she is, and where she is? Is she living, or is she dead?'

'She is living, and in good health,' said the dwarf; 'and better, and braver, and happier, and lovelier than ever; and if you make haste, you will see her and her family at Moffat to-morrow afternoon. They are to pass there on a journey, but it is an express one, and I am sent to you with that token, to inform you of the circumstance, that you may have it in your power to see and embrace your beloved daughter once before you die.'

'And am I to meet my Mary at Moffat? Come away, little, dear, welcome body, thou blessed of heaven, come away, and taste of an auld shepherd's best cheer, and I'll gang foot for foot with you to Moffat, and my auld wife shall gang foot for foot with us too. I tell you, little, blessed, and welcome crile, come alone with me.'

'I may not tarry to enter your house, or taste of your cheer, good shepherd,' said the being. 'May plenty still be within your walls, and a thankful heart to enjoy it! But my directions are neither to taste meat nor drink in this country, but to haste back to her that sent me. Go – haste, and make ready, for you have no time to lose.'

'At what time will she be there?' cried Andrew, flinging the plaid from him to run home with the tidings.

'Precisely when the shadow of the Holy Cross falls due east,' cried the dwarf; and turning round, he hasted on his way.

When old Jean Linton saw her husband coming hobbling and running home without his plaid, and having his doublet flying wide open, she had no doubt that he had lost his wits; and, full of anxiety, she met him at the side of the kail-yard. 'Gudeness preserve us a' in our right senses, Andrew Burnet, what's the matter wi' you, Andrew Burnet?'

'Stand out o' my gate, wife, for, d'ye see, I am rather in a haste, Jean Linton.'

'I see that indeed, gudeman; but stand still, and tell me what has putten you *in* sic a haste. Ir ye dementit?'

'Na, na; gudewife, Jean Linton, I'm no dementit – I'm only gaun away till Moffat.'

'O, gudeness pity the poor auld body! How can ye gang to Moffat, man? Or what have ye to do at Moffat? Dinna ye mind that the morn is the day o' our solemnity?'

'Haud out o' my gate, auld wife, and dinna speak o' solemnities to me. I'll keep it at Moffat the morn. Ay, gudewife, and ye shall keep it at Moffat, too. What d'ye think o' that, woman? Too-whoo! ye dinna ken the metal that's in an auld body till it be tried.'

'Andrew – Andrew Burnet!'

'Get awa' wi' your frightened looks, woman; and haste ye, gang and fling me out my Sabbath-day claes. And, Jean Linton, my woman, d'ye hear, gang and pit on your bridal gown, and your silk hood, for ye maun be at Moffat the morn too; and it is mair nor time we were awa'. Dinna look sae surprised, woman, till I tell ye, that our ain Mary is to meet us at Moffat the morn.'

'Oh, Andrew! dinna sport wi' the feelings of an auld forsaken heart!'

'Gude forbid, my auld wife, that I should ever sport wi' feelings o' yours,' cried Andrew, bursting into tears; 'they are a' as sacred to me as breathings frae the Throne o' Grace. But it is true that I tell ye; our dear bairn is to meet us at Moffat the morn, wi' a son in every hand; and we maun e'en gang and see her aince again, and kiss her and bless her afore we dee.'

The tears now rushed from the old woman's eyes like fountains, and dropped from her sorrow-worn cheeks to the earth, and then, as with a spontaneous movement, she threw her skirt over her head, kneeled down at her husband's feet, and poured out her soul in thanksgiving to her Maker. She then rose up, quite deprived of her senses through joy, and ran crouching away on the road, towards Moffat, as if hasting beyond her power to be at it. But Andrew brought her back; and they prepared themselves for their journey.

Kirkstyle being twenty miles from Moffat, they set out on the afternoon of Tuesday, the 16th of September; slept that night at a place called Turnbery Shiel, and were in Moffat next day by noon. Wearisome was the remainder of the day to that aged couple; they wandered about conjecturing by what road their daughter would come, and how she would come attended. 'I have made up my mind on baith these matters,' said Andrew; 'at first I thought it was likely that she would come out of the east, because a' our blessings come frae that airt; but finding now that would be o'er near to the very road we hae come oursells, I now take it for granted she'll come frae the south; and I just think I see her leading a bonny boy in every hand, and a servant lass carrying a bit bundle ahint her.'

The two now walked out on all the southern roads, in hopes to meet their Mary, but always returned to watch the shadow of the Holy Cross; and, by the time it fell due east, they could do nothing but stand in the middle of the street, and look round them in all directions. At length, about half a mile out on the Dumfries road, they perceived a poor beggar woman approaching with two children following close to her, and another beggar a good way behind. Their eyes were instantly riveted on these objects; for Andrew thought he perceived his friend the dwarf in the one that was behind; and now all other earthly objects were to them nothing, save these approaching beggars. At that moment a gilded chariot entered the village from the south, and drove by them at full speed, having two livery-men before, and two behind, clothed in green and gold, 'Ach-wow! the vanity of worldly grandeur!' ejaculated Andrew, as the splendid vehicle went thundering by; but neither he nor his wife deigned to look at it farther, their whole attention being fixed on the group of beggars. 'Ay, it is just my woman,' said Andrew, 'it is just hersell; I ken her gang yet, sair pressed down wi' poortith although she be. But I dinna care how poor she be, for baith her and hers sall be welcome to my fireside as lang as I hae ane.'

While their eyes were thus strained, and their hearts melting with tenderness and pity, Andrew felt something embracing his knees, and, on looking down, there was his Mary, blooming in splendour and beauty, kneeling at his feet. Andrew uttered a loud hysterical scream of joy, and clasped her to his bosom; and old Jean Linton stood trembling, with her arms spread, but durst not close them on so splendid a creature, till her daughter first enfolded her in a fond embrace, and then she hung upon her and wept. It was a wonderful event – a restoration without a parallel. They indeed beheld their Mary, their long-lost darling; they held her in their embraces, believed in her identity, and were satisfied. Satisfied, did I say? They were happy beyond the lot of mortals. She had just alighted from her chariot; and, perceiving her aged parents standing together, she ran and kneeled at their feet. They now retired into the hostel, where Mary presented her two sons to her father and mother. They spent the evening in every social endearment; and Mary loaded the good old couple with rich presents, watched over them till midnight, when they both fell into a deep and happy sleep, and then she remounted her chariot, and was driven away. If she was any more seen in Scotland, I never heard of it; but her parents rejoiced in the thoughts of her happiness till the day of their death.

The Open Door

Margaret Oliphant

I took the house of Brentwood on my return from India in 18–,
for the temporary accommodation of my family, until I could
find a permanent home for them. It had many advantages which
made it peculiarly appropriate. It was within reach of Edinburgh,
and my boy Roland, whose education had been considerably
neglected, could go in and out to school, which was thought to
be better for him than either leaving home altogether or staying
there always with a tutor. The first of these expedients would
have seemed preferable to me, the second commended itself to
his mother. The doctor, like a judicious man, took the midway
between. 'Put him on his pony, and let him ride into the High
School every morning; it will do him all the good in the world,'
Dr. Simson said; 'and when it is bad weather there is the train.'
His mother accepted the solution of the difficulty more easily
than I could have hoped; and our pale-faced boy, who had never
known anything more invigorating than Simla, began to encounter the brisk breezes of the North in the subdued severity of
the month of May. Before the time of the vacation in July we
had the satisfaction of seeing him begin to acquire something of
the brown and ruddy complexion of his schoolfellows. The
English system did not commend itself to Scotland in these days.
There was no little Eton at Fettes; nor do I think, if there had
been, that a genteel exotic of that class would have tempted either
my wife or me. The lad was doubly precious to us, being the
only one left us of many; and he was fragile in body we believed,

and deeply sensitive in mind. To keep him at home, and yet to send him to school – to combine the advantages of the two systems – seemed to be everything that could be desired. The two girls also found at Brentwood everything they wanted. They were near enough to Edinburgh to have masters and lessons as many as they required for completing that never-ending education which the young people seem to require nowadays. Their mother married me when she was younger than Agatha, and I should like to see them improve upon their mother! I myself was then no more than twenty-five – an age at which I see the young fellows now groping about them, with no notion what they are going to do with their lives. However, I suppose every generation has a conceit of itself which elevates it, in its own opinion, above that which comes after it.

Brentwood stands on that fine and wealthy slope of country, one of the richest in Scotland, which lies between the Pentland Hills and the Firth. In clear weather you could see the blue gleam – like a bent bow, embracing the wealthy fields and scattered houses – of the great estuary on one side of you; and on the other the blue heights, not gigantic like those we had been used to, but just high enough for all the glories of the atmosphere, the play of clouds, and sweet reflections, which give to a hilly country an interest and a charm which nothing else can emulate. Edinburgh, with its two lesser heights – the Castle and the Calton Hill – its spires and towers piercing through the smoke, and Arthur's Seat lying crouched behind, like a guardian no longer very needful, taking his repose beside the well-beloved charge, which is now, so to speak, able to take care of itself without him – lay at our right hand. From the lawn and drawing-room windows we could see all these varieties of landscape. The colour was sometimes a little chilly, but sometimes, also, as animated and full of vicissitude as a drama. I was never tired of it. Its colour and freshness revived the eyes which had grown weary of arid plains and blazing skies. It was always cheery, and fresh, and full of repose.

The village of Brentwood lay almost under the house, on the other side of the deep little ravine, down which a stream – which ought to have been a lovely, wild, and frolicsome little river – flowed between its rocks and trees. The river, like so many in that district, had, however, in its earlier life been sacrificed to trade, and was grimy with paper-making. But this did not affect our pleasure in it so much as I have known it to affect other streams. Perhaps our water was more rapid – perhaps less clogged with dirt and refuse. Our side of the dell was charmingly *accidenté,* and clothed with fine trees, through which various paths wound down to the river-side and to the village bridge which crossed the stream. The village lay in the hollow, and climbed, with very prosaic houses, the other side. Village architecture does not flourish in Scotland. The blue slates and the grey stone are sworn foes to the picturesque; and though I do not, for my own part, dislike the interior of an old-fashioned pewed and galleried church, with its little family settlements on all sides, the square box outside, with its bit of a spire like a handle to lift it by, is not an improvement to the landscape. Still, a cluster of houses on differing elevations – with scraps of garden coming in between, a hedgerow with clothes laid out to dry, the opening of a street with its rural sociability, the women at their doors, the slow waggon lumbering along – gives a centre to the landscape. It was cheerful to look at, and convenient in a hundred ways. Within ourselves we had walks in plenty, the glen being always beautiful in all its phases, whether the woods were green in the spring or ruddy in the autumn. In the park which surrounded the house were the ruins of the former mansion of Brentwood, a much smaller and less important house than the solid Georgian edifice which we inhabited. The ruins were picturesque, however, and gave importance to the place. Even we, who were but temporary tenants, felt a vague pride in them, as if they somehow reflected a certain consequence upon ourselves. The old building had the remains of a tower, an indistinguishable mass of mason-work, overgrown with ivy, and the shells of walls attached to this were half filled up with soil. I had never examined it closely, I am ashamed to say. There was a large room, or what had been a large room, with the lower part of the windows still existing, on the principal floor, and underneath other windows, which were perfect, though half filled up with fallen soil, and waving with a wild growth of brambles and chance growths of all kinds. This was the oldest part of all. At a little distance were some very commonplace and disjointed fragments of the building, one of them suggesting a certain pathos by its very commonness and the complete wreck which it showed. This was the end of a low gable, a bit of grey wall, all encrusted with lichens, in which was a common doorway. Probably it had been a servants' entrance, a back-door, or opening into what are called 'the offices' in Scotland. No offices remained to be entered – pantry and kitchen had all been swept out of being; but there stood the doorway open and vacant, free to all the winds, to the rabbits, and every wild creature. It struck my eye, the first time I went to Brentwood, like a melancholy comment upon a life that was over. A door that led to nothing – closed once perhaps with anxious care, bolted and guarded, now void of any meaning. It impressed me, I remember, from the first; so perhaps it may be said that my mind was prepared to attach to it an importance, which nothing justified.

The summer was a very happy period of repose for us all. The warmth of Indian suns was still in our veins. It seemed to us that we could never have enough of the greenness, the dewiness, the freshness of the northern landscape. Even its mists were pleasant to us, taking all the fever out of us, and pouring in vigour and refreshment. In autumn we followed the fashion of the time, and went away for change which we did not in the least require. It was when the family had settled down for the winter, when the days were short and dark, and the rigorous reign of frost upon us, that the incidents occurred which alone could justify me in intruding upon the world my private affairs. These incidents were, however, of so curious a character, that I hope my inevitable references to my own family and pressing personal interests will meet with a general pardon.

I was absent in London when these events began. In London an old Indian plunges back into the interests with which all his previous life has been associated, and meets old friends at every step. I had been circulating among some half-dozen of these – enjoying the return to my former life in shadow, though I had been so thankful in substance to throw it aside – and had missed some of my home letters, what with going down from Friday to Monday to old Benbow's place in the country, and stopping on the way back to dine and sleep at Sellar's and to take a look into Cross's stables, which occupied another day. It is never safe to miss one's letters. In this transitory life, as the Prayer-book says, how can one ever be certain what is going to happen? All was well at home. I knew exactly (I thought) what they would have to say to me: 'The weather has been so fine, that Roland has not once gone by train, and he enjoys the ride beyond anything.' 'Dear papa, be sure that you don't forget anything, but bring us so-and-so and so-and-so' – a list as long as my arm. Dear girls and dearer mother! I would not for the world have forgotten their commissions, or lost their little letters, for all the Benbows and Crosses in the world.

But I was confident in my home-comfort and peacefulness. When I got back to my club, however, three or four letters were lying for me, upon some of which I noticed the 'immediate,' 'urgent,' which old-fashioned people and anxious people still believe will influence the post-office and quicken the speed of the mails. I was about to open one of these, when the club porter brought me two telegrams, one of which, he said, had arrived the night before. I opened, as was to be expected, the last first, and this was what I read: 'Why don't you come or answer? For God's sake, come. He is much worse.' This was a thunderbolt to fall upon a man's head who had only one son, and he the light of his eyes! The other telegram, which I opened with hands trembling so much that I lost time by my haste, was to much the same purport: 'No better; doctor afraid of brain-fever. Calls for you day and night. Let nothing detain you.' The first thing I did was to look up the time-tables to see if there was any way of getting off sooner than by the night-train, though I knew well enough there was not; and then I read the letters, which furnished, alas! too clearly, all the details. They told me that the boy had been pale for some time, with a scared look. His mother had noticed it before I left home, but would not say anything to alarm me. This look had increased day by day; and soon it was observed that Roland came home at a wild gallop through the park, his pony panting and in foam, himself 'as white as a sheet,' but with the perspiration streaming from his forehead. For a long time he had resisted all questioning, but at length had developed such strange changes of mood, showing a reluctance to go to school, a desire to be fetched in the carriage at night – which was a ridiculous piece of luxury – an unwillingness to go out into the grounds, and nervous start at every sound, that his mother had insisted upon an explanation. When the boy – our boy Roland, who had never known what fear was – began to talk to her of voices he had heard in the park, and shadows that had appeared to him among the ruins, my wife promptly put him to bed and sent for Dr. Simson – which, of course, was the only thing to do.

I hurried off that evening, as may be supposed, with an anxious heart. How I got through the hours before the starting of the train, I cannot tell. We must all be thankful for the quickness of the railway when in anxiety; but to have thrown myself into a postchaise as soon as horses could be put to, would have been a relief. I got to Edinburgh very early in the blackness of the winter morning, and scarcely dared look the man in the face at whom I gasped 'What news?' My wife had sent the brougham for me, which I concluded, before the man spoke, was a bad sign. His answer was that stereotyped answer which leaves the imagination so wildly free – 'Just the same.' Just the same! What might that mean? The horses seemed to me to creep along the long dark country-road. As we dashed through the park, I thought I heard some one moaning among the trees, and clenched my fist at him (whoever he might be) with fury. Why had the fool of a woman at the gate allowed any one to come in to disturb the quiet of the place? If I had not been in such hot haste to get home, I think I should have stopped the carriage and got out to see what tramp it was that had made an entrance, and chosen my grounds, of all places in the world – when my boy was ill! – to grumble and groan in. But I had no reason to complain of our slow pace here. The horses flew like lightning along the intervening path, and drew up at the door all panting, as if they had run a race. My wife stood waiting to receive me with a pale face, and a candle in her hand, which made her look paler still as the wind blew the flame about. 'He is sleeping,' she said in a whisper, as if her voice might wake him. And I replied, when I could find my voice, also in a whisper, as though the jingling of the horses' furniture and the sound of their hoofs must not have been more dangerous. I stood on the steps with her a moment, almost afraid to go in, now that I was here; and it seemed to me that I saw without observing, if I may say so, that the horses were unwilling to turn round, though their stables lay that way, or that the men were unwilling. These things occurred to me afterwards, though at the moment I was not capable of anything but to ask questions and to hear of the condition of the boy.

I looked at him from the door of his room, for we were afraid to go near, lest we should disturb that blessed sleep. It looked like actual sleep – not the lethargy into which my wife told me he would sometimes fall. She told me everything in the next room, which communicated with his, rising now and then and going to the door of communication; and in this there was much that was very startling and confusing to the mind. It appeared that ever since the winter began, since it was early dark and night had fallen before his return from school, he had been hearing voices among the ruins – at first only a groaning, he said, at which his pony was as much alarmed as he was, but by degrees a voice. The tears ran down my wife's cheeks as she described to me how he would start up in the night and cry out, 'Oh, mother, let me in! oh, mother, let me in!' with a pathos which rent her heart. And she sitting there all the time, only longing to do everything his heart could desire! But though she would try to soothe him, crying, 'You are at home, my darling. I am here. Don't you know me? Your mother is here,' he would only stare at her, and after a while spring up again with the same cry. At other times he would be quite reasonable, she said, asking eagerly when I was coming, but declaring that he must go with me as soon as I did so, 'to let them in.' 'The doctor thinks his nervous system must have received a shock,' my wife said. 'Oh, Henry, can it be that we have pushed him on too much with his work – a delicate boy like Roland? – and what is his work in comparison with his health? Even you would think little of honours or prizes if it hurt the boy's health.' Even I! as if I were an inhuman father sacrificing my child to my ambition. But I would not increase her trouble by taking any notice. After a while they persuaded me to lie down, to rest, and to eat – none of which things had been possible since I received their letters. The mere fact of being on the spot, of course, in itself was a great thing; and when I knew that I would be called in a moment, as soon as he was awake and wanted me, I felt capable, even in the dark, chill morning twilight, to snatch an hour or two's sleep. As it happened, I was so worn out with the strain of anxiety, and he so quieted and consoled by knowing I had come, that I was not disturbed till the afternoon, when the twilight had again settled down. There was just daylight enough to see his face when I went to him; and what a change in a fortnight! He was paler and more worn, I thought, than even in those dreadful days in the plains before we left India. His hair seemed to me to have grown long and lank; his eyes were like blazing lights projecting out of his white face. He got hold of my hand in a cold and tremulous clutch, and waved to everybody to go away. 'Go away – even mother,' he said – 'go away.' This went to her heart, for she did not like that even I should have more of the boy's confidence than herself; but my wife has never been a woman to think of herself, and she left us alone. 'Are they all gone?' he said, eagerly. 'They would not let me speak. The doctor treated me as if I were a fool. You know I am not a fool, papa.'

'Yes, yes, my boy, I know; but you are ill, and quiet is so necessary. You are not only not a fool, Roland, but you are reasonable and understand. When you are ill you must deny yourself; you must not do everything that you might do being well.'

He waved his thin hand with a sort of indignation. 'Then, father, I am not ill,' he cried. 'Oh, I thought when you came you would not stop me – you would see the sense of it! What do you think is the matter with me, all of you? Simson is well enough, but he is only a doctor. What do you think is the matter with me? I am no more ill than you are. A doctor, of course, he thinks you are ill the moment he looks at you – that's what he's there for – and claps you into bed.'

'Which is the best place for you at present, my dear boy.'

'I made up my mind,' cried the little fellow, 'that I would stand it till you came home. I said to myself, I won't frighten mother and the girls. But now, father,' he cried, half jumping out of bed, 'it's not illness – it's a secret.'

His eyes shone so wildly, his face was so swept with strong feeling, that my heart sank within me. It could be nothing but fever that did it, and fever had been so fatal. I got him into my arms to put him back into bed. 'Roland,' I said, humouring the poor child, which I knew was the only way, 'if you are going to tell me this secret to do any good, you know you must be quite quiet, and not excite yourself. If you excite yourself, I must not let you speak.'

'Yes, father,' said the boy. He was quiet directly, like a man, as if he quite understood. When I had laid him back on his pillow, he looked up at me with that grateful, sweet look with which children, when they are ill, break one's heart, the water coming into his eyes in his weakness. 'I was sure as soon as you were here you would know what to do,' he said.

'To be sure, my boy. Now keep quiet, and tell it all out like a man.' To think I was telling lies to my own child I for I did it only to humour him, thinking, poor little fellow, his brain was wrong.

'Yes, father. Father, there is some one in the park – some one that has been badly used.'

'Hush, my dear; you remember, there is to be no excitement. Well, who is this somebody, and who has been ill-using him? We will soon put a stop to that.'

'Ah,' cried Roland, 'but it is not so easy as you think. I don't know who it is. It is just a cry. Oh, if you could hear it! It gets into my head in my sleep. I heard it as clear as clear; and they think that I am dreaming – or raving perhaps,' the boy said, with a sort of disdainful smile.

This look of his perplexed me; it was less like fever than I thought. 'Are you quite sure you have not dreamt it, Roland?' I said.

'Dreamt? – that!' He was springing up again when he suddenly bethought himself, and lay down flat with the same sort of smile on his face. 'The pony heard it too,' he said. 'She jumped as if she had been shot. If I had not grasped at the reins – for I was frightened, father —'

'No shame to you, my boy,' said I, though I scarcely knew why.

'If I hadn't held to her like a leech, she'd have pitched me over her head, and she never drew breath till we were at the door. Did the pony dream it?' he said, with a soft disdain, yet indulgence for my foolishness. Then he added slowly: 'It was only a cry the first time, and all the time before you went away. I wouldn't tell you, for it was so wretched to be frightened. I thought it might be a hare or a rabbit snared, and I went in the morning and looked, but there was nothing. It was after you went I heard it really first, and this is what he says.' He raised himself on his elbow close to me, and looked me in the face.

' "Oh, mother, let me in! oh, mother, let me in!" ' As he said the words a mist came over his face, the mouth quivered, the soft features all melted and changed, and when he had ended these pitiful words; dissolved in a shower of heavy tears.

Was it a hallucination? Was it the fever of the brain? Was it the disordered fancy caused by great bodily weakness? How could I tell? I thought it wisest to accept it as if it were all true.

'This is very touching, Roland,' I said.

'Oh, if you had just heard it, father! I said to myself, "if father heard it he would do something"; but mamma, you know, she's given over to Simson, and that fellow's a doctor, and never thinks of anything but clapping you into bed.'

'We must not blame Simson for being a doctor, Roland.'

'No, no,' said my boy, with delightful toleration and indulgence; 'oh, no; that's the good of him – that's what he's for; I know that. But you – you are different; you are just father: and you'll do something – directly, papa, directly – this very night.'

'Surely,' I said. 'No doubt, it is some little lost child.'

He gave me a sudden, swift look, investigating my face as though to see whether, after all, this was everything my eminence as 'father' came to – no more than that? Then he got hold of my shoulder, clutching it with his thin hand: 'Look here,' he said, with a quiver in his voice; 'suppose it wasn't – living at all!'

'My dear boy, how then could you have heard it?' I said.

He turned away from me, with a pettish exclamation – 'As if you didn't know better than that!'

'Do you want to tell me it is a ghost?' I said.

Roland withdrew his hand; his countenance assumed an aspect of great dignity and gravity; a slight quiver remained about his lips. 'Whatever it was – you always said we were not to call names. It was something – in trouble. Oh, father, in terrible trouble!'

'But, my boy,' I said – I was at my wits' end – 'if it was a child that was lost, or any poor human creature – but, Roland, what do you want me to do?'

'I should know if I was you,' said the child, eagerly. 'That is what I always said to myself – "Father will know." Oh, papa, papa, to have to face it night after night, in such terrible, terrible trouble! and never to be able to do it any good. I don't want to cry; it's like a baby, I know; but what can I do else? – out there all by itself in the ruin, and nobody to help it. I can't bear it, I can't bear it!' cried my generous boy. And in his weakness he burst out, after many attempts to restrain it, into a great childish fit of sobbing and tears.

I do not know that I ever was in a greater perplexity in my life; and afterwards, when I thought of it, there was something comic in it too. It is bad enough to find your child's mind possessed with the conviction that he has seen – or heard – a ghost. But that he should require you to go instantly and help that ghost, was the most bewildering experience that had ever come my way. I am a sober man myself, and not superstitious – at least any more than everybody is superstitious. Of course I do not believe in ghosts; but I don't deny, any more than other people, that there are stories which I cannot pretend to understand. My blood got a sort of chill in my veins at the idea that Roland should be a ghost-seer; for that generally means a hysterical temperament and weak health, and all that men most hate and fear for their children. But that I should take up his ghost and right its wrongs, and save it from its trouble, was such a mission as was enough to confuse any man. I did my best to console my boy without giving any promise of this astonishing kind; but he was too sharp for me. He would have none of my caresses. With sobs breaking in at intervals upon his voice, and the rain-drops hanging on his eyelids, he yet returned to the charge.

'It will be there now – it will be there all the night. Oh think, papa, think, if it was me! I can't rest for thinking of it. Don't!' he cried, putting away my hand – 'don't! You go and help it, and mother can take care of me.'

'But, Roland, what can I do?'

My boy opened his eyes, which were large with weakness and fever, and gave me a smile such, I think, as sick children only know the secret of. 'I was sure you would know as soon as you came. I always said – "Father will know": and mother,' he cried, with a softening of repose upon his face, his limbs relaxing, his form sinking with a luxurious ease in his bed – 'mother can come and take care of me.'

I called her, and saw him turn to her with the complete dependence of a child, and then I went away and left them, as perplexed a man as any in Scotland. I must say, however, I had this consolation, that my mind was greatly eased about Roland. He might be under a hallucination, but his head was clear enough, and I did not think him so ill as everybody else did. The girls were astonished even at the ease with which I took it. 'How do you think he is?' they said in a breath, coming round me, laying hold of me. 'Not half so ill as I expected,' I said; 'not very bad at all.' 'Oh, papa, you are a darling,' cried Agatha, kissing me, and crying upon my shoulder; while little Jeanie, who was as pale as Roland, clasped both her arms round mine, and could not speak at all. I knew nothing about it, not half so much as Simson; but they believed in me; they had a feeling that all would go right now. God is very good to you when your children look to you like that. It makes one humble, not proud. I was not worthy of it; and then I recollected that I had to act the part of a father to Roland's ghost, which made me almost laugh, though I might just as well have cried. It was the strangest mission that ever was entrusted to mortal man.

It was then I remembered suddenly the looks of the men when they turned to take the brougham to the stables in the dark that morning; they had not liked it, and the horses had not liked it. I remembered that even in my anxiety about Roland I had heard them tearing along the avenue back to the stables, and had made a memorandum mentally that I must speak of it. It seemed to me that the best thing I could do was to go to the stables now and make a few inquiries. It is impossible to fathom the minds of rustics; there might be some devilry of practical joking, for anything I knew; or they might have some interest in getting up a bad reputation for the Brentwood avenue. It was getting dark by the time I went out, and nobody who knows the country will need to be told how black is the darkness of a November night under high laurel-bushes and yew-trees. I walked into the heart of the shrubberies two or three times, not seeing a step before me, till I came out upon the broader carriage-road, where the trees opened a little, and there was a faint grey glimmer of sky visible, under which the great limes and elms stood darkling like ghosts; but it grew black again as I approached the corner where the ruins lay. Both eyes and ears were on the alert, as may be supposed; but I could see nothing in the absolute gloom, and, so far as I can recollect, I heard nothing. Nevertheless, there came a strong impression upon me that somebody was there. It is a sensation which most people have felt. I have seen when it has been strong enough to awake me out of sleep, the sense of some one looking at me. I suppose my imagination had been affected by Roland's story; and the mystery of the darkness is always full of suggestions. I stamped my feet violently on the gravel to rouse myself, and called out sharply, 'Who's there?' Nobody answered, nor did I expect any one to answer, but the impression had been made. I was so foolish that I did not like to look back, but went sideways, keeping an eye on the gloom behind. It was with great relief that I spied the light in the stables, making a sort of oasis in the darkness. I walked very quickly into the midst of that lighted and cheerful place, and thought the clank of the groom's pail one of the pleasantest sounds I had ever heard. The coachman was the head of this little colony, and it was to his house I went to pursue my investigations. He was a native of the district, and had taken care of the place in the absence of the family for years; it was impossible but that he must know everything that was going on, and all the traditions of the place. The men, I could see, eyed me anxiously when I thus appeared at such an hour among them, and followed me with their eyes to Jarvis's house, where he lived alone with his old wife, their children being all married and out in the world. Mrs. Jarvis met me with anxious questions. How was the poor young gentleman? but the others knew, I could see by their faces, that not even this was the foremost thing in my mind.

'Noises? – och aye, there'll be noises – the wind in the trees, and the water soughing down the glen. As for tramps, Cornel, no, there's little o' that kind of cattle about here; and Merran at the gate's a careful body.' Jarvis moved about with some embarrassment from one leg to another as he spoke. He kept in the shade, and did not look at me more than he could help. Evidently his mind was perturbed, and he had reasons for keeping his own counsel. His wife sat by, giving him a quick look now and then, but saying nothing. The kitchen was very snug, and warm, and bright – as different as could be from the chill and mystery of the night outside.

'I think you are trifling with me, Jarvis,' I said.

'Triflin', Cornel? no me. What would I trifle for? If the deevil himsel' was in the auld hoose, I have no interest in't one way or another —'

'Sandy, hold your peace!' cried his wife imperatively.

'And what am I to hold my peace for, wi' the Cornel standing there asking a' thae questions? I'm saying, if the deevil himsel' —'

'And I'm telling ye hold your peace!' cried the woman, in great excitement. 'Dark November weather and lang nichts, and us that ken a' we ken. How daur ye name – a name that shouldna be spoken?' She threw down her stocking and got up, also in great agitation. 'I tell't ye you never could keep it. It's no a thing that will hide; and the haill toun kens as weel as you or me. Tell the Cornel straight out – or see, I'll do it. I dinna hold wi' your secrets; and a secret that the haill toun kens!' She snapped her fingers with an air of large disdain. As for Jarvis, ruddy and big as he was, he shrank to nothing before this decided woman. He repeated to her two or three times her own abjuration, 'Hold your peace!' then, suddenly changing his tone, cried out, 'Tell him then, confound ye! I'll wash my hands o't. If a' the ghosts in Scotland were in the auld hoose, is that ony concern o' mine?'

After this I elicited without much difficulty the whole story. In the opinion of the Jarvises, and of everybody about, the certainty that the place was haunted was beyond all doubt. As Sandy and his wife warmed to the tale, one tripping up another in their eagerness to tell everything, it gradually developed as distinct a superstition as I ever heard, and not without poetry and pathos. How long it was since the voice had been heard first, nobody could tell with certainty. Jarvis's opinion was that his father, who had been coachman at Brentwood before him, had never heard anything about it, and that the whole thing had arisen within the last ten years, since the complete dismantling of the old house: which was a wonderfully modern date for a tale so well authenticated. According to these witnesses, and to several whom I questioned afterwards, and who were all in perfect agreement, it was only in the months of November and December that 'the visitation' occurred. During these months, the darkest of the year, scarcely a night passed without the recurrence of these inexplicable cries. Nothing, it was said, had ever been seen – at least nothing that could be identified. Some people, bolder or more imaginative than the others, had seen the darkness moving, Mrs. Jarvis said, with unconscious poetry. It began when night fell and continued, at intervals, till day broke. Very often it was only an inarticulate cry and moaning, but sometimes the words which had taken possession of my poor boy's fancy had been distinctly audible – 'Oh, mother, let me in!' The Jarvises were not aware that there had ever been any investigation into it. The estate of Brentwood had lapsed into the hands of a distant branch of the family, who had lived but little there; and of the many people who had taken it, as I had done, few had remained through two Decembers. And nobody had taken the trouble to make a very close examination into the facts. 'No, no,' Jarvis said, shaking his head, 'No, no, Cornel. Wha wad set themsels up for a laughin'-stock to a' the country-side, making a wark about a ghost? Naebody believes in ghosts. It bid to be the wind in the trees, the last gentleman said, or some effec' o' the water wrastlin' among the rocks. He said it was a' quite easy explained: but he gave up the hoose. And when you cam, Cornel, we were awfu' anxious you should never hear. What for should I have spoiled the bargain and hairmed the property for no-thing?'

'Do you call my child's life nothing?' I said in the trouble of the moment, unable to restrain myself. 'And instead of telling this all to me, you have told it to him – to a delicate boy, a child unable to sift evidence, or judge for himself, a tender-hearted young creature —'

I was walking about the room with an anger all the hotter that I felt it to be most likely quite unjust. My heart was full of bitterness against the stolid retainers of a family who were content to risk other people's children and comfort rather than let the house lie empty. If I had been warned I might have taken precautions, or left the place, or sent Roland away, a hundred things which now I could not do; and here I was with my boy in a brain-fever, and his life, the most precious life on earth, hanging in the balance, dependent on whether or not I could get to the reason of a commonplace ghost-story! I paced about in high wrath, and seeing what I was to do; for, to take Roland away, even if he were able to travel, would not settle his agitated mind; and I feared even that a scientific explanation of refracted sound, or reverberation, or any other of the easy certainties with which we elder men are silenced, would have very little effect upon the boy.

'Cornel,' said Jarvis, solemnly, 'and *she'll* bear me witness – the young gentleman never heard a word from me – no, nor from either groom or gardener; I'll gie ye my word for that. In the first place, he's no a lad that invites ye to talk. There are some that are, and some that are na. Some will draw ye on, till ye've tellt them a' the clatter of the toun, and a' ye ken, and whiles mair. But Maister Roland, his mind's fu' of his books. He's aye civil and kind, and a fine lad; but no that sort. And ye see it's for a' our interest, Cornel, that you should stay at Brentwood. I took it upon me mysel' to pass the word – "No a syllable to Maister Roland, nor to the young leddies – no a syllable." The women-servants, that have little reason to be out at night, ken little or nothing about it. And some think it grand to have a ghost so long as they're no in the way of coming across it. If you had been tellt the story to begin with, maybe ye would have thought so yourself.'

This was true enough, though it did not throw any light upon my perplexity. If we had heard of it to start with, it is possible that all the family would have considered the possession of a ghost a distinct advantage. It is the fashion of the times. We never think what a risk it is to play with young imaginations, but cry out, in the fashionable jargon, 'A ghost! – nothing else was wanted to make it perfect.' I should not have been above this myself. I should have smiled, of course, at the idea of the ghost at all, but then to feel that it was mine would have pleased my vanity. Oh, yes, I claim no exemption. The girls would have been delighted. I could fancy their eagerness, their interest, and excitement. No; if we had been told, it would have done no good – we should have made the bargain all the more eagerly, the fools that we are. 'And there has been no attempt to investigate it,' I said, 'to see what it really is?'

'Eh, Cornel,' said the coachman's wife, 'wha would investigate, as ye call it, a thing that nobody believes in? Ye would be the laughing-stock of a' the country-side, as my man says.'

'But you believe in it,' I said, turning upon her hastily. The woman was taken by surprise. She made a step backward out of my way.

'Lord, Cornel, how ye frichten a body! Me! – there's awful strange things in this world. An unlearned person doesna ken what to think. But the minister and the gentry they just laugh in your face. Inquire into the thing that is not! Na, na, we just let it be.'

'Come with me, Jarvis,' I said, hastily, 'and we'll make an attempt at least. Say nothing to the men or to anybody. I'll come back after dinner, and we'll make a serious attempt to see what it is, if it is anything. If I hear it – which I doubt – you may be sure I shall never rest till I make it out. Be ready for me about ten o'clock.'

'Me, Cornel!' Jarvis said, in a faint voice. I had not been looking at him in my own preoccupation, but when I did so, I found that the greatest change had come over the fat and ruddy coachman. 'Me, Cornel!' he repeated, wiping the perspiration from his brow. His ruddy face hung in flabby folds, his knees knocked together, his voice seemed half extinguished in his throat. Then he began to rub his hands and smile upon me in a deprecating, imbecile way, 'There's nothing I wouldna do to pleasure ye, Cornel,' taking a step further back. 'I'm sure she kens I've aye said I never had to do with a mair fair, weelspoken gentleman —' Here Jarvis came to a pause, again looking at me, rubbing his hands.

'Well?' I said.

'But eh, sir!' he went on, with the same imbecile yet insinuating smile, 'if ye'll reflect that I am no used to my feet. With a horse atween my legs, or the reins in my hand, I'm maybe nae worse than other men; but on fit, Cornel – It's no the – bogles; – but I've been cavalry, ye see,' with a little hoarse laugh, 'a' my life. To face a thing ye didna understan' – on your feet, Cornel —'

'Well, sir, if *I* do it,' said I tartly, 'why shouldn't you?'

'Eh, Cornel, there's an awfu' difference. In the first place, ye tramp about the haill country-side, and think naething of it; but a walk tires me mair than a hunard miles' drive; and then ye'e a gentleman, and do your ain pleasure; and you're no so auld as me; and it's for your ain bairn, ye see, Cornel; and then —'

'He believes in it, Cornel, and you dinna believe in it,' the woman said.

'Will you come with me?' I said, turning to her.

She jumped back, upsetting her chair in her bewilderment.

'Me!' with a scream, and then fell into a sort of hysterical laugh. 'I wouldna say but what I would go; but what would the folk say to hear of Cornel Mortimer with an auld silly woman at his heels?'

The suggestion made me laugh too, though I had little inclination for it. 'I'm sorry you have so little spirit, Jarvis,' I said. 'I must find some one else, I suppose.'

Jarvis, touched by this, began to remonstrate, but I cut him short. My butler was a soldier who had been with me in India, and was not supposed to fear anything – man or devil – certainly not the former; and I felt that I was losing time. The Jarvises were too thankful to get rid of me. They attended me to the door with the most anxious courtesies. Outside, the two grooms stood close by, a little confused by my sudden exit. I don't know if perhaps they had been listening – at least standing as near as possible, to catch any scrap of the conversation. I waved my hand to them as I went past, in answer to their salutations, and it was very apparent to me that they also were glad to see me go.

And it will be thought very strange, but it would be weak not to add, that I myself, though bent on the investigation I have spoken of, pledged to Roland to carry it out, and feeling that my boy's health, perhaps his life, depended on the result of my inquiry – I felt the most unaccountable reluctance to pass these ruins on my way home. My curiosity was intense; and yet it was all my mind could do to pull my body along. I daresay the scientific people would describe it the other way, and attribute my cowardice to the state of my stomach. I went on; but if I had followed my impulse, I should have turned and bolted. Everything in me seemed to cry out against it; my heart thumped, my pulses all began, like sledge-hammers, beating against my ears and every sensitive part. It was very dark, as I have said; the old house, with its shapeless tower, loomed a heavy mass through the darkness, which was only not entirely so solid as itself. On the other hand, the great dark cedars of which we were so proud seemed to fill up the night. My foot strayed out of the path in my confusion and the gloom together, and I brought myself up with a cry as I felt myself knock against something solid. What was it? The contact with hard stone and lime, and prickly bramble-bushes, restored me a little to myself. 'Oh, it's only the old gable,' I said aloud, with a little laugh to reassure myself. The rough feeling of the stones reconciled me. As I groped about thus, I shook off my visionary folly. What so easily explained as that I should have strayed from the path in the darkness? This brought me back to common existence, as if I had been shaken by a wise hand out of all the silliness of superstition. How silly, it was, after all! What did it matter which path I took? I laughed again, this time with better heart – when suddenly, in a moment, the blood was chilled in my veins, a shiver stole along my spine, my faculties seemed to forsake me. Close by me at my side, at my feet, there was a sigh. No, not a groan, not a moaning, not anything so tangible – a perfectly soft, faint, inarticulate sigh. I sprang back, and my heart stopped beating. Mistaken! no, mistake was impossible. I heard it as clearly as I hear myself speak; a long, soft, weary sigh, as if drawn to the utmost, and emptying out a load of sadness that filled the breast. To hear this in the solitude, in the dark, in the night (though it was still early), had an effect which I cannot describe. I feel it now – something cold creeping over me, up into my hair, and down to my feet, which refused to move. I cried out with a trembling voice, 'Who is there?' as I had done before – but there was no reply.

I got home – I don't quite know how; but in my mind there was no longer any indifference as to the thing, whatever it was, that haunted these ruins. My scepticism disappeared like a mist. I was as firmly determined that there was something as Roland was. I did not for a moment pretend to myself that it was possible I could be deceived; there were movements and noises which I understood all about, cracklings of small branches in the frost, and little rolls of gravel on the path, such as have a very eerie sound sometimes, and perplex you with wonder as to who has done it, *when there is no real mystery*; but I assure you all these little movements of nature don't affect you one bit *when there is something*. I understood *them*. I did not understand the sigh. That was not simple nature; there was meaning in it – feeling, the soul of a creature invisible. This is the thing that human nature trembles at – a creature invisible, yet with sensations, feelings, a power somehow of expressing itself. I had not the same sense of unwillingness to turn my back upon the scene of the mystery which I had experienced in going to the stables; but I almost ran home, impelled by eagerness to get everything done that had to be done in order to apply myself to finding it out. Bagley was in the hall as usual when I went in. He was always there in the afternoon, always with the appearance of perfect occupation, yet, so far as I know, never doing anything. The door was open, so that I hurried in without any pause, breathless; but the sight of his calm regard, as he came to help me off with my overcoat, subdued me in a moment. Anything out of the way, anything incomprehensible, faded to nothing in the presence of Bagley. You saw and wondered how he was made: the parting of his hair, the tie of his white neckcloth, the fit of his trousers, all perfect as works of art; but you could see how they were done, which makes all the difference. I flung myself upon him, so to speak, without waiting to note the extreme unlikeness of the man to anything of the kind I meant. 'Bagley,' I said, 'I want you to come out with me to-night to watch for —'

'Poachers, Colonel,' he said, a gleam of pleasure running all over him.

'No, Bagley; a great deal worse,' I cried.

'Yes, Colonel; at what hour, sir?' the man said; but then I had not told him what it was.

It was ten o'clock when we set out. All was perfectly quiet indoors. My wife was with Roland, who had been quite calm, she said, and who (though, no doubt, the fever must run its course) had been better since I came. I told Bagley to put on a thick greatcoat over his evening coat, and did the same myself – with strong boots; for the soil was like a sponge, or worse.

Talking to him, I almost forgot what we were going to do. It was darker even than it had been before, and Bagley kept very close to me as we went along. I had a small lantern in my hand, which gave us a partial guidance. We had come to the corner where the path turns. On one side was the bowling-green, which the girls had taken possession of for their croquet-ground – a wonderful enclosure surrounded by high hedges of holly, three hundred years old and more; on the other, the ruins. Both were black as night; but before we got so far, there was a little opening in which we could just discern the trees and the lighter line of the road. I thought it best to pause there and take breath. 'Bagley,' I said, 'there is something about these ruins I don't understand. It is there I am going. Keep your eyes open and your wits about you. Be ready to pounce upon any stranger you see – anything, man or woman. Don't hurt, but seize – anything you see.' 'Colonel,' said Bagley, with a little tremor in his breath, 'they do say there's things there – as is neither man nor woman.' There was no time for words. 'Are you game to follow me, my man? that's the question,' I said. Bagley fell in without a word, and saluted. I knew then I had nothing to fear.

We went, so far as I could guess, exactly as I had come, when I heard that sigh. The darkness, however, was so complete that all marks, as of trees or paths, disappeared. One moment we felt our feet on the gravel, another sinking noiselessly into the slippery grass, that was all. I had shut up my lantern, not wishing to scare any one, whoever it might be. Bagley followed, it seemed to me, exactly in my footsteps as I made my way, as I supposed, towards the mass of the ruined house. We seemed to take a long time groping along seeking this; the squash of the wet soil under our feet was the only thing that marked our progress. After a while I stood still to see, or rather feel, where we were. The darkness was very still, but no stiller than is usual in a winter's night. The sounds I have mentioned – the crackling of twigs, the roll of a pebble, the sound of some rustle in the dead leaves, or creeping creature on the grass – were audible when you listened, all mysterious enough when your mind is disengaged, but to me cheering now as signs of the livingness of nature, even in the death of the frost. As we stood still there came up from the trees in the glen the prolonged hoot of an owl. Bagley started with alarm, being in a state of general nervousness, and not knowing what he was afraid of. But to me the sound was encouraging and pleasant, being so comprehensible. 'An owl,' I said, under my breath. 'Y—es, Colonel,' said Bagley, his teeth chattering. We stood still about five minutes, while it broke into the still brooding of the air, the sound widening out in circles, dying upon the darkness. This sound, which is not a cheerful one, made me almost gay. It was natural, and relieved the tension of the mind. I moved on with new courage, my nervous excitement calming down.

When all at once, quite suddenly, close to us, at our feet, there broke out a cry. I made a spring backwards in the first moment of surprise and horror, and in doing so came sharply against the same rough masonry and brambles that had struck me before. This new sound came upwards from the ground – a low, moaning, wailing voice, full of suffering and pain. The contrast between it and the hoot of the owl was indescribable; the one with a wholesome wildness and naturalness that hurt nobody – the other a sound that made one's blood curdle, full of human misery. With a great deal of fumbling – for in spite of everything I could do to keep up my courage my hands shook – I managed to remove the slide of my lantern. The light leaped out like something living, and made the place visible in a moment. We were what would have been inside the ruined building had anything remained but the gable-wall which I have described. It was close to us, the vacant doorway in it going out straight into the blackness outside. The light showed the bit of wall, the ivy glistening upon it in clouds of dark green, the bramble-branches waving, and below, the open door – a door that led to nothing. It was from this the voice came which died out just as the light flashed upon this strange scene. There was a moment's silence, and then it broke forth again. The sound was so near, so penetrating, so pitiful, that, on the nervous start I gave, the light fell out of my hand. As I groped for it in the dark my hand was clutched by Bagley, who I think must have dropped upon his knees; but I was too much perturbed myself to think much of this. He clutched at me in the confusion of his terror, forgetting all his usual decorum. 'For God's sake, what is it, sir?' he gasped. If I yielded, there was evidently an end of both of us. 'I can't tell,' I said, 'any more than you; that's what we've got to find out: up, man, up!' I pulled him to his feet. 'Will you go round and examine the other side, or will you stay here with the lantern?' Bagley gasped at me with a face of horror. 'Can't we stay together, Colonel?' he said – his knees were trembling under him. I pushed him against the corner of the wall, and put the light into his hands. 'Stand fast till I come back; shake yourself together, man; let nothing pass you,' I said. The voice was within two or three feet of us, of that there could be no doubt.

I went myself to the other side of the wall, keeping close to it. The light shook in Bagley's hand, but tremulous though it was, it shone out through the vacant door, one oblong block of light marking all the crumbling corners and hanging masses of foliage. Was that something dark huddled in a heap by the side of it? I pushed forward across the light in the doorway, and fell upon it with my hands; but it was only a juniper-bush growing close against the wall. Meanwhile, the sight of my figure crossing the doorway had brought Bagley's nervous excitement to a height: he flew at me, gripping my shoulder. 'I've got him, Colonel! I've got him!' he cried, with a voice of sudden exultation. He thought it was a man, and was at once relieved. But at that moment the voice burst forth again between us, at our feet – more close to us than any separate being could be. He dropped off from me, and fell against the wall, his jaw dropping as if he were dying. I suppose, at the same moment, he saw that it was me whom he had clutched. I, for my part, had scarcely more command of myself. I snatched the light out of his hand, and flashed it all about me wildly. Nothing – the juniper-bush which I thought I had never seen before, the heavy growth of the glistening ivy, the brambles waving. It was close to my ears now, crying, crying, pleading as if for life. Either I heard the same words Roland had heard, or else, in my excitement, his imagination got possession of mine. The voice went on, growing into distinct articulation, but wavering about, now from one point, now from another, as if the owner of it were moving slowly back and forward – 'Mother! mother!' and then an outburst of wailing. As my mind steadied, getting accustomed (as one's mind gets accustomed to anything), it seemed to me as if some uneasy, miserable creature was pacing up and down before a closed door. Sometimes – but that must have been excitement – I thought I heard a sound like knocking, and then another burst, 'Oh, mother! mother!' All this close, close to the space where I was standing with my lantern – now before me, now behind me: a creature restless, unhappy, moaning, crying, before the vacant doorway, which no one could either shut or open more.

'Do you hear it, Bagley? do you hear what it is saying?' I cried, stepping in through the doorway. He was lying against the wall – his eyes glazed, half dead with terror. He made a motion of his lips as if to answer me, but no sounds came; then lifted his hand with a curious imperative movement as if ordering me to be silent and listen. And how long I did so I cannot tell. It began to have an interest, an exciting hold upon me, which I could not describe. It seemed to call up visibly a scene any one could understand – a something shut out, restlessly wandering to and fro; sometimes the voice dropped, as if throwing itself down – sometimes wandered off a few paces, growing sharp and clear. 'Oh, mother, let me in! oh, mother, mother, let me in! oh, let me in!' every word was clear to me. No wonder the boy had gone wild with pity. I tried to steady my mind upon Roland, upon his conviction that I could do something, but my head swam with the excitement, even when I partially overcame the terror. At last the words died away, and there was a sound of sobs and moaning.

I cried out, 'In the name of God who are you?' with a kind of feeling in my mind that to use the name of God was profane, seeing that I did not believe in ghosts or anything supernatural; but I did it all the same, and waited, my heart giving a leap of terror lest there should be a reply. Why this should have been I cannot tell, but I had a feeling that if there was an answer, it would be more than I could bear. But there was no answer; the moaning went on, and then, as if it had been real, the voice rose, a little higher again, the words recommenced, 'Oh, mother, let me in! oh, mother, let me in!' with an expression that was heart-breaking to hear.

As if it had been real! What do I mean by that? I suppose I got less alarmed as the thing went on. I began to recover the use of my senses – I seemed to explain it all to myself by saying that this had once happened, that it was a recollection of a real scene. Why there should have seemed something quite satisfactory and composing in this explanation I cannot tell, but so it was. I began to listen almost as if it had been a play, forgetting Bagley, who, I almost think, had fainted, leaning against the wall. I was startled out of this strange spectatorship that had fallen upon me by the sudden rush of something which made my heart jump once more, a large black figure in the doorway waving its arms. 'Come in! come in! come in!' it shouted out hoarsely at the top of a deep bass voice, and then poor Bagley fell down senseless across the threshold. He was less sophisticated than I – he had not been able to bear it any longer. I took him for something supernatural, as he took me, and it was some time before I awoke to the necessities of the moment. I remembered only after, that from the time I began to give my attention to the man, I heard the other voice no more. It was some time before I brought him to. It must have been a strange scene; the lantern making a luminous spot in the darkness, the man's white face lying on the black earth, I over him, doing what I could for him. Probably I should have been thought to be murdering him had any one seen us. When at last I succeeded in pouring a little brandy down his throat he sat up and looked about him wildly. 'What's up?' he said; then recognising me, tried to struggle to his feet with a faint 'Beg your pardon, Colonel.' I got him home as best I could, making him lean upon my arm. The great fellow was as weak as a child. Fortunately he did not for some time remember what had happened. From the time Bagley fell the voice had stopped, and all was still.

'You've got an epidemic in your house, Colonel,' Simson said to me next morning. 'What's the meaning of it all? Here's your butler raving about a voice. This will never do, you know; and so far as I can make out, you are in it too.'

'Yes, I am in it, doctor. I thought I had better speak to you. Of course you are treating Roland all right – but the boy is not raving, he is as sane as you or me. It's all true.'

'As sane as – I – or you. I never thought the boy insane. He's got cerebral excitement, fever. I don't know what you've got. There's something very queer about the look of your eyes.'

'Come,' said I, 'you can't put us all to bed, you know. You had better listen and hear the symptoms in full.'

The doctor shrugged his shoulders, but he listened to me patiently. He did not believe a word of the story, that was clear; but he heard it all from beginning to end. 'My dear fellow,' he said, 'the boy told me just the same. It's an epidemic. When one person falls a victim to this sort of thing, it's as safe as can be – there's always two or three.'

'Then how do you account for it?' I said.

'Oh, account for it! – that's a different matter; there's no accounting for the freaks our brains are subject to. If it's delusion; if it's some trick of the echoes or the winds – some phonetic disturbance or other —'

'Come with me to-night, and judge for yourself,' I said.

Upon this he laughed aloud, then said, 'That's not such a bad idea; but it would ruin me for ever if it were known that John Simson was ghost-hunting.'

'There it is,' said I; 'you dart down on us who are unlearned with your phonetic disturbances, but you daren't examine what the thing really is for fear of being laughed at. That's science!'

'It's not science – it's common-sense,' said the doctor. 'The thing has delusion on the front of it. It is encouraging an unwholesome tendency even to examine. What good could come of it? Even if I am convinced, I shouldn't believe.'

'I should have said so yesterday; and I don't want you to be convinced or to believe,' said I. 'If you prove it to be a delusion, I shall be very much obliged to you for one. Come; somebody must go with me.'

'You are cool,' said the doctor. 'You've disabled this poor fellow of yours, and made him – on that point – a lunatic for life; and now you want to disable me. But for once, I'll do it. To save appearance, if you'll give me a bed, I'll come over after my last rounds.'

It was agreed that I should meet him at the gate, and that we should visit the scene of last night's occurrences before we came to the house, so that nobody might be the wiser. It was scarcely possible to hope that the cause of Bagley's sudden illness should not somehow steal into the knowledge of the servants at least, and it was better that all should be done as quietly as possible. The day seemed to me a very long one. I had to spend a certain part of it with Roland, which was a terrible ordeal for me – for what could I say to the boy? The improvement continued, but he was still in a very precarious state, and the trembling vehemence with which he turned to me when his mother let the room filled me with alarm. 'Father!' he said, quietly. 'Yes, my boy; I am giving my best attention to it – all is being done that I can do. I have not come to any conclusion – yet. I am neglecting nothing you said,' I cried. What I could not do was to give his active mind any encouragement to dwell upon the mystery. It was a hard predicament, for some satisfaction had to be given him. He looked at me very wistfully, with the great blue eyes which shone so large and brilliant out of his white and worn face. 'You must trust me,' I said. 'Yes, father. Father understands,' he said to himself, as if to soothe some inward doubt. I left him as soon as I could. He was about the most precious thing I had on earth, and his health my first thought; but yet somehow, in the excitement of this other subject, I put that aside, and preferred not to dwell upon Roland, which was the most curious part of it all.

That night at eleven I met Simson at the gate. He had come by train, and I let him in gently myself. I had been so much absorbed in the coming experiment that I passed the ruins in going to meet him, almost without thought, if you can understand that. I had my lantern; and he showed me a coil of taper which he had ready for use. 'There is nothing like light,' he said, in his scoffing tone. It was a very still night, scarcely a sound, but not so dark. We could keep the path without difficulty as we went along. As we approached the spot we could hear a low moaning, broken occasionally by a bitter cry. 'Perhaps that is your voice,' said the doctor; 'I thought it must be something of the kind. That's a poor brute caught in some of these infernal traps of yours; you'll find it among the bushes somewhere.' I said nothing. I felt no particular fear, but a triumphant satisfaction in what was to follow. I led him to the spot where Bagley and I had stood on the previous night. All was silent as a winter night could be – so silent that we heard far off the sound of the horses in the stables, the shutting of a window at the house. Simson lighted his taper and went peering about, poking into all the corners. We looked like two conspirators lying in wait for some unfortunate traveller; but not a sound broke the quiet. The moaning had stopped before we came up; a star or two shone over us in the sky, looking down as if surprised at our strange proceedings. Dr. Simson did nothing but utter subdued laughs under his breath. 'I thought as much,' he said. 'It is just the same with tables and all other kinds of ghostly apparatus; a sceptic's presence stops everything. When I am present nothing ever comes off. How long do you think it will be necessary to stay here? Oh, I don't complain; only, when *you* are satisfied, *I* am – quite.'

I will not deny that I was disappointed beyond measure by this result. It made me look like a credulous fool. It gave the doctor such a pull over me as nothing else could. I should point all his morals for years to some, and his materialism, his scepticism, would be increased beyond endurance. 'It seems, indeed,' I said, 'that there is to be no —' 'Manifestation,' he said, laughing; 'that is what all the mediums say. No manifestations, in consequence of the presence of an unbeliever.' His laugh sounded very uncomfortable to me in the silence; and it was now near midnight. But that laugh seemed the signal; before it died away the moaning we had heard before was resumed. It started from some distance off, and came towards us, nearer and nearer, like some one walking along and moaning to himself. There could be no idea now that it was a hare caught in a trap. The approach was slow, like that of a weak person, with little halts and pauses. We heard it coming along the grass straight towards the vacant doorway. Simson had been a little startled by the first sound. He said hastily, 'That child has no business to be out so late.' But he felt, as well as I, that this was no child's voice. As it came nearer, he grew silent, and, going to the doorway with his taper, stood looking out towards the sound. The taper being unprotected blew about in the night air, though there was scarcely any wind. I threw the light of my lantern steady and white across the same space. It was a blaze of light in the midst of the blackness. A little icy thrill had gone over me at the first sound, but as it came close, I confess that my only feeling was satisfaction. The scoffer could scoff no more. The light touched his own face, and showed a very perplexed countenance. If he was afraid, he concealed it with great success, but he was perplexed. And then all that had happened on the previous night was enacted once more. It fell strangely upon me with a sense of repetition. Every cry, every sob seemed the same as before. I listened almost without any emotion at all in my own person, thinking of its effect upon Simson. He maintained a very bold front on the whole. All that coming and going of the voice was, if our ears could be trusted, exactly in front of the vacant, blank doorway, blazing full of light, which caught and shone in the glistening leaves of the great hollies at a little distance. Not a rabbit could have crossed the turf without being seen; but there was nothing. After a time, Simson, with a certain caution and bodily reluctance, as it seemed to me, went out with his roll of taper into this space. His figure showed against the holly in full outline. Just at this moment the voice sank, as was its custom, and seemed to fling itself down at the door. Simson recoiled violently, as if some one had come up against him, then turned, and held his taper low as if examining something. 'Do you see anybody?' I cried in a whisper, feeling the chill of nervous panic steal over me at this action. 'It's nothing but a – confounded juniper-bush,' he said. This I knew very well to be nonsense, for the juniper-bush was on the other side. He went about after this round and round, poking his taper everywhere, then returned to me on the inner side of the wall. He scoffed no longer; his face was contracted and pale. 'How long does this go on?' he whispered to me, like a man who does not wish to interrupt some one who is speaking. I had become too much perturbed myself to remark whether the successions and changes of the voice were the same as last night. It suddenly went out in the air almost as he was speaking, with a soft, reiterated sob dying away. If there had been anything to be seen, I should have said that the person was at that moment crouching on the ground close to the door.

We walked home very silent afterwards. It was only when we were in sight of the house that I said, 'What do you think of it?' 'I can't tell what to think of it,' he said, quickly. He took – though he was a very temperate man – not the claret I was going to offer him, but some brandy from the tray, and swallowed it almost undiluted. 'Mind you, I don't believe a word of it,' he said, when he had lighted his candle; 'but I can't tell what to think,' he turned round to add, when he was half-way upstairs.

All of this, however, did me no good with the solution of my problem. I was to help this weeping, sobbing thing, which was already to me as distinct a personality as anything I knew – or what should I say to Roland? It was on my heart that my boy would die if I could not find some way of helping this creature. You may be surprised that I should speak of it in this way. I did not know if it was man or woman; but I no more doubted that it was a soul in pain than I doubted my own being; and it was my business to soothe this pain – to deliver it, if that was possible. Was ever such a task given to an anxious father trembling for his only boy? I felt in my heart, fantastic as it may appear, that I must fulfil this somehow, or part with my child; and you may conceive that rather than do that I was ready to die. But even my dying would not have advanced me – unless by bringing me into the same world with that seeker at the door.

Next morning Simson was out before breakfast, and came in with evident signs of the damp grass on his boots, and a look of worry and weariness, which did not say much for the night he had passed. He improved a little after breakfast, and visited his two patients, for Bagley was still an invalid. I went out with him on his way to the train, to hear what he had to say about the boy. 'He is going on very well,' he said; 'there are no complications as yet. But mind you, that's not a boy to be trifled with, Mortimer. Not a word to him about last night.' I had to tell him then of my last interview with Roland, and of the impossible demand he had made upon me – by which, though he tried to laugh, he was much discomposed, as I could see. 'We must just perjure ourselves all round,' he said, 'and swear you exorcized it'; but the man was too kind-hearted to be satisfied with that. 'It's frightfully serious for you, Mortimer. I can't laugh as I should like to. I wish I saw a way out of it, for your sake. By the way,' he added shortly, 'didn't you notice that juniper-bush on the left-hand side?' 'There was one on the right hand of the door. I noticed you made that mistake last night.' 'Mistake!' he cried, with a curious low laugh, pulling up the collar of his coat as though he felt the cold – 'there's no juniper there this morning, left or right.

Just go and see.' As he stepped into the train a few minutes after, he looked back upon me and beckoned me for a parting word. 'I'm coming back to-night,' he said.

I don't think I had any feeling about this as I turned away from that common bustle of the railway, which made my private preoccupations feel so strangely out of date. There had been a distinct satisfaction in my mind before that his scepticism had been so entirely defeated. But the more serious part of the matter pressed upon me now. I went straight from the railway to the manse, which stood on a little plateau on the side of the river opposite to the woods of Brentwood. The minister was one of a class which is not so common in Scotland as it used to be. He was a man of good family, well educated in the Scotch way, strong in philosophy, not so strong in Greek, strongest of all in experience – a man who had 'come across,' in the course of his life, most people of note that had ever been in Scotland – and who was said to be very sound in doctrine, without infringing the toleration with which old men, who are good men, are generally endowed. He was old-fashioned; perhaps he did not think so much about the troublous problems of theology as many of the young men, nor ask himself any hard questions about the Confession of Faith – but he understood human nature, which is perhaps better. He received me with a cordial welcome. 'Come away, Colonel Mortimer,' he said; 'I'm all the more glad to see you, that I feel it's a good sign for the boy. He's doing well? – God be praised – and the Lord bless him and keep him. He has many a poor body's prayers – and that can do nobody harm.'

'He will need them all, Dr. Moncrieff,' I said, 'and your counsel too.' And I told him the story – more than I had told Simson. The old clergyman listened to me with many suppressed exclamations, and at the end the water stood in his eyes.

'That's just beautiful,' he said. 'I do not mind to have heard anything like it; it's as fine as Burns when he wished deliverance to one – that is prayed for in no kirk. Ay, ay! so he would have you console the poor lost spirit? God bless the boy! There's something more than common in that, Colonel Mortimer. And also the faith of him in his father! – I would like to put that into a sermon.' Then the old gentleman gave me an alarmed look, and said, 'No, no; I was not meaning a sermon; but I must write it down for the *Children's Record*.' I saw the thought that passed through his mind. Either he thought, or he feared I would think, of a funeral sermon. You may believe this did not make me more cheerful.

I can scarcely say that Dr. Moncrieff gave me any advice. How could any one advise on such a subject? But he said, 'I think I'll come too. I'm an old man; I'm less liable to be frighted than those that are further off the world unseen. It behoves me to think of my own journey there. I've no cut-and-dry beliefs on the subject. I'll come too; and maybe at the moment the Lord will put into our heads what to do.'

This gave me a little comfort – more than Simson had given me. To be clear about the cause of it was not my grand desire. It was another thing that was in my mind – my boy. As for the poor soul at the open door, I had no more doubt, as I have said, of its existence than I had of my own. It was no ghost to me. I knew the creature, and it was in trouble. That was my feeling about it, as it was Roland's. To hear it first was a great shock to my nerves, but not now; a man will get accustomed to anything. But to do something for it was the great problem; how was I to be service-able to a being that was invisible, that was mortal no longer? 'Maybe at the moment the Lord will put it into our heads.' This is very old-fashioned phraseology, and a week before, most likely, I should have smiled (though always with kindness) at Dr. Moncrieff's credulity; but there was a great comfort, whether rational or otherwise I cannot say, in the mere sound of the words.

The road to the station and the village lay through the glen – not by the ruins; but though the sunshine and the fresh air, and the beauty of the trees, and the sound of the water were all very soothing to the spirits, my mind was so full of my own subject that I could not refrain from turning to the right hand as I got to the top of the glen, and going straight to the place which I may call the scene of all my thoughts. It was lying full in the sunshine, like all the rest of the world. The ruined gable looked due east, and in the present aspect of the sun the light streamed down through the doorway as our lantern had done, throwing a flood of light upon the damp grass beyond. There was a strange suggestion in the open door – so futile, a kind of emblem of vanity – all free around, so that you could go where you pleased, and yet that semblance of an enclosure – that way of entrance, unnecessary, leading to nothing. And why any creature should pray and weep to get in – to nothing: or be kept out – by nothing! You could not dwell upon it, or it made your brain go round. I remembered however, what Simson said about the juniper, with a little smile on my own mind as to the inaccuracy of recollection, which even a scientific man will be guilty of. I could see now the light of my lantern gleaming upon the wet glistening surface of the spiky leaves at the right hand – and he ready to go to the stake for it that it was the left! I went round to make sure. And then I saw what he had said. Right or left there was no juniper at all. I was confounded by this, though it was entirely a matter of detail: nothing at all: a bush of brambles waving, the grass growing up to the very walls. But after all, though it gave me a shock for a moment, what did that matter? There were marks as if a number of footsteps had been up and down in front of the door; but these might have been our steps; and all was bright, and peaceful, and still. I poked about the other ruin – the larger ruins of the old house – for some time, as I had done before. There were marks upon the grass here and there, I could not call them footsteps, all about; but that told for nothing one way or another. I had examined the ruined rooms closely the first day. They were half filled up with soil and *débris*, withered brackens and bramble – no refuge for any one there. It vexed me that Jarvis should see me coming from that spot when he came up to me for his orders. I don't know whether my nocturnal expeditions had got wind among the servants. But there was a significant look in his face. Something in it I felt was like my own sensation when Simson in the midst of his scepticism was struck dumb. Jarvis felt satisfied that his veracity had been put beyond question. I never spoke to a servant of mine in such a peremptory tone before. I sent him away 'with a flea in his lug,' as the man described it afterwards. Interference of any kind was intolerable to me at such a moment.

But what was strangest of all was, that I could not face Roland. I did not go up to his room as I would have naturally done at once. This the girls could not understand. They saw there was some mystery in it. 'Mother has gone to lie down,' Agatha said; 'he has had such a good night.' 'But he wants you so, papa!' cried little Jeanie, always with her two arms embracing mine in a pretty way she had. I was obliged to go at last – but what could I say? I could only kiss him, and tell him to keep still – that I was doing all I could. There is something mystical about the patience of a child. 'It will come all right won't it, father?' he said. 'God grant it may! I hope so, Roland.' 'Oh yes, it will come all right.' Perhaps he understood that in the midst of my anxiety I could not stay with him as I should have done otherwise. But the girls were more surprised than it is possible to describe. They looked at me with wondering eyes. 'If I were ill, papa, and you only stayed with me a moment, I should break my heart,' said Agatha. But the boy had a sympathetic feeling. He knew that of my own will I would not have done it. I shut myself up in the library, where I could not rest, but kept pacing up and down like a caged beast. What could I do? and if I could do nothing, what would become of my boy? These were the questions that, without ceasing, pursued each other through my mind.

Simson came out to dinner, and when the house was all still, and most of the servants in bed, we went out and met Dr. Moncrieff, as we had appointed, at the head of the glen. Simson, for his part, was disposed to scoff at the doctor. 'If there are to be any spells, you know, I'll cut the whole concern,' he said. I did not make him any reply. I had not invited him; he could go or come as he pleased. He was very talkative, far more than suited my humour, as we went on. 'One thing is certain, you know, there must be some human agency,' he said. 'It is all bosh about apparitions. I never have investigated the laws of sound to any great extent, and there's a great deal in ventriloquism that we don't know much about.' 'If it's the same to you,' I said, 'I wish you'd keep all that to yourself, Simson. It doesn't suit my state of mind.' 'Oh, I hope I know how to respect idiosyncrasy,' he said. The very tone of his voice irritated me beyond measure. These scientific fellows, I wonder people put up with them as they do, when you have no mind for their cold-blooded confidence. Dr. Moncrieff met us about eleven o'clock, the same time as on the previous night. He was a large man, with a venerable countenance and white hair – old, but in full vigour, and thinking less of a cold night walk than many a younger man. He had his lantern as I had. We were fully provided with means of lighting the place, and we were all of us resolute men. We had a rapid consultation as we went up, and the result was that we divided to different posts. Dr. Moncrieff remained inside the wall – if you can call that inside where there was no wall but one. Simson placed himself on the side next the ruins, so as to intercept any communication with the old house, which was what his mind was fixed upon. I was posted on the other side. To say that nothing could come near without being seen was self-evident. It had been so also on the previous night. Now, with our three lights in the midst of the darkness, the whole place seemed illuminated. Dr. Moncrieff's lantern, which was a large one, without any means of shutting up – an old-fashioned lantern with a pierced and ornamental top – shone steadily, the rays shooting out of it upward into the gloom. He placed it on the grass, where the middle of the room, if this had been a room, would have been. The usual effect of the light streaming out of the doorway was prevented by the illumination which Simson and I on either side supplied. With these differences, everything seemed as on the previous night.

And what occurred was exactly the same, with the same air of repetition, point for point, as I had formerly remarked. I declare that it seemed to me as if I were pushed against, put aside, by the owner of the voice as he paced up and down in his trouble – though these are perfectly futile words, seeing that the stream of light from my lantern, and that from Simson's taper, lay broad and clear, without a shadow, without the smallest break, across the entire breadth of the grass. I had ceased even to be alarmed, for my part. My heart was rent with pity and trouble – pity for the poor suffering human creature that moaned and pleaded so, and trouble for myself and my boy. God! if I could not find any help – and what help could I find? – Roland would die.

We were all perfectly still till the first outburst was exhausted, as I knew (by experience) it would be. Dr. Moncrieff, to whom it was new, was quite motionless on the other side of the wall, as we were in our places. My heart had remained almost at its usual beating during the voice. I was used to it; it did not rouse all my pulses as it did at first. But just as it threw itself sobbing at the door (I cannot use other words), there suddenly came something which sent the blood coursing through my veins and my heart into my mouth. It was a voice inside the wall – the minister's well-known voice. I would have been prepared for it in any kind of adjuration, but I was not prepared for what I heard. It came out with a sort of stammering, as if too much moved for utterance. 'Willie, Willie! Oh, God preserve us! is it you?'

These simple words had an effect upon me that the voice of the invisible creature had ceased to have. I thought the old man, whom I had brought into this danger, had gone mad with terror. I made a dash round to the other side of the wall, half crazed myself with the thought. He was standing where I had left him, his shadow thrown vague and large upon the grass by the lantern which stood at his feet. I lifted my own light to see his face as I rushed forward. He was very pale, his eyes wet and glistening, his mouth quivering with parted lips. He neither saw nor heard me. We that had gone through this experience before, had crouched towards each other to get a little strength to bear it. But he was not even aware that I was there. His whole being seemed absorbed in anxiety and tenderness. He held out his hands, which trembled, but it seemed to me with eagerness, not fear. He went on speaking all the time. 'Willie, if it is you – and it's you, if it is not a delusion of Satan – Willie, lad! why come ye here frighting them that know you not? Why came ye not to me?'

He seemed to wait for an answer. When his voice ceased, his countenance, every line moving, continued to speak. Simson gave me another terrible shock, stealing into the open doorway with his light, as much awe-stricken, as wildly curious, as I. But the minister resumed, without seeing Simson, speaking to some one else. His voice took a tone of expostulation —

'Is this right to come here? Your mother's gone with your name on her lips. Do you think she would ever close her door on her own lad? Do ye think the Lord will close the door, ye faint-hearted creature? No! – I forbid ye! I forbid ye!' cried the old man. The sobbing voice had begun to resume its cries. He made a step forward, calling out the last words in a voice of command. 'I forbid ye! Cry out no more to man. Go home, ye wandering spirit! go home! Do you hear me? – me that christened ye, that have struggled with ye, that have wrestled for ye with the Lord!' Here the loud tones of his voice sank into tenderness. 'And her too, poor woman! poor woman! her you are calling upon. She's no here. You'll find her with the Lord. Go there and seek her, not here. Do you hear me, lad? go after her there: He'll let you in, though it's late. Man, take heart! if you will lie and sob and greet, let it be at heaven's gate, and no your poor mother's ruined door.'

He stopped to get his breath: and the voice had stopped, not as it had done before, when its time was exhausted and all its repetitions said, but with a sobbing catch in the breath as if over-ruled. Then the minister spoke again, 'Are you hearing me, Will? Oh, laddie, you've liked the beggarly elements all your days. Be done with them now. Go home to the Father – the Father! Are you hearing me?' Here the old man sank down upon his knees, his face raised upwards, his hands held up with a tremble in them, all white in the light in the midst of the darkness. I resisted as long as I could, though I cannot tell why – then I, too, dropped upon my knees. Simson all the time stood in the doorway, with an expression in his face such as words could not tell, his under lip drooped, his eyes wild, staring. It seemed to be to him, that image of blank ignorance and wonder, that we were praying. All the time the voice, with a low arrested sobbing, lay just where he was standing, as I thought.

'Lord,' the minister said – 'Lord, take him into Thy ever-lasting habitations. The mother he cries to is with Thee. Who can open to him but Thee? Lord, when is it too late for Thee, or what is too hard for Thee? Lord, let that woman there draw him into her! Let her draw him into her!'

I sprang forward to catch something in my arms that flung itself wildly within the door. The illusion was so strong, that I never paused till I felt my forehead graze against the wall and my hands clutch the ground – for there was nobody there to save from falling, as in my foolishness I thought. Simson held out his hand to me to help me up. He was trembling and cold, his lower lip hanging, his speech almost inarticulate. 'It's gone,' he said, stammering – 'it's gone!' We leant upon each other for a moment, trembling so much both of us that the whole scene trembled as if it were going to dissolve and disappear; and yet as long as I live I will never forget it – the shining of the strange lights, the blackness all round, the kneeling figure with all the whiteness of the light concentrated on its white venerable head and uplifted hands. A strange solemn stillness seemed to close all round us. By intervals a single syllable, 'Lord! Lord!' came from the old minister's lips. He saw none of us, nor thought of us. I never knew how long we stood, like sentinels guarding him at his prayers, holding our lights in a confused dazed way, not knowing what we did. But at last he rose from his knees, and standing up at his full height, raised his arms, as the Scotch manner is at the

end of a religious service, and solemnly gave the apostolical
benediction – to what? to the silent earth, the dark woods, the
wide breathing atmosphere – for we were but spectators gasping
an Amen!

It seemed to me that it must be the middle of the night, as we
all walked back. It was in reality very late. Dr. Moncrieff put his
arm into mine. He walked slowly, with an air of exhaustion. It
was as if we were coming from a deathbed. Something hushed
and solemnized the very air. There was that sense of relief in it
which there always is at the end of a death-struggle. And nature
persistent, never daunted, came back in all of us, as we returned
into the ways of life. We said nothing to each other, indeed, for
a time; but when we got clear of the trees and reached the opening
near the house, where we could see the sky, Dr. Moncrieff himself
was the first to speak. 'I must be going,' he said; 'it's very late,
I'm afraid. I will go down the glen, as I came.'

'But not alone. I am going with you, doctor.'

'Well, I will not oppose it. I am an old man and agitation
wearies more than work. Yes; I'll be thankful of your arm. To-
night, Colonel, you've done me more good turns than one.'

I pressed his hand on my arm, not feeling able to speak. But
Simson, who turned with us, and who had gone along all this
time with his taper flaring, in entire unconsciousness, came to
himself, apparently at the sound of our voices, and put out that
wild little torch with a quick movement, as if of shame. 'Let me
carry your lantern' he said; 'it is heavy.' He recovered with a
spring, and in a moment, from the awe-stricken spectator he had
been, became himself sceptical and cynical. 'I should like to ask
you a question,' he said. 'Do you believe in Purgatory, Doctor?
It's not in the tenets of the Church, so far as I know.'

'Sir,' said Dr. Moncrieff, 'an old man like me is sometimes
not very sure what he believes. There is just one thing I am
certain of – and that is the loving-kindness of God.'

'But I thought that was in this life. I am no theologian —'

'Sir,' said the old man, again with a tremor in him which I

could feel going over all his frame, 'if I saw a friend of mine within the gates of hell, I would not despair but his Father would take him by the hand still – if he cried like *yon*.'

'I allow it is very strange – very strange. I cannot see through it. That there must be human agency, I feel sure. Doctor, what made you decide upon the person and the name?'

The minister put out his hand with the impatience which a man might show if he were asked how he recognized his brother.

'Tuts!' he said, in familiar speech – then more solemnly, 'how should I not recognize a person that I know better – far better – than I know you?'

'Then you saw the man?'

Dr. Moncrieff made no reply. He moved his hand again with a little impatient movement, and walked on, leaning heavily on my arm. And we went on for a long time without another word, threading the dark paths, which were steep and slippery with the damp of the winter. The air was very still – not more than enough to make a faint sighing in the branches, which mingled with the sound of the water to which we were descending. When we spoke again, it was about indifferent matters – about the height of the river, and the recent rains. We parted with the minister at his own door, where his old housekeeper appeared in great perturbation, waiting for him. 'Eh, me, minister! the young gentleman will be worse?' she cried.

'Far from that – better. God bless him!' Doctor Moncrieff said.

I think if Simson had begun again to me with his questions, I should have pitched him over the rocks as we returned up the glen; but he was silent, by a good inspiration. And the sky was clearer than it had been for many nights, shining high over the trees, with here and there a star faintly gleaming through the wilderness of dark and bare branches. The air, as I have said, was very soft in them, with a subdued and peaceful cadence. It was real, like every natural sound, and came to us like a hush of peace and relief. I thought there was a sound in it as of the breath of a sleeper, and it seemed clear to me that Roland must be sleeping, satisfied and calm. We went up to his room when we went in. There we found the complete hush of rest. My wife looked up out of a doze, and gave me a smile; 'I think he is a great deal better: but you are very late,' she said in a whisper, shading the light with her hand that the doctor might see his patient. The boy had got back something like his own colour. He woke as we stood all round his bed. His eyes had the happy half-awakened look of childhood, glad to shut again, yet pleased with the interruption and glimmer of the light. I stooped over him and kissed his forehead, which was moist and cool. 'All is well, Roland,' I said. He looked up at me with a glance of pleasure, and took my hand and laid his cheek upon it, and so went to sleep.

For some nights after, I watched among the ruins, spending all the dark hours up to midnight patrolling about the bit of wall which was associated with so many emotions; but I heard nothing, and saw nothing beyond the quiet course of nature: nor, so far as I am aware, has anything been heard again. Dr. Moncrieff gave me the history of the youth, whom he never hesitated to name. I did not ask, as Simson did, how he recognised him. He had been a prodigal – weak, foolish, easily imposed upon, and 'led away,' as people say. All that we had heard had passed actually in life, the Doctor said. The young man had come home thus a day or two after his mother died – who was no more than the housekeeper in the old house – and distracted with the news, had thrown himself down at the door and called upon her to let him in. The old man could scarcely speak of it for tears. To me it seemed as if – heaven help us, how little do we know about anything! – a scene like that might impress itself somehow upon the hidden heart of nature. I do not pretend to know how, but the repetition had struck me at the time as, in its terrible strangeness and incomprehensibility, almost mechanical – as if the unseen actor could not exceed or vary, but was bound to re-enact the whole. One thing that struck me, however, greatly, was the likeness between the old minister and my boy in the manner of regarding these strange phenomena. Dr. Moncrieff was not terrified, as I had been myself, and all the rest of us. It was no 'ghost,' as I fear we all vulgarly considered it, to him – but a poor creature whom he knew under these conditions, just as he had known him in the flesh, having no doubt of his identity. And to Roland it was the same. This spirit in pain – if it was a spirit – this voice out of the unseen – was a poor fellow-creature in misery, to be succoured and helped out of his trouble, to my boy. He spoke to me quite frankly about it when he got better. 'I knew father would find out some way,' he said. And this was when he was strong and well, and all idea that he would turn hysterical or become a seer of visions had happily passed away.

I must add one curious fact which does not seem to me to have any relation to the above, but which Simson made great use of, as the human agency which he was determined to find somehow. We had examined the ruins very closely at the time of these occurrences; but afterwards, when all was over, as we went casually about them one Sunday afternoon in the idleness of that unemployed day, Simson with his stick penetrated an old window which had been entirely blocked up with fallen soil. He jumped down into it in great excitement, and called me to follow. There we found a little hole – for it was more a hole than a room – entirely hidden under the ivy ruins, in which there was a quantity of straw laid in a corner, as if some one had made a bed there, and some remains of crusts about the floor. Some one had lodged there, and not very long before, he made out; and that this unknown being was the author of all the mysterious sounds we heard he is convinced. 'I told you it was human agency,' he said, triumphantly. He forgets, I suppose, how he and I stood with our lights seeing nothing, while the space between us was audibly traversed by something that could speak, and sob, and suffer.

There is no argument with men of this kind. He is ready to get up a laugh against me on this slender ground. 'I was puzzled myself – I could not make it out – but I always felt convinced human agency was at the bottom of it. And here it is – and a clever fellow he must have been,' the Doctor says.

Bagley left my service as soon as he got well. He assured me it was no want of respect; but he could not stand 'them kind of things,' and the man was so shaken and ghastly that I was glad to give him a present and let him go. For my own part, I made a point of staying out the time, two years, for which I had taken Brentwood; but I did not renew my tenancy. By that time we had settled, and found for ourselves a pleasant home of our own.

I must add that when the doctor defies me, I can always bring back gravity to his countenance, and a pause in his railing, when I remind him of the juniper-bush. To me that was a matter of little importance. I could believe I was mistaken. I did not care about it one way or other; but on his mind the effect was different. The miserable voice, the spirit in pain, he could think of as the result of ventriloquism, or reverberation, or – anything you please: an elaborate prolonged hoax executed somehow by the tramp that had found a lodging in the old tower. But the juniper-bush staggered him. Things have effects so different on the minds of different men.

The Gray Wolf

George Macdonald

One evening-twilight in spring, a young English student, who
had wandered northwards as far as the outlying fragments of
Scotland called the Orkney and Shetland Islands, found himself
on a small island of the latter group, caught in a storm of wind
and hail, which had come on suddenly. It was in vain to look
about for any shelter; for not only did the storm entirely obscure
the landscape, but there was nothing around him save a desert
moss.

At length, however, as he walked on for mere walking's sake,
he found himself on the verge of a cliff, and saw, over the brow
of it, a few feet below him, a ledge of rock, where he might find
some shelter from the blast, which blew from behind. Letting
himself down by his hands, he alighted upon something that
crunched beneath his tread, and found the bones of many small
animals scattered about in front of a little cave in the rock,
offering the refuge he sought. He went in, and sat upon a stone.
The storm increased in violence, and as the darkness grew he
became uneasy, for he did not relish the thought of spending the
night in the cave. He had parted from his companions on the
opposite side of the island, and it added to his uneasiness that
they must be full of apprehension about him. At last there came
a lull in the storm, and the same instant he heard a footfall,
stealthy and light as that of a wild beast, upon the bones at the
mouth of the cave. He started up in some fear, though the least
thought might have satisfied him that there could be no very

dangerous animals upon the island. Before he had time to think, however, the face of a woman appeared in the opening. Eagerly the wanderer spoke. She started at the sound of his voice. He could not see her well, because she was turned towards the darkness of the cave.

'Will you tell me how to find my way across the moor to Shielness?' he asked.

'You cannot find it tonight,' she answered, in a sweet tone, and with a smile that bewitched him, revealing the whitest of teeth.

'What am I to do, then?"

'My mother will give you shelter, but that is all she has to offer.'

'And that is far more than I expected a minute ago,' he replied. 'I shall be most grateful.'

She turned in silence and left the cave. The youth followed.

She was barefooted, and her pretty brown feet went catlike over the sharp stones, as she led the way down a rocky path to the shore. Her garments were scanty and torn, and her hair blew tangled in the wind. She seemed about five and twenty, lithe and small. Her long fingers kept clutching and pulling nervously at her skirts as she went. Her face was very gray in complexion, and very worn, but delicately formed, and smooth-skinned. Her thin nostrils were tremulous as eyelids, and her lips, whose curves were faultless, had no colour to give sign of indwelling blood. What her eyes were like he could not see, for she had never lifted the delicate films of her eyelids.

At the foot of the cliff they came upon a little hut leaning against it, and having for its inner apartment a natural hollow within. Smoke was spreading over the face of the rock, and the grateful odour of food gave hope to the hungry student. His guide opened the door of the cottage; he followed her in, and saw a woman bending over a fire in the middle of the floor. On the fire lay a large fish broiling. The daughter spoke a few words, and the mother turned and welcomed the stranger. She had an old and very wrinkled, but honest face, and looked troubled. She dusted the only chair in the cottage, and placed it for him by the side of the fire, opposite the one window, whence he saw a little patch of yellow sand over which the spent waves spread themselves out listlessly. Under this window there was a bench, upon which the daughter threw herself in an unusual posture, resting her chin upon her hand. A moment after, the youth caught the first glimpse of her blue eyes. They were fixed upon him with a strange look of greed, amounting to craving, but, as if aware that they belied or betrayed her, she dropped them instantly. The moment she veiled them, her face, notwithstanding its colourless complexion, was almost beautiful.

When the fish was ready, the old woman wiped the deal table, steadied it upon the uneven floor, and covered it with a piece of fine table-linen. She then laid the fish on a wooden platter, and invited the guest to help himself. Seeing no other provision, he pulled from his pocket a hunting knife, and divided a portion from the fish, offering it to the mother first.

'Come, my lamb,' said the old woman; and the daughter approached the table. But her nostrils and mouth quivered with disgust.

The next moment she turned and hurried from the hut.

'She doesn't like fish,' said the old woman, 'and I haven't anything else to give her.'

'She does not seem in good health,' he rejoined.

The woman answered only with a sigh, and they ate their fish with the help of a little rye bread. As they finished their supper, the youth heard the sound as of the pattering of a dog's feet upon the sand close to the door; but ere he had time to look out of the window, the door opened, and the young woman entered. She looked better, perhaps from having just washed her face. She drew a stool to the corner of the fire opposite him. But as she sat down, to his bewilderment, and even horror, the student spied a single drop of blood on her white skin within her torn dress. The woman brought out a jar of whisky, put a rusty old kettle on the fire, and took her place in front of it. As soon as the water boiled, she proceeded to make some toddy in a wooden bowl.

Meantime the youth could not take his eyes off the young woman, so that at length he found himself fascinated, or rather bewitched. She kept her eyes for the most part veiled with the loveliest eyelids fringed with darkest lashes, and he gazed entranced; for the red glow of the little oil-lamp covered all the strangeness of her complexion. But as soon as he met a stolen glance out of those eyes unveiled, his soul shuddered within him. Lovely face and craving eyes alternated fascination and repulsion.

The mother placed the bowl in his hands. He drank sparingly, and passed it to the girl. She lifted it to her lips, and as she tasted – only tasted it – looked at him. He thought the drink must have been drugged and have affected his brain. Her hair smoothed itself back, and drew her forehead backwards with it; while the lower part of her face projected towards the bowl, revealing, ere she sipped, her dazzling teeth in strange prominence. But the same moment the vision vanished; she returned the vessel to her mother, and rising, hurried out of the cottage.

Then the old woman pointed to a bed of heather in one corner with a murmured apology; and the student, wearied both with the fatigues of the day and the strangeness of the night, threw himself upon it, wrapped in his cloak. The moment he lay down, the storm began afresh, and the wind blew so keenly through the crannies of the hut, that it was only by drawing his cloak over his head that he could protect himself from its currents. Unable to sleep, he lay listening to the uproar which grew in violence, till the spray was dashing against the window. At length the door opened, and the young woman came in, made up the fire, drew the bench before it, and lay down in the same strange posture, with her chin propped on her hand and elbow, and her face turned towards the youth. He moved a little; she dropped her head, and lay on her face, with her arms crossed beneath her forehead. The mother had disappeared.

Drowsiness crept over him. A movement of the bench roused

him, and he fancied he saw some four-footed creature as tall as a large dog trot quietly out of the door. He was sure he felt a rush of cold wind. Gazing fixedly through the darkness, he thought he saw the eyes of the damsel encountering his, but a glow from the falling together of the remnants of the fire revealed clearly enough that the bench was vacant. Wondering what could have made her go out in such a storm, he fell fast asleep.

In the middle of the night he felt a pain in his shoulder, came broad awake, and saw the gleaming eyes and grinning teeth of some animal close to his face. Its claws were in his shoulder, and its mouth in the act of seeking his throat. Before it had fixed its fangs, however, he had its throat in one hand, and sought his knife with the other. A terrible struggle followed; but regardless of the tearing claws, he found and opened his knife. He had made one futile stab, and was drawing it for a surer, when, with a spring of the whole body, and one wildly contorted effort, the creature twisted its neck from his hold, and with something betwixt a scream and a howl, darted from him. Again he heard the door open; again the wind blew in upon him, and it continued blowing; a sheet of spray dashed across the floor, and over his face. He sprung from his couch and bounded to the door.

It was a wild night – dark, but for the flash of whiteness from the waves as they broke within a few yards of the cottage; the wind was raving, and the rain pouring down the air. A gruesome sound as of mingled weeping and howling came from somewhere in the dark. He turned again into the hut and closed the door, but could find no way of securing it.

The lamp was nearly out, and he could not be certain whether the form of the young woman was upon the bench or not. Overcoming a strong repugnance, he approached it, and put out his hands – there was nothing there. He sat down and waited for the daylight: he dared not sleep any more.

When the day dawned at length, he went out yet again, and looked around. The morning was dim and gusty and gray. The wind had fallen, but the waves were tossing wildly. He wandered up and down the little strand, longing for more light.

At length he heard a movement in the cottage. By and by the voice of the old woman called to him from the door.

'You're up early, sir. I doubt you didn't sleep well.'

'Not very well,' he answered. 'But where is your daughter?'

'She's not awake yet,' said the mother. 'I'm afraid I have but a poor breakfast for you. But you'll take a dram and a bit of fish. It's all I've got.'

Unwilling to hurt her, though hardly in good appetite, he sat down at the table. While they were eating, the daughter came in, but turned her face away and went to the farther end of the hut. When she came forward after a minute or two, the youth saw that her hair was drenched, and her face whiter than before. She looked ill and faint, and when she raised her eyes, all their fierceness had vanished, and sadness had taken its place. Her neck was now covered with a cotton handkerchief. She was modestly attentive to him, and no longer shunned his gaze. He was gradually yielding to the temptation of braving another night in the hut, and seeing what would follow, when the old woman spoke.

'The weather will be broken all day, sir,' she said. 'You had better be going, or your friends will leave without you.'

Ere he could answer, he saw such a beseeching glance on the face of the girl, that he hesitated, confused. Glancing at the mother, he saw the flash of wrath in her face. She rose and approached her daughter, with her hand lifted to strike her. The young woman stooped her head with a cry. He darted round the table to interpose between them. But the mother had caught hold of her; the handkerchief had fallen from her neck; and the youth saw five blue bruises on her lovely throat – the marks of the four fingers and the thumb of a left hand. With a cry of horror he darted from the house, but as he reached the door he turned. His hostess was lying motionless on the floor, and a huge gray wolf came bounding after him.

There was no weapon at hand. Instinctively, he set himself

202

firm, leaning a little forward, with half outstretched arms, and hands curved ready to clutch again at the throat upon which he had left those pitiful marks. But the creature as she sprung eluded his grasp, and just as he expected to feel her fangs, he found a woman weeping on his bosom, with her arms around his neck. The next instant, the gray wolf broke from him, and bounded howling up the cliff. Recovering himself as he best might, the youth followed, for it was the only way to the moor above, across which he must now make his way to find his companions.

All at once he heard the sound of a crunching of bones – not as if a creature was eating them, but as if they were ground by the teeth of rage and disappointment; looking up, he saw close above him the mouth of the little cavern in which he had taken refuge the day before. Summoning all his resolution, he passed it slowly and softly. From within came the sounds of a mingled moaning and growling.

Having reached the top, he ran at full speed for some distance across the moor before venturing to look behind him. When at length he did so, he saw, against the sky, the girl standing on the edge of the cliff, wringing her hands. One solitary wail crossed the space between. She made no attempt to follow him, and he reached the opposite shore in safety.

The Return of the Native

William Croft Dickinson

About a year after the end of World War II, when I was still an officer in the American Intelligence, and stationed in London, I decided to seize the opportunity of visiting Scotland and seeing, for the first time, the land of my folk. I had little difficulty in obtaining a fortnight's leave and, after spending a week-end in Edinburgh, I hired a small car to drive to Arisaig and Morar – the district from which I knew my forbears had emigrated some two hundred years ago.

Setting off from Edinburgh on the Monday morning, I made that marvellous drive through Callander, Lochearnhead, and Tyndrum, and on through Glencoe to Ballachulish, where I put up for the night. Passing through Balquhidder country on my way from Callander to Tyndrum, I had recalled the story of assembled Macgregors swearing their oaths on the severed head of a royal forester; and, as I had passed through Glencoe, I had recalled the tragedy of sleeping MacDonalds who were massacred by those to whom they had given food and shelter. Yet that night, in the inn at Ballachulish, as I brooded over the stories of the past, I little thought that I myself was soon to be touched by the past – touched too closely for my liking – and simply because I, too, was a MacDonald, though a MacDonald of a different sept from the MacIans of Glencoe.

The Tuesday morning broke fine and clear. Leaving Ballachulish, I crossed by the ferry and took the lovely road by the shores of Loch Linnhe and Loch Eil, and on to Glenfinnan, where Prince Charlie's standard was raised, and where I thought the monument a poor thing to commemorate so stirring an event. From Glenfinnan the scenery became more wonderful still, as the narrow road, still 'unimproved', twisted and turned on its ledge between the hills and the sea: and I remembered I was on 'The Road to the Isles'.

It may be that my head was too full of the tales of the Young Chevalier, or it may be that my eyes strayed too often to the beauty of land and sea: I do not know. But, almost too late, I caught sight of an enormous boulder crashing down the hillside and almost on top of my car. Braking hard, and wrenching the wheel violently to the right, I lost control of the car and ran into the bank of the hill, while the boulder, missing the front of the car by inches, thundered across the road and bounded over the opposite verge.

Slightly shaken, I got out to see what damage I had done, and, as I did so, I was astonished to see an old woman standing on the other side of the road just where the boulder had crashed across. For a moment I wondered how she had escaped; then, something in her appearance made me look at her more closely. I was startled to see that her dark and deep-set eyes were glaring at me with a look of intense hate. I saw, too, that water was dripping from her clothes and that her grey hair was hanging round her shoulders, dank and wet. And, looking at her, I experienced a strange sense of danger, or it might even have been fear, which it is wholly impossible to describe.

So we stood, facing one another, and myself in a kind of trance, until, suddenly the woman turned away and, apparently stepping down from the road, disappeared over the edge. Recovering my wits, I ran across the road, only to pull myself up with a jerk. On that side of the road, and guarded only by a single strand of wire, there was a sheer drop of a hundred feet or more to the rocks on the loch-side below. Had I wrenched my wheel the other way, or had that boulder crashed into my small car, broadside on, nothing could have saved me.

I made myself look again at that sheer drop. What had happened to the old woman? There was no sign of her anywhere. Not even a ghastly huddle of body and clothes on the rocks below. Yet I had seen her clearly enough; and she had stepped down from the road at this very spot. And why had she glared at me with such bitter hate? Surely I had not fallen asleep at the wheel and dreamed the whole thing – a boulder crashing down and a malevolent old hag with dripping clothes?

I walked slowly back to the car, trying to puzzle things out. Fortunately the car was not badly damaged: a buckled wing and little more. But it was firmly wedged in the bank and would not move. I sat down beside it and waited for help. And help soon came in the shape of a delivery van; its driver fortunately had a length of rope; and within a few minutes he had hauled me clear.

'You were lucky in your skid,' he said, cheerfully. 'Had you skidded the other way you'd have finished driving for good. And it would have been pretty difficult to recover your remains for the funeral. However, all's well now. And that front wheel seems all right, too. But it's queer the way you managed to skid on a dry surface like this.'

'I didn't skid,' I replied, slowly. 'I was trying to avoid a boulder that was rolling down the hillside on to the road.'

'Boulder!' he answered, looking me hard in the eye. 'It's the first time I've heard of a boulder rolling down on to this road. And I've driven over it six days a week for the last twelve years or so.' Then, still looking me straight in the eye, he wavered a little and condescended to add: 'However, strange things do happen. But I'd like to know where that boulder came from. So long.'

He waved a friendly hand, got into his van, and drove off, leaving me alone with uncomfortable thoughts. I was positive I had not fallen asleep. I was equally positive that a large boulder had missed my car by inches. And what of that old woman with her dank hair and dripping clothes, who might almost have risen from the waters of the loch below, and who, after glaring at me with burning hate, had apparently been swallowed up in the waters again? If not, where had she gone? And who was she, anyway? How did she fit in? 'Well,' I said to myself, resignedly, 'strange things certainly do happen. But I'd be glad of an explanation, if anyone could give it.'

I stepped into my car, started the engine, and drove on again. Possibly I was more shaken than I had at first realized, and possibly I was worried with my thoughts; certainly I now crawled along the road, through Arisaig, and on to Morar. I remember that when at last I pulled into the drive of my hotel I felt as though a great burden had suddenly been lifted from my back.

Morar is a lovely spot, with its stretch of silver sand and with the islands of Rum, Eigg and Muck standing like sentinels in the sea. Inland, I found delightful walks, especially one by the side of the loch. In a couple of days the old woman of my adventure on the road from Glenfinnan had become a puzzling memory, and nothing more.

I had reached Morar on the Tuesday evening. Wednesday and Thursday I spent in lazily wandering about, or in lying in the heather and feeling how good, for a time, was a life of ease. On Friday, much against my inclination, I caught up with some long-delayed mail from home and then, in the early evening, took a short walk that led to the falls, where the waters of the loch, at that time still unharnessed for electric power, poured through a gorge before finding their way to the sea.

I had scrambled down a steep and narrow path that led to the foot of the falls, and had taken my stance on a boulder there, when a noise, rising above the thunder of the falls, made me turn round. I was only half-interested, and I turned round casually, but, to my horror, I saw a large rock hurtling down the narrow path on which I stood. How I managed to make the right decision in a split second of time, I shall never know. I flung myself down behind the boulder on which I was standing. The rock struck it with a mighty crack, bounced harmlessly over my head, and plunged into the whirlpool at the bottom of the falls.

Dazed and trembling, I carefully picked myself up. Then pain made itself felt, and I discovered that I had injured my left knee by throwing myself down to the ground. Would I be able to climb back again to the top of the path? I looked up at that steep and broken slope, and my heart suddenly jumped into my throat. An old woman with dank grey hair, and with clothes that were dripping wet, was glaring at me from above; glaring at me with intense hate, as three days before she had glared at me on the road from Glenfinnan. And again, though this time far more pronounced, I felt the same strange fear, and, with it, a weakness that seemed to affect every part of me.

I gripped the boulder beside me with both hands, frightened lest I should fall backwards into the whirlpool below. Gradually the weakness passed. Then, summoning the little courage that was left in me, I began a slow and painful crawl on hands and knees, taking advantage of every turn in the path, and praying constantly that no other rock would be hurled against me from above. When, at long last, I reached the top of the path, I lay there completely exhausted and unable to take a further step. The old woman was nowhere to be seen.

As I lay there, worn out and riddled with fear, my mind strove vainly to grapple with accidents that were beyond all reasoning. I now knew definitely that I had not fallen asleep at the wheel of my car. I knew, too, that twice a fiend of an old woman had tried to send me to the shades from which I was convinced she herself had risen. I had had enough. If, all unwittingly, I had disturbed the haunts of some avenging 'ghost', the only answer was to leave her haunts forthwith. Call me a coward, if you like; and coward I certainly became! But, then and there, I determined to return to Edinburgh and the safety of its streets.

I limped slowly back to the hotel, intending to pack my bags and depart. Yet, as soon as I had reached the hotel, a new fear struck me. To leave forthwith would mean driving through Arisaig, and on to Glenfinnan, by night. I couldn't face it. I knew that even driving along that road by day I should be crawling at a snail's pace, and looking to the right and left of me all the time. I even had thoughts of driving the odd four miles into Mallaig and there putting myself and my car on the boat. In the end I decided to stay the night, and to leave on the Saturday morning.

After dinner I told the landlord of my decision to leave early the next morning. I excused myself by reference to some urgent business that had arisen from my mail; and, in expressing my appreciation of the comfort of my stay, murmured something of my regret at having to leave so soon, and before I had even made any attempt to trace my ancestors who had come from Morar about two hundred years ago.

'Have you seen Father MacWilliam?' came his unexpected reply.

'No,' I answered. 'Why do you ask?'

'Well, it will be this way,' he said. 'The Father knows the history of Morar. He's been at the books and the papers these many years. And he's the one who would be telling you about your own folks, way past, if, indeed, there is anything to be known of them at all.'

'Could I call upon him now?' I asked eagerly.

'Indeed you could; but he'd be out.'

I looked at him in surprise.

'He'd be out, for he's in my own parlour this very time. Come you with me, and you can have a talk with him before you go.'

Full of interest, I was led to the back of the hotel, where Father MacWilliam, a plump and rosy-faced priest, was snugly ensconced in an easy-chair, and deep in the pages of an enormous book.

'Father, I've brought you Mr John MacDonald,' said my host, without further ado. 'He's for leaving tomorrow, but he'd be glad if you could be telling him of his people who, it would seem, came from these parts may be two hundred years ago. If I were to let the two of you talk together, maybe he'll be learning

209

something of what he wants to know.'

The priest gave me a warm smile of welcome, and somehow managed to unfold himself out of his chair. The landlord gave us a nod, and left the two of us together.

'John MacDonald,' said the priest, looking at me. 'It tells me nothing. Everyone here is a MacDonald. Every man, woman and child. God bless them all. Could you tell me more?'

I had to confess that I couldn't. All I knew was that my forbears had left Morar, or some place in its vicinity, about the 1750s. That, and no more.

Father MacWilliam shook his head. ' 'Tis no use,' he said. 'I can be of no help to you, much as I would have liked. Too many MacDonalds have left these parts – and sometimes I think too many have stayed on. But there, you've had a good time for the few days you've been here. And that's aye something.'

'Yes,' I answered slowly, and then, with a sudden desire to unburden myself, 'a good enough time if it hadn't been for an old woman who has twice tried to stone me to death.'

'What?' shouted the priest, his eyes suddenly blazing. 'You will be telling me that! Were her clothes dripping with water? Did you see, man, did you see?'

'Yes,' I answered, quickly. 'They were dripping wet. And she glared at me with such hatred in her eyes that I knew she was trying to kill me. Who is she? Or what is she?'

'I know only too well what she is,' he replied, slowly and quietly. 'And I know now who you are, John MacDonald, and I can give you your forbears. I'm thinking 'tis well you'll be leaving when the morning comes. But tell me your tale, and I'll tell you mine.'

Briefly I told him of my two encounters – on the road from Glenfinnan, and on the path by the falls. I told him, too, of the feeling of fear that had come to me. 'But why,' I protested, 'why should this old hag – ghost or spirit or fiend or whatever she is – hate me, a complete stranger, and try to murder me?'

'Because you are no stranger,' answered the priest, gravely.

210

'You are a MacDonald of Grianan, and the curse is on you and all your kin. That's why. And there's more to it. The same curse made your own people sell all, pack up, and sail across the seas in the year 1754. And though I'd be the last man to be frightening you, I shall be glad when you're back in your own land again.'

'But the thing's impossible,' I burst out, even though my own experiences had told me the very contrary.

'Not at all,' he replied firmly. 'Doesn't the Holy Book itself speak of evil and foul spirits? And didn't an evil spirit attack the seven sons of Sceva, leaping upon them, and driving them away, wounded and naked?'

'Well, what is the curse?' I demanded impatiently.

'That the stones of the earth shall crush you and all your kin,' answered the priest, looking at me sadly. 'And I'd be glad to be seeing you escape.'

'But why should there be such a curse?' I pleaded.

'Listen, my son. Away back in the seventeenth century the MacDonalds of Grianan were big folk, holding their land by charter of the king and with a right of judging the people on their land – even with a right of *furca et fossa*, a right of "gallows and pit", a gallows for hanging guilty men, and a pit for drowning guilty women. And in that time, when many a poor woman was put to death because she was reputed to be a witch, Angus MacDonald of Grianan, you'll forgive me, was a cruel man. Then it was that Isabel MacKenzie, a poor creature on his lands, was accused of witchcraft because a neighbour's cow had sickened and died. Isabel MacKenzie was condemned to death, and Angus MacDonald the cruel man, decreed it should be death by drowning. Did not his own charter say so? That poor creature was tied by her wrists to the length of a rope; the rope was tied to a boat; and Angus himself, with the others of his house, rowed out into the loch, dragging her behind them till at last she was drowned.

'Then, it is said, as the waters slowly ended her unhappy life, she cursed Angus and all his kin. "The waters of the loch shall drown me, but the stones of the earth shall crush you and all

211

your kin – *Pronnaidh clachan na talmhainn thu 's do chinneadh uile.*" '

The priest paused, 'And so it has been,' he continued, with a sigh. 'Angus laughed, as the years passed and he still lived. But one night, in a storm of wind, the chimney of his house was blown down and the stones of it fell through the roof and crushed him to death where he lay in his bed.

'Alastair, his son, was of finer mould. I can find no word of his doing wrong to man or beast. Yet he, too, was to die. There was a jetty to be built – and this was maybe a full twenty years after his father had died – and Alastair had gone down to see the men at the work. There was a tackle of some kind for lifting the heavy stones, and, somehow, a stone slipped from the tackle. It fell on him and crushed him to death.

'Then it was that people began to look at Grianan and quietly, among themselves, began to talk of the curse. And then it was that the MacDonalds of Grianan began to die more quickly. Always there was a stone of the earth in the way of their dying; and some of them, with their last words, would be speaking of strange things – of a woman with burning eyes, and whose clothes were wet with the waters of the loch. And, in the end, one, Roderick MacDonald, having seen his own father crushed to death by a millstone that was firmly fixed and yet somehow broke loose, sold his lands and his cattle, and sailed to America with his wife and child.

'And you, my son,' said Father MacWilliam, laying his hand gently on my arm, 'you are come of Roderick's stock. Yet I see some comfort for you. In all the papers that I have read, Isabel MacKenzie's curse never failed before. Twice it has failed to touch you. To me it would seem that her evil power is on the wane. I shall pray for you. But I shall still be glad to see you gone.'

'And I can do nothing?' I asked lamely.

'Nothing, save to put your trust in God,' he answered. 'And to remember that the power of the Lord is greater than all the powers of evil.'

Again he touched me lightly on the arm, looked kindly at me, and went out.

To be quite frank, I do not remember very clearly how I passed the rest of that evening. I was already completely unnerved, and now the story of my own house, the house that had the curse upon it, occupied my mind to the exclusion of all else. I wanted company. I wanted to have people around me. And yet my mind was never on the talk that they made. I am ashamed to think how boorish and uncivil I must have seemed. I am ashamed, too, to think of the drink that I took. I freely admit that terror had taken hold of me. Terror of being left alone. Terror of going to my bed. I drank in the bar, trying to make friends with complete strangers and yet thinking always of an old woman and her curse on my kin. In the end, I am told, I had to be carried to bed by the local doctor and a guest at the hotel. For a time, drink had ousted terror.

I do not know what time it was when I awoke. It was already daylight – but daylight breaks early in the Highlands in summer time. My head ached violently. Then I remembered my heavy drinking, and, with that, I remembered its cause. But what had awakened me? The wind was blowing strongly and yet, I assured myself, not strongly enough to bring a chimney-stack crashing down. But what was that? My ears caught a strange noise that seemed to come from the corridor outside my room. At once all my terror returned. I sat up in bed. There was the noise again! A shuffling noise. And something more. A noise that came between each shuffle. What was it? A shuffle; a strange dull thump; a shuffle; a thump. And drawing nearer all the time.

I tried to shout, but I could only croak like a feeble frog. I jumped out of bed, trembling from head to foot. How could I escape? Outside, in the corridor, a hell-hag, dead three hundred years ago, was coming to me, coming to crush me to death with a stone. A stone! That was the noise I could hear! She was pushing it before her, pushing it up to my door!

213

I looked wildly round. Thank God! The window! Flinging it wide open, I climbed quickly out, and, hanging from the window-ledge by my hands, let myself drop. As I landed on the ground I fell over backwards and, at the same instant, there came a heavy thud at my feet and the soft garden-earth splashed over me. I lay there, paralyzed with fear.

Then, slowly, I raised my head to look. A large stone had embedded itself in the ground exactly where I had dropped and exactly where I would have been had I not fallen over on my back. The curse was still upon me, and my life was to end with a stone.

I sprang to my feet, and, strangely, found my voice again. With a wild cry I ran across the garden, my injured knee sending quivers of hot pain up my thigh. And immediately I was held in a fast grip. Trembling and overwrought, I whimpered like a beaten cur, only to be at once calmed and reassured. I had run straight into the arms of Father MacWilliam.

'You are safe, my son,' came his gentle voice, as he still held me in his arms. 'Safe and saved. The powers of darkness shall trouble you no more. I have wrestled, even as Jacob wrestled at Peniel. Come with me to my own house. The Lord forgive me: I should have taken you there before.'

Paying no attention to the confused hubbub that now came from the hotel, he led me gently across the road – its stones feeling smooth and cool to my bare feet – and over the open moor-land to the church. There he took me into his house and put me in his own bed. On the instant, I fell into peaceful sleep.

Late the next morning I awoke to find my clothes on a chair by my bed. I washed and dressed, and went downstairs. A wise and gentle priest was awaiting me. He gave me breakfast, and then took me to my car which, with all my luggage packed and neatly stowed on the rear seat, was standing at his gate. 'There you are, my son,' he said. 'The curse is at an end. You can take any road and drive on it as freely as you wish – though,' he added, with a twinkle in his eye, 'always observing the laws that are enforced by the police.' He gave me his blessing, and wished me God-speed. With unashamed tears in my eyes, I thanked him again and again. At last I drove away.

Without a qualm, without fear of any kind, I drove back through Arisaig and Glenfinnan, ran back through Ballachulish and Callander, and so to Edinburgh.

Yet my tale has not quite ended.

On my way back, I stopped at Ballachulish for a very late lunch at the inn. As I ate alone in the dining-room, I heard two men talking outside by the open window.

'That was a mighty queer business last night, though I could get nothing out of the landlord when I tried to pump him this morning.'

'Yes, but the fellow was obviously drunk. He had to be carried to bed, you know.'

'I agree, old man. All the same, there was more to it than that. As you know, my room was next to his, and, just before he gave that awful yell which woke up everybody, I'd already been wakened by a strange kind of bumping noise which I couldn't fathom. I got up and looked out of the window, thinking the noise was probably coming from outside – and it may well have been that coping-stone, which had obviously worked loose, and which the wind may have been lifting slightly before it fell.

'However, that's not what I was going to say. As I looked out of the window, there, in the clear light of the early morning, I was astonished to see the local priest standing in the middle of the lawn, with one arm raised above his head, while a dishevelled old woman crouched and cowered before him. The very next second I saw this fellow climb out of his window and drop down. There was a crash as the coping-stone fell. And, with that, he jumped up, gave his appalling yell, and rushed straight into the arms of the priest. Where the old woman had gone to I don't know. She just seemed to disappear. And what she and the priest were doing . . .'

'What an extraordinary . . . Did you . . .'

The men had moved away, and their voices were fading. I tiptoed as fast as I could to the window and strained my ears. But I could catch only a few more words.

'And another queer thing – when I dashed out into the corridor in my bare feet it seemed to be soaking wet all along its length.'

The White Cat of Drumgunniol

J. S. Le Fanu

There is a famous story of a white cat, with which we all become acquainted in the nursery. I am going to tell a story of a white cat very different from the amiable and enchanted princess who took that disguise for a season. The white cat of which I speak was a more sinister animal.

The traveller from Limerick toward Dublin, after passing the hills of Killaloe upon the left, as Keeper Mountain rises high in view, finds himself gradually hemmed in, up the right, by a range of lower hills. An undulating plain that dips gradually to a lower level than that of the road interposes, and some scattered hedge-rows relieve its somewhat wild and melancholy character.

One of the few human habitations that send up their films of turf-smoke from that lonely plain, is the loosely-thatched, earth-built dwelling of a 'strong farmer,' as the more prosperous of the tenant-farming classes are termed in Munster. It stands in a clump of trees near the edge of a wandering stream, about half-way between the mountains and the Dublin road, and had been for generations tenanted by people named Donovan.

In a distant place, desirous of studying some Irish records which had fallen into my hands, and inquiring for a teacher capable of instructing me in the Irish language, a Mr. Donovan, dreamy, harmless, and learned, was recommended to me for the purpose.

I found that he had been educated as a Sizar in Trinity College, Dublin. He now supported himself by teaching, and the special

217

direction of my studies, I suppose, flattered his national partial-
ities, for he unbosomed himself of much of his long-reserved
thoughts, and recollections about his country and his early days.
It was he who told me this story, and I mean to repeat it, as
nearly as I can, in his own words.

I have myself seen the old farm-house, with its orchard of
huge moss grown apple trees. I have looked round on the peculiar
landscape; the roofless, ivied tower, that two hundred years
before had afforded a refuge from raid and rapparee, and which
still occupies its old place in the angle of the haggard; the bush-
grown 'liss,' that scarcely a hundred and fifty steps away records
the labours of a bygone race; the dark and towering outline of
old Keeper in the background; and the lonely range of furze and
heath-clad hills that form a nearer barrier, with many a line of
grey rock and clump of dwarf oak or birch. The pervading sense
of loneliness made it a scene not unsuited for a wild and unearthly story. And I could quite fancy how, seen in the grey of a
wintry morning, shrouded far and wide in snow, or in the
melancholy glory of an autumnal sunset, or in the chill splendour
of a moonlight night, it might have helped to tone a dreamy
mind like honest Dan Donovan's to superstition and a proneness
to the illusions of fancy. It is certain, however, that I never
anywhere met with a more simple-minded creature, or one on
whose good faith I could more entirely rely.

When I was a boy, said he, living at home at Drumgunniol, I
used to take my Goldsmith's *Roman History* in my hand and go
down to my favourite seat, the flat stone, sheltered by a hawthorn
tree beside the little lough, a large and deep pool, such as I have
heard called a tarn in England. It lay in the gentle hollow of a
field that is overhung toward the north by the old orchard, and
being a deserted place was favourable to my studious quietude.

One day reading here, as usual, I wearied at last, and began to
look about me, thinking of the heroic scenes I had just been
reading of. I was as wide awake as I am at this moment, and I
saw a woman appear at the corner of the orchard and walk down

the slope. She wore a long, light grey dress, so long that it seemed to sweep the grass behind her, and so singular was her appearance in a part of the world where female attire is so inflexibly fixed by custom, that I could not take my eyes off her. Her course lay diagonally from corner to corner of the field, which was a large one, and she pursued it without swerving.

When she came near I could see that her feet were bare, and that she seemed to be looking steadfastly upon some remote object for guidance. Her route would have crossed me – had the tarn not interposed – about ten or twelve yards below the point at which I was sitting. But instead of arresting her course at the margin of the lough, as I had expected, she went on without seeming conscious of its existence, and I saw her, as plainly as I see you, sir, walk across the surface of the water, and pass, without seeming to see me, at about the distance I had calculated.

I was ready to faint from sheer terror. I was only thirteen years old then, and I remember every particular as if it had happened this hour.

The figure passed through the gap at the far corner of the field, and there I lost sight of it. I had hardly strength to walk home, and was so nervous, and ultimately so ill, that for three weeks I was confined to the house, and could not bear to be alone for a moment. I never entered that field again, such was the horror with which from that moment every object in it was clothed. Even at this distance of time I should not like to pass through it.

This apparition I connected with a mysterious event; and, also, with a singular liability, that has for nearly eight years distinguished, or rather afflicted, our family. It is no fancy. Everybody in that part of the country knows all about it. Everybody connected what I had seen with it.

I will tell it all to you as well as I can.

When I was about fourteen years old – that is about a year after the sight I had seen in the lough field – we were one night expecting my father home from the fair of Killaloe. My mother

219

sat up to welcome him home, and I with her, for I liked nothing better than such a vigil. My brothers and sisters, and the farm servants, except the men who were driving home the cattle from the fair, were asleep in their beds. My mother and I were sitting in the chimney corner chatting together, and watching my father's supper, which was kept hot over the fire. We knew that he would return before the men who were driving home the cattle, for he was riding, and told us that he would only wait to see them fairly on the road, and then push homeward.

At length we heard his voice and the knocking of his loaded whip at the door, and my mother let him in. I don't think I ever saw my father drunk, which is more than most men of my age, from the same part of the country, could say of theirs. But he could drink his glass of whisky as well as another, and he usually came home from fair or market a little merry and mellow, and with a jolly flush in his cheeks.

To-night he looked sunken, pale and sad. He entered with the saddle and bridle in his hand, and he dropped them against the wall, near the door, and put his arms round his wife's neck, and kissed her kindly.

'Welcome home, Meehal,' said she, kissing him heartily.

'God bless you, mavourneen,' he answered.

And hugging her again, he turned to me, who was plucking him by the hand, jealous of his notice. I was little, and light of my age, and he lifted me up in his arms, and kissed me, and my arms being about his neck, he said to my mother:

'Draw the bolt, acuishla.'

She did so, and setting me down very dejectedly, he walked to the fire and sat down on a stool, and stretched his feet toward the glowing turf, leaning with his hands on his knees.

'Rouse up, Mick, darlin',' said my mother, who was growing anxious, 'and tell me how did the cattle sell, and did everything go lucky at the fair, or is there anything wrong with the landlord, or what in the world is it that ails you, Mick, jewel?'

'Nothin', Molly. The cows sould well, thank God, and there's nothin' fell out between me an' the landlord, an' everything's the same way. There's no fault to find anywhere.'

'Well, then, Mickey, since so it is, turn round to your hot supper, and ate it, and tell us is there anything new.'

'I got my supper, Molly, on the way, and I can't ate a bit,' he answered.

'Got your supper on the way, an' you knowin' 'twas waiting for you at home, an' your wife sittin' up an' all!' cried my mother, reproachfully.

'You're takin' a wrong meanin' out of what I say,' said my father. 'There's something happened that leaves me that I can't ate a mouthful, and I'll not be dark with you, Molly, for, maybe, it ain't very long I have to be here, an' I'll tell you what it was. It's what I've seen, the white cat.'

'The Lord between us and harm!' exclaimed my mother, in a moment as pale and as chap-fallen as my father; and then, trying to rally, with a laugh, she said: 'Ha! 'tis only funnin' me you are. Sure a white rabbit was snared a Sunday last, in Grady's wood; an' Teigue seen a big white rat in the haggard yesterday.'

' 'Twas neither rat nor rabbit was in it. Don't ye think but I'd know a rat or a rabbit from a big white cat, with green eyes as big as halfpennies, and its back riz up like a bridge, trottin' on and across me, and ready, if I dar' stop, to rub its sides against my shins, and maybe to make a jump and seize my throat, if that it's a cat, at all, an' not something worse?'

As he ended his description in a low tone, looking straight at the fire, my father drew his big hand across his forehead once or twice, his face being damp and shining with the moisture of fear, and he sighed, or rather groaned, heavily.

My mother had relapsed into panic, and was praying again in her fear. I, too, was terribly frightened, and on the point of crying, for I knew all about the white cat.

Clapping my father on the shoulder, by way of encouragement, my mother leaned over him, kissing him, and at last began to cry. He was wringing her hands in his, and seemed in great trouble.

'There was nothin' came into the house with me?' he asked, in a very low tone, turning to me.

'There was nothin', father,' I said, 'but the saddle and bridle that was in your hand.'

'Nothin' white kem in at the doore wid me,' he repeated.

'Nothin' at all,' I answered.

'So best,' said my father, and making the sign of the cross, he began mumbling to himself, and I knew he was saying his prayers.

Waiting for a while, to give him time for this exercise, my mother asked him where he first saw it.

'When I was riding up the bohereen,' – the Irish term meaning a little road, such as leads up to a farm-house – 'I bethought myself that the men was on the road with the cattle, and no one to look to the horse barrin' myself, so I thought I might as well leave him in the crooked field below, an' I tuck him there, he bein' cool, and not a hair turned, for I rode him aisy all the way. It was when I turned, after lettin' him go – the saddle and bridle bein' in my hand – that I saw it, pushin' out o' the long grass at the side o' the path, an' it walked across it, in front of me, an' then back again, before me, the same way, an' sometimes at one side, an' then at the other, lookin' at me wid them shinin' eyes; and I consayted I heard it growlin' as it kep' beside me – as close as ever you see – till I kem up to the doore, here, an' knocked an' called, as ye heerd me.'

Now, what was it, in so simple an incident, that agitated my father, my mother, myself, and finally, every member of this rustic household, with a terrible foreboding? It was this that we, one and all, believed that my father had received, in thus encountering the white cat, a warning of his approaching death.

The omen had never failed hitherto. It did not fail now. In a week after my father took the fever that was going, and before a month he was dead.

222

My honest friend, Dan Donovan, paused here; I could perceive that he was praying, for his lips were busy, and I concluded that it was for the repose of that departed soul.

In a little while he resumed.

It is eighty years now since that omen first attached to my family. Eighty years? Ay, is it. Ninety is nearer the mark. And I have spoken to many old people, in those earlier times, who had a distinct recollection of everything connected with it.

It happened in this way.

My grand-uncle, Connor Donovan, had the old farm of Drumgunniol in his day. He was richer than ever my father was, or my father's father either, for he took a short lease of Balraghan, and made money of it. But money won't soften a hard heart, and I'm afraid my grand-uncle was a cruel man – a profligate man he was, surely, and that is mostly a cruel man at heart. He drank his share, too, and cursed and swore, when he was vexed, more than was good for his soul, I'm afraid.

At that time there was a beautiful girl of the Colemans, up in the mountains, not far from Capper Cullen. I'm told that there are no Colemans there now at all, and that family has passed away. The famine years made great changes.

Ellen Coleman was her name. The Colemans were not rich. But, being such a beauty, she might have made a good match. Worse than she did for herself, poor thing, she could not.

Con Donovan – my grand-uncle, God forgive him! – sometimes in his rambles saw her at fairs or patterns, and he fell in love with her, as who might not?

He used her ill. He promised her marriage, and persuaded her to come away with him; and, after all, he broke his word. It was just the old story. He tired of her, and he wanted to push himself in the world; and he married a girl of the Collopys, that had a great fortune – twenty-four cows, seventy sheep, and a hundred and twenty goats.

He married this Mary Collopy, and grew richer than before;

and Ellen Coleman died broken-hearted. But that did not trouble the strong farmer much.

He would have liked to have children, but he had none, and this was the only cross he had to bear, for everything else went much as he wished.

One night he was returning from the fair of Nenagh. A shallow stream at that time crossed the road – they have thrown a bridge over it, I am told, some time since – and its channel was often dry in summer weather. When it was so, as it passes close by the old farm-house of Drumgunniol, without a great deal of winding, it makes a sort of road, which people then used as a short cut to reach the house by. Into this dry channel, as there was plenty of light from the moon, my grand-uncle turned his horse, and when he had reached the two ash-trees at the meering of the farm he turned his horse short into the river-field, intending to ride through the gap at the other end, under the oak-tree, and so he would have been within a few hundred yards of his door.

As he approached the 'gap' he saw, or thought he saw, with a slow motion, gliding along the ground toward the same point, and now and then with a soft bound, a white object, which he described as being no bigger than his hat, but what it was he could not see, as it moved along the hedge and disappeared at the point to which he was himself tending.

When he reached the gap the horse stopped short. He urged and coaxed it in vain. He got down to lead it through, but it recoiled, snorted, and fell into a wild trembling fit. He mounted it again. But its terror continued, and it obstinately resisted his caresses and his whip. It was bright moonlight, and my grand-uncle was chafed by the horse's resistance, and, seeing nothing to account for it, and being so near home, what little patience he possessed forsook him, and, plying his whip and spur in earnest, he broke into oaths and curses.

All on a sudden the horse sprang through, and Con Donovan, as he passed under the broad branch of the oak, saw clearly a woman standing on the bank beside him, her arm extended, with the hand of which, as he flew by, she struck him a blow upon the shoulders. It threw him forward upon the neck of the horse, which, in wild terror, reached the door at a gallop, and stood there quivering and steaming all over.

Less alive than dead, my grand-uncle got in. He told his story, at least, so much as he chose. His wife did not quite know what to think. But that something very bad had happened she could not doubt. He was very faint and ill, and begged that the priest should be sent for forthwith. When they were getting him to his bed they saw distinctly the marks of five fingerpoints on the flesh of his shoulder, where the spectral blow had fallen. These singular marks – which they said resembled in tint the hue of a body struck by lightning – remained imprinted on his flesh, and were buried with him.

When he had recovered sufficiently to talk with the people about him – speaking, like a man at his last hour, from a burdened heart, and troubled conscience – he repeated his story, but said he did not see, or, at all events, know, the face of the figure that stood in the gap. No one believed him. He told more about it to the priest than to others. He certainly had a secret to tell. He might as well have divulged it frankly, for the neighbours all knew well enough that it was the face of dead Ellen Coleman that he had seen.

From that moment my grand-uncle never raised his head. He was a scared, silent, broken-spirited man. It was early summer then, and at the fall of the leaf in the same year he died.

Of course there was a wake, such as beseemed a strong farmer so rich as he. For some reason the arrangements of this ceremonial were a little different from the usual routine.

The usual practice is to place the body in the great room, or kitchen, as it is called, of the house. In this particular case there was, as I told you, for some reason, an unusual arrangement. The body was placed in a small room that opened upon the greater one. The door of this, during the wake, stood open. There were candles about the bed, and pipes and tobacco on the table, and stools for such guests as chose to enter, the door standing open for their reception.

The body, having been laid out, was left alone, in this smaller room, during the preparations for the wake. After nightfall one of the women, approaching the bed to get a chair which she had left near it, rushed from the room with a scream, and, having recovered her speech at the further end of the 'kitchen,' and surrounded by a gaping audience, she said, at last:

'May I never sin, if his face bain't riz up again the back o' the bed, and he starin' down to the doore, wid eyes as big as pewter plates, that id be shinin' in the moon!'

'Arra, woman! Is it cracked you are?' said one of the farm boys as they are termed, being men of any age you please.

'Agh, Molly, don't be talkin', woman! 'Tis what ye consayted it, goin' into the dark room, out o' the light. Why didn't ye take a candle in your fingers, ye aumadhaun?' said one of her female companions.

'Candle, or no candle; I seen it,' insisted Molly. 'An' what's more, I could a' most tak' my oath I seen his arum, too, stretchin' out o' the bed along the flure, three times as long as it should be, to take hould o' me be the fut.'

'Nansinse, ye fool, what id he want o' yer fut?' exclaimed one scornfully.

'Gi' me the candle, some o' yez – in the name o' God,' said old Sal Doolan, that was straight and lean, and a woman that could pray like a priest almost.

'Give her a candle,' agreed all.

But whatever they might say, there wasn't one among them that did not look pale and stern enough as they followed Mrs. Doolan, who was praying as fast as her lips could patter, and leading the van with a tallow candle, held like a taper, in her fingers.

The door was half open, as the panic-stricken girl had left it; and holding the candle on high the better to examine the room, she made a step or so into it.

If my grand-uncle's hand had been stretched along the floor, in the unnatural way described, he had drawn it back again under the sheet that covered him. And tall Mrs. Doolan was in no danger of tripping over his arm as she entered. But she had not gone more than a step or two with her candle aloft, when, with a drowning face, she suddenly stopped short, staring at the bed which was now fully in view.

'Lord, bless us, Mrs. Doolan, ma'am, come back,' said the woman next her, who had fast hold of her dress, or her 'coat,' as they call it, and drawing her backwards with a frightened pluck, while a general recoil among her followers betokened the alarm which her hesitation had inspired.

'Whisht, will yez?' said the leader, peremptorily, 'I can't hear my own ears wid the noise ye're makin', an' which iv yez let the cat in here, an' whose cat is it?' she asked, peering suspiciously at a white cat that was sitting on the breast of the corpse.

'Put it away, will yez?' she resumed, with horror at the profanation. 'Many a corpse as I shtretched and crossed in the bed, the likes o' that I never seen yet. The man o' the house, wid a brute baste like that mounted on him, like a phooka, Lord forgi' me for namin' the like in this room. Dhrive it away, some o' yez! out o' that, this minute, I tell ye.'

Each repeated the order, but no one seemed inclined to execute it. They were crossing themselves, and whispering their conjectures and misgivings as to the nature of the beast, which was no cat of that house, nor one that they had ever seen before. On a sudden, the white cat placed itself on the pillow over the head of the body, and having from that place glared for a time at them over the features of the corpse, it crept softly along the body towards them, growling low and fiercely as it drew near.

Out of the room they bounced, in dreadful confusion, shutting the door fast after them, and not for a good while did the hardiest venture to peep in again.

The white cat was sitting in its old place, on the dead man's breast, but this time it crept quietly down the side of the bed, and disappeared under it, the sheet which was spread like a coverlet, and hung down nearly to the floor, concealing it from view.

Praying, crossing themselves, and not forgetting a sprinkling of holy water, they peeped, and finally searched, poking spades, 'wattles,' pitchforks and such implements under the bed. But the cat was not to be found, and they concluded that it had made its escape among their feet as they stood near the threshold. So they secured the door carefully, with hasp and padlock.

But when the door was opened next morning they found the white cat sitting, as if it had never been disturbed, upon the breast of the dead man.

Again occurred very nearly the same scene with a like result, only that some said they saw the cat afterwards lurking under a big box in a corner of the outer-room, where my grand-uncle kept his leases and papers, and his prayer-book and beads.

Mrs. Doolan heard it growling at her heels wherever she went; and although she could not see it, she could hear it spring on the back of her chair when she sat down, and growl in her ear, so that she would bounce up with a scream and a prayer, fancying that it was on the point of taking her by the throat.

And the priest's boy, looking round the corner, under the branches of the old orchard, saw a white cat sitting under the little window of the room where my grand-uncle was laid out and looking up at the four small panes of glass as a cat will watch a bird.

The end of it was that the cat was found on the corpse again, when the room was visited, and do what they might, whenever the body was left alone, the cat was found again in the same ill-omened contiguity with the dead man. And this continued, to the scandal and fear of the neighbourhood, until the door was opened finally for the wake.

My grand-uncle being dead, and, with all due solemnities, buried, I have done with him. But not quite yet with the white cat. No banshee ever yet was more inalienably attached to a family than this ominous apparition is to mine. But there is this

difference. The banshee seems to be animated with an affection-
ate sympathy with the bereaved family to whom it is hereditarily
attached, whereas this thing has about it a suspicion of malice. It
is the messenger simply of death. And its taking the shape of a
cat – the coldest, and they say, the most vindictive of brutes – is
indicative of the spirit of its visit.

When my grandfather's death was near, although he seemed
quite well at the time, it appeared not exactly, but very nearly in
the same way in which I told you it showed itself to my father.

The day before my Uncle Teigue was killed by the bursting of
his gun, it appeared to him in the evening, at twilight, by the
lough, in the field where I saw the woman who walked across
the water, as I told you. My uncle was washing the barrel of his
gun in the lough. The grass is short there, and there is no cover
near it. He did not know how it approached but the first he saw
of it, the white cat was walking close round his feet, in the
twilight, with an angry twist of its tail, and a green glare in its
eyes, and do what he would, it continued walking round and
round him, in larger or smaller circles, till he reached the orchard,
and there he lost it.

My poor Aunt Peg – she married one of the O'Brians, near
Oolah – came to Drumgunniol to go to the funeral of a cousin
who died about a mile away. She died herself, poor woman, only
a month after.

Coming from the wake, at two or three o'clock in the morning,
as she got over the stile into the farm of Drumgunniol, she saw
the white cat at her side, and it kept close beside her, she ready
to faint all the time, till she reached the door of the house, where
it made a spring up into the white-thorn tree that grows close by,
and so it parted from her. And my little brother Jim saw it also,
just three weeks before he died. Every member of our family
who dies, or takes his death-sickness, at Drumgunniol, is sure to
see the white cat, and no one of us who sees it need hope for
long life after.

The Child that Went with the Fairies

J. S. Le Fanu

Eastward of the old city of Limerick, about ten Irish miles under the range of mountains known as the Slieveelim hills, famous as having afforded Sarsfield a shelter among their rocks and hollows, when he crossed them in his gallant descent upon the cannon and ammunition of King William, on its way to the beleaguering army, there runs a very old and narrow road. It connects the Limerick road to Tipperary with the old road from Limerick to Dublin, and runs by bog and pasture, hill and hollow, straw-thatched village, and roofless castle, not far from twenty miles.

Skirting the healthy mountains of which I have spoken, at one part it becomes singularly lonely. For more than three Irish miles it traverses a deserted country. A wide, black bog, level as a lake, skirted with copse, spreads at the left, as you journey northward, and the long and irregular line of mountain rises at the right, clothed in heath, broken with lines of grey rock that resemble the bold and irregular outlines of fortifications, and riven with many a gully, expanding here and there into rocky and wooded glens, which open as they approach the road.

A scanty pasturage, on which browsed a few scattered sheep or kine, skirts this solitary road for some miles, and under shelter of a hillock, and of two or three great ash-trees, stood, not many years ago, the little thatched cabin of a widow named Mary Ryan.

Poor was this widow in a land of poverty. The thatch had acquired the grey tint and sunken outlines, that show how the alternations of rain and sun have told upon that perishable shelter.

But whatever other dangers threatened, there was one well provided against by the care of other times. Round the cabin stood half a dozen mountain ashes, as the rowans, inimical to witches, are there called. On the worn planks of the door were nailed two horse-shoes, and over the lintel and spreading along the thatch, grew, luxuriant, patches of that ancient cure for many maladies, and prophylactic against the machinations of the evil one, the house-leek. Descending into the doorway, in the *chiaroscuro* of the interior, when your eye grew sufficiently accustomed to that dim light, you might discover, hanging at the head of the widow's wooden-roofed bed, her beads and a phial of holy water.

Here certainly were defences and bulwarks against the intrusion of that unearthly and evil power, of whose vicinity this solitary family were constantly reminded by the outline of Lisnavoura, that lonely hill-haunt of the 'good people,' as the fairies are called euphemistically, whose strangely dome-like summit rose not half a mile away, looking like an outwork of the long line of mountain that sweeps by it.

It was at the fall of the leaf, and an autumnal sunset threw the lengthening shadow of haunted Lisnavoura, close in front of the solitary little cabin, over the undulating slopes and sides of Slieveelim. The birds were singing among the branches in the thinning leaves of the melancholy ash-trees that grew at the roadside in front of the door. The widow's three younger children were playing on the road, and their voices mingled with the evening song of the birds. Their elder sister, Nell, was 'within in the house,' as their phrase is, seeing after the boiling of the potatoes for supper.

Their mother had gone down to the bog, to carry up a hamper of turf on her back. It is, or was at least, a charitable custom – and if not disused, long may it continue – for the wealthier people when cutting their turf and stacking it in the bog, to make a smaller stack for the behoof of the poor, who were welcome to take from it so long as it lasted, and thus the potato pot was kept boiling, and hearth warm that would have been cold enough but for that good-natured bounty, through wintry months.

Moll Ryan trudged up the steep 'bohereen' whose banks were overgrown with thorn and brambles, and stooping under her burden, re-entered her door, where her dark-haired daughter Nell met her with a welcome, and relieved her of her hamper.

Moll Ryan looked round with a sigh of relief, and drying her forehead, uttered the Munster ejaculation:

'Eiah, wisha! It's tired I am with it, God bless it. And where's the craythurs, Nell?'

'Playin' out on the road, mother; didn't ye see them and you comin' up?'

'No; there was no one before me on the road,' she said, uneasily; 'not a soul, Nell; and why didn't ye keep an eye on them?'

'Well, they're in the haggard, playin' there, or round by the back o' the house. Will I call them in?'

'Do so, good girl, in the name o' God. The hens is comin' home, see, and the sun was just down over Knockdoulah, an' I comin' up.'

So out ran tall, dark-haired Nell, and standing on the road, looked up and down it; but not a sign of her two little brothers, Con and Bill, or her little sister, Peg, could she see. She called them; but no answer came from the little haggard, fenced with straggling bushes. She listened, but the sound of their voices was missing. Over the stile, and behind the house she ran – but there all was silent and deserted.

She looked down toward the bog, as far as she could see; but they did not appear. Again she listened – but in vain. At first she had felt angry, but now a different feeling overcame her, and she grew pale. With an undefined boding she looked toward the heathy boss of Lisnavoura, now darkening into the deepest purple against the flaming sky of sunset.

Again she listened with a sinking heart, and heard nothing

but the farewell twitter and whistle of the birds in the bushes around. How many stories had she listened to by the winter hearth, of children stolen by the fairies, at nightfall, in lonely places! With this fear she knew her mother was haunted.

No one in the country round gathered her little flock about her so early as this frightened widow, and no door 'in the seven parishes' was barred so early.

Sufficiently fearful, as all young people in that part of the world are of such dreaded and subtle agents, Nell was even more than usually afraid of them, for her terrors were infected and redoubled by her mother's. She was looking towards Lisnavoura in a trance of fear, and crossed herself again and again, and whispered prayer after prayer. She was interrupted by her mother's voice on the road calling her loudly. She answered, and ran round to the front of the cabin, where she found her standing.

'And where in the world's the craythurs – did ye see sight o' them anywhere?' cried Mrs. Ryan, as the girl came over the stile.

'Arrah! mother, 'tis only what they're run down the road a bit. We'll see them this minute coming back. It's like goats they are, climbin' here and runnin' there; an' if I had them here, in my hand, maybe I wouldn't give them a hiding all round.'

'May the Lord forgive you, Nell! the childhers gone. They're took, and not a soul near us, and Father Tom three miles away! And what'll I do, or who's to help us this night? Oh, wirristhru, wirristhru! The craythurs is gone!'

'Whisht, mother, be aisy: don't ye see them comin' up?'

And then she shouted in menacing accents, waving her arm, and beckoning the children, who were seen approaching on the road, which some little way off made a slight dip, which had concealed them. They were approaching from the westward, and from the direction of the dreaded hill of Lisnavoura.

But there were only two of the children, and one of them, the little girl, was crying. Their mother and sister hurried forward to meet them, more alarmed than ever.

'Where is Billy – where is he?' cried the mother, nearly

breathless, so soon as she was within hearing.

'He's gone – they took him away; but they said he'll come back again,' answered little Con, with the dark brown hair.

'He's gone away with the grand ladies,' blubbered the little girl.

'What ladies – where? Oh, Leum, asthora! My darlin', are you gone away at last? Where is he? Who took him? What ladies are you talkin' about? What way did he go?' she cried in distraction.

'I couldn't see where he went, mother; 'twas like as if he was going to Lisnavoura.'

With a wild exclamation the distracted woman ran on towards the hill alone, clapping her hands, and crying aloud the name of her lost child.

Scared and horrified, Nell, not daring to follow, gazed after her, and burst into tears; and the other children raised high their lamentations in shrill rivalry.

Twilight was deepening. It was long past the time when they were usually barred securely within their habitation. Nell led the younger children into the cabin, and made them sit down by the turf fire, while she stood in the open door, watching in great fear for the return of her mother.

After a long while they did see their mother return. She came in and sat down by the fire, and cried as if her heart would break.

'Will I bar the doore, mother?' asked Nell.

'Ay, do – didn't I lose enough, this night, without lavin' the doore open, for more o' yez to go; but first take an' sprinkle a dust o' the holy waters over ye, acuishla, and bring it here till I throw a taste iv it over myself and the craythurs; an' I wondher, Nell, you'd forget to do the like yourself, lettin' the craythurs out so near nightfall. Come here and sit on my knees, asthora, come to me, mavourneen, and hould me fast, in the name o' God, and I'll hould you fast that none can take yez from me, and tell me all about it, and what it was – the Lord between us and harm – an' how it happened, and who was in it.'

And the door being barred, the two children, sometimes speaking together, often interrupting one another, often interrupted by their mother, managed to tell this strange story, which I had better relate connectedly and in my own language.

The Widow Ryan's three children were playing, as I have said, upon the narrow old road in front of her door. Little Bill or Leum, about five years old, with golden hair and large blue eyes, was a very pretty boy, with all the clear tints of healthy childhood, and that gaze of earnest simplicity which belongs not to town children of the same age. His little sister Peg, about a year older, and his brother Con, a little more than a year elder than she, made up the little group.

Under the great old ash-trees, whose last leaves were falling at their feet, in the light of an October sunset, they were playing with the hilarity and eagerness of rustic children, clamouring together, and their faces were turned toward the west and storied hill of Lisnavoura.

Suddenly a startling voice with a screech called to them from behind, ordering them to get out of the way, and turning, they saw a sight, such as they never beheld before. It was a carriage drawn by four horses that were pawing and snorting, in impatience, as if just pulled up. The children were almost under their feet, and scrambled to the side of the road next their own door.

This carriage and all its appointments were old-fashioned and gorgeous, and presented to the children, who had never seen anything finer than a turf car, and once, an old chaise that passed that way from Killaloe, a spectacle perfectly dazzling.

Here was antique splendour. The harness and trappings were scarlet, and blazing with gold. The horses were huge, and snow white, with great manes, that as they tossed and shook them in the air, seemed to stream and float sometimes longer and sometimes shorter, like so much smoke – their tails were long, and tied up in bows of broad scarlet and gold ribbon. The coach itself was glowing with colours, gilded and emblazoned. There were footmen in gay liveries, and three-cocked hats, like the coachman's; but he had a great wig, like a judge's, and their hair was frizzed out and powdered, and a long thick 'pigtail,' with a bow to it, hung down the back of each.

All these servants were diminutive, and ludicrously out of proportion with the enormous horses of the equipage, and had sharp, sallow features, and small, restless fiery eyes, and faces of cunning and malice that chilled the children. The little coachman was scowling and showing his white fangs under his cocked hat, and his little blazing beads of eyes were quivering with fury in their sockets as he whirled his whip round and round over their heads, till the lash of it looked like a streak of fire in the evening sun, and sounded like the cry of a legion of 'fillapoueeks' in the air.

'Stop the princess on the highway!' cried the coachman, in a piercing treble.

'Stop the princess on the highway!' piped each footman in turn, scowling over his shoulder down on the children, and grinding his keen teeth.

The children were so frightened they could only gape and turn white in their panic. But a very sweet voice from the open window of the carriage reassured them, and arrested the attack of the lackeys.

A beautiful and 'very grand-looking' lady was smiling from it on them, and they all felt pleased in the strange light of that smile.

'The boy with the golden hair, I think,' said the lady, bending her large and wonderfully clear eyes on little Leum.

The upper sides of the carriage were chiefly of glass, so that the children could see another woman inside, whom they did not like so well.

This was a black woman, with a wonderfully long neck, hung round with many strings of large variously-coloured beads, and on her head was a sort of turban of silk striped with all the colours of the rainbow, and fixed in it was a golden star.

This black woman had a face as thin almost as a death's-head, with high cheekbones, and great goggle eyes, the whites of which, as well as her wide range of teeth, showed in brilliant contrast with her skin, as she looked over the beautiful lady's shoulder, and whispered something in her ear.

'Yes; the boy with the golden hair, I think,' repeated the lady.

And her voice sounded sweet as a silver bell in the children's ears, and her smile beguiled them like the light of an enchanted lamp, as she leaned from the window with a look of ineffable fondness on the golden-haired boy, with the large blue eyes; insomuch that little Billy, looking up, smiled in return with a wondering fondness, and when she stooped down, and stretched her jewelled arms towards him, he stretched his little hands up, and how they touched the other children did not know; but, saying, 'Come and give me a kiss, my darling,' she raised him, and he seemed to ascend in her small fingers as lightly as a feather, and she held him in her lap and covered him with kisses.

Nothing daunted, the other children would have been only too happy to change places with their favoured little brother. There was only one thing that was unpleasant, and a little frightened them, and that was the black woman, who stood and stretched forward, in the carriage as before. She gathered a rich silk and gold handkerchief that was in her fingers up to her lips, and seemed to thrust ever so much of it, fold after fold, into her capacious mouth, as they thought to smother her laughter, with which she seemed convulsed, for she was shaking and quivering, as it seemed, with suppressed merriment; but her eyes, which remained uncovered, looked angrier than they had ever seen eyes look before.

But the lady was so beautiful they looked on her instead, and she continued to caress and kiss the little boy on her knee; and smiling at the other children she held up a large russet apple in her fingers, and the carriage began to move slowly on, and with a nod inviting them to take the fruit, she dropped it on the road from the window; it rolled some way beside the wheels, they following, and then she dropped another, and then another, and so on. And the same thing happened to all; for just as either of the children who ran beside had caught the rolling apple, somehow it slipt into a hole or ran into a ditch, and looking up they saw the lady drop another from the window, and so the chase was taken up and continued till they got, hardly knowing how far they had gone, to the old cross-road that leads to Owney. It seemed that there the horses' hoofs and carriage wheels rolled up a wonderful dust, which being caught in one of those eddies that whirl the dust up into a column, on the calmest day, enveloped the children for a moment, and passed whirling on towards Lisnavoura, the carriage, as they fancied, driving in the centre of it; but suddenly it subsided, the straws and leaves floated to the ground, the dust dissipated itself, but the white horses and the lackeys, the gilded carriage, the lady and their little golden-haired brother were gone.

At the same moment suddenly the upper rim of the clear setting sun disappeared behind the hill of Knockdoula, and it was twilight. Each child felt the transition like a shock – and the sight of the rounded summit of Lisnavoura, now closely overhanging them, struck them with a new fear.

They screamed their brother's name after him, but their cries were lost in the vacant air. At the same time they thought they heard a hollow voice say, close to them, 'Go home.'

Looking round and seeing no one, they were scared, and hand in hand – the little girl crying wildly, and the boy white as ashes, from fear, they trotted homeward, at their best speed, to tell, as we have seen, their strange story.

Molly Ryan never more saw her darling. But something of the lost little boy was seen by his former playmates.

Sometimes when their mother was away earning a trifle at hay-making, and Nelly washing the potatoes for their dinner, or 'beatling' clothes in the little stream that flows in the hollow close by, they saw the pretty face of little Billy peeping in archly at the door, and smiling silently at them, and as they ran to embrace him, with cries of delight, he drew back, still smiling archly, and when they got out into the open day, he was gone, and they could see no trace of him anywhere.

This happened often, with slight variations in the circumstances of the visit. Sometimes he would peep for a longer time, sometimes for a shorter time, sometimes his little hand would come in, and, with bended finger, beckon them to follow; but always he was smiling with the same arch look and wary silence – and always he was gone when they reached the door. Gradually these visits grew less and less frequent, and in about eight months they ceased altogether, and little Billy, irretrievably lost, took rank in their memories with the dead.

One wintry morning, nearly a year and a half after his disappearance, their mother having set out for Limerick soon after cock-crow, to sell some fowls at the market, the little girl, lying by the side of her elder sister, who was fast asleep, just at the grey of the morning heard the latch lifted softly, and saw little Billy enter and close the door gently after him. There was light enough to see that he was barefoot and ragged, and looked pale and famished. He went straight to the fire, and cowered over the turf embers, and rubbed his hands slowly, and seemed to shiver as he gathered the smouldering turf together.

The little girl clutched her sister in terror and whispered, 'Waken, Nelly, waken; here's Billy come back!'

Nelly slept soundly on, but the little boy, whose hands were extended close over the coals, turned and looked toward the bed, it seemed to her, in fear, and she saw the glare of the embers reflected on his thin cheek as he turned toward her. He rose and went, on tiptoe, quickly to the door, in silence, and let himself out as softly as he had come in.

After that, the little boy was never seen any more by any one of his kindred.

'Fairy doctors,' as the dealers in the preternatural, who in such cases were called in, are termed, did all that in them lay – but in vain. Father Tom came down, and tried what holier rites could do, but equally without result. So little Billy was dead to mother, brother, and sisters; but no grave received him. Others whom affection cherished, lay in holy ground, in the old church-yard of Abington, with headstone to mark the spot over which the survivor might kneel and say a kind prayer for the peace of the departed soul. But there was no landmark to show where little Billy was hidden from their loving eyes, unless it was in the old hill of Lisnavoura, that cast its long shadow at sunset before the cabin-door; or that, white and filmy in the moonlight, in later years, would occupy his brother's gaze as he returned from fair or market, and draw from him a sigh and a prayer for the little brother he had lost so long ago, and was never to see again.

Hertford O'Donnell's Warning

Mrs J. H. Riddell

Many a year ago, before chloroform was thought of, there lived in an old rambling house in Gerrard Street, Soho, a young Irishman called Hertford O'Donnell.

After Hertford O'Donnell he was entitled to write M.R.C.S., for he had studied hard to gain this distinction, and the elder surgeons at Guy's (his hospital) considered him, in their secret hearts, one of the most rising operators of the day.

Having said chloroform was unknown at the time this story opens, it will strike my readers that, if Hertford O'Donnell were a rising and successful operator in those days, of necessity he combined within himself a larger number of striking qualities than are by any means necessary to form a successful operator in these.

There was more than mere hand skill, more than even thorough knowledge of his profession, needful for the man who, dealing with conscious subjects, essayed to rid them of some of the diseases to which flesh is heir. There was greater courage required in the manipulator of old than is altogether essential now. Then, as now, a thorough mastery of his instruments – a steady hand – a keen eye – a quick dexterity, were indispensable to a good operator; but, added to all these things, there were formerly required a pulse which knew no quickening – a mental strength which never faltered – a ready power of adaptation in unexpected circumstances – fertility of resource in difficult cases, and a brave front under all emergencies.

If I refrain from adding that a hard as well as a courageous heart was an important item in the programme, it is only out of deference to general opinion, which, amongst other delusions, clings to the belief that courage and hardness are antagonistic qualities.

Hertford O'Donnell, however, was hard as steel. He understood his work, and he did it thoroughly; but he cared no more for quivering nerves and contracting muscles, for screams of agony, for faces white with pain, and teeth clenched in the extremity of anguish, than he did for the stony countenance of the dead, which sometimes in the dissecting room appalled younger and less experienced men.

He had no sentiment, and he had no sympathy. The human body was to him an ingenious piece of mechanism, which it was at once a pleasure and a profit to understand. Precisely as Brunel loved the Thames Tunnel, or any other singular engineering feat, so O'Donnell loved a patient on whom he operated successfully, more especially if the ailment possessed by the patient were of a rare and difficult character.

And for this reason he was much liked by all who came under his hands, for patients are apt to mistake a surgeon's interest in their cases for interest in themselves; and it was gratifying to John Dicks, plasterer, and Timothy Regan, labourer, to be the happy possessors of remarkable diseases, which produced a cordial understanding between them and the handsome Irishman.

If he were hard and cool at the moment of hewing them to pieces, that was all forgotten, or remembered only as a virtue, when, after being discharged from hospital like soldiers who have served in a severe campaign, they met Mr. O'Donnell in the street, and were accosted by that rising individual, just as though he considered himself nobody.

He had a royal memory, this stranger in a strange land, both for faces and cases; and, like the rest of his countrymen, he never felt it beneath his dignity to talk cordially to corduroy and fustian.

In London, as at Calgillan, he never held back his tongue

from speaking a cheery or a kindly word. His manners were pliable enough, if his heart were not; and the porters, and the patients, and the nurses, and the students at Guy's all were pleased to see Hertford O'Donnell.

Rain, hail, sunshine, it was all the same; there was a life, and a brightness about the man which communicated itself to those with whom he came in contact. Let the mud out in Smithfield be a foot deep, or the London fog thick as pea-soup, Mr. O'Donnell never lost his temper, never uttered a surly reply to the gate-keeper's salutation, but spoke out blithely and cheerfully to his pupils and his patients, to the sick and to the well, to those below and to those above him.

And yet, spite of all these good qualities – spite of his handsome face, his fine figure, his easy address and his unquestionable skill as an operator, the dons, who acknowledged his talent, shook their heads gravely when two or three of them, in private and solemn conclave, talked confidentially of their younger brother.

If there were many things in his favour, there were more in his disfavour. He was Irish – not merely by the accident of birth, which might have been forgiven, since a man cannot be held accountable for such caprices of Nature, but by every other accident and design which is objectionable to the orthodox and respectable and representative English mind.

In speech, appearance, manner, habits, modes of expression, habits of life, Hertford O'Donnell was Irish. To the core of his heart he loved the island which he, nevertheless, declared he never meant to revisit; and amongst the English he moved, to all intents and purposes, a foreigner who was resolved, so said the great prophets at Guy's, to go to destruction as fast as he could and let no man hinder him.

'He means to go the whole length of his tether,' observed one of the ancient wiseacres to another; which speech implied a conviction that Hertford O'Donnell, having sold himself to the Evil One, had determined to dive the full length of his rope into wickedness before being pulled to the shore where even wickedness is negative – where there are no mad carouses, no wild, sinful excitement, nothing but impotent wailing and gnashing of teeth.

A reckless, graceless, clever, wicked devil – going to his natural home as fast as in London a man can possibly progress thither: this was the opinion his superiors held of the man who lived all alone with a housekeeper and her husband (who acted as butler) in his big house near Soho.

Gerrard Street was not then an utterly shady and forgotten locality: carriage patients found their way to the rising young surgeon – some great personages thought it not beneath them to fee an individual whose consulting rooms were situated on what was even then the wrong side of Regent Street. He was making money; and he was spending it; he was over head and ears in debt – useless, vulgar debt – senselessly contracted, never bravely faced. He had lived at an awful pace ever since he came to London, at a pace which only a man who hopes and expects to die young can ever travel.

Life! what good was it? Death! was he a child, or a woman, or a coward, to be afraid of that hereafter? God knew all about the trifle which had upset his coach better than the dons at Guy's; and he did not dread facing his Maker, and giving an account to Him, even of the disreputable existence he had led since he came to London.

Hertford O'Donnell knew the world pretty well, and the ways thereof were to him as roads often traversed; therefore, when he said that at the day of judgment he felt certain he should come off better than many of those who censured him, it may be assumed that, although his views of post-mortem punishment were vague, unsatisfactory, and infidel, still his information as to the peccadilloes of his neighbours was such as consoled himself.

And yet, living all alone in the old house near Soho Square, grave thoughts would intrude frequently into the surgeon's mind

– thoughts which were, so to say, italicized by peremptory letters, and still more peremptory visits, from people who wanted money.

Although he had many acquaintances, he had no single friend, and accordingly these thoughts were received and brooded over in solitude, in those hours when, after returning from dinner or supper, or congenial carouse, he sat in his dreary room smoking his pipe and considering means and ways, chances and certainties.

In good truth he had started in London with some vague idea that as his life in it would not be of long continuance, the pace at which he elected to travel could be of little consequence; but the years since his first entry into the metropolis were now piled one on the top of another, his youth was behind him, his chances of longevity, spite of the way he had striven to injure his constitution, quite as good as ever. He had come to that time in existence, to that narrow strip of table land whence the ascent of youth and the descent of age are equally discernible – when, simply because he has lived for so many years, it strikes a man as possible he may have to live for just as many more, with the ability for hard work gone, with the boon companions scattered abroad, with the capacity for enjoying convivial meetings a mere memory, with small means, perhaps, with no bright hopes, with the pomp and the equipage, and the fairy carriages, and the glamour which youth flings over earthly objects, faded away like the pageant of yesterday, while the dreary ceremony of living has to be gone through to-day and to-morrow and the morrow after, as though the gay cavalcade and the martial music, and the glittering helmets and the prancing steeds were still accompanying the wayfarer to his journey's end.

Ah! my friends, there comes a moment when we must all leave the coach with its four bright bays, its pleasant outside freight, its cheery company, its guard who blows the horn so merrily through villages and along lonely country roads.

Long before we reach that final stage, where the black

business claims us for its own especial property, we have to bid good-bye to all easy thoughtless journeying, and betake ourselves, with what zest we will, to traversing the common of Reality. There is no royal road across it that ever I heard of. From the king on his throne to the labourer who vaguely imagines what manner of being a king is, we have all to tramp across that desert at one period of our lives, at all events, and that period usually is when, as I have said, a man starts to find the hopes and the strength and the buoyancy of youth left behind, while years and years of life lie stretching out before him.

Even supposing a man's spring-time to have been a cold and ungenial one, with bitter easterly winds and nipping frosts, biting the buds and retarding the blossom, still it was spring for all that – spring, with the young green leaves sprouting forth, with the flowers unfolding tenderly, with the songs of birds and the rush of waters, with the summer before and the autumn afar off, and winter remote as death and eternity; but when once the trees have donned their summer foliage, when the pure white blossoms have disappeared, and a gorgeous red and orange, and purple blaze of many-coloured flowers fills the gardens; then, if there comes a wet, dreary day, the idea of autumn and winter is not so difficult to realise. When once twelve o'clock is reached, the evening and night become facts, not possibilities; and it was of the afternoon and the evening and the night, Hertford O'Donnell sat thinking on the Christmas Eve when I crave permission to introduce him to my readers.

A good-looking man, ladies considered him. A tall, dark-complexioned, black-haired, straight-limbed, deeply, divinely blue-eyed fellow, with a soft voice, with a pleasant brogue, who had ridden like a Centaur over the loose stone walls in Connemara, who had danced all night at the Dublin balls, who had walked over the Bennebeola mountains, gun in hand, day after day without weariness: who had led a mad, wild life while 'studying for a doctor' – as the Irish phrase goes – in Dublin, and who, after the death of his eldest brother left him free to return to Calgillan and pursue the usual utterly useless, utterly purposeless, utterly pleasant life of an Irish gentleman possessed of health, birth, and expectations, suddenly kicked over the paternal traces, bade adieu to Calgillan Castle and the blandishments of a certain beautiful Miss Clifden, beloved of his mother, and laid out to be his wife, walked down the avenue without even so much company as a gossoon to carry his carpet-bag, shook the dust from his feet at the lodge-gates, and took his seat on the coach, never once looking back at Calgillan, where his favourite mare was standing in the stable, his greyhounds chasing one another round the home paddock, his gun at half-cock in his dressing-room, and his fishing-tackle all in order and ready for use.

He had not kissed his mother nor asked for his father's blessing; he left Miss Clifden arrayed in her brand-new riding-habit, without a word of affection or regret; he had spoken no syllable of farewell to any servant about the place; only when the old woman at the lodge bade him good morning and God-blessed his handsome face, he recommended her bitterly to look well at it, for she would never see it more.

Twelve years and a half had passed since then without either Nancy Blake or any other one of the Calgillan people having set eyes on Master Hertford's handsome face. He had kept his vow to himself – he had not written home; he had not been indebted to mother or father for even a tenpenny-piece during the whole of that time; he had lived without God – so far as God ever lets a man live without him – and his own private conviction was that he could get on very well without either. One thing only he felt to be needful – money; money to keep him when the evil days of sickness, or age, or loss of practice came upon him. Though a spendthrift, he was not a simpleton. Around him he saw men, who, having started with fairer prospects than his own, were nevertheless reduced to indigence; and he knew that what had happened to others might happen to himself.

An unlucky cut, slipping on a bit of orange-peel in the street, the merest accident imaginable, is sufficient to change opulence to beggary in the life's programme of an individual whose income depends on eye, on nerve, on hand; and besides the consciousness of this fact, Hertford O'Donnell knew that beyond a certain point in his profession progress was not easy.

It did not depend quite on the strength of his own bow or shield whether he counted his earnings by hundreds or thousands. Work may achieve competence; but mere work cannot, in a profession at all events, compass wealth.

He looked around him, and he perceived that the majority of great men – great and wealthy – had been indebted for their elevation more to the accidents of birth, patronage, connection, or marriage than to personal ability.

Personal ability, no doubt, they possessed; but then, little Jones, who lived in Frith Street, and who could barely keep himself and his wife and family, had ability, too, only he lacked the concomitants of success.

He wanted something or some one to puff him into notoriety – a brother at court – a lord's leg to mend – a rich wife to give him prestige in society; and, lacking this something or some one, he had grown grey-haired and faint-hearted in the service of that world which utterly despises its most obsequious servants.

'Clatter along the streets with a pair of hired horses, snub the middle classes, and drive over the commonalty – that is the way to compass wealth and popularity in England,' said Hertford O'Donnell bitterly; and, as the man desired wealth and popularity, he sat before his fire, with a foot on each hob, and a short pipe in his mouth, considering how he might best obtain the means to clatter along the streets in his carriage, and splash plebeians with mud from his wheels like the best.

In Dublin he could, by means of his name and connection, have done well; but then he was not in Dublin, neither did he want to be. The bitterest memories of his life were inseparable from the name of the Green Island, and he had no desire to return to it.

Besides, in Dublin, heiresses are not quite so plentiful as in London; and an heiress, Hertford O'Donnell had decided, would do more for him than years of steady work.

A rich wife could clear him of debt, introduce him to fashionable practice, afford him that measure of social respectability which a medical bachelor invariably lacks; deliver him from the loneliness of Gerrard Street, and the domination of Mr. and Mrs. Coles.

To most men, deliberately bartering away their dependence for money seems so prosaic a business that they strive to gloss it over even to themselves, and to assign every reason for their choice, save that which is really the influencing one.

Not so, however, with Hertford O'Donnell. He sat beside the fire scoffing over his proposed bargain – thinking of the lady's age – her money-bags – her desirable house in town – her seat in the country – her snobbishness – her folly.

'It would be a fitting ending,' he sneered; 'and why I did not settle the matter to-night passes my comprehension. I am not a fool, to be frightened with old women's tales; and yet I must have turned white. I felt I did, and she asked me whether I was ill. And then to think of my being such an idiot as to ask her if she had heard anything like a cry, as though she would be likely to hear *that* – she, with her poor *parvenu* blood, which, I often imagine, must have been mixed with some of her father's strong pickling vinegar. What the deuce could I have been dreaming about? I wonder what it really was?' and Hertford O'Donnell pushed his hair back from his forehead and took another draught from the too familiar tumbler, which was placed conveniently on the chimney piece.

'After expressly making up my mind to propose, too!' he mentally continued. 'Could it have been conscience – that myth, which somebody, who knew nothing of the matter, said "makes cowards of us all?" I don't believe in conscience; and even if there be such a thing capable of being developed by sentiment and cultivation, why should it trouble me? I have no intention of wronging Miss Janet Price Ingot – not the least. Honestly and fairly I shall marry her; honestly and fairly I shall act by her. An old wife is not exactly an ornamental article of furniture in a man's house; and I do not know that the fact of her being well gilded makes her look any more ornamental. But she shall have no cause for complaint; and I will go and dine with her to-morrow and settle the matter.'

Having arrived at which resolution, Mr. O'Donnell arose, kicked down the fire – burning hollow – with the heel of his boot, knocked the ashes out of his pipe, emptied his tumbler, and bethought him it was time to go to bed. He was not in the habit of taking rest so early as a quarter to twelve o'clock; but he felt unusually weary – tired mentally and bodily – and lonely beyond all power of expression.

'The fair Janet would be better than this,' he said, half aloud; and then, with a start and a shiver and a blanched face, he turned sharply round, whilst a low, sobbing, wailing cry echoed mourn-fully through the room. No form of words could give an idea of the sound. The plaintiveness of the Eolian harp – that plaintive-ness which so soon affects and lowers the highest spirits – would have seemed wildly gay in comparison to the sadness of the cry which seemed floating in the air. As the summer wind comes and goes amongst the trees, so that mournful wail came and went – came and went. It came in a rush of sound, like a gradual crescendo managed by a skilful musician, and it died away like a lingering note, so that the listener could scarcely tell the exact moment when it faded away into silence.

I say faded away, for it disappeared as the coast line disappears in the twilight, and there was utter stillness in the apartment.

Then for the first time, Hertford O'Donnell looked at his dog, and, beholding the creature crouched into a corner beside the fireplace, called upon him to come out.

His voice sounded strange, even to himself, and apparently the dog thought so too, for he made no effort to obey the summons.

'Come out, sir,' his master repeated, and then the animal came crawling reluctantly forward, with his hair on end, his eyes almost starting from his head, trembling violently, as the surgeon, who caressed him, felt.

'So you heard it, Brian?' he said to the dog. 'And so your ears are sharper than hers, old fellow? It's a mighty queer thing to think of, being favoured with a visit from a banshee in Gerrard Street; and as the lady has travelled so far, I only wish I knew whether there is any sort of refreshment she would like to take after her long journey.'

He spoke loudly and with a certain mocking defiance, seeming to think the phantom he addressed would reply; but when he stopped at the end of his sentence, no sound came through the stillness. There was utter silence in the room – silence broken only by the falling of the cinders on the hearth, and the breathing of the dog.

'If my visitor would tell me,' he proceeded, 'for whom this lamentation is being made, whether for myself, or for some member of my illustrious family, I should feel immensely obliged. It seems too much honour for a poor surgeon to have such attention paid him. Good heavens! What is that?' he exclaimed, as a ring, loud and peremptory, woke all the echoes in the house, and brought his housekeeper, in a state of distressing dishabille, 'out of her warm bed,' as she subsequently stated, to the head of the staircase.

Across the hall Hertford O'Donnell strode, relieved at the prospect of speaking to any living being. He took no precaution of putting up the chain, but flung the door wide. A dozen burglars would have proved welcome in comparison to that ghostly intruder; and, as I have said, he threw the door open, admitting a rush of wet, cold air, which made poor Mrs. Coles's few remaining teeth chatter in her head.

'Who is there? – what do you want?' asked the surgeon, seeing no person, and hearing no voice. 'Who is there? – why the devil can't you speak?'

251

But when even this polite exhortation failed to elicit an answer, he passed out into the night, and looked up the street, and down the street, to see nothing but the drizzling rain and the blinking lights.

'If this goes on much longer, I shall soon think I must be either mad or drunk,' he muttered, as he re-entered the house and locked and bolted the door once more.

'Lord's sake! what is the matter, sir?' asked Mrs. Coles, from the upper flight, careful only to reveal the borders of her nightcap to Mr. O'Donnell's admiring gaze 'Is anybody killed? – have you to go out, sir?'

'It was only a runaway ring,' he answered, trying to reassure himself with an explanation he did not in his heart believe.

'Runaway! – I'd runaway them,' murmured Mrs. Coles, as she retired to the conjugal couch, where Coles was, to quote her own expression, 'snoring like a pig through it all.' Almost immediately afterwards she heard her master ascend the stairs and close his bedroom door.

'Madam will surely be too much of a gentlewoman to intrude here,' thought the surgeon, scoffing even at his own fears; but when he lay down he did not put out his light, and he made Brian leap up and crouch on the coverlet beside him.

The man was fairly frightened, and would have thought it no discredit to his manhood to acknowledge as much. He was not afraid of death, he was not afraid of trouble, he was not afraid of danger; but he was afraid of the banshee; and as he lay with his hand on the dog's head, he thought over all the stories he had ever heard about this family retainer in the days of his youth. He had not thought about her for years and years. Never before had he heard her voice himself. When his brother died, she had not thought it necessary to travel up to Dublin and give him notice of the impending catastrophe. 'If she had, I would have gone down to Calgillan, and perhaps saved his life,' considered the surgeon. 'I wonder who this is for! If for me, that will settle my debts and my marriage. If I could be quite certain it was either of the old people, I would start for Ireland to-morrow.' And then vaguely his mind wandered on to think of every banshee story he had ever heard in his life. About the beautiful lady with the wreath of flowers, who sat on the rocks below Red Castle, in the County Antrim, crying till one of the sons died for love of her; about the Round Chamber at Dunluce, which was swept clean by the banshee every night; about the bed in a certain great house in Ireland, which was slept in constantly, although no human being passed ever in or out after dark; about that general officer who, the night before Waterloo, said to a friend, 'I have heard the banshee, and shall not come off the field alive to-morrow; break the news gently to poor Carry;' and who, nevertheless, coming safe off the field, had subsequently news about poor Carry broken tenderly and pitifully to him; about the lad who, aloft in the rigging, hearing through the night a sobbing and wailing coming over the waters, went down to the captain and told him he was afraid they were somehow out of their reckoning, just in time to save the ship, which when morning broke, they found, but for his warning, would have been on the rocks. It was blowing great guns, and the sea was all fret and turmoil, and they could sometimes see in the trough of the waves, as down a valley, the cruel black reefs they had escaped.

On deck the captain stood speaking to the boy who had saved them, and asking how he knew of their danger; and when the lad told him, the captain laughed, and said her ladyship had been outwitted that time.

But the boy answered, with a grave shake of his head, that the warning was either for him or his, and that if he got safe to port there would be bad tidings waiting for him from home; whereupon the captain bade him go below, and get some brandy and lie down.

He got the brandy, and he laid down, but he never rose again; and when the storm abated – when a great calm succeeded to the previous tempest – there was a very solemn funeral at sea; and on their arrival at Liverpool the captain took a journey to Ireland to tell a widowed mother how her only son died, and to bear his few effects to the poor, desolate soul.

And Hertford O'Donnell thought again about his own father, riding full-chase across country, and hearing, as he galloped by a clump of plantation, something like a sobbing and wailing. The hounds were in full cry; but he still felt, as he afterwards expressed it, that there was something among those trees he could not pass; and so he jumped off his horse, and hung the reins over the branch of a fir and beat the cover well, but not a thing could he find in it.

Then, for the first time in his life, Miles O'Donnell turned his horse's head *from* the hunt, and, within a mile of Calgillan, met a man running to tell him Mr. Martin's gun had burst and hurt him badly.

And he remembered the story, also, of how Mary O'Donnell, his great-aunt, being married to a young Englishman, heard the banshee as she sat one evening waiting for his return; and of how she, thinking the bridge by which he often came home unsafe for horse and man, went out in a great panic, to meet and entreat him go round by the main road for her sake. Sir Everard was riding alone in the moonlight, making straight for the bridge, when he beheld a figure dressed all in white upon it. Then there was a crash, and the figure disappeared.

The lady was rescued and brought back to the hall; but next morning there were two dead bodies within its walls – those of Lady Eyreton and her still-born son.

Quicker than I write them, these memories chased one another through Hertford O'Donnell's brain; and there was one more terrible memory than any, which would recur to him, concerning an Irish nobleman who, seated alone in his great town-house in London, heard the banshee, and rushed out to get rid of the phantom, which wailed in his ear, nevertheless, as he strode down Piccadilly. And then the surgeon remembered how he went with a friend to the opera, feeling sure that there no banshee, unless she had a box, could find admittance, until suddenly he heard her singing up amongst the highest part of the scenery, with a terrible mournfulness, with a pathos which made the prima donna's tenderest notes seem harsh by comparison.

As he came out, some quarrel arose between him and a famous fire-eater, against whom he stumbled; and the result was that the next afternoon there was a new Lord —, *vice* Lord —, killed in a duel with Captain Bravo.

Memories like these are not the most enlivening possible; they are apt to make a man fanciful, and nervous, and wakeful; but as time ran on, Hertford O'Donnell fell asleep, with his candle still burning and Brian's cold nose pressed against his hand.

He dreamt of his mother's family – the Hertfords, of Artingbury, Yorkshire, far-off relatives of Lord Hertford – so far off that even Mrs. O'Donnell held no clue to the genealogical maze.

He thought he was at Artingbury, fishing; that it was a misty summer's morning and the fish rising beautifully. In his dream he hooked one after another, and the boy who was with him threw them into the basket.

At last there was one more difficult to land than the others; and the boy, in his eagerness to watch the sport, drew nearer and nearer to the brink, while the fisher, intent on his prey, failed to notice his companion's danger.

Suddenly there was a cry, a splash, and the boy disappeared from sight.

Next instant he rose again, however, and then, for the first time, Hertford O'Donnell saw his face.

It was one he knew well.

In a moment he plunged into the water, and struck out for the lad. He had him by the hair, he was turning to bring him back to land, when the stream suddenly changed into a wide, wild, shoreless sea, where the billows were chasing one another with a mad, demoniac mirth.

For a while O'Donnell kept the lad and himself afloat. They were swept under the waves, and came forth again, only to see larger waves rushing towards them; but through all the surgeon never loosened his hold until a tremendous billow engulfing them both, tore the boy from him.

With the horror of that he awoke, to hear a voice saying quite distinctly: 'Go to the hospital! – go at once!'

The surgeon started up in bed, rubbed his eyes and looked about him. The candle was flickering faintly in its socket. Brian, with his ears pricked forward, had raised his head at his master's sudden jump.

Everything was quiet, but still those words were ringing in his ear —

'Go to the hospital! – go at once!'

The tremendous peal of the bell overnight, and this sentence, seemed to be simultaneous.

That he was wanted at Guy's – wanted imperatively – came to O'Donnell like an inspiration.

Neither sense nor reason had anything to do with the conviction that roused him out of bed, and made him dress as speedily as possible and grope his way down the staircase, Brian following.

He opened the front door and passed out into the darkness. The rain was over, and the stars were shining as he pursued his way down Newport Market, and thence, winding in and out in a south-east direction, through Lincoln's Inn Fields and Old Square to Chancery Lane, whence he proceeded to St. Paul's.

Along the deserted streets he resolutely continued his walk. He did not know what he was going to Guy's for. Some instinct was urging him on, and he neither strove to combat nor control it. Only once had the thought of turning back occurred, and that was at the archway leading into Old Square. There he had paused for a moment, asking himself whether he were not gone stark, staring mad; but Guy's seemed preferable to the haunted house in Gerrard Street, and he walked resolutely on, determining to say, if any surprise were expressed at his appearance, that he had been sent for.

On, thinking of many things: of his wild life in London; of the terrible cry he had heard overnight – that terrible wail which he could not drive away from his memory, even as he entered Guy's, and confronted the porter, who said:

'You have just been sent for, sir; did you meet the messenger?'

Like one in a dream, Hertford O'Donnell heard him; like one in a dream, also, he asked what was the matter.

'Bad accident, sir: fire; fall of a balcony – unsafe – old building. Mother and child – a son; child with compound fracture of thigh.' This, the joint information of porter and house-surgeon, mingled together, and made a roar in Mr. O'Donnell's ears like the sound of the sea breaking on a shingly shore.

Only one sentence he understood perfectly – 'Immediate amputation necessary.' At this point he grew cool; he was the careful, cautious, successful surgeon in a moment.

'The child, you say?' he answered; 'let me see him.'

In the days of which I am writing, the two surgeons had to pass a staircase leading to the upper stories. On the lower step of this staircase, partially in shadow, Hertford O'Donnell beheld as he came forward, an old woman seated.

An old woman with streaming grey hair, with attenuated arms, with head bowed forward, with scanty clothing, with bare feet; who never looked up at their approach, but sat unnoticing, shaking her head and wringing her hands in an extremity of grief.

'Who is that?' asked Mr. O'Donnell, almost involuntarily.

'Who is what?' demanded his companion.

'That – that woman,' was the reply.

'What woman?'

'There – are you blind? – seated on the bottom step of the staircase. What is she doing?' persisted Mr. O'Donnell.

'There is no woman near us,' his companion answered, looking at the rising surgeon very much as though he suspected him of seeing double.

'No woman!' scoffed Hertford. 'Do you expect me to

disbelieve the evidence of my own eyes?' and he walked up to the figure, meaning to touch it.

But as he essayed to do so, the woman seemed to rise in the air and float away, with her arms stretched high up over her head, uttering such a wail of pain, and agony, and distress, as caused the Irishman's blood to curdle.

'My God! did you hear that?' he said to his companion.

'What?' was the reply.

Then, although he knew the sound had fallen on deaf ears, he answered —

'The wail of the banshee! Some of my people are doomed!'

'I trust not,' answered the house-surgeon.

With nerves utterly shaken, Mr. O'Donnell walked forward to the accident ward. There, with his face shaded from the light, lay his patient – a young boy, with a compound fracture of the thigh.

In that ward, in the face of actual pain or danger capable of relief, the surgeon had never known faltering nor fear; and now he carefully examined the injury, felt the pulse, inquired as to the treatment pursued, and ordered the sufferer to be carried to the operating room.

While he was laying out his instruments he heard the boy lying on the table murmur faintly —

'Tell her not to cry so – tell her not to cry.'

'What is he talking about?' Hertford O'Donnell inquired.

'The nurse says he has been speaking about some woman crying ever since he came in – his mother, most likely,' answered one of the attendants.

'He is delirious, then?' observed the surgeon.

'No, sir,' pleaded the boy excitedly. 'No; it is that woman – that woman with the grey hair. I saw her looking from the upper window before the balcony gave way. She has never left me since, and she won't be quiet, wringing her hands and crying.'

'Can you see her now?' Hertford O'Donnell inquired, stepping to the side of the table. 'Point out where she stands.'

Then the lad stretched forth a feeble finger in the direction of the door, where clearly, as he had seen her seated on the stairs, the surgeon saw a woman standing – a woman with grey hair and scanty clothing, and upstretched arms and bare feet.

'A word with you, sir,' O'Donnell said to the house surgeon, drawing him back from the table. 'I cannot perform this operation: send for some other person. I am ill; I am incapable.'

'But,' pleaded the other, 'there is no time to get anyone else. We sent for Mr. — before we troubled you, but he was out of town, and all the rest of the surgeons live so far away. Mortification may set in at any moment, and —' then Hertford O'Donnell fell fainting on the floor.

How long he lay in that dead-like swoon I cannot say: but when he returned to consciousness, the principal physician of Guy's was standing beside him in the cold grey light of the Christmas morning.

'The boy?' murmured O'Donnell faintly.

'Now, my dear fellow, keep yourself quiet,' was the reply.

'The boy?' he repeated irritably. 'Who operated?'

'No one,' Dr. — answered. 'It would have been useless cruelty. Mortification had set in, and —'

Hertford O'Donnell turned his face to the wall, and his friend could not see it.

'Do not distress yourself,' went on the physician kindly. 'Allington says he could not have survived the operation in any case. He was quite delirious from the first, raving about a woman with grey hair, and —'

'Yes, I know,' Hertford O'Donnell interrupted; 'and the boy had a mother, they told me, or I dreamt it.'

'Yes; bruised and shaken, but not seriously injured.'

'Has she blue eyes and fair hair – fair hair rippling and wavy? Is she white as a lily, with just a faint flush of colour in her cheeks? Is she young, and trusting, and innocent? No; I am wandering. She must be nearly thirty now. Go, for God's sake, and tell me if you can find a woman that you could imagine having been as a girl such as I describe.'

'Irish?' asked the doctor; and O'Donnell made a gesture of assent.

'It is she then,' was the reply; 'a woman with the face of an angel.'

'A woman who should have been my wife,' the surgeon answered; 'whose child was my son.'

'Lord help you!' ejaculated the doctor. Then Hertford O'Donnell raised himself from the sofa where they had laid him, and told his companion the story of his life – how there had been bitter feud between his people and her people – how they were divided by old animosities and by difference of religion – how they had met by stealth, and exchanged rings and vows, all for nought – how his family had insulted hers, so that her father, wishful for her to marry a kinsman of his own, bore her off to a far-away land, and made her write him a letter of eternal farewell – how his own parents had kept all knowledge of the quarrel from him till she was utterly beyond his reach – how they had vowed to discard him unless he agreed to marry according to their wishes – how he left home, and came to London, and pushed his fortune. All this Hertford O'Donnell repeated; and when he had finished, the bells were ringing for morning service – ringing loudly – ringing joyfully: 'Peace on earth, good will towards men.'

But there was little peace that morning for Hertford O'Donnell. He had to look on the face of his dead son, wherein he beheld, as though reflected, the face of the boy in his dream.

Stealthily he followed his friend, and beheld, with her eyes closed, her cheeks pale and pinched, her hair thinner, but still falling like a veil over her, the love of his youth, the only woman he had ever loved devotedly and unselfishly.

There is little space left here to tell of how the two met at last – of how the stone of the years seemed suddenly rolled away from the tomb of their past, and their youth arose and returned to them, amid their tears.

She had been true to him, through persecution, through

contumely, through kindness, which was more trying; through shame, and grief, and poverty, she had been loyal to the lover of her youth; and before the new year dawned there came a letter from Calgillan, saying that the banshee had been heard there, and praying Hertford, if he was still alive, to let bygones be bygones, in consideration of the long years of estrangement – the anguish and remorse of his afflicted parents.

More than that, Hertford O'Donnell, if a reckless man, was an honourable one; and so, on the Christmas Day, when he was to have proposed for Miss Ingot, he went to that lady and told her how he had wooed and won in the years of his youth one who, after many days, was miraculously restored to him. And from the hour in which he took her into his confidence he never thought her either vulgar or foolish, but rather he paid homage to the woman who, when she had heard the whole tale repeated, said simply, 'Ask her to come to me till you claim her – and God bless you both.'

The Haunted Haven

A. E. Ellis

Attention all shipping. The Meteorological Office issued the following gale warning at 1600 hours: south-westerly gale, force eight, imminent in sea areas Irish Sea, Lundy, and Fastnet.

In the south-eastern angle of St Bride's Bay, sheltered from the south-west winds by the projecting tongue of land that ends in Wooltack Point, nestles the little fishing village of Ticklas Haven, which consists of an inn, a compact group of cottages, a stout jetty partly fashioned out of the living rock, and two snug little coves or havens, one on each side of the jetty. In the more northerly of these tiny bays ten or a dozen fishing smacks may usually be seen riding at their moorings, or lying in lopsided idleness at ebb tide. In the other cove, although it appears more sheltered and suitable in every way for use as a harbour, never a boat will be seen, nor any signs of human occupation, such as the lobster-pots, coils of rope, nets and tarpaulins, which litter the foreshore of the north cove.

Four steep roads converge upon the village, two from the landward side and two from the coast to the north and the south-west. About a furlong up the more southerly of the landward roads, a hundred and fifty feet above the cluster of cottages in the haven, stands a ruined house, still known in the village as the Doctor's House, although now deserted for some thirty years. Little remains of this once imposing and substantial dwelling, a mansion in comparison with the fishermen's cottages it dominates, save the ivy-grown walls, through which the Atlantic gales shriek and wail, and the heavy wooden gate, which creaks and bangs in the wind like demoniac artillery.

For a quiet and restful summer resort Ticklas Haven is hard to beat, and I congratulated myself on my good fortune in not only discovering so cosy a nook, but in securing comfortable lodging at the inn. The landlord was a kindly and intelligent man, some fifty years of age, and his wife a cheerful and competent house-wife and an excellent cook. My days were mostly spent fishing for mackerel in the bay, taking long tramps up and down the rugged coast, or simply lolling amongst the soft lush grass on the cliff-tops, drinking in the glorious panorama of St Bridge's Bay, as it sweeps round in a majestic curve from Ramsey Island in the north to the Isle of Skomer in the south. When the weather was too boisterous for outdoor pursuits, there was the snug bar-parlour of the inn, and the rough but genial society of the fishermen who frequented it. It was there that I was sitting one August evening when the radio in the bar gave utterance to that ominous gale warning.

At the mention of south-westerly gales, I perceived a sudden start amongst the fishermen present, and apprehensive glances were exchanged. Several boats were to be seen fishing in the bay, and one or two of the men walked to the door and peered out anxiously at the distant smacks.

'Glad I'm not out there now,' muttered one old salt.

'Hope my son William'll get in before dark,' said another.

This display of alarm was surprising, for the bay is sheltered to a great extent from the south-west wind, and in any case the boats were all near enough in to make harbour before being overtaken by the oncoming gale, of which the sky was already giving ample warning. I remarked as much to the innkeeper, who agreed that the boats were in no real danger, but added that nobody in Ticklas Haven would willingly be out in the bay, or even in the neighbourhood of the harbour, after nightfall, when the wind blew strongly from the south-west: it amounted to a fixed tradition with them. I at once became eager to learn the origin of this strange superstition, and besought the landlord to enlighten me further.

'Well, it's a strange story,' replied the innkeeper, 'and I can best begin by showing you a picture that a painter who stayed here many years ago gave to my grandfather, when he was landlord of this inn.'

So saying, he led the way into a back parlour and pointed to an oil-painting hanging on the wall in a dark corner. I took it down and carried it to the window, and saw that it represented the harbour at Ticklas Haven as seen from the beach at low tide. Although about eighty years old, the painting might almost have been done yesterday, for everything was depicted much as it is now, with one striking exception. The north haven, where now all the boats are kept, was in the picture practically deserted, except for some children at play on the sand, whilst the south haven presented just such a scene of activity as would be expected in so excellent a harbour. Half a dozen fishing-boats lay high and dry at its entrance, while on the shingle sat a group of fishermen mending sails and nets. Two or three women were carrying baskets of fish up towards the village, and the usual litter of gear was scattered over the foreshore. In fact the two little inlets presented an aspect just the reverse of their present-day appearance.

'Why is it,' I asked, 'that the south haven, which seems so clearly the better of the two, has now been abandoned in favour of the other, which was apparently in use in your grandfather's day?'

'That is precisely what I am about to tell you,' replied the landlord.

The Innkeeper's Story

When I was a lad that south haven was still used, as you see it in that picture, and very few boats put into the north haven, which is, as you observe, less sheltered and convenient.

There lived in the village in those days three brothers, who worked for their uncle, the owner of a fishing-boat and gear. They were tall, strong young fellows, these three brothers, but of a morose disposition, and mixed little with other folk in the village. They were very hardy and fearless and would put to sea in all but the most tempestuous weather, usually accompanied by their uncle, who was a first-rate seaman and could handle a craft in all seas. He was a grasping old ruffian, however, and on the strength of his ownership of the boat he appropriated most of the profits of the fishing and allowed his nephews barely enough to live upon, with the understanding that on his death they would inherit his property. His niggardliness was a source of much discontent amongst the brothers, who bore their uncle no affection and only continued to work for him in the expectation of some day possessing his wealth, which, owing to economy and judicious investment was pretty considerable for a man in his position.

One spring night – I was seventeen at the time – the four put to sea, although it was beginning to blow up a gale from the south-west and the crews of none of the other boats would venture out. We watched them beating out past the Stack Rocks till they were hidden by the rain and darkness, and some of us wondered whether we should ever see them again.

Early next morning the boat returned, with no fish, and without the uncle. The brothers' story was that he had been carried overboard by a huge wave and had at once disappeared. It was useless to search for him and they were themselves in great peril. They had a very rough time getting back and the boat and gear were badly damaged. The three brothers seemed more upset about the accident than one might have expected, considering the unfriendly relations existing between them and their uncle, by whose death they now became comparatively well off. They were loud in their expressions of grief at their loss and repeatedly cursed their folly in putting to sea on such a night.

Two days later the uncle's body was washed ashore in the south haven, where it was found by a fisherman in the early morning actually caught on the anchor of his own boat. The body was carried up to the quay, where it was noticed that there was a long, livid bruise across the right temple. The doctor, who lived in that big house, now a ruin, up the hill, examined the corpse, and at the inquest expressed the opinion that the bruise had been inflicted before death and had been caused by a severe blow from some blunt instrument, such as a club – or perhaps a tiller.

The coroner looked up sharply at this, and asked if the bruise might not equally well have been caused by the deceased striking his head against the mast or the gunwale of the boat in falling overboard. The doctor agreed that that might have been the cause of the injury, but added that he could not believe that such a severe blow could have been inflicted in such a manner.

The eldest brother was then re-examined as to what precisely took place, and deposed that his uncle had been knocked overboard by the boom suddenly swinging over and striking him on the head. This fresh testimony was corroborated by the other brothers, although previously they had all repeatedly affirmed that their uncle was simply washed overboard by a wave and had made no mention of the boom. The jury, however, brought in a verdict of 'death by misadventure'. The coroner was later criticized for not excluding two of the brothers from the court while the first was giving evidence. The deceased was buried next day in the churchyard at Walwyn's Castle. That was near the end of April.

In the last week of May the youngest of the three brothers slipped on the jetty when landing from the boat one dark night, there being a heavy sea running due to a strong south-west wind, and broke his neck on the rocks in the south haven below.

Towards the end of June the eldest brother, being harbour-bound by a south-westerly gale, was gathering mussels and limpets on the rocks at the far side of the south haven, when a large stone fell from the cliff above and smashed in his skull.

Within a month the surviving brother was overtaken by a

sudden squall, coming up from the south-west, while fishing out by Grassholm, and was washed ashore, together with the wreck of his boat, about a week later, at almost the identical spot where his uncle's body had been found. The boat, so battered as to be no longer seaworthy, was hauled up on the shingle and left there to rot.

The violent deaths of these three brothers, following so regularly one after the other, considered together with the suspicious circumstances attending their uncle's death, gave cause for much gossip amongst the village folk, and what had at first been but a vague uneasiness developed into a general conviction that there had been foul play.

Some nine months after the death of the last of the brothers, we had a spell of very rough weather, with strong gales from the south-west, and the fishermen were idle for weeks on end. A large amount of driftwood was cast up during these storms and the men employed themselves in gathering and storing this for firewood. There was one old man in particular, now too infirm ever to go out fishing, who was to be seen early and late collecting this wood, and at low tide was always hobbling about the haven like some ungainly sea-bird, leaving off only when it grew too dark to see.

One stormy night the old man failed to return home and a search was made at daybreak. We had not far to look: his body was found wedged among the rocks in the south haven, with a ragged cut across the forehead. On his face was such a look of horror as I pray I may never see again. The doctor said that in his opinion the old man had received a bad fright and had started to run away, but had tripped over a boulder and stunned himself. He had then been drowned by the incoming tide. What on earth could have so terrified him was a mystery.

Some three months later, when the wind was again blowing strongly from the south-west, a girl of fifteen, daughter of one of the fishermen, went over to the rocks beyond the south haven to collect shellfish. She stayed too long and was cut off by the flowing tide, but her parents were not worried, for she was quite safe and had taken some food with her, and would be able to get back when the tide was low again at about ten p.m. The sea was too rough for a boat to approach the rocks, and there was no way up the cliff, so she was just left to wait.

At half-past ten that night the girl suddenly burst into her home, screaming wildly and clearly crazed with terror. She had gone completely out of her mind and howled and raved like a maniac. Her cries soon attracted a crowd to the cottage and someone went and fetched the doctor. He could do nothing to calm the child, however, and had to put her under sedation. After being left under observation for a day or two she was taken away to the asylum, where she died soon afterwards without recovering her reason.

The most extraordinary feature of this sad case was what the poor child kept repeating in her insane ravings. It was all about 'dead men': 'the four dead men,' she would screech, 'the dead men in the boat!', and could utter nothing but incoherent phrases about 'the dead men'.

This second case of severe fright, following so soon after the death of the old wood-gatherer, and in the same place, namely the south haven, created a considerable stir amongst the villagers, and their fears were further increased by a peculiar occurrence which had been noticed several times and by many witnesses, including myself, namely that on the morning following a south-westerly gale tracks were seen in the sand leading down to the sea from the derelict boat, as if it had been launched and beached again during the night. This was humanly impossible, as the brothers' boat could not have floated for a single minute, but there the tracks always were at dawn after a high wind from the south-west, provided they had not been obliterated by the flowing tide.

One evening, shortly after the death of the poor demented girl, the doctor came into the bar-parlour here and asked to have a few words with my father in private. They came into this back room and the doctor told my father that he had been all around the village endeavouring to persuade someone to spend a night with him by the wrecked fishing-boat in the south haven when next the south-west wind blew a gale, in order to try and solve the mystery of those tracks in the sand, but not a man would go near the place after dark for love or money. The doctor then asked my father if he would watch with him, for otherwise he would go alone, and it was desirable to have more than one witness of whatever took place. My father, though not at all liking the job, eventually undertook to keep the doctor company.

It was not until the autumn equinoctial gales began that a suitable opportunity for the investigation occurred, but at last the wind blew so strongly from the south-west that the boats were unable to put to sea. At about ten o'clock one cloudy night the doctor called in for my father and the pair of them went down to the south haven. They found a sheltered corner amongst the rocks in full view of the wrecked boat, where they made themselves as comfortable as they could and began their watch. My father afterwards said that he had experienced only one thing in his life more unpleasant than the beginning of that vigil, and that was its end.

The wind, now blowing a whole gale, sent dense masses of black clouds hurtling across the moon, which intermittently shone forth upon as wild a scene as could be imagined. Even in this sheltered corner of the bay the breakers were dashing high up the rocks, while, farther out, the sea seemed to have gone mad and was foaming in tempestuous fury like a living thing in torment. No fishing-boat could have weathered such a storm for a moment.

So fiercely magnificent was the view across the bay that the two watchers became absorbed in contemplating it and forgot about the boat on which they were supposed to be keeping an eye. Suddenly my father's gaze was diverted by a movement on the sand below and he grasped the doctor's arm and pointed. There, half way between its normal resting place and the edge of the surf, was the wreck of the fishing-smack, while four men, two on each side, were hauling it down the beach!

The doctor gave a shout and began to clamber down from his perch on the rocks, but the men at the boat seemed not to hear the cry; they rapidly dragged the derelict down to the sea, launched it, and climbed aboard. Two of the men put out oars and started to row, one took the helm, while the fourth stationed himself in the bows. Then the old tub, with great rents in her sides and a hole in the bottom that a man could have crawled through, put out to sea and was quickly lost to view.

My father and the doctor stood by the edge of the sea like men thunderstruck until the incoming tide wet their legs and recalled them to themselves. They then went up the beach to make sure that it was the wreck that had thus been miraculously launched, and found that it was indeed gone. There could be no shadow of doubt that four men had put to sea in a near hurricane with a boat which would not normally have floated for ten seconds. There was nothing for it but to await the possible return of these uncanny mariners, so the two men returned to their former position on the rocks and kept a tireless watch upon the stormy sea.

Shortly after two o'clock in the morning their vigilance was rewarded by the sight of a boat approaching from the direction of the Stack Rocks. It drew rapidly inshore, and proved to be the old fishing-boat with her mysterious crew, who appeared quite unaffected by the mountainous seas and beached the boat as easily as if it had been a dead calm. The four men then dragged the boat up to its habitual place on the shingle and moved off in single file towards the village.

The doctor immediately jumped down and ran across the beach so as to intercept them, followed by my father. These two reached the foot of the quay where they waited for the four men to come up. On they came, walking stiffly in line, until they were abreast of the watchers, when the clouds covering the moon blew away and there was revealed a spectacle that sent my father

270

tearing blindly across the beach and turned the doctor sick and faint where he stood.

Those four men were the long dead and buried brothers and their uncle!

The doctor, rallying from the first shock, continued to gaze in horror as they passed. In front, marching with no movement beyond a mechanical swinging of the legs, was the old man, a great, livid weal across the side of his forehead. Behind him, with the same mechanical gait, stalked his three nephews, the first with his head all crushed and bloody, the next swollen and bloated and covered with a tangle of seaweed, and the third with his head hanging on one side at a horrible angle. So the four dead men walked up from the sea, and the doctor, overcome with dreadful nausea, collapsed in a dead faint.

The spray blowing over the jetty brought the doctor round from his fainting fit and he tottered to his feet. The ghastly procession had vanished, so he went in search of my father, whom he found lying insensible on the shingle in the north haven, having fallen and struck his head on the prow of a boat. Help was summoned and my father was carried home, but it was many days before he was sufficiently recovered to attend to business and he never altogether got over the shock he received on that awful night. Meanwhile the doctor resolved to have the old fishing-boat destroyed, in the hope of putting a stop to these supernatural proceedings. Not a soul in the place would now go near it, so the doctor, single-handed, built up a pile of brushwood around the wreck and set it alight. The whole thing was soon consumed and the ashes were cast into the sea so that not a trace remained.

At eleven o'clock that very night, as I was shutting up the inn, four men passed up the street walking stiffly in single file. I hastily closed and locked the door and ran up to my bedroom, the window of which overlooked the street. It was too dark to see much, but something about the figures filled me with dread, and the rearmost carried his head at an unnatural angle. I watched them until they turned up the hill leading to the doctor's house, and then went to bed. A little later I fancied I heard a scream coming from the hill, but it was not repeated and may merely have been a seagull crying.

Next day the woman who used to 'do' for the doctor came back to the village in great distress, saying that she had found the door open and the doctor gone. Search was made along the shore and all over the neighbourhood, but without success. A few days later the doctor's body was washed ashore by a high tide in the south haven and was deposited on the very spot where he had burnt the boat.

So now you can understand why we at Ticklas Haven avoid that south haven and fear the south-west wind.

'But do the dead men still haunt the haven when the sou'wester blows?' I asked.

'Nobody ever goes there to see,' replied the innkeeper.

The Judge's House

Bram Stoker

When the time for his examination drew near Malcolm Malcolmson made up his mind to go somewhere to read by himself. He feared the attractions of the seaside, and also he feared completely rural isolation, for of old he knew its charms, and so he determined to find some unpretentious little town where there would be nothing to distract him. He refrained from asking suggestions from any of his friends, for he argued that each would recommend some place of which he had knowledge, and where he had already acquaintances. As Malcolmson wished to avoid friends he had no wish to encumber himself with the attention of friends' friends, and so he determined to look out for a place for himself. He packed a portmanteau with some clothes and all the books he required, and then took ticket for the first name on the local time-table which he did not know.

When at the end of three hours' journey he alighted at Benchurch, he felt satisfied that he had so far obliterated his tracks as to be sure of having a peaceful opportunity of pursuing his studies. He went straight to the one inn which the sleepy little place contained, and put up for the night. Benchurch was a market town, and once in three weeks was crowded to excess, but for the remainder of the twenty-one days it was as attractive as a desert. Malcolmson looked around the day after his arrival to try to find quarters more isolated than even so quiet an inn as 'The Good Traveller' afforded. There was only one place which took his fancy, and it certainly satisfied his wildest ideas regarding quiet; in fact, quiet was not the proper word to apply to it – desolation was the only term conveying any suitable idea of its isolation. It was an old rambling, heavy-built house of the Jacobean style, with heavy gables and windows, unusually small, and set higher than was customary in such houses, and was surrounded with a high brick wall massively built. Indeed, on examination, it looked more like a fortified house than an ordinary dwelling. But all these things pleased Malcolmson. 'Here,' he thought, 'is the very spot I have been looking for, and if I can only get opportunity of using it I shall be happy.' His joy was increased when he realised beyond doubt that it was not at present inhabited.

From the post-office he got the name of the agent, who was rarely surprised at the application to rent a part of the old house. Mr Carnford, the local lawyer and agent, was a genial old gentleman, and frankly confessed his delight at anyone being willing to live in the house.

'To tell you the truth,' said he, 'I should be only too happy, on behalf of the owners, to let anyone have the house rent free for a term of years if only to accustom the people here to see it inhabited. It has been so long empty that some kind of absurd prejudice has grown up about it, and this can be best put down by its occupation – if only,' he added with a sly glance at Malcolmson, 'by a scholar like yourself, who wants its quiet for a time.'

Malcolmson thought it needless to ask the agent about the 'absurd prejudice'; he knew he would get more information, if he should require it, on that subject from other quarters. He paid his three months' rent, got a receipt, and the name of an old woman who would probably undertake to 'do' for him, and came away with the keys in his pocket. He then went to the landlady of the inn, who was a cheerful and most kindly person, and asked her advice as to such stores and provisions as he would be likely to require. She threw up her hands in amazement when he told her where he was going to settle himself.

'Not in the Judge's House!' she said, and grew pale as she spoke. He explained the locality of the house, saying that he did not know its name. When he had finished she answered:

'Aye, sure enough – sure enough the very place. It is the Judge's House sure enough.' He asked her to tell him about the place, why so called, and what there was against it. She told him that it was so called locally because it had been many years before – how long she could not say, as she was herself from another part of the country, but she thought it must have been a hundred years or more – the abode of a judge who was held in great terror on account of his harsh sentences and his hostility to prisoners at Assizes. As to what there was against the house itself she could not tell. She had often asked, but no one could inform her; but there was a general feeling that there was *something*, and for her own part she would not take all the money in Drinkwater's Bank and stay in the house an hour by herself. Then she apologised to Malcolmson for her disturbing talk.

'It is too bad of me, sir, and you – and a young gentleman, too – if you will pardon me saying it, going to live there all alone. If you were my boy – and you'll excuse me for saying it – you wouldn't sleep there a night, not if I had to go there myself and pull the big alarm bell that's on the roof!' The good creature was so manifestly in earnest, and was so kindly in her intentions, that Malcomson, although amused, was touched. He told her kindly how much he appreciated her interest in him, and added:

'But, my dear Mrs Witham, indeed you need not be concerned about me! A man who is reading for the Mathematical Tripos has too much to think of to be disturbed by any of these mysterious "somethings," and his work is of too exact and prosaic a kind to allow of his having any corner in his mind for mysteries of any kind. Harmonical Progression, Permutations and Combinations, and Elliptic Functions have sufficient mysteries for me!' Mrs Witham kindly undertook to see after his commissions, and he went himself to look for the old woman who had been recommended to him. When he returned to the Judge's House with her, after an interval of a couple of hours, he found Mrs Witham herself waiting with several men and boys carrying parcels, and an upholsterer's man with a bed in a cart, for she said, though tables and chairs might be all very well, a bed that hadn't been aired for mayhap fifty years was not proper for young bones to lie on. She was evidently curious to see the inside of the house; and though manifestly so afraid of the 'somethings' that at the slightest sound she clutched on to Malcomson, whom she never left for a moment, went over the whole place.

After his examination of the house, Malcomson decided to take up his abode in the great dining-room, which was big enough to serve for all his requirements; and Mrs Witham, with the aid of the charwoman, Mrs Dempster, proceeded to arrange matters. When the hampers were brought in and unpacked, Malcomson saw that with much kind forethought she had sent from her own kitchen sufficient provisions to last for a few days. Before going she expressed all sorts of kind wishes; and at the door turned and said:

'And perhaps, sir, as the room is big and draughty it might be well to have one of those big screens put round your bed at night – though, truth to tell, I would die myself if I were to be so shut in with all kinds of – of "things," that put their heads round the sides, or over the top, and look on me!' The image which she had called up was too much for her nerves, and she fled incontinently.

Mrs Dempster sniffed in a superior manner as the landlady disappeared, and remarked that for her own part she wasn't afraid of all the bogies in the kingdom.

'I'll tell you what it is, sir,' she said; 'bogies is all kinds and sorts of things – except bogies! Rats and mice, and beetles; and creaky doors, and loose slates, and broken panes, and stiff drawer handles, that stay out when you pull them and then fall down in the middle of the night. Look at the wainscot of the room! It is old – hundreds of years old! Do you think there's no rats and beetles there! And do you imagine, sir, that you won't see none of them? Rats is bogies, I tell you, and bogies is rats; and don't you get to think anything else!'

'Mrs Dempster,' said Malcomson gravely, making her a polite bow, 'you know more than a Senior Wrangler! And let me say, that, as a mark of esteem for your indubitable soundness of head and heart, I shall, when I go, give you possession of this house, and let you stay here by yourself for the last two months of my tenancy, for four weeks will serve my purpose.'

'Thank you kindly, sir!' she answered, 'but I couldn't sleep away from home a night. I am in Greenhow's Charity, and if I slept a night away from my rooms I should lose all I have got to live on. The rules is very strict; and there's too many watching for a vacancy for me to run any risks in the matter. Only for that, sir, I'd gladly come here and attend on you altogether during your stay.'

'My good woman,' said Malcomson hastily, 'I have come here on purpose to obtain solitude; and believe me that I am grateful to the late Greenhow for having so organised his admirable charity – whatever it is – that I am perforce denied the opportunity of suffering from such a form of temptation! Saint Anthony himself could not be more rigid on the point!'

The old woman laughed harshly. 'Ah, you young gentlemen,' she said, 'you don't fear for naught; and belike you'll get all the solitude you want here.' She set to work with her cleaning; and by nightfall, when Malcomson returned from his walk – he always had one of his books to study as he walked – he found the room swept and tidied, a fire burning in the old hearth, the lamp lit, and the table spread for supper with Mrs Witham's excellent fare. 'This is comfort, indeed,' he said, as he rubbed his hands.

When he had finished his supper, and lifted the tray to the other end of the great oak dining-table, he got out his books again, put fresh wood on the fire, trimmed his lamp, and set himself down to a spell of real hard work. He went on without pause till about eleven o'clock, when he knocked off for a bit to fix his fire and lamp, and to make himself a cup of tea. He had always been a tea-drinker, and during his college life had sat late at work and had taken tea late. The rest was a great luxury to him, and he enjoyed it with a sense of delicious, voluptuous ease. The renewed fire leaped and sparkled, and threw quaint shadows through the great old room; and as he sipped his hot tea he revelled in the sense of isolation from his kind. Then it was that he began to notice for the first time what a noise the rats were making.

'Surely,' he thought, 'they cannot have been at it all the time I was reading. Had they been, I must have noticed it!' Presently, when the noise increased, he satisfied himself that it was really new. It was evident that at first the rats had been frightened at the presence of a stranger, and the light of fire and lamp; but that as the time went on they had grown bolder and were now disporting themselves as was their wont.

How busy they were! and hark to the strange noises! Up and down behind the old wainscot, over the ceiling and under the floor they raced, and gnawed, and scratched! Malcomson smiled to himself as he recalled to mind the saying of Mrs Dempster, 'Bogies is rats, and rats is bogies!' The tea began to have its effect of intellectual and nervous stimulus, he saw with joy another long spell of work to be done before the night was past, and in the sense of security which it gave him, he allowed himself the luxury of a good look round the room. He took his lamp in one hand, and went all around, wondering that so quaint and beautiful an old house had been so long neglected. The carving of the oak on the panels of the wainscot was fine, and on and round the doors and windows it was beautiful and of rare merit. There were some old pictures on the walls, but they were coated so thick with dust and dirt that he could not distinguish any detail of them, though he held his lamp as high as he could over his head. Here and there as he went round he saw some crack or hole blocked for a moment by the face of a rat with its bright eyes glittering in the light, but in an instant it was gone, and a squeak and a scamper followed. The thing that most struck him, however, was the rope of the great alarm bell on the roof, which hung down in a corner of the room on the right-hand side of the fireplace. He pulled up close to the hearth a great high-backed carved oak chair, and sat down to his last cup of tea. When this was done he made up the fire, and went back to his work, sitting at the corner of the table, having the fire to his left. For a little while the rats disturbed him somewhat with their perpetual scampering, but he got accustomed to the noise as one does to the ticking of a clock or to the roar of moving water; and he became so immersed in his work that everything in the world, except the problem which he was trying to solve, passed away from him.

He suddenly looked up, his problem was still unsolved, and there was in the air that sense of the hour before the dawn, which is so dread to doubtful life. The noise of the rats had ceased. Indeed it seemed to him that it must have ceased but lately and that it was the sudden cessation which had disturbed him. The fire had fallen low, but still it threw out a deep red glow. As he looked he started in spite of his *sang froid*.

There on the great high-backed carved oak chair by the right side of the fire-place sat an enormous rat, steadily glaring at him with baleful eyes. He made a motion to it as though to hunt it away, but it did not stir. Then he made the motion of throwing something. Still it did not stir, but showed its great white teeth angrily, and its cruel eyes shone in the lamplight with an added vindictiveness.

Malcomson felt amazed, and seizing the poker from the hearth ran at it to kill it. Before, however, he could strike it, the rat, with a squeak that sounded like the concentration of hate, jumped upon the floor, and, running up the rope of the alarm bell, disappeared in the darkness beyond the range of the green-shaded lamp. Instantly, strange to say, the noisy scampering of the rats in the wainscot began again.

By this time Malcomson's mind was quite off the problem;

and as a shrill cock-crow outside told him of the approach of morning, he went to bed and to sleep.

He slept so sound that he was not even waked by Mrs Dempster coming in to make up his room. It was only when she had tidied up the place and got his breakfast ready and tapped on the screen which closed in his bed that he woke. He was a little tired still after his night's hard work, but a strong cup of tea soon freshened him up and, taking his book, he went out for his morning walk, bringing with him a few sandwiches lest he should not care to return till dinner time. He found a quiet walk between high elms some way outside the town, and here he spent the greater part of the day studying his Laplace. On his return he looked in to see Mrs Witham and to thank her for her kindness. When she saw him coming through the diamond-paned bay window of her sanctum she came out to meet him and asked him in. She looked at him searchingly and shook her head as she said:

'You must not overdo it, sir. You are paler this morning than you should be. Too late hours and too hard work on the brain isn't good for any man! But tell me, sir, how did you pass the night? Well, I hope? But, my heart! sir, I was glad when Mrs Dumpster told me this morning that you were all right and sleeping sound when she went in.'

'Oh, I was all right,' he answered smiling, 'the "somethings" didn't worry me, as yet. Only the rats; and they had a circus, I tell you, all over the place. There was one wicked looking old devil that sat up on my own chair by the fire, and wouldn't go till I took the poker to him, and then he ran up the rope of the alarm bell and got to somewhere up the wall or the ceiling – I couldn't see where, it was so dark.'

'Mercy on us,' said Mrs Witham, 'an old devil, and sitting on a chair by the fireside! Take care, sir! take care! There's many a true word spoken in jest.'

'How do you mean? 'Pon my word I don't understand.'

'An old devil! The old devil, perhaps. There! sir, you needn't laugh,' for Malcomson had broken into a hearty peal. 'You young folks thinks it easy to laugh at things that makes older ones shudder. Never mind, sir! never mind! Please God, you'll laugh all the time. It's what I wish you myself!' and the good lady beamed all over in sympathy with his enjoyment, her fears gone for a moment.

'Oh, forgive me!' said Malcomson presently. 'Don't think me rude; but the idea was too much for me – that the old devil himself was on the chair last night!' And at the thought he laughed again. Then he went home to dinner.

This evening the scampering of the rats began earlier; indeed it had been going on before his arrival, and only ceased whilst his presence by its freshness disturbed them. After dinner he sat by the fire for a while and had a smoke; and then, having cleared his table, began to work as before. Tonight the rats disturbed him more than they had done on the previous night. How they scampered up and down and under and over! How they squeaked, and scratched, and gnawed! How they, getting bolder by degrees, came to the mouths of their holes and to the chinks and cracks and crannies in the wainscoting till their eyes shone like tiny lamps as the firelight rose and fell. But to him, now doubtless accustomed to them, their eyes were not wicked; only their playfulness touched him. Sometimes the boldest of them made sallies out on the floor or along the mouldings of the wainscot. Now and again as they disturbed him Malcomson made a sound to frighten them, smiting the table with his hand or giving a fierce 'Hsh, hsh,' so that they fled straightway to their holes.

And so the early part of the night wore on; and despite the noise Malcomson got more and more immersed in his work.

All at once he stopped, as on the previous night, being overcome by a sudden sense of silence. There was not the faintest sound of gnaw, or scratch, or squeak. The silence was as of the grave. He remembered the odd occurrence of the previous night, and instinctively he looked at the chair standing close by the fireside. And then a very odd sensation thrilled through him.

There, on the great old high-backed carved oak chair beside the fireplace sat the same enormous rat, steadily glaring at him with baleful eyes.

Instinctively he took the nearest thing to his hand, a book of logarithms, and flung it at it. The book was badly aimed and the rat did not stir, so again the poker performance of the previous night was repeated; and again the rat, being closely pursued, fled up the rope of the alarm bell. Strangely too, the departure of this rat was instantly followed by the renewal of the noise made by the general rat community. On this occasion, as on the previous one, Malcomson could not see at what part of the room the rat disappeared, for the green shade of his lamp left the upper part of the room in darkness, and the fire had burned low.

On looking at his watch he found it was close on midnight; and, not sorry for the *divertissement*, he made up his fire and made himself his nightly pot of tea. He had got through a good spell of work, and thought himself entitled to a cigarette; and so he sat on the great carved oak chair before the fire and enjoyed it. Whilst smoking he began to think that he would like to know where the rat disappeared to, for he had certain ideas for the morrow not entirely disconnected with a rat-trap. Accordingly he lit another lamp and placed it so that it would shine well into the right-hand corner of the wall by the fireplace. Then he got all the books he had with him, and placed them handy to throw at the vermin. Finally he lifted the rope of the alarm bell and placed the end of it on the table, fixing the extreme end under the lamp. As he handled it he could not help noticing how pliable it was, especially for so strong a rope, and one not in use. 'You could hang a man with it,' be thought to himself. When his preparations were made he looked around, and said complacently:

'There now, my friend, I think we shall learn something of you this time!' He began his work again, and though as before somewhat disturbed at first by the noise of the rats, soon lost himself in his propositions and problems.

Again he was called to his immediate surroundings suddenly.

This time it might not have been the sudden silence only which took his attention; there was a slight movement of the rope, and the lamp moved. Without stirring, he looked to see if his pile of books was within range, and then cast his eye along the rope. As he looked he saw the great rat drop from the rope on the oak armchair and sit there glaring at him. He raised a book in his right hand, and taking careful aim, flung it at the rat. The latter, with a quick movement, sprang aside and dodged the missile. He then took another book, and a third, and flung them one after another at the rat, but each time unsuccessfully. At last, as he stood with a book poised in his hand to throw, the rat squeaked and seemed afraid. This made Malcomson more than ever eager to strike, and the book flew and struck the rat a resounding blow. It gave a terrified squeak, and turning on his pursuer a look of terrible malevolence, ran up the chair-back and made a great jump to the rope of the alarm bell and ran up it like lightning. The lamp rocked under the sudden strain, but it was a heavy one and did not topple over. Malcomson kept his eyes on the rat, and saw it by the light of the second lamp leap to a moulding of the wainscot and disappear through a hole in one of the great pictures which hung on the wall, obscured and invisible through its coating of dirt and dust.

'I shall look up my friend's habitation in the morning,' said the student, as he went over to collect his books. The third picture from the fireplace; I shall not forget.' He picked up the books one by one, commenting on them as he lifted them. '*Conic Sections* he does not mind, nor *Cycloidal Oscillations*, nor the *Principia*, nor *Quaternions*, nor *Thermodynamics*. Now for the book that fetched him!' Malcomson took it up and looked at it. As he did so he started, and a sudden pallor overspread his face. He looked round uneasily and shivered slightly, as he murmured to himself:

'The Bible my mother gave me! What an odd coincidence.' He sat down to work again, and the rats in the wainscot renewed their gambols. They did not disturb him, however; somehow their presence gave him a sense of companionship. But he could not attend to his work, and after striving to master the subject on which he was engaged gave it up in despair, and went to bed as the first streak of dawn stole in through the eastern window.

He slept heavily but uneasily, and dreamed much; and when Mrs Dempster woke him late in the morning he seemed ill at ease, and for a few minutes did not seem to realise exactly where he was. His first request rather surprised the servant.

'Mrs Dempster, when I am out today I wish you would get the steps and dust or wash those pictures – specially that one the third from the fireplace – I want to see what they are.'

Late in the afternoon Malcomson worked at his books in the shaded walk, and the cheerfulness of the previous day came back to him as the day wore on, and he found that his reading was progressing well. He had worked out to a satisfactory conclusion all the problems which had as yet baffled him, and it was in a state of jubilation that he paid a visit to Mrs Witham at 'The Good Traveller.' He found a stranger in the cosy sitting-room with the landlady, who was introduced to him as Dr Thornhill. She was not quite at ease, and this, combined with the doctor's plunging at once into a series of questions, made Malcomson come to the conclusion that his presence was not an accident, so without preliminary he said:

'Dr Thornhill, I shall with pleasure answer you any question you may choose to ask me if you will answer me one question first.'

The doctor seemed surprised, but he smiled and answered at once, 'Done! What is it?'

'Did Mrs Witham ask you to come here and see me and advise me?'

Dr Thornhill for a moment was taken aback, and Mrs Witham got fiery red and turned away; but the doctor was a frank and ready man, and he answered at once and openly:

'She did: but she didn't intend you to know it. I suppose it was my clumsy haste that made you suspect. She told me that she did not like the idea of your being in that house all by yourself, and that she thought you took too much strong tea. In fact, she wants me to advise you if possible to give up the tea and the very late hours. I was a keen student in my time, so I suppose I may take the liberty of a college man, and without offence, advise you not quite as a stranger.'

Malcomson with a bright smile held out his hand. 'Shake! as they say in America,' he said. 'I must thank you for your kindness and Mrs Witham too, and your kindness deserves a return on my part. I promise to take no more strong tea — no tea at all till you let me — and I shall go to bed tonight at one o'clock at latest. Will that do?'

'Capital,' said the doctor. 'Now tell us all that you noticed in the old house,' and so Malcomson then and there told in minute detail all that had happened in the last two nights. He was interrupted every now and then by some exclamation from Mrs Witham, till finally when he told of the episode of the Bible the landlady's pent-up emotions found vent in a shriek; and it was not till a stiff glass of brandy and water had been administered that she grew composed again. Dr Thornhill listened with a face of growing gravity, and when the narrative was complete and Mrs Witham had been restored he asked:

'The rat always went up the rope of the alarm bell?'

'Always.'

'I suppose you know,' said the Doctor after a pause, 'what the rope is?'

'No!'

'It is,' said the Doctor slowly, 'the very rope which the hangman used for all the victims of the Judge's judicial rancour!' Here he was interrupted by another scream from Mrs Witham, and steps had to be taken for her recovery. Malcomson having looked at his watch, and found that it was close to his dinner hour, had gone home before her complete recovery.

When Mrs Witham was herself again she almost assailed the Doctor with angry questions as to what he meant by putting such horrible ideas into the poor young man's mind. 'He has quite enough there already to upset him,' she added. Dr Thornhill replied.

'My dear madam, I had a distinct purpose in it! I wanted to draw his attention to the bell rope, and to fix it there. It may be that he is in a highly over-wrought state, and has been studying too much, although I am bound to say that he seems as sound and healthy a young man, mentally and bodily, as ever I saw – but then the rats – and that suggestion of the devil.' The doctor shook his head and went on. 'I would have offered to go and stay the first night with him but that I felt sure it would have been a cause of offence. He may get in the night some strange fright or hallucination; and if he does I want him to pull that rope. All alone as he is it will give us warning, and we may reach him in time to be of service. I shall be sitting up pretty late tonight and shall keep my ears open. Do not be alarmed if Benchurch gets a surprise before morning.'

'Oh, Doctor, what do you mean? What do you mean?'

'I mean this; that possibly – nay, more probably – we shall hear the great alarm bell from the Judge's House tonight,' and the Doctor made about as effective an exit as could be thought of.

When Malcomson arrived home he found that it was a little after his usual time, and Mrs Dempster had gone away – the rules of Greenhow's Charity were not to be neglected. He was glad to see that the place was bright and tidy with a cheerful fire and a well-trimmed lamp. The evening was colder than might have been expected in April, and a heavy wind was blowing with such rapidly-increasing strength that there was every promise of a storm during the night. For a few minutes after his entrance the noise of the rats ceased; but so soon as they became accustomed to his presence they began again. He was glad to hear them, for he felt once more the feeling of companionship in their noise, and his mind ran back to the strange fact that they only ceased to manifest themselves when that other – the great rat with the baleful eyes – came upon the scene. The reading-lamp only was lit and its green shade kept the ceiling and the upper part of the room in darkness, so that the cheerful light from the hearth spreading over the floor and shining on the white cloth laid over the end of the table was warm and cheery. Malcomson sat down to his dinner with a good appetite and a buoyant spirit. After his dinner and a cigarette he sat steadily down to work, determined not to let anything disturb him, for he remembered his promise to the doctor, and made up his mind to make the best of the time at his disposal.

For an hour or so he worked all right, and then his thoughts began to wander from his books. The actual circumstances around him, the calls on his physical attention, and his nervous susceptibility were not to be denied. By this time the wind had become a gale, and the gale a storm. The old house, solid though it was, seemed to shake to its foundations, and the storm roared and raged through its many chimneys and its queer old gables, producing strange, unearthly sounds in the empty rooms and corridors. Even the great alarm bell on the roof must have felt the force of the wind, for the rope rose and fell slightly, as though the bell were moved a little from time to time, and the limber rope fell on the oak floor with a hard and hollow sound.

As Malcomson listened to it he bethought himself of the doctor's words, 'It is the rope which the hangman used for the victims of the Judge's judicial rancour,' and he went over to the corner of the fireplace and took it in his hand to look at it. There seemed a sort of deadly interest in it, and as he stood there he lost himself for a moment in speculation as to who these victims were, and the grim wish of the Judge to have such a ghastly relic ever under his eyes. As he stood there the swaying of the bell on the roof still lifted the rope now and again; but presently there came a new sensation – a sort of tremor in the rope, as though something was moving along it.

Looking up instinctively Malcomson saw the great rat coming slowly down towards him, glaring at him steadily. He dropped the rope and started back with a muttered curse, and the rat turning ran up the rope again and disappeared, and at the same instant Malcomson became conscious that the noise of the rats, which had ceased for a while, began again.

All this set him thinking, and it occurred to him that he had not investigated the lair of the rat or looked at the pictures, as he had intended. He lit the other lamp without the shade, and, holding it up, went and stood opposite the third picture from the fireplace on the right-hand side where he had seen the rat disappear on the previous night.

At the first glance he started back so suddenly that he almost dropped the lamp, and a deadly pallor overspread his face. His knees shook, and heavy drops of sweat came on his forehead, and he trembled like an aspen. But he was young and plucky, and pulled himself together, and after the pause of a few seconds stepped forward again, raised the lamp, and examined the picture which had been dusted and washed, and now stood out clearly

It was of a judge dressed in his robes of scarlet and ermine. His face was strong and merciless, evil, crafty, and vindictive, with a sensual mouth, hooked nose of ruddy colour, and shaped like the beak of a bird of prey. The rest of the face was of a cadaverous colour. The eyes were of peculiar brilliance and with a terribly malignant expression. As he looked at them, Malcomson grew cold, for he saw there the very counterpart of the eyes of the great rat. The lamp almost fell from his hand, he saw the rat with its baleful eyes peering out through the hole in the corner of the picture, and noted the sudden cessation of the noise of the other rats. However, he pulled himself together, and went on with his examination of the picture.

The Judge was seated in a great high-backed carved oak chair, on the right-hand side of a great stone fireplace where, in the corner, a rope hung down from the ceiling, its end lying coiled on the floor. With a feeling of something like horror, Malcomson recognised the scene of the room as it stood, and gazed around him in an awestruck manner as though he expected to find some strange presence behind him. Then he looked over to the corner of the fireplace – and with a loud cry he let the lamp fall from his hand.

There, in the judge's arm-chair, with the rope hanging behind, sat the rat with the Judge's baleful eyes, now intensified and with a fiendish leer. Save for the howling of the storm without there was silence.

The fallen lamp recalled Malcomson to himself. Fortunately it was of metal, and so the oil was not spilt. However, the practical need of attending to it settled at once his nervous apprehensions. When he had turned it out, he wiped his brow and thought for a moment.

'This will not do,' he said to himself. 'If I go on like this I shall become a crazy fool. This must stop! I promised the doctor I would not take tea. Faith, he was pretty right! My nerves must have been getting into a queer state. Funny I did not notice it. I never felt better in my life. However, it is all right now, and I shall not be such a fool again.'

Then he mixed himself a good stiff glass of brandy and water and resolutely sat down to his work.

It was nearly an hour when he looked up from his book, disturbed by the sudden stillness. Without, the wind howled and roared louder than ever, and the rain drove in sheets against the windows, beating like hail on the glass; but within there was no sound whatever save the echo of the wind as it roared in the great chimney, and now and then a hiss as a few raindrops found their way down the chimney in a lull of the storm. The fire had fallen low and had ceased to flame, though it threw out a red glow. Malcomson listened attentively, and presently heard a thin, squeaking noise, very faint. It came from the corner of the room where the rope hung down, and he thought it was the creaking of the rope on the floor as the swaying of the bell raised and lowered it. Looking up, however, he saw in the dim light the great rat clinging to the rope and gnawing it. The rope was already nearly gnawed through – he could see the lighter colour where the strands were laid bare. As he looked the job was completed, and the severed end of the rope fell clattering on the oaken floor, whilst for an instant the great rat remained like a knob or tassel at the end of the rope, which now began to sway to and fro. Malcomson felt for a moment another pang of terror as he thought that now the possibility of calling the outer world to his assistance was cut off, but an intense anger took its place, and seizing the book he was reading he hurled it at the rat. The blow was well aimed, but before the missile could reach him the rat dropped off and struck the floor with a soft thud. Malcomson instantly rushed over towards him, but it darted away and disappeared in the darkness of the shadows of the room. Malcomson felt that his work was over for the night, and determined then and there to vary the monotony of the proceedings by a hunt for the rat, and took off the green shade of the lamp so as to insure a wider spreading light. As he did so the gloom of the upper part of the room was relieved, and in the new flood of light, great by comparison with the previous darkness, the pictures on the wall stood out boldly. From where he stood, Malcomson saw right opposite to him the third picture on the wall from the right of the fireplace. He rubbed his eyes in surprise, and then a great fear began to come upon him.

In the centre of the picture was a great irregular patch of brown canvas, as fresh as when it was stretched on the frame. The background was as before, with chair and chimney-corner and rope, but the figure of the Judge had disappeared.

Malcomson, almost in a chill of horror, turned slowly round, and then he began to shake and tremble like a man in a palsy. His strength seemed to have left him, and he was incapable of action or movement, hardly even of thought. He could only see and hear.

There, on the great high-backed carved oak chair sat the judge in his robes of scarlet and ermine, with his baleful eyes glaring vindictively, and a smile of triumph on the resolute, cruel mouth, as he lifted with his hands a black cap. Malcomson felt as if the blood was running from his heart, as one does in moments of prolonged suspense. There was a singing in his ears. Without, he could hear the roar and howl of the tempest, and through it, swept on the storm, came the striking of midnight by the great chimes in the market place. He stood for a space of time that seemed to him endless still as a statue, and with wide-open, horror-struck eyes, breathless. As the clock struck, so the smile of triumph on the Judge's face intensified, and at the last stroke of midnight he placed the black cap on his head.

Slowly and deliberately the Judge rose from his chair and picked up the piece of the rope of the alarm bell which lay on the floor, drew it through his hands as if he enjoyed its touch, and then deliberately began to knot one end of it, fashioning it into a noose. This he tightened and tested with his foot, pulling hard at it till he was satisfied and then making a running noose of it, which he held in his hand. Then he began to move along the table on the opposite side to Malcomson keeping his eyes on him until he had passed him, when with a quick movement he stood in front of the door. Malcomson then began to feel that he was trapped, and tried to think of what he should do. There was some fascination in the Judge's eyes, which he never took off him, and he had, perforce, to look. He saw the Judge approach – still keeping between him and the door – and raise the noose and throw it towards him as if to entangle him. With a great effort he made a quick movement to one side, and saw the rope fall beside him, and heard it strike the oaken floor. Again the Judge raised the noose and tried to ensnare him, ever keeping his baleful eyes fixed on him, and each time by a mighty effort the student just managed to evade it. So this went on for many times, the Judge seeming never discouraged nor discomposed at failure, but playing as a cat does with a mouse. At last in despair, which had reached its climax, Malcomson cast a quick glance round him. The lamp seemed to have blazed up, and there was a fairly good light in the room. At the many rat-holes and in the chinks and crannies of the wainscot he saw the rats' eyes; and this aspect, that was purely physical, gave him a gleam of comfort. He looked around and saw that the rope of the great alarm bell was laden with rats. Every inch of it was covered with them, and more and more were pouring through the small circular hole in the ceiling whence it emerged, so that with their weight the bell was beginning to sway.

Hark! it had swayed till the clapper had touched the bell. The sound was but a tiny one, but the bell was only beginning to sway, and it would increase.

At the sound the Judge, who had been keeping his eyes fixed on Malcolmson, looked up, and a scowl of diabolical anger overspread his face. His eyes fairly glowed like hot coals, and he stamped his foot with a sound that seemed to make the house shake. A dreadful peal of thunder broke overhead as he raised the rope again, whilst the rats kept running up and down the rope as though working against time. This time, instead of throwing it, he drew close to his victim, and held open the noose as he approached. As he came closer there seemed something paralysing in his very presence, and Malcolmson stood rigid as a corpse. He felt the Judge's icy fingers touch his throat as he adjusted the rope. The noose tightened – tightened. Then the Judge, taking the rigid form of the student in his arms, carried him over and placed him standing in the oak chair, and stepping up beside him, put his hand up and caught the end of the swaying rope of the alarm bell. As he raised his hand the rats fled squeaking, and disappeared through the hole in the ceiling. Taking the end of the noose which was round Malcolmson's neck he tied it to the hanging-bell rope, and then descending pulled away the chair.

When the alarm bell of the Judge's House began to sound a crowd soon assembled. Lights and torches of various kinds appeared, and soon a silent crowd was hurrying to the spot. They knocked loudly at the door, but there was no reply. Then they burst in the door, and poured into the great dining-room, the doctor at the head.

There at the end of the rope of the great alarm bell hung the body of the student, and on the face of the Judge in the picture was a malignant smile.

The Brown Man

Gerald Griffin

All sorts of cattle he did eat,
Some say he eat up trees,
And that the forest sure he would,
Devour up by degrees.
For houses and churches, were to him geese and turkeys,
He ate all, and left none behind,
But some stones, dear Jack, which he could not crack,
Which on the hills you'll find.

The Dragon of Wantley

The common Irish expression of 'the seven devils,' does not, it would appear, owe its origin to the supernatural influences ascribed to that numeral, from its frequent association with the greatest and most solemn occasions of theological history. If one were disposed to be fancifully metaphysical upon the subject, it might not be amiss to compare credulity to a sort of mental prism, by which the great volume of the light of speculative superstition is refracted in a manner precisely similar to that of the material, every day sun, the great refractor thus showing only *blue* devils to the dwellers in the good city of London, *orange* and *green* devils to the inhabitants of the sister (or rather step-daughter), island, and so forward until the seven component hues are made out, through the other nations of the earth. But what has this to do with the story? In order to answer that question, the story must be told.

In a lonely cabin, in a lonely glen, on the shores of a lonely lough, in one of the most lonesome districts of west Munster, lived a lone woman named Guare. She had a beautiful girl, a daughter named Nora. Their cabin was the only one within three miles round them every way. As to their mode of living, it was simple enough, for all they had was one little garden of white cabbage, and they had eaten that down to a few heads between them, a sorry prospect in a place where even handful of *prischoc* weed was not to be had without sowing it.

It was a very fine morning in those parts, for it was only snowing and hailing, when Nora and her mother were sitting at the door of their little cottage, and laying out plans for the next day's dinner. On a sudden, a strange horseman rode up to the door. He was strange in more ways than one. He was dressed in brown, his hair was brown, his eyes were brown, his boots were brown, he rode a brown horse, and he was followed by a brown dog.

'I'm come to marry you, Nora Guare,' said the Brown Man.

'Ax my mother fusht, if you plaise, sir,' said Nora, dropping him a curtsy.

'You'll not refuse, ma'am,' said the Brown Man to the old mother, 'I have money enough, and I'll make your daughter a lady, with servants at her call, and all manner of fine doings about her.' And so saying, he flung a purse of gold into the widow's lap.

'Why then the heavens speed you and her together, take her away with you, and make much of her,' said the old mother, quite bewildered with all the money.

'Agh, agh,' said the Brown Man, as he placed her on his horse behind him without more ado. 'Are you all ready now?'

'I am!' said the bride. The horse snorted, and the dog barked, and almost before the word was out of her mouth, they were all whisked away out of sight. After travelling a day and a night, faster than the wind itself, the Brown Man pulled up his horse in the middle of the Mangerton mountain, in one of the most lonesome places that eye ever looked on.

'Here is my estate,' said the Brown Man.

'A'then, is it this wild bog you call an estate?' said the bride.

'Come in, wife; this is my palace,' said the bridegroom.

'What! a clay-hovel, worse than my mother's!'

They dismounted, and the horse and the dog disappeared in an instant, with a horrible noise, which the girl did not know whether to call snorting, barking, or laughing.

'Are you hungry?' said the Brown Man. 'If so, there is your dinner.'

'A handful of raw white-eyes,[1] and a grain of salt!'

'And when you are sleepy, here is your bed,' he continued, pointing to a little straw in a corner, at sight of which Nora's limbs shivered and trembled again. It may be easily supposed that she did not make a very hearty dinner that evening, nor did her husband neither.

In the dead of the night, when the clock of Mucruss Abbey had just tolled one, a low neighing at the door, and a soft barking at the window were heard. Nora feigned sleep. The Brown Man passed his hand over her eyes and face. She snored. 'I'm coming,' said he, and he arose gently from her side. In half an hour after she felt him by her side again. He was cold as ice.

The next night the same summons came. The Brown Man rose. The wife feigned sleep. He returned, cold. The morning came.

The next night came. The bell tolled at Mucruss, and was heard across the lakes. The Brown Man rose again, and passed a light before the eyes of the feigning sleeper. None slumber so sound as they who will not wake. Her heart trembled, but her frame was quiet and firm. A voice at the door summoned the husband.

'You are very long coming. The earth is tossed up, and I am hungry. Hurry! Hurry! Hurry! if you would not lose all.'

[1] A kind of potato

296

'I'm coming!' said the Brown Man. Nora rose and followed instantly. She beheld him at a distance winding through a lane of frostnipt sallow trees. He often paused and looked back, and once or twice retraced his steps to within a few yards of the tree, behind which she had shrunk. The moon-light, cutting the shadow close and dark about her, afforded the best concealment. He again proceeded, and she followed. In a few minutes they reached the old Abbey of Mucruss. With a sickening heart she saw him enter the church-yard. The wind rushed through the huge yew-tree and startled her. She mustered courage enough, however, to reach the gate of the church-yard and look in. The Brown Man, the horse, and the dog, were there seated by an open grave, eating something; and glancing their brown, fiery eyes about in every direction. The moonlight shone full on them and her. Looking down towards her shadow on the earth, she started with horror to observe it move, although she was herself perfectly still. It waved its black arms, and motioned her back. What the feasters said, she understood not, but she seemed still fixed in the spot. She looked once more on her shadow; it raised one hand, and pointed the way to the lane; then slowly rising from the ground, and confronting her, it walked rapidly off in that direction. She followed as quickly as might be.

She was scarcely in her straw, when the door creaked behind, and her husband entered. He lay down by her side, and started.

'Uf! Uf!' said she, pretending to be just awakened, 'how cold you are, my love!'

'Cold, inagh? Indeed you're not very warm yourself, my dear, I'm thinking.'

'Little admiration I shouldn't be warm, and you laving me alone this way at night, till my blood is snow broth, no less.'

'Umph!' said the Brown Man, as he passed his arm round her waist. 'Ha! your heart is beating fast?'

'Little admiration it should. I am not well, indeed. Them pzaties and salt don't agree with me at all.'

'Umph!' said the Brown Man.

The next morning as they were sitting at the breakfast-table together, Nora plucked up a heart, and asked leave to go to see her mother. The Brown Man, who ate nothing, looked at her in a way that made her think he knew all. She felt her spirit die away within her.

'If you only want to see your mother,' said he, 'there is no occasion for your going home. I will bring her to you here. I didn't marry you to be keeping you gadding.'

The Brown Man then went out and whistled for his dog and his horse. They both came; and in a very few minutes they pulled up at the old widow's cabin-door.

The poor woman was very glad to see her son-in-law, though she did not know what could bring him so soon.

'Your daughter sends her love to you, mother,' says the Brown Man, the villain, 'and she'd be obliged to you for a *loand* of a *shoot* of your best clothes, as she's going to give a grand party, and the dress-maker has disappointed her.'

'To be sure and welcome,' said the mother; and making up a bundle of clothes, she put them into his hands.

'Whogh! whogh!' said the horse as they drove off, 'that was well done. Are we to have a mail of her?'

'Easy, ma-coppuleen, and you'll get your 'nough before night,' said the Brown Man, 'and you likewise, my little dog.'

'Boh!' cried the dog, 'I'm in no hurry – I hunted down a doe this morning that was fed with milk from the horns of the moon.'

Often in the course of that day did Nora Guare go to the door, and cast her eye over the weary flat before it, to discern, if possible, the distant figures of her bridegroom and mother. The dusk of the second evening found her alone in the desolate cot. She listened to every sound. At length the door opened, and an old woman, dressed in a new *jock*, and leaning on a staff, entered the hut. 'O mother, are you come?' said Nora, and was about to rush into her arms, when the old woman stopped her.

'Whist! whist! my child! – I only stepped in before the man to know how you like him? Speak softly, in dread he'd hear you –

he's turning the horse loose, in the swamp, abroad, over.'

'O mother, mother! such a story!'

'Whisht! easy again – how does he use you?'

'Sarrow worse. That straw my bed, and them white-eyes – and bad ones they are – all my diet. And 'tisn't that same, only —'

'Whisht! easy, again! He'll hear you, may be – Well?'

'I'd be easy enough only for his own doings. Listen, mother. The fusht night, I came about twelve o'clock —'

'Easy, speak easy, eroo!'

'He got up at the call of the horse and the dog, and staid out a good hour. He ate nothing next day. The second night, and the second day, it was the same story. The third —'

'Husht! husht! Well, the third night?'

'The third night I said I'd watch him. Mother, don't hold my hand so hard . . . He got up, and I got up after him . . . Oh, don't laugh, mother, for 'tis frightful . . . I followed him to Mucruss church-yard . . . Mother, mother, you hurt my hand . . . I looked in at the gate – there was great moonlight there, and I could see every thing as plain as day.'

'Well, darling – husht! softly! What did you see?'

'My husband by the grave, and the horse, . . . Turn your head aside, mother, for your breath is very hot . . . and the dog and they eating. – Ah, you are not my mother!' shrieked the miserable girl, as the Brown Man flung off his disguise, and stood before her, grinning worse than a blacksmith's face through a horse-collar. He just looked at her one moment, and then darted his long fingers into her bosom, from which the red blood spouted in so many streams. She was very soon out of all pain, and a merry supper the horse, the dog, and the Brown Man had that night, by all accounts.

The Tale of the Piper

Donn Byrne

I first saw him as I rode from the Irish village into the gates of
Destiny – a burly man with a moustache, a cheap suit of Glasgow
reach-me-downs, a cap with a twisted brim, and the most evilly
insolent eyes I have ever seen in a human face. At the sight of
him Pelican, that wisest and steadiest of horses, reared; and I felt
a savage gust of hatred rise in me.

'Now, who are you?' I asked; 'and what are you doing here?'

'The same question from me to you.' And his eyes were
studiedly insulting.

An unaccountable rage made me tremble. I shook out the
thong of the hunting-crop, and edged Pelican towards him.

'I am the Younger of Destiny,' I informed him; 'and when I
pass, all folk in Destiny do me the honour of uncovering.'

He fumbled with his cap and took it off. His hair was shaggy
and matted, like a wild man's.

'I am a piper your uncle, Sir Valentine Macfarlane, sent
from the High Country of Scotland home here to await his
coming.'

I said no more and rode in. My Aunt Jenepher told me of my
Uncle Valentine's letter which Morag, her Islay maid, had read
to her. My Uncle Valentine had met the man in an inn in
Argyllshire, where he was stalking deer. 'None knows anything
about him, and he is most reticent about himself; but I am
persuaded he is the best piper in the world. Also, he may help
revive the lost art of piping in Ireland.'

'Now, if he had only sent me a pair of Ayrshire ploughmen,' I grumbled.

At dinner that night the man threw his reeds over his shoulder and played outside the dining-room window. He broke into the rollicking country air of the 'Palatine's Daughter.' I don't know what he did to it with the knowledge of his art, but out of that tune of frolicsome rural love-making he produced an atmosphere which made me uncomfortable, as though some cad were telling foul stories. He swung from that into, 'Thorroo a Warralla,' the 'Funeral of the Barrel' – a noted drinking song of how a barrel of porter went dry after a day's flax-pulling. But the picture evoked was not that of country men drinking healthily at a crossroads, but of a thieves' kitchen, where dreadful blowsy women, as of Hogarth, lay drunk with their rat-faced cut-purses . . .

'Stop that man, James Carabine,' said my Aunt Jenepher.

He played no more under our window, but in the Irish village the next day he piped 'The Desperate Battle,' that music that only a great piper can touch, and that night the only faction fight we had had in Destiny for forty years broke out and raged until the police from the neighbouring villages were rushed in. He played 'The Belles of Perth' to the men from the fields, and for days afterwards I saw maidservants and young girls in the farmhouses around with red eyelids. And a young under-gardener flung down his spade and said out of nothing, to nobody: 'I'm sick of the women in this untoward place.' And one morning I heard him play, '*Iss fada may an a walla shuh*' – 'I'm a long time in this one town' – and my own feet took an itch for the road.

I said to my Aunt Jenepher at luncheon, 'I was thinking now, with the winter coming, I'll give up hunting for this one season, and go and see Egypt maybe, or go as far as India. A young man ought to see the world a bit.'

'Shall we talk about it tonight, Kerry?' said my Aunt Jenepher. She asked me to go with her into the garden after luncheon,

sent Carabine for the piper. He arrived with his instrument
under his arm.

'You have never played for me yet, piper.'

'Your ladyship has never asked me.' There was a solid dignity
about him.

'I suppose you have many tunes,' said my Aunt Jenepher.

'What I say now would be immodest in another man, but
true in me: no piper has more tunes. I have the lost tunes of
McCrimmon. I have tunes that were lost before McCrimmon's
day – old, dark tunes. Also tunes of my own making.'

'Will you play me the tune of the fishermen, piper, as they
raise the brown sails: "Christ, Who walked on the sea, guard us
poor fisher folk"!'

'I am sorry, my lady, but I have not that tune.'

'Please play me Bruce's Hymn: "God of Battles"!'

'That also, my lady, is a tune I have not.'

'Then a merry song, piper, which you must know: "The
Marriage Feast which took place in Cana"!'

He was stolid as a rock. 'I am afraid I have not that either.'

'One of your favourite tunes is: "I'm a long while in this one
town"?'

He bowed with a nobleman's courtesy.

'It is a choice tune,' he said slowly, 'a darling tune.'

'Then play it, piper, then play it,' said my Aunt Jenepher. 'And
as you are playing it' – she rose up suddenly from the seat and
looked at him with her blind eyes – 'in God's name, go!'

'I was to wait,' said the piper, 'until Sir Valentine returned.'

Both Carabine and I made a step towards him. My
Aunt Jenepher must have felt us. 'Please, Kerry! Please, James
Carabine!'

'Piper, my brother Valentine will not wish you to stay here an
instant longer than I would have you stay, and I would not have
you stay at all.'

'Then I had better go,' the piper said. And he swung his reeds
to his shoulder; struck the piper's swagger.

302

'Do you need money for the road?' my Aunt Jenepher asked.

'I need nothing.'

'But you do, piper,' said my Aunt Jenepher softly. 'I shall pray for you tonight.'

He dropped the pipes from his shoulder and turned around. 'I thank your ladyship,' he said simply; 'but I fear it is late for that.'

'Nevertheless, I shall,' said my Aunt Jenepher.

He turned and went away from us down the garden path, and what became of him is not known. He did not play his pipes as he went, but held them crumpled under his arm, and his walk was more like the rapid amble of an animal than the step of a man. I was convinced that were I to look in the gravel I should find not a footprint of a man, but the slot of an animal. But I did not look. I was afraid.

The Whistling Room

William Hope Hodgson

Carnacki shook a friendly fist at me as I entered, late. Then he opened the door into the dining room and ushered the four of us – Jessop, Arkright, Taylor and myself – in to dinner.

We dined well, as usual, and equally as usual Carnacki was pretty silent during the meal. At the end we took our wine and cigars to our accustomed positions and Carnacki – having got himself comfortable in his big chair – began without any preliminary:

'I have just got back from Ireland, again,' he said. 'And I thought you chaps would be interested to hear my news. Besides, I fancy I shall see the thing clearer after I have told it all out straight. I must tell you this, though, at the beginning – up to the present moment I have been utterly and completely "stumped." I have tumbled upon one of the most peculiar cases of "haunting" – or devilment of some sort – that I have come against. Now listen.

'I have been spending the last few weeks at Iastrae Castle, about twenty miles North-East of Galway. I got a letter about a month ago from a Mr. Sid K. Tassoc, who it seemed had bought the place lately and moved in, only to find that he had got a very peculiar piece of property.

'When I reached there he met me at the station, driving a jaunting-car and drove me up to the castle, which by the way, he called a "house-shanty." I found that he was "pigging it" there with his boy brother and another American who seemed to be half-servant and half-companion. It appears that all the servants had left the place, in a body, as you might say, and now they were managing among themselves, assisted by some day-help.

'The three of them got together a scratch feed and Tassoc told me all about the trouble whilst we were at table. It is most extraordinary and different from anything that I have had to do with, though that Buzzing Case was very queer too.

'Tassoc began right in the middle of his story. "We've got a room in this shanty," he said, "which has got a most infernal whistling in it, sort of haunting it. The thing starts any time, you never know when, and it goes on until it frightens you. It's not ordinary whistling and it isn't the wind. Wait till you hear it.'

' "We're all carrying guns," said the boy, and slapped his coat pocket.

' "As bad as that?" I said, and the older brother nodded. "I may be soft," he replied, "but wait till you've heard it. Sometimes I think it's some infernal thing and the next moment I'm just as sure that someone's playing a trick on us."

' "Why?" I asked. "What is to be gained?"

' "You mean," he said, "that people usually have some good reason for playing tricks as elaborate as this. Well, I'll tell you. There's a lady in this province by the name of Miss Donnehue who's going to be my wife, this day two months. She's more beautiful than they make them, and so far as I can see, I've just stuck my head into an Irish hornet's nest. There's about a score of hot young Irishmen been courting her these two years gone and now that I've come along and cut them out they feel raw against me. Do you begin to understand the possibilities?"

' "Yes," I said. "Perhaps I do in a vague sort of way, but I don't see how all this affects the room?"

' "Like this," he said. "When I'd fixed it up with Miss Donnehue I looked out for a place and bought this little house-shanty. Afterwards I told her – one evening during dinner – that I'd decided to tie up here. And then she asked me whether I wasn't afraid of the whistling room. I told her it must have been thrown in gratis, as I'd heard nothing about it. There were some of her men friends present and I saw a smile go round. I found out after a bit of questioning that several people have bought this place during the last twenty-odd years. And it was always on the market again, after a trial.

' "Well, the chaps started to bait me a bit and offered to take bets after dinner that I'd not stay six months in this shanty. I looked once or twice at Miss Donnehue so as to be sure I was 'getting the note' of the talkee-talkee, but I could see that she didn't take it as a joke at all. Partly, I think, because there was a bit of a sneer in the way the men were tackling me and partly because she really believes there is something in this yarn of the whistling room.

' "However, after dinner I did what I could to even things up with the others. I nailed all their bets and screwed them down good and safe. I guess some of them are going to be hard hit, unless I lose; which I don't mean to. Well, there you have practically the whole yarn."

' "Not quite," I told him. "All that I know is that you have bought a castle with a room in it that is in some way 'queer,' and that you've been doing some betting. Also, I know that your servants have got frightened and run away. Tell me something about the whistling?"

' "O, that!" said Tassoc. "That started the second night we were in. I'd had a good look round the room in the daytime, as you can understand; for the talk up at Arlestrae – Miss Donnehue's place – had me wonder a bit. But it seems just as usual as some of the other rooms in the old wing only perhaps a bit more lonesome feeling. But that may be only because of the talk about it, you know.

' "The whistling started about ten o'clock on the second night, as I said. Tom and I were in the library when we heard an awfully queer whistling coming along the East Corridor – the room is in the East Wing, you know.

' " 'That's that blessed ghost!' I said to Tom and we collared the lamps off the table and went up to have a look. I tell you, even as we dug along the corridor it took me a bit in the throat, it was so beastly queer. It was a sort of tune in a way, but more as if a devil or some rotten thing were laughing at you and going to get round at your back. That's how it makes you feel.

' "When we got to the door we didn't wait, but rushed it open, and then I tell you the sound of the thing fairly hit me in the face. Tom said he got it the same way – sort of felt stunned and bewildered. We looked all round and soon got so nervous, we just cleared out and I locked the door.

' "We came down here and had a stiff peg each. Then we landed fit again and began to feel we'd been nicely had. So we took sticks and went out into the grounds, thinking after all it must be some of these confounded Irishmen working the ghost-trick on us. But there was not a leg stirring.

' "We went back into the house and walked over it and then paid another visit to the room. But we simply couldn't stand it. We fairly ran out and locked the door again. I don't know how to put it into words, but I had a feeling of being up against something that was rottenly dangerous. You know! We've carried our guns ever since.

' "Of course we had a real turn-out of the room next day and the whole house-place, and we even hunted round the grounds but there was nothing queer. And now I don't know what to think, except that the sensible part of me tells me that it's some plan of these Wild Irishmen to try to take a rise out of me."

' "Done anything since?" I asked him.

' "Yes," he said. "Watched outside of the door of the room at night and chased round the grounds and sounded the walls and floor of the room. We've done everything we could think of and it's beginning to get on our nerves, so we sent for you."

'By this time we had finished eating. As we rose from the table Tassoc suddenly called out: – "Ssh! Hark!"

'We were instantly silent, listening. Then I heard it, an extra-ordinary hooning whistle, monstrous and inhuman, coming from

307

far away through corridors to my right.

' "By God!" said Tassoc, "and it's scarcely dark yet! Collar those candles, both of you and come along."

'In a few moments we were all out of the door and racing up the stairs. Tassoc turned into a long corridor and we followed, shielding our candles as we ran. The sound seemed to fill all the passage as we drew near, until I had the feeling that the whole air throbbed under the power of some wanton Immense Force – a sense of an actual taint, as you might say, of monstrosity all about us.

'Tassoc unlocked the door then, giving it a push with his foot, jumped back and drew his revolver. As the door flew open the sound beat out at us with an effect impossible to explain to one who has not heard it – with a certain, horrible personal note in it, as if in there in the darkness you could picture the room rocking and creaking in a mad, vile glee to its own filthy piping and whistling and hooning, and yet all the time aware of you in particular. To stand there and listen was to be stunned by Realisation. It was as if someone showed you the mouth of a vast pit suddenly and said: That's Hell. And you *knew* that they had spoken the truth. Do you get it, even a little bit?

'I stepped a pace into the room and held the candle over my head and looked quickly round. Tassoc and his brother joined me and the man came up at the back and we all held our candles high. I was deafened with the shrill, piping hoon of the whistling and then, clear in my ear something seemed to be saying to me: "Get out of here – quick! Quick! Quick!"

'As you chaps know, I never neglect that sort of thing. Sometimes it may be nothing but nerves, but as you will remember, it was just such a warning that saved me in the "Grey Dog" Case and in the "Yellow Finger" Experiments, as well as other times. Well, I turned sharp round to the others: "Out!" I said. "For God's sake, *out* quick!" And in an instant I had them into the passage.

'There came an extraordinary yelling scream into the hideous whistling and then, like a clap of thunder, an utter silence. I slammed the door, and locked it. Then, taking the key, I looked round at the others. They were pretty white and I imagine I must have looked that way too. And there we stood a moment, silent.

' "Come down out of this and have some whisky," said Tassoc, at last, in a voice he tried to make ordinary; and he led the way. I was the back man and I knew we all kept looking over our shoulders. When we got downstairs Tassoc passed the bottle round. He took a drink himself and slapped his glass on to the table. Then sat down with a thud.

' "That's a lovely thing to have in the house with you, isn't it!" he said. And directly afterwards: "What on earth made you hustle us all out like that, Carnacki?"

' "Something seemed to be telling me to get out, *quick*," I said. "Sounds a bit silly – superstitious, I know, but when you are meddling with this sort of thing you've got to take notice of queer fancies and risk being laughed at."

'I told him then about the "Grey Dog" business and he nodded a lot to that. "Of course," I said, "this may be nothing more than those would-be rivals of yours playing some funny game, but personally, though I'm going to keep an open mind, I feel that there is something beastly and dangerous about this thing."

'We talked for a while longer and then Tassoc suggested billiards, which we played in a pretty half-hearted fashion, and all the time cocking an ear to the door as you might say, for sounds; but none came, and later after coffee he suggested early bed and a thorough overhaul of the room on the morrow.

'My bedroom was in the newer part of the castle and the door opened into the picture gallery. At the East end of the gallery was the entrance to the corridor of the East Wing; this was shut off from the gallery by two old and heavy oak doors which looked rather odd and quaint beside the more modern doors of the various rooms.

'When I reached my room I did not go to bed, but began to unpack my instrument-trunk, of which I had retained the key. I intended to take one or two preliminary steps at once in my investigation of the extraordinary whistling.

'Presently, when the castle had settled into quietness, I slipped out of my room and across to the entrance of the great corridor. I opened one of the low, squat doors and threw the beam of my pocket searchlight down the passage. It was empty and I went through the doorway and pushed-to the oak behind me. Then along the great passage-way, throwing my light before and behind and keeping my revolver handy.

'I had hung a "protection belt" of garlic round my neck and the smell of it seemed to fill the corridor and give me assurance; for as you all know, it is a wonderful "protection" against the more usual Aeiirii forms of semi-materialisation by which I supposed the whistling might be produced, though at that period of my investigation I was still quite prepared to find it due to some perfectly natural cause, for it is astonishing the enormous number of cases that prove to have nothing abnormal in them.

'In addition to wearing the necklet I had plugged my ears loosely with garlic and as I did not intend to stay more than a few minutes in the room, I hoped to be safe.

'When I reached the door and put my hand into my pocket for the key I had a sudden feeling of sickening funk. But I was not going to back out if I could help it. I unlocked the door and turned the handle. Then I gave the door a sharp push with my foot, as Tassoc had done, and drew my revolver, though I did not expect to have any use for it, really.

'I shone the searchlight all round the room and then stepped inside with a disgustingly horrible feeling of walking slap into a waiting Danger. I stood a few seconds, expectant, and nothing happened and the empty room showed bare from corner to corner. And then, you know, I realised that the room was full of an abominable silence – can you understand that? A sort of purposeful silence, just as sickening as any of the filthy noises the Things have power to make. Do you remember what I told you about that "Silent Garden" business? Well this room had just that same *malevolent* silence – the beastly quietness of a thing that is looking at you and not seeable itself, and thinks that it has got you. O, I recognised it instantly and I shipped the top off my lantern so as to have light over the *whole* room.

'Then I set-to working like fury and keeping my glance all about me. I sealed the two windows with lengths of human hair, right across, and sealed them at every frame. As I worked a queer, scarcely perceptible tenseness stole into the air of the place and the silence seemed, if you can understand me, to grow more solid. I knew then that I had no business there without "full protection," for I was practically certain that this was no mere Aeiirii development, but one of the worse forms as the Saiitii, that "Grunting Man" case – you know.

'I finished the window and hurried over to the great fireplace. This is a huge affair and has a queer gallows-iron, I think they are called, projecting from the back of the arch. I sealed the opening with seven human hairs – the seventh crossing the six others.

'Then just as I was making an end, a low, mocking whistle grew in the room. A cold, nervous prickling went up my spine and round my forehead from the back. The hideous sound filled all the room with an extraordinary, grotesque parody of human whistling, too gigantic to be human – as if something gargantuan and monstrous made the sounds softly. As I stood there a last moment, pressing down the final seal, I had little doubt but that I had come across one of those rare and horrible cases of the *Inanimate* reproducing the functions of the *Animate*. I made a grab for my lamp and went quickly to the door, looking over my shoulder and listening for the thing that I expected. It came just as I got my hand upon the handle – a squeal of incredible, malevolent anger, piercing through the low hooning of the whistling. I dashed out, slamming the door and locking it.

'I leant a little against the opposite wall of the corridor, feeling rather funny for it had been a hideously narrow squeak . . . "thyr be noe sayfetie to be gained bye gayrds of holieness when the monyster hath pow'r to speak throe woode and stoene." So runs the passage in the Sigsand MS. and I proved it in that "Nodding Door" business. There is no protection against this particular form of monster, except possibly for a fractional period of time; for it can reproduce itself in or take to its purposes the very protective material which you may use and has power to "*forme wythine the pentycle*," though not immediately. There is, of course, the possibility of the Unknown Last Line of the Saaamaaa Ritual being uttered but it is too uncertain to count upon and the danger is too hideous and even then it has no power to protect for more than "maybe fyve beats of the harte" as the Sigsand has it.

'Inside of the room there was now a constant, mediatative, hooning whistling, but presently this ceased and the silence seemed worse for there is such a sense of hidden mischief in a silence.

'After a little I sealed the door with crossed hairs and then cleared off down the great passage and so to bed.

'For a long time I lay awake, but managed eventually to get some sleep. Yet, about two o'clock I was waked by the hooning whistling of the room coming to me, even through the closed doors. The sound was tremendous and seemed to beat through the whole house with a presiding sense of terror. As if (I remember thinking) some monstrous giant had been holding mad carnival with itself at the end of that great passage.

'I got up and sat on the edge of the bed, wondering whether to go along and have a look at the seal and suddenly there came a thump on my door and Tassoc walked in with his dressing-gown over his pyjamas.

' "I thought it would have waked you so I came along to have a talk," he said. "I can't sleep. Beautiful! Isn't it?"

' "Extraordinary!" I said, and tossed him my case.

'He lit a cigarette and we sat and talked for about an hour, and all the time that noise went on down at the end of the big corridor.

'Suddenly Tassoc stood up:

' "Let's take our guns and go and examine the brute," he said, and turned towards the door.

' "No!" I said. "By Jove – NO! I can't say anything definite yet but I believe that room is about as dangerous as it well can be."

' "Haunted – *really* haunted?" he asked, keenly and without any of his frequent banter.

'I told him, of course, that I could not say a definite *yes* or *no* to such a question, but that I hoped to be able to make a statement soon. Then I gave him a little lecture on the False Re-Materialisation of the Animate-Force through the Inanimate-Inert. He began then to understand the particular way in which the room might be dangerous, if it were really the subject of a manifestation.

'About an hour later the whistling ceased quite suddenly and Tassoc went off again to bed. I went back to mine also, and eventually got another spell of sleep.

'In the morning I walked along to the room. I found the seals on the door intact. Then I went in. The window seals and the hair were all right, but the seventh hair across the great fireplace was broken. This set me thinking. I knew that it might, very possibly, have snapped, through my having tensioned it too highly; but then, again, it might have been broken by something else. Yet it was scarcely possible that a man, for instance, could have passed between the six unbroken hairs for no one would ever have noticed them, entering the room that way, you see; but just walked through them, ignorant of their very existence.

'I removed the other hairs and the seals. Then I looked up the chimney. It went up straight and I could see blue sky at the top. It was a big, open flue and free from any suggestion of hiding places or corners. Yet, of course, I did not trust to any such casual examination and after breakfast I put on my overalls and climbed to the very top, sounding all the way, but I found nothing.

'Then I came down and went over the whole of the room – floor, ceiling and the walls, mapping them out in six-inch squares and sounding with both hammer and probe. But there was nothing unusual.

'Afterwards I made a three-weeks' search of the whole castle in the same thorough way, but found nothing. I went even further then for at night, when the whistling commenced, I made a microphone test. You see, if the whistling were mechanically produced this test would have made evident to me the working of the machinery if there were any such concealed within the walls. It certainly was an up-to-date method of examination, as you must allow.

'Of course I did not think that any of Tassoc's rivals had fixed up any mechanical contrivance, but I thought it just possible that there had been some such thing for producing the whistling made away back in the years, perhaps with the intention of giving the room a reputation that would insure its being free of inquisitive folk. You see what I mean? Well of course it was just possible, if this were the case, that someone knew the secret of the machinery and was utilising the knowledge to play this devil of a prank on Tassoc. The microphone test of the walls would certainly have made this known to me, as I have said, but there was nothing of the sort in the castle so that I had practically no doubt at all now but that it was a genuine case of what is popularly termed "haunting."

'All this time, every night, and sometimes most of each night the hooning whistling of the Room was intolerable. It was as if an Intelligence there knew that steps were being taken against it and piped and hooned in a sort of mad, mocking contempt. I tell you, it was as extraordinary as it was horrible. Time after time I went along – tiptoeing noiselessly on stockinged feet – to the sealed floor (for I always kept the Room sealed). I went at all hours of the night and often the whistling inside would seem to change to a brutally jeering note, as though the half-animate monster saw me plainly through the shut door. And all the time as I would stand, watching, the hooning of the whistling would seem to fill the whole corridor so that I used to feel a precious lonely chap messing about there with one of Hell's mysteries.

'And every morning I would enter the room and examine the different hairs and seals. You see, after the first week, I had stretched parallel hairs all along the walls of the room and along the ceiling, but over the floor which was of polished stone I had set out little colourless wafers, tacky-side uppermost. Each wafer was numbered and they were arranged after a definite plan so that I should be able to trace the exact movements of any living thing that went across.

'You will see that no material being or creature could possibly have entered that room without leaving many signs to tell me about it. But nothing was ever disturbed and I began to think that I should have to risk an attempt to stay a night in the room in the Electric Pentacle. Mind you, I *knew* that it would be a crazy thing to do, but I was getting stumped and ready to try anything.

'Once, about midnight, I did break the seal on the door and have a quick look in, but I tell you, the whole Room gave one mad yell and seemed to come towards me in a great belly of shadows as if the walls had bellied in towards me. Of course, that must have been fancy. Anyway, the yell was sufficient and I slammed the door and locked it, feeling a bit weak down my spine. I wonder whether you know the feeling.

'And then when I had got to that state of readiness for anything I made what, at first, I thought was something of a discovery:

'It was about one in the morning and I was walking slowly round the castle, keeping in the soft grass. I had come under the shadow of the East Front and far above me I could hear the vile, hooning whistling of the Room up in the darkness of the unlit wing. Then suddenly, a little in front of me, I heard a man's voice speaking low, but evidently in glee:

' "By George! You chaps, but I wouldn't care to bring a wife home to that!" it said, in the tone of the cultured Irish.

'Someone started to reply, but there came a sharp exclamation and then a rush and I heard footsteps running in all directions. Evidently the men had spotted me.

'For a few seconds I stood there feeling an awful ass. After all, *they* were at the bottom of the haunting! Do you see what a big fool it made me seem? I had no doubt but that they were some of Tassoc's rivals and here I had been feeling in every bone that I had hit a genuine Casel And then, you know, there came the memory of hundreds of details that made me just as much in doubt again. Anyway, whether it was natural or ab-natural, there was a great deal yet to be cleared up.

'I told Tassoc next morning what I had discovered and through the whole of every night for five nights we kept a close watch round the East Wing, but there was never a sign of anyone prowling about and all this time, almost from evening to dawn, that grotesque whistling would hoon incredibly, far above us in the darkness.

'On the morning after the fifth night I received a wire from here which brought me home by the next boat. I explained to Tassoc that I was simply bound to come away for a few days, but told him to keep up the watch round the castle. One thing I was very careful to do and that was to make him absolutely promise never to go into the Room between sunset and sunrise. I made it clear to him that we knew nothing definite yet, one way or the other, and if the Room were what I had first thought it to be, it might be a lot better for him to die first than enter it after dark.

'When I got here and had finished my business I thought you chaps would be interested and also I wanted to get it all spread out clear in my mind, so I rang you up. I am going over again tomorrow and when I get back I ought to have something pretty extraordinary to tell you. By the way, there is a curious thing I forgot to tell you. I tried to get a phonographic record of the whistling, but it simply produced no impression on the wax at all. That is one of the things that has made me feel queer.

'Another extraordinary thing is that the microphone will not magnify the sound – will not even transmit it, seems to take no account of it and acts as if it were non-existent. I am absolutely and utterly stumped up to the present. I am a wee bit curious to see whether any of you dear clever heads can make daylight of it. I cannot – not yet.'

He rose to his feet.

'Good-night, all,' he said, and began to usher us out abruptly, but without offence, into the night.

A fortnight later he dropped us each a card and you can imagine that I was not late this time. When we arrived Carnacki took us straight into dinner and when we had finished and all made ourselves comfortable he began again, where he had left off:

'Now just listen quietly, for I have got something very queer to tell you. I got back late at night and I had to walk up to the castle as I had not warned them that I was coming. It was bright moonlight, so that the walk was rather a pleasure than otherwise. When I got there the whole place was in darkness and I thought I would go round outside to see whether Tassoc or his brother was keeping watch. But I could not find them anywhere and concluded that they had got tired of it and gone off to bed.

'As I returned across the lawn that lies below the front of the East Wing I caught the hooning whistling of the Room coming down strangely clear through the stillness of the night. It had a peculiar note in it I remember – low and constant, queerly meditative. I looked up at the window, bright in the moonlight, and got a sudden thought to bring a ladder from the stable-yard and try to get a look into the Room from the outside.

'With this notion I hunted round at the back of the castle among the straggle of the office and presently found a long, fairly light ladder, though it was heavy enough for one, goodness knows! I thought at first that I should never get it reared. I managed at last and let the ends rest very quietly against the wall a little below the sill of the larger window. Then, going silently, I went up the ladder. Presently I had my face above the sill and was looking in, alone with the moonlight.

'Of course the queer whistling sounded louder up there, but it still conveyed that peculiar sense of something whistling quietly to itself – can you understand? Though for all the meditative lowness of the note, the horrible, gargantuan quality was distinct – a mighty parody of the human, as if I stood there and listened to the whistling from the lips of a monster with a man's soul.

'And then, you know, I saw something. The floor in the middle of the huge, empty room was puckered upwards in the centre into a strange, soft-looking mound parted at the top into an everchanging hole that pulsated to that great, gentle hooning. At times, as I watched, I saw the heaving of the indented mound gap across with a queer, inward suction as with the drawing of an enormous breath, then the thing would dilate and pout once more to the incredible melody. And suddenly as I stared, dumb, it came to me that the thing was living. I was looking at two enormous, blackened lips, blistered and brutal, there in the pale moonlight . . .

'Abruptly they bulged out to a vast pouting mound of force and sound, stiffened and swollen and hugely massive and clean-cut in the moonbeams. And a great sweat lay heavy on the vast upper-lip. In the same moment of time the whistling had burst into a mad screaming note that seemed to stun me, even where I stood, outside of the window. And then the following moment I was staring blankly at the solid, undisturbed floor of the room – smooth, polished stone flooring from wall to wall. And there was an absolute silence.

'You can picture me staring into the quiet Room and knowing what I knew. I felt like a sick, frightened child and I wanted to slide *quietly* down the ladder and run away. But in that very instant I heard Tassoc's voice calling to me from within the Room for help, *help*. My God! but I got such an awful dazed feeling and I had a vague, bewildered notion that after all, it was the Irishmen who had got him in there and were taking it out of him. And then the call came again and I burst the window and jumped in to help him. I had a confused idea that the call had come from within the shadow of the great fireplace and I raced across to it, but there was no one there.

' "Tassoc!" I shouted, and my voice went empty-sounding round the great apartment, and then in a flash *I knew that Tassoc had never called*. I whirled round, sick with fear, towards the window and as I did so a frightful, exultant whistling scream burst through the Room. On my left the end wall had bellied-in towards me in a pair of gargantuan lips, black and utterly monstrous, to within a yard of my face. I fumbled for a mad instant at my revolver; not for *it*, but myself, for the danger was a thousand times worse than death. And then suddenly the Unknown Last Line of the Saaamaaa Ritual was whispered quite audibly in the room. Instantly the thing happened that I have known once before. There came a sense as of dust falling continually and monotonously and I knew that my life hung uncertain and suspended for a flash in a brief, reeling vertigo of unseeable things. Then *that* ended and I knew that I might live. My soul and body blended again and life and power came to me. I dashed furiously at the window and hurled myself out head-foremost, for I can tell you that I had stopped being afraid of death. I crashed down on to the ladder and slithered, grabbing and grabbing and so came some way or other alive to the bottom. And there I sat in the soft, wet grass with the moonlight all about me and far above through the broken window of the Room, there was a low whistling.

'That is the chief of it. I was not hurt and I went round to the front and knocked Tassoc up. When they let me in we had a long yarn over some good whisky – for I was shaken to pieces – and I explained things as much as I could. I told Tassoc that the Room would have to come down and every fragment of it be burned in a blast-furnace erected within a pentacle. He nodded. There was nothing to say. Then I went to bed.

'We turned a small army on to the work and within ten days that lovely thing had gone up in smoke and what was left was calcined and clean.

'It was when the workmen were stripping the panelling that I got hold of a sound notion of the beginnings of that beastly development. Over the great fireplace, after the great oak panels had been torn down, I found that there was let into the masonry a scrollwork of stone with on it an old inscription in ancient Celtic, that here in this room was burned Dian Tiansay, Jester of King Alzof, who made the Song of Foolishness upon King Ernore of the Seventh Castle.

'When I got the translation clear I gave it to Tassoc. He was tremendously excited for he knew the old tale and took me down to the library to look at an old parchment that gave the story in detail. Afterwards I found that the incident was well-known about the countryside, but always regarded more as a legend, than as history. And no one seemed ever to have dreamt that the old East Wing of Iastrae Castle was the remains of the ancient Seventh Castle.

'From the old parchment I gathered that there had been a pretty dirty job done, away back in the years. It seems that King Alzof and King Ernore had been enemies by birthright, as you might say truly, but that nothing more than a little raiding had occurred on either side for years until Dian Tiansay made the Song of Foolishness upon King Ernore and sang it before King Alzof, and so greatly was it appreciated that King Alzof gave the jester one of his ladies to wife.

'Presently all the people of the land had come to know the song and so it came at last to King Ernore who was so angered that he made war upon his old enemy and took and burned him and his castle; but Dian Tiansay, the jester, he brought with him to his own place and having torn his tongue out because of the song which he had made and sung, he imprisoned him in the Room in the East Wing (which was evidently used for unpleasant purposes), and the jester's wife he kept for himself, having a fancy for her prettiness.

'But one night, Dian Tiansay's wife was not to be found and in the morning they discovered her lying dead in her husband's arms and he sitting, whistling the Song of Foolishness, for he had no longer the power to sing it.

'Then they roasted Dian Tiansay in the great fireplace – probably from that self-same "gallows-iron" which I have already mentioned. And until he died Dian Tiansay "ceased not to whistle" the Song of Foolishness which he could no longer sing. But afterwards "in that room" there was often heard at night the sound of something whistling and there "grew a power in that room" so that none dared to sleep in it. And presently, it would seem, the King went to another castle for the whistling troubled him.

'There you have it all. Of course, that is only a rough rendering of the translation from the parchment. It's a bit quaint! Don't you think so?'

'Yes,' I said, answering for the lot. 'But how did the thing grow to such a tremendous manifestation?'

'One of those cases of continuity of thought producing a positive action upon the immediate surrounding material,' replied Carnacki. 'The development must have been going forward through centuries, to have produced such a monstrosity. It was a true instance of Saiitii manifestation which I can best explain by likening it to a living spiritual fungus which involves the very structure of the aether-fibre itself and, of course, in so doing acquires an essential control over the "material-substance" involved in it. It is impossible to make it plainer in a few words.'

'What broke the seventh hair?' asked Taylor.

But Carnacki did not know. He thought it was probably nothing but being too severely tensioned. He also explained that they found out that the men who had run away had not been up to mischief, but had come over secretly merely to hear the whistling which, indeed, had suddenly become the talk of the whole countryside.

'One other thing,' said Arkright, 'have you any idea what governs the use of the Unknown Last Line of the Saaamaaa Ritual? I know, of course, that it was used by the Ab-human

Priests in the Incantation of the Raaee, but what used it on your behalf and what made it?'

'You had better read Harzam's Monograph and my Addenda to it, on Astral and "Astarral" Co-ordination and Interference,' said Carnacki. 'It is an extraordinary subject and I can only say here that the human-vibration may not be insulated from the "astarral" (as is always believed to be the case in interferences by the Ab-human), without immediate action being taken by those Forces which govern the spinning of the outer circle. In other words, it is being proved, time after time, that there is some inscrutable Protective Force constantly intervening between the human-soul (not the body, mind you) and the Outer Monstrosities. Am I clear?'

'Yes, I think so,' I replied. 'And you believe that the Room had become the material expression of the ancient Jester – that his soul, rotted with hatred, had bred into a monster – eh?' I asked.

'Yes,' said Carnacki, nodding. 'I think you've put my thought rather neatly. It is a queer coincidence that Miss Donnehue is supposed to be descended (so I heard since) from the same King Ernore. It makes one think some rather curious thoughts, doesn't it? The marriage coming on and the Room waking to fresh life. If she had gone into that room, ever . . . eh? IT had waited a long time. Sins of the fathers. Yes, I've thought of that. They're to be married next week and I am to be best man, which is a thing I hate. And he won his bets, rather! Just think, *if* ever she had gone into that room. Pretty horrible, eh?'

He nodded his head, grimly, and we four nodded back. Then he rose and took us collectively to the door and presently thrust us forth in friendly fashion on to the Embankment and into the fresh night air.

'Good night,' we all called back and went to our various homes.

If she had, eh? If she had? That is what I kept thinking.

Teig O'Kane and the Corpse

Douglas Hyde

There was once a grown-up lad in the County Leitrim, and he was strong and lively, and the son of a rich farmer. His father had plenty of money, and he did not spare it on the son. Accordingly, when the boy grew up he liked sport better than work, and, as his father had no other children, he loved this one so much that he allowed him to do in everything just as it pleased himself. He was very extravagant, and he used to scatter the gold money as another person would scatter the white. He was seldom to be found at home, but if there was a fair, or a race, or a gathering within ten miles of him, you were dead certain to find him there. And he seldom spent a night in his father's house, but he used to be always out rambling, and, like Shawn Bwee long ago, there was

grádh gach cailin i mbrollach a léine,

'the love of every girl in the breast of his shirt,' and it's many's the kiss he got and he gave, for he was very handsome, and there wasn't a girl in the country but would fall in love with him, only for him to fasten his two eyes on her, and it was for that someone made this rann on him —

Look at the rogue, it's for kisses he's rambling,
It isn't much wonder, for that was his way;
He's like an old hedgehog, at night he'll be scrambling

323

From this place to that, but he'll sleep in the day.

At last he became very wild and unruly. He wasn't to be seen day or night in his father's house, but always rambling or going on his kailee[1] from place to place and from house to house, so that the old people used to shake their heads and say to one another, 'It's easy seen what will happen to the land when the old man dies; his son will run through it in a year, and it won't stand him that long itself.'

He used to be always gambling and card-playing and drinking, but his father never minded his bad habits, and never punished him. But it happened one day that the old man was told that the son had ruined the character of a girl in the neighbourhood, and he was greatly angry, and he called the son to him, and said to him, quietly and sensibly – 'Avic,' says he, 'you know I loved you greatly up to this, and I never stopped you from doing your choice thing whatever it was, and I kept plenty of money with you, and I always hoped to leave you the house and land, and all I had after myself would be gone; but I heard a story of you today that has disgusted me with you. I cannot tell you the grief that I felt when I heard such a thing of you, and I tell you now plainly that unless you marry that girl I'll leave house and land and everything to my brother's son. I never could leave it to anyone who would make so bad a use of it as you do yourself, deceiving women and coaxing girls. Settle with yourself now whether you'll marry that girl and get my land as a fortune with her, or refuse to marry her and give up all that was coming to you; and tell me in the morning which of the two things you have chosen.'

'Och! *Domnoo Sheery*! father, you wouldn't say that to me, and I such a good son as I am. Who told you I wouldn't marry the girl?' says he.

But his father was gone, and the lad knew well enough that he

[1] night visit

324

would keep his word too; and he was greatly troubled in his mind, for as quiet and as kind as the father was, he never went back on a word that he had once said, and there wasn't another man in the country who was harder to bend than he was.

The boy did not know rightly what to do. He was in love with the girl indeed, and he hoped to marry her sometime or other, but he would much sooner have remained another while as he was, and follow on at his old tricks – drinking, sporting, and playing cards; and, along with that, he was angry that his father should order him to marry, and should threaten him if he did not do it.

'Isn't my father a great fool,' says he to himself. 'I was ready enough, and only too anxious, to marry Mary; and now since he threatened me, faith I've a great mind to let it go another while.'

His mind was so much excited that he remained between two notions as to what he should do. He walked out into the night at last to cool his heated blood, and went on to the road. He lit a pipe, and as the night was fine he walked and walked on, until the quick pace made him begin to forget his trouble. The night was bright, and the moon half full. There was not a breath of wind blowing, and the air was calm and mild. He walked on for nearly three hours, when he suddenly remembered that it was late in the night, and time for him to turn. 'Musha! I think I forgot myself,' says he; 'it must be near twelve o'clock now.'

The word was hardly out of his mouth, when he heard the sound of many voices, and the trampling of feet on the road before him. 'I don't know who can be out so late at night as this, and on such a lonely road,' said he to himself.

He stood listening, and he heard the voices of many people talking through other, but he could not understand what they were saying. 'Oh, wirra!' says he, 'I'm afraid. It's not Irish or English they have; it can't be they're Frenchmen!' He went on a couple of yards further, and he saw well enough by the light of the moon a band of little people coming towards him, and they were carrying something big and heavy with them. 'Oh, murder!'

says he to himself, 'sure it can't be that they're the good people that's in it!' Every rib of hair that was on his head stood up, and there fell a shaking on his bones, for he saw that they were coming to him fast.

He looked at them again, and perceived that there were about twenty little men in it, and there was not a man at all of them higher than about three feet or three feet and a half, and some of them were grey, and seemed very old. He looked again, but he could not make out what was the heavy thing they were carrying until they came up to him, and then they all stood round about him. They threw the heavy thing down on the road, and he saw on the spot that it was a dead body.

He became as cold as the Death, and there was not a drop of blood running in his veins when an old little grey maneen came up to him and said, 'Isn't it lucky we met you, Teig O'Kane?'

Poor Teig could not bring out a word at all, nor open his lips, if he were to get the world for it, and so he gave no answer.

'Teig O'Kane,' said the little grey man again, 'isn't it timely you met us?'

Teig could not answer him.

'Teig O'Kane,' says he, 'the third time, isn't it lucky and timely that we met you?'

But Teig remained silent, for he was afraid to return an answer, and his tongue was as if it was tied to the roof of his mouth.

The little grey man turned to his companions, and there was joy in his bright little eye. 'And now,' says he, 'Teig O'Kane hasn't a word, we can do with him what we please. Teig, Teig,' says he, 'you're living a bad life, and we can make a slave of you now, and you cannot withstand us, for there's no use in trying to go against us. Lift that corpse.'

Teig was so frightened that he was only able to utter the two words, 'I won't'; for as frightened as he was he was obstinate and stiff, the same as ever.

'Teig O'Kane won't lift the corpse,' said the little maneen, with a wicked little laugh, for all the world like the breaking of a lock of dry kippeens, and with a little harsh voice like the striking of a cracked bell. 'Teig O'Kane won't lift the corpse – make him lift it'; and before the word was out of his mouth they had all gathered round poor Teig, and they all talking and laughing through each other.

Teig tried to run from them, but they followed him, and a man of them stretched out his foot before him as he ran, so that Teig was thrown in a heap on the road. Then before he could rise up the fairies caught him, some by the hands and some by the feet, and they held him tight, in a way that he could not stir, with his face against the ground. Six or seven of them raised the body then, and pulled it over to him, and left it down on his back. The breast of the corpse was squeezed against Teig's back and shoulders, and the arms of the corpse were thrown around Teig's neck. Then they stood back from him a couple of yards, and let him get up. He rose, foaming at the mouth and cursing, and he shook himself, thinking to throw the corpse off his back. But his fear and his wonder were great when he found that the two arms had a tight hold round his own neck, and that the two legs were squeezing his hips firmly, and that, however strongly he tried, he could not throw it off, any more than a horse can throw off its saddle. He was terribly frightened then, and he thought he was lost. 'Ochone! for ever,' said he to himself, 'it's the bad life I'm leading that has given the good people this power over me. I promise to God and Mary, Peter and Paul, Patrick and Bridget, that I'll mend my ways for as long as I have to live, if I come clear out of this danger – and I'll marry the girl.'

The little grey man came up to him again, and said he to him, 'Now, Teig*een*,' says he, 'you didn't lift the body when I told you to lift it, and see how you were made to lift it; perhaps when I tell you to bury it, you won't bury it until you're made to bury it!'

'Anything at all that I can do for your honour,' said Teig, 'I'll do it,' for he was getting sense already, and if it had not been for the great fear that was on him, he never would have let that civil word slip out of his mouth.

The little man laughed a sort of laugh again. 'You're getting quiet now, Teig,' says he. 'I'll go bail but you'll be quiet enough before I'm done with you. Listen to me now, Teig O'Kane, and if you don't obey me in all I'm telling you to do, you'll repent it. You must carry with you this corpse that is on your back to Teampoll-Démus, and you must bring it into the church with you, and make a grave for it in the very middle of the church, and you must raise up the flags and put them down again the very same way, and you must carry the clay out of the church and leave the place as it was when you came, so that no one could know that there had been anything changed. But that's not all. Maybe that the body won't be allowed to be buried in that church; perhaps some other man has the bed, and, if so, it's likely he won't share it with this one. If you don't get leave to bury it in Teampoll-Démus, you must carry it to Carrick-fhad-vic-Orus, and bury it in the churchyard there; and if you don't get it into that place, take it with you to Teampoll-Ronan; and if that churchyard is closed on you, take it to Imlogue-Fada; and if you're not able to bury it there, you've no more to do than to take it to Kill-Breedya, and you can bury it there without hindrance. I cannot tell you what one of those churches is the one where you will have leave to bury that corpse under the clay, but I know that it will be allowed you to bury him at some church or other of them. If you do this work rightly, we will be thankful to you, and you will have no cause to grieve; but if you are slow or lazy, believe me we shall take satisfaction of you.'

When the grey little man had done speaking, his comrades laughed and clapped their hands together. 'Glic! Glic! Hwee! Hwee!' they all cried; 'go on, go on, you have eight hours before you till daybreak, and if you haven't this man buried before the sun rises, you're lost.' They struck a fist and a foot behind on him, and drove him on in the road. He was obliged to walk, and to walk fast, for they gave him no rest.

He thought himself that there was not a wet path, or a dirty boreen, or a crooked contrary road in the whole county, that he had not walked that night. The night was at times very dark, and whenever there would come a cloud across the moon he could see nothing, and then he used often to fall. Sometimes he was hurt, and sometimes he escaped, but he was obliged always to rise on the moment and to hurry on. Sometimes the moon would break out clearly, and then he would look behind him and see the little people following at his back. And he heard them speaking amongst themselves, talking and crying out, and screaming like a flock of sea-gulls; and if he was to save his soul he never understood as much as one word of what they were saying.

He did not know how far he had walked, when at last one of them cried out to him, 'Stop here!' He stood, and they all gathered round him.

'Do you see those withered trees over there?' says the old boy to him again. 'Teampoll-Démus is among those trees, and you must go in there by yourself, for we cannot follow you or go with you. We must remain here. Go on boldly.'

Teig looked from him, and he saw a high wall that was in places half broken down, and an old grey church on the inside of the wall, and about a dozen withered old trees scattered here and there round it. There was neither leaf nor twig on any of them, but their bare crooked branches were stretched out like the arms of an angry man when he threatens. He had no help for it, but was obliged to go forward. He was a couple of hundred yards from the church, but he walked on, and never looked behind him until he came to the gate of the churchyard. The old gate was thrown down, and he had no difficulty in entering. He turned then to see if any of the little people were following him, but there came a cloud over the moon, and the night became so dark that he could see nothing. He went into the churchyard, and he walked up the old grassy pathway leading to the church. When he reached the door, he found it locked. The door was large and strong, and he did not know what to do. At last he drew out his knife with difficulty, and stuck it in the wood to try if it were not rotten, but it was not.

'Now,' said he to himself, 'I have no more to do; the door is shut, and I can't open it.'

Before the words were rightly shaped in his own mind, a voice in his ear said to him, 'Search for the key on the top of the door, or on the wall.'

He started. 'Who is that speaking to me?' he cried, turning round; but he saw no one. The voice said in his ear again, 'Search for the key on the top of the door, or on the wall.'

'What's that?' said he, and the sweat running from his forehead; 'who spoke to me?'

'It's I, the corpse, that spoke to you!' said the voice.

'Can you talk?' said Teig.

'Now and again,' said the corpse.

Teig searched for the key, and he found it on the top of the wall. He was too much frightened to say any more, but he opened the door wide, and as quickly as he could, and he went in, with the corpse on his back. It was as dark as pitch inside, and poor Teig began to shake and tremble.

'Light the candle,' said the corpse.

Teig put his hand in his pocket, as well as he was able, and drew out a flint and steel. He struck a spark out of it, and lit a burnt rag he had in his pocket. He blew it until it made a flame, and he looked round him. The church was very ancient, and part of the wall was broken down. The windows were blown in or cracked, and the timber of the seats were rotten. There were six or seven old iron candle-sticks left there still, and in one of these candlesticks Teig found the stump of an old candle, and he lit it. He was still looking round him on the strange and horrid place in which he found himself, when the cold corpse whispered in his ear, 'Bury me now, bury me now; there is a spade and turn the ground.' Teig looked from him, and he saw a spade lying beside the altar. He took it up, and he placed the blade under a flag that was in the middle of the aisle, and leaning all his weight on the handle of the spade, he raised it. When the first flag was raised it was not hard to raise the others near it, and he moved three or four of them out of their places. The clay that was under them was soft and easy to dig, but he had not thrown up more than three or four shovelfuls when he felt the iron touch something soft like flesh. He threw up three or four more shovelfuls from around it, and then he saw that it was another body that was buried in the same place.

'I am afraid I'll never be allowed to bury the two bodies in the same hole,' said Teig, in his own mind. 'You corpse, there on my back,' says he, 'will you be satisfied if I bury you down here?' But the corpse never answered him a word.

'That's a good sign,' said Teig to himself. 'Maybe he's getting quiet,' and he thrust the spade down in the earth again. Perhaps he hurt the flesh of the other body, for the dead man that was buried there stood up in the grave, and shouted an awful shout. 'Hoo! hoo!! hoo!!! Go! go!! go!!! or you're a dead, dead, dead man!' And then he fell back in the grave again. Teig said afterwards, that of all the wonderful things he saw that night, that was the most awful to him. His hair stood upright on his head like the bristles of a pig, the cold sweat ran off his face, and then came a tremour over all his bones, until he thought that he must fall.

But after a while he became bolder, when he saw that the second corpse remained lying quietly there, and he threw in the clay on it again, and he smoothed it overhead, and he laid down the flags carefully as they had been before. 'It can't be that he'll rise up any more,' said he.

He went down the aisle a little further, and drew near to the door, and began raising the flags again, looking for another bed for the corpse on his back. He took up three or four flags and put them aside, and then he dug the clay. He was not long digging until he laid bare an old woman without a thread upon her but her shirt. She was more lively than the first corpse, for he had scarcely taken any of the clay away from about her, when she sat

331

up and began to cry, 'Ho, you bodach![2] Ha, you bodach! Where has he been that he got no bed?'

Poor Teig drew back, and when she found that she was getting no answer, she closed her eyes gently, lost her vigour, and fell back quietly and slowly under the clay. Teig did to her as he had done to the man – he threw the clay back on her, and left the flags down overhead.

He began digging again near the door, but before he had thrown up more than a couple of shovelfuls, he noticed a man's hand laid bare by the spade. 'By my soul, I'll go no further, then,' said he to himself; 'what use is it for me?' And he threw the clay in again on it, and settled the flags as they had been before.

He left the church then, and his heart was heavy enough, but he shut the door and locked it, and left the key where he found it. He sat down on a tombstone that was near the door, and began thinking. He was in great doubt what he should do. He laid his face between his two hands, and cried for grief and fatigue, since he was dead certain at this time that he never would come home alive. He made another attempt to loosen the hands of the corpse that were squeezed round his neck, but they were as tight as if they were clamped; and the more he tried to loosen them, the tighter they squeezed him. He was going to sit down once more, when the cold, horrid lips of the dead man said to him, 'Carrickfhad-vic-Orus,' and he remembered the command of the good people to bring the corpse with him to that place if he should be unable to bury it where he had been.

He rose up, and looked about him. 'I don't know the way,' he said.

As soon as he had uttered the word, the corpse stretched out suddenly its left hand that had been tightened round his neck, and kept it pointing out, showing him the road he ought to follow. Teig went in the direction that the fingers were stretched, and

[2]clown

332

passed out of the churchyard. He found himself on an old rutty, stony road, and he stood still again, not knowing where to turn. The corpse stretched out its bony hand a second time, and pointed out to him another road – not the road by which he had come when approaching the old church. Teig followed that road, and whenever he came to a path or road meeting it, the corpse always stretched out its hand and pointed with its fingers, showing him the way he was to take.

Many was the cross-road he turned down, and many was the crooked boreen he walked, until he saw from him an old burying-ground at last, beside the road, but there was neither church nor chapel nor any other building in it. The corpse squeezed him tightly, and he stood. 'Bury me, bury me in the burying-ground,' said the voice.

Teig drew over towards the old burying-place, and he was not more than about twenty yards from it, when, raising his eyes, he saw hundreds and hundreds of ghosts – men, women, and children – sitting on the top of the wall round about, or standing on the inside of it, or running backwards and forwards, and pointing at him, while he could see their mouths opening and shutting as if they were speaking, though he heard no word, nor any sound amongst them at all.

He was afraid to go forward, so he stood where he was, and the moment he stood, all the ghosts became quiet, and ceased moving. Then Teig understood that it was trying to keep him from going in, that they were. He walked a couple of yards forwards, and immediately the whole crowd rushed together towards the spot to which he was moving, and they stood so thickly together that it seemed to him that he never could break through them, even though he had a mind to try. But he had no mind to try it. He went back broken and dispirited, and when he had gone a couple of hundred yards from the burying-ground, he stood again, for he did not know what way he was to go. He heard the voice of the corpse in his ear, saying, 'Teampoll-Ronan,' and the skinny hand was stretched out again, pointing him out the road.

As tired as he was, he had to walk, and the road was neither short nor even. The night was darker than ever, and it was difficult to make his way. Many was the toss he got, and many a bruise they left on his body. At last he saw Teampoll-Ronan from him in the distance, standing in the middle of the burying-ground. He moved over towards it, and thought he was all right and safe, when he saw no ghosts nor anything else on the wall, and he thought he would never be hindered now from leaving his load off him at last. He moved over to the gate, but as he was passing in, he tripped on the threshold. Before he could recover himself, something that he could not see seized him by the neck, by the hands, and by the feet, and bruised him, and shook him, and choked him, until he was nearly dead; and at last he was lifted up, and carried more than a hundred yards from that place, and then thrown down in an old dyke, with the corpse still clinging to him.

He rose up, bruised and sore, but feared to go near the place again, for he had seen nothing the time he was thrown down and carried away.

'You corpse, up on my back?' said he, 'shall I go over again to the churchyard?' – but the corpse never answered him. 'That's a sign you don't wish me to try it again,' said Teig.

He was now in great doubt as to what he ought to do, when the corpse spoke in his ear, and said, 'Imlogue-Fada.'

'Oh, murder!' said Teig, 'must I bring you there? If you keep me long walking like this, I tell you I'll fall under you.'

He went on, however, in the direction the corpse pointed out to him. He could not have told, himself, how long he had been going, when the dead man behind suddenly squeezed him, and said, 'There!'

Teig looked from him, and he saw a little low wall, that was so broken down in places that it was no wall at all. It was in a great wide field, in from the road; and only for three or four great stones at the corners, that were more like rocks than stones, there was nothing to show that there was either graveyard or burying ground there.

'Is this Imlogue-Fada? Shall I bury you here?' said Teig.

'Yes,' said the voice.

'But I see no grave or gravestone, only this pile of stones,' said Teig.

The corpse did not answer, but stretched out its long fleshless hand to show Teig the direction in which he was to go. Teig went on accordingly, but he was greatly terrified, for he remembered what had happened to him at the last place. He went on, 'with his heart in his mouth,' as he said himself afterwards; but when he came to within fifteen or twenty yards of the little low square wall, there broke out a flash of lightning, bright yellow and red, with blue streaks in it, and went round about the wall in one course, and it swept by as fast as the swallow in the clouds, and the longer Teig remained looking at it the faster it went, till at last it became like a bright ring of flame round the old graveyard, which no one could pass without being burnt by it. Teig never saw, from the time he was born, and never saw afterwards, so wonderful or so splendid a sight as that was. Round went the flame, white and yellow and blue sparks leaping out from it as it went, and although at first it had been no more than a thin, narrow line, it increased slowly until it was at last a great broad band, and it was continually getting broader and higher, and throwing out more brilliant sparks, till there was never a colour on the ridge of the earth that was not to be seen in that fire; and lightning never shone and flame never flamed that was so shining and so bright as that.

Teig was amazed; he was half dead with fatigue, and he had no courage left, to approach the wall. There fell a mist over his eyes, and there came a soorawn[3] in his head, and he was obliged to sit down upon a great stone to recover himself. He could see nothing but the light, and he could hear nothing but the whirr of

[3]vertigo

it as it shot round the paddock faster than a flash of lightning.

As he sat there on the stone, the voice whispered once more in his ear, 'Kill-Breedya'; and the dead man squeezed him so tightly that he cried out. He rose again, sick, tired, and trembling, and went forward as he was directed. The wind was cold, and the road was bad, and the load upon his back was heavy, and the night was dark, and he himself was nearly worn out, and if he had had very much farther to go he must have fallen dead under his burden.

At last the corpse stretched out its hand, and said to him, 'Bury me there.'

'This is the last burying-place,' said Teig in his own mind; 'and the little grey man said I'd be allowed to bury him in some of them, so it must be this; it can't be but they'll let him in here.'

The first faint streak of the ring of day was appearing in the east, and the clouds were beginning to catch fire, but it was darker than ever, for the moon was set, and there were no stars.

'Make haste, make haste!' said the corpse; and Teig hurried forward as well as he could to the graveyard, which was a little place on a bare hill, with only a few graves in it. He walked boldly in through the open gate, and nothing touched him, nor did he either hear or see anything. He came to the middle of the ground, and then stood up and looked round him for a spade or shovel to make a grave. As he was turning round and searching, he suddenly perceived what startled him greatly – a newly-dug grave right before him. He moved over to it, and looked down, and there at the bottom he saw a black coffin. He clambered down into the hole and lifted the lid, and found that (as he thought it would be) the coffin was empty. He had hardly mounted up out of the hole, and was standing on the brink, when the corpse, which had clung to him for more than eight hours, suddenly relaxed its hold of his neck, and loosened its shins from round his hips, and sank down with a *plop* into the open coffin.

Teig fell down on his two knees at the brink of the grave, and gave thanks to God. He made no delay then, but pressed down the coffin lid in its place, and threw in the clay over it with his two hands, and when the grave was filled up, he stamped and leaped on it with his feet, until it was firm and hard, and then he left the place.

The sun was fast rising as he finished his work, and the first thing he did was to return to the road, and look out for a house to rest himself in. He found an inn at last; and lay down upon a bed there, and slept till night. Then he rose up and ate a little, and fell asleep again till morning. When he awoke in the morning he hired a horse and rode home. He was more than twenty-six miles from home where he was, and he had come all that way with the dead body on his back in one night.

All the people at his own home thought that he must have left the country, and they rejoiced greatly when they saw him come back. Everyone began asking him where he had been, but he would not tell anyone except his father.

He was a changed man from that day. He never drank too much; he never lost his money over cards; and especially he would not take the world and be out late by himself of a dark night.

He was not a fortnight at home until he married Mary, the girl he had been in love with, and it's at their wedding the sport was, and it's he was the happy man from that day forward, and it's all I wish that we may be as happy as he was.

The Ghost in the Machine

Kevin Carolan

'You're sending me to Ireland. What is this – some kind of joke!'

Jack Ross was never normally aggressive with more senior colleagues in the company, but he was worried. Aged thirty-five, he was on the fast track to promotion to the board of directors. Ireland sounded like a sideline into some kind of dead-end job. Despite his best efforts to control it, the concern showed in his voice.

The other man replied calmly. 'Don't worry, Jack. This is no joke. In fact, it's a big job that is a great opportunity for you.'

Milton Bain was Managing Director (Europe) of Communi-com Inc. He was normally affable enough, although people said that he smiled only with his mouth and not with his eyes. It was generally accepted in the company that you crossed him at your peril. Bain got to the point.

'You've probably heard that we're building a big new computer factory in Ireland – it's the new Alpha 10 workstation. The problem is that the construction of the plant is running behind schedule. I want *you* to go to Ireland and take charge of the factory – technically you'll be Production Director. Sort out the problems, and get us first to market. I'm due to go back to the States in a year's time. Do a good job, and I'll be happy to propose you to the board as my successor.'

Ross was not totally convinced. 'But why Ireland? It seems a long way from the main customers. Wouldn't Britain or Germany make more sense?'

'Look, we get EU grants to build the plant, and then the Irish government lets us off any taxes on the profits. It's a no-brainer!'

Bain then fixed Ross with an unblinking gaze.

'I can rely on you, Jack, can't I?'

Put that way Ross had to accept it. Within four hours he was on a flight to Dublin. The factory itself was on the west of Ireland, near the city of Limerick, but he had to fly to Dublin first to spend a couple of days with the bankers to the project. On the plane over he wondered what it would be like. An Englishman himself, he was used to flying all over the US and the Continent, but had never been to Ireland. The discussions with the bankers were fairly relaxed and amicable, and they took place in better restaurants than he was expecting. Ross looked forward to returning to Dublin. It also became clear how critical it was to get the project back on time. The plant was due to be finished in six months, but construction was already a month behind.

It was quick and easy to get to Limerick. There was a modern jet rather than the turboprop aircraft he was expecting. The airport itself was surprisingly large and modern. Landing formalities were few, and he soon found himself in a taxi heading west to the little town of Boolebeg where the plant was located. The road quickly dwindled into a simple narrow lane, but traffic was light and they made good speed. Once they left Limerick behind fields replaced the houses, although Ross was in no mood to enjoy the scenery. Dublin had been warm and sunny, but the weather here was dark and overcast, with a steady drizzle of rain.

Plant Manager Jim Plunkett showed him the little bungalow, near the plant, where he would be living. Plunkett had reddish-fair hair and green eyes in a broad face, with an easy, warm manner.

'It's fairly basic, but you should be comfortable here. Breakfast and lunch are available from the staff canteen at the normal times and Doreen, the cleaner, will come in twice a week. She'll take care of any laundry or shopping you want done. There's also a quite decent pub in the town where you can get reasonable food – that's where most of us have our dinner. I hope that you will join us tonight. It will give you a chance to meet some of the staff.'

'I will,' replied Ross, 'but show me around the plant first.'

'Are you sure?' Plunkett's smile faltered. 'Operations have shut down for the night – there'll be nothing going on. Wouldn't you be better off looking round in the morning?'

'No, I want to see it now.' Ross realised that he ought to soften his tone. There was no point getting people's backs up on his first day on site. 'But I'd be pleased to go with you to the pub afterwards.'

The site was triangular, about six acres in size. One side was the road, another the sea, with the longest side a gentle slope up into the hills. As they walked in Ross saw the familiar glass and concrete shape of a Communicom factory. He couldn't restrain himself any longer.

'I hear we're a month behind schedule on the construction programme. So what's the problem? It all looks fine to me.'

Plunkett shrugged his shoulders! 'It's not too bad really. We're actually ahead of plan on the main assembly and distribution plant; it's practically ready. The problem lies with the semi-conductor testing room on the far side.'

Ross felt his heart leap. This was good news. The semi-conductor testing room was a key part of the factory, but it was only a small building which could be knocked up in a hurry if need be.

'So? That shouldn't take long.'

Plunkett looked embarrassed. 'There's been trouble with the workmen. It's the site, you see. The only place where we can put the testing room is on the side of the plant facing the hill, and the construction workers are being awkward about it.'

'What sort of awkward?'

'Well . . . well, a lot of them are local lads, and they have funny ideas. This may be a computer factory, but this area was the back of beyond until recently. The locals are a superstitious lot, and they say that it would bring bad luck to disturb the mound.'

'Mound – what mound?'

'Well, it's more like a very small hill covered with trees. According to local folklore, sometime in the last century Farmer Reilly tried to plough it up, and was found dead in his bed that night. Since then everybody has left it alone.'

At that, Ross insisted that they should stop looking over the plant, and go and see this mysterious hillock. Plunkett took a torch. When they got there Ross couldn't see what the fuss was all about. It looked like an ordinary field, with a slight bump in the corner, and with a few straggly trees on top. They soon left the plant and went on to the pub in the village for supper, which was ample in size if basic in taste. Plunkett introduced him to everybody, and Ross soon got to know them. After a while the excitement of the new boss's arrival died down as the workers got used to his presence. Ross was able to use the opportunity to chat to Brian Doolan, the construction foreman.

'They tell me,' he said, 'that you've been having problems with the construction.' Doolan looked tough, solid and self-assured. To Ross's ear his Irish accent seemed sharper, jerkier and more abrupt than most of the men present.

'I wouldn't say that,' he replied. 'We're just a little bit behind on the side extension. The main plant is ahead of schedule.'

'That's a bit like saying that the car's ready to go except for the tyres.' Ross's tone was curt. 'What's all this rubbish about superstition?'

Doolan smiled. He beckoned Ross to a corner, and spoke quietly.

'I'm a Dublin man, you know. It's all nonsense to me. But this is the west of Ireland. Until recently all they did here was cut turf and raise cows. You can give a peasant a computer but he's still a peasant. They're priest-ridden here, and they still believe in the little people.'

'Leprechauns?'

'That's what the ignorant call them. In the Irish tradition they're called the *Sidhe*. The locals round here think it's bad luck even to talk about them. Did you see those trees on that little mound? Those are ash trees. According to the old sayings, ash trees keep the little people away.'

'Look, uh, Brian, it's very important for the company that the plant is completed on time. Do people realise that they could be threatened with the sack unless they get on with their work?'

'You can't do that here,' replied Doolan. 'This is Ireland, not Thatcher's Britain. Fire a batch of workers and you'd get the Government down on you like a ton of bricks – they might even take back the grant they made to attract the company here in the first place.'

'Well, how do we build the wretched thing?'

Doolan leaned forward and whispered in Ross's ear. The man's breath stank of beer and tobacco.

'I have an idea. Next week it's St Patrick's Day, and the whole plant will shut down for a four-day long weekend. I could fly in some lads I know from Dublin. I'm sure we could sort it out in a couple of days. Of course, working on Patrick's Day is a great burden – we'd need special holiday pay rates.'

'How much is special?'

'A thousand pounds a day for me, and three hundred each for the lads required.'

'How many lads?'

'Three plus myself.'

'You don't get paid unless you complete the job!'

'Done!'

That night Ross went cheerfully to bed. Once he turned the light off he realised how dark and quiet it was in the country – quite unlike the cities he was used to. He woke up in the night from what he thought was a dream. He seemed to see a small dark figure, moving about in the room. It was not possible to distinguish any details, yet the figure seemed to possess great solidity. There was just the impression of an intensely black shape silhouetted against the lesser darkness of the room. In the morning sunshine he dismissed it, and for the next week all seemed well.

St Patrick's Day came. Ross told Doolan and Plunkett to meet him at the plant at eight o'clock sharp. For once the normal overcast conditions gave way to sunshine, although there was a biting wind coming off from the sea. Doolan had, in fact, four labourers with him. It did not take long get the chainsaws going, and within two hours the trees had been cut down. Digging out the roots took a lot longer, and at four o'clock they called it a day. That night, in the pub with Doolan and Plunkett, Ross drank more than he was used to. He felt optimistic for the first time since he had come to Boolebeg. Things really seemed to be looking up.

He woke up suddenly around 3 a.m. He had the dream again. This time there seemed to be two figures in the darkness. His eyes strained to make out any details, but it was impossible in the gloom. There was also seemed a sense of limited space, as if the bedroom itself had shrunk in size. He wanted to get away, but escape was impossible. To reassure himself, Ross put the lights on and looked around the house. Everything looked normal. There was a distinct chill in the air, but he convinced himself that this was hardly surprising, living as he did so close to the cold winds from the sea.

The next day was cold, wet and overcast, and a steady drizzle made it an unpleasant day to be out in the open. They only had one mechanical digger, so progress was slow. Doolan and the other workmen were wearing thick overalls and boots as they worked. Ross and Plunkett found their thin raincoats too cold to stand around in for long, and around ten o'clock they retreated to the main plant. Plunkett led the way to the small executive suite on the fourth floor, where some sandwiches had been left. As they went up Ross praised the intricate interweaving pattern on the wood panelling in the lift. Plunkett replied that this had been made by local craftsmen and based on ancient Celtic scrollwork. He added that he thought the staff were pleased at the attempts made by the company to give the factory a distinctively Irish character. They made themselves a warm and pleasant breakfast of coffee and sandwiches. Ross led the way to his office. He was annoyed that the sign he had ordered, *John E Ross PhD, Production Director*, had not yet been put on the door. He thought to himself how slow these people were; in New York they would have had the boss's nameplate up on the first day he ordered it. He saw Plunkett look appraisingly round the office.

'What are you looking at, Jim?'

'Just looking round, Jack. I haven't been here since Alex left. I see you've taken down the pictures he had on the wall.'

'Yeah, I think an office should be plain and functional, not all cluttered up. But tell me, why did Alexander leave? I heard in London that it was abrupt, but that was all. Was there a problem between him and Bain?'

'Yes.'

Plunkett looked extremely embarrassed. His hands were crossed across his chest and his eyes seemed glued to the floor. Clearly something odd had been going on. Ross wondered whether Alexander had been involved in some kind of dubious financial deal, and whether that was the real reason the plant was behind schedule. Typical of Bain not to tell him

'It's like this, Jack. All I know is that Bain accused Alex of "going native". There was a big row between them, and Alex left suddenly.'

'Do you know what the row was about?'

'The mound. You see, Alex's teenage daughter Peggy has suffered from bad asthma for years. Somehow she got involved with some travellers – gypsies – who live on the other side of the hill. There's some alleged "wise-woman", Mother Ryan, who lives in the camp there. She treated Peggy with herbal remedies, and the kid got better. After that Peggy treated the Ryan woman as some kind of guru. Anyway, she heard from her father about the plans for the semiconductor testing room, and told Mother Ryan about them. The old woman somehow persuaded Peggy that it would be bad for her family if the mound was demolished. Alex was crazy enough to believe her, and he even argued with Mr Bain about it.'

Ross looked out of the window. He saw that the workmen had totally levelled off the mound, and were now starting to dig the foundations of the testing room. This seemed a good time to ring London. Why not use the speakerphone to show Plunkett how close he was to Milton Bain?

'Milt? Hi, it's Jack here. I just thought you were due for an update. Things were slipping here, but I've tightened them up. It'll be tight, but we shouldn't be more than two weeks behind schedule when we start production.'

Ross actually thought there was a good chance of starting on time, but it was always sensible to have a bit of leeway. The voice on the other end of the line did not sound impressed.

'That's good, Jack, but not good enough. I hear that ABC Systems are launching their new workstation in the autumn. We've got to have the Alpha 10 ready for shipment in September. You can work out what that means – we've got have to production started by end July. I know that's a month earlier than we thought. Sure it's a tough schedule – but you can do it, can't you, Jack?'

Ross almost choked, but he could not afford to let Bain down.

'Sure, Milt, we'll manage it somehow.'

Feeling depressed, he rang off. The telephone rang again about ten minutes later. He thought it would Bain checking something else, but to his surprise it was Doolan on an internal line.

'Boss, come here at once!'

'What is it?'

'Boss, it's best you just come and look.'

Ross got there within minutes. The men had dug trenches going down about four feet. Odd-looking pieces of stone stuck out from some of the edges. The digger had come to a stop. The driver was standing by the side of the vehicle. He appeared upset. Doolan pointed to what looked like brown sticks caught in the prongs of the digger. Ross couldn't see what the fuss was about.

'So, what's the problem?'

'Boss, those are bones. We're digging into a grave! If we'd have known that, me and the boys would never have taken the job on.'

Ross thought quickly.

'Look, lads, if it's a grave, it must be an old one. Some of those trees must have been over a hundred years old. So there's nothing to worry about.'

'It's older than that, Jack.' Plunkett spoke quietly. 'Look over there, just under the prongs. You see that thing shining over there – it's a bronze *torque*. This is not an ordinary grave – it's an ancient barrow. We ought to tell the Museum of Ancient History in Dublin about this. It could be an important archaeological site.'

'Damn, damn, damn!' Ross's mind went into overdrive. His foot was tapping and he had to bite his lip to stop himself from shouting that he could not care less about their stupid superstitions, or what he thought they could do with their Irish museum. He wanted to scream at these imbeciles that the only thing that mattered was to get the job done. With a great effort of will he took control of himself. The key thing was to keep the situation quiet. It would be a disaster if Irish archaeologists got involved – the excavations could last for months.

'Look.' Ross smiled weakly. 'I know it may look old, but it probably isn't. Why go to all the trouble of getting the authorities in? Let's just keep it quiet and get on with the job.'

For about twenty minutes he argued and harangued the other men. Doolan and the other workmen refused to touch the bones, but for an extra bonus they agreed to keep their mouths shut about the find. Doolan said they would continue to build the foundations if Ross and Plunkett cleared the bones away. Ross turned to Plunkett.

'Right, Jim, you start removing the bones while I go and get a cardboard box to put them in. I'll come back and help you in a minute.'

'Sorry, Jack, I'm not touching them either.' Ross was astonished to hear Plunkett contradict him.

'I'm not superstitious, but I'm not going to break the law. It's up to you if you don't want to tell the authorities, but I don't want to be involved any more. I'm going home now – I'll see you at work on Monday as normal.' With that Plunkett walked away.

Ross made a mental note to put a black mark on Plunkett's record when he got back to London. There seemed nothing for it but to do it himself, so he went into the plant to get a big box. The workmen sat on the ground eating their sandwiches and drinking tea as they watched him pick up the bones. Ross could feel the damp coming through his shoes as he trudged through the thick, heavy clay. There were the remains of two skeletons, plus some filthy rags, and some curiously carved bits of bone or ivory that might have been a necklace. He had to rake around with Doolan's fork to be certain that he had removed all the bones. Lastly he picked up the *torque*. The yellow metal had been cast in a scrolling pattern to look like twisted hair. After two hours' hard work he had finished. He left Doolan to get on with the foundations, and put the box in the safe room. The door was double locked. Plunkett had the only other key to the room.

The hard, physical labour had been exhausting. Ross staggered into the lift to go to the executive washroom. Once he got there he looked at himself in the mirror, under the bright neon lights. Ross thought that he looked like a tramp, a man in an expensive suit that was torn and covered in mud. His face looked drawn. Then he noticed his hands. The mud on them seemed a curious red colour, almost like blood. He washed and washed his hands, but the clay was sticky, and the stain didn't seem to go away entirely. To Ross this seemed mute evidence that proved his illegal digging. In a panic he scrubbed the hands with a brush until the skin was almost raw, but he did not feel certain that the red hue had fully gone.

Ross went home feeling shattered, and collapsed into bed in his underclothes, throwing his ruined suit on the floor. He slept fitfully, his dreams stuck in a recurrent pattern. He was alone in the factory, but felt quite safe. *They* could not get him here, not with all the powerful lights on. Then there was a power cut. He saw some small, dark figures coming towards him. Their features were not visible in the gloom, but he seemed to see sharp teeth and long, claw-like hands. He ran, but did not know which way to go in the darkness. There was the pressure of long, bony hands on his back – at which point he woke up. The next night Ross was afraid to go to sleep, but the dream did not reoccur. By Monday morning he was feeling refreshed. Ross was pleased to see that Doolan had fulfilled his part of the bargain. The brick foundations of the testing room rose about four feet above the ground where the mound had once stood.

That morning Plunkett was invited up to his office. Neither spoke about the events of the previous week.

'Jim, I just wondered about the systems in the factory. What happens, for example, if there is a power cut?'

'There's no problem. We have a back-up generator which automatically starts up if the power is off for more than ten seconds.'

'What about the computer systems controlling the plant – how robust are they?'

'Everything is fault-tolerant to the highest degree. All the key systems – electricity and lights, water, security plus odds and sods like the lifts – are run by a master operating-system that essentially uses two minicomputers. In the unlikely event of one going down, the other has adequate capacity to run the whole thing. We use software that was designed for the space shuttle. You can't hack into the computers from outside either – there is a "firewall" to prevent hackers trying to come in from the Internet. But why do you ask?'

Ross shrugged. 'I just want to be sure that everything will work when we need it to. As you know, we're only a month away from prototype production.'

The next four weeks were a blaze of activity for everyone in the factory, as they rushed to get ready. The day came to run the prototype. Ross almost ran to work. At ten o'clock he pressed the button. Nothing happened. He pressed it again. Nothing happened. Plunkett checked all the contacts, which looked fine. It was agreed that it must be a software problem. The chief programmer was summoned. He bent over a keyboard and his fingers started flickering out commands. After about fifteen minutes he stood up, shaking his head.

'It's very strange. There's a file in the system which wasn't there yesterday. It doesn't look like a virus, but it seems to be interfering with the instructions. It is curious. I can't seem to read it, nor does it seem to be written in any kind of programming language I recognise.'

Suddenly the printer burst forth into life, spilling out pages and pages of paper.

'Turn that damned thing off,' screamed Ross.

'I can't,' the programmer replied. 'I didn't instruct it to print, and I can't seem to instruct it to stop printing.'

Plunkett walked over and calmly pulled the plug of the printer out of its socket. The printing stopped.

Ross looked at the sheets of paper lying on the floor. All of them seemed covered with a meaningless scribble of letters. He picked one up to show Plunkett.

'Look at this gibberish, Jim. What the hell's gone wrong with the software?' He glared at the programmer.

'It's not gibberish, Jack. It's the Old Irish, Gaelic. We had to learn it at school.'

'Well, what does it say?'

'I don't know. I hated learning the Gaelic at school, it was worse than the Latin the monks made us study. I can recognise it, but I can't read it. But here in Limerick we're in the *Gaeltacht*, one of the few places where it hasn't entirely died out. There must be someone in the factory who can read it.'

After a few minutes a middle-aged woman was found who claimed to know Gaelic. Ross could not contain his impatience.

'Are you sure you can read it?'

'Sure? And me just after a course in the Gaelic!'

Ross handed her the paper in his hand. She read intently.

'The first sentence: *Bhearfad a rogha dhoibh, imeacht sa bhaile no fanuint*, means "I shall give them a choice, to go away to their homeland, or to stay". The second is: *Tiocfaidh se nuair is lu a bheidh coinne againn leis* – which in English is: "He will come when they least expect it." '

The other sheets of paper also contained similar paradoxical pronouncements. A mysterious person was going to come, there would be suffering, and then there would be peace.

It meant nothing to Ross. For two days the programming team struggled to get the system up and running, but without success. They made one breakthrough, however. The weird code could be traced back, via the network, to the safe room. Ross was sceptical as no computer equipment was kept there, but was forced to accept Plunkett's point that someone could have taken a portable computer into the safe room and downloaded the stuff into the system. They went down to see. The door was locked. Inside it was just as Ross had left it. There was no sign of any computer equipment. Plunkett spoke first.

'What's in that box? Maybe that's the source of the problem.'

'None of your business, Jim. It's my stuff.'

'Sweet Jasus, Ross, is that where you put the bones?'

'I said it's none of your business. Now, are you sure you haven't been in here, left the door unlocked or something?'

'I certainly haven't.'

'Good. But to be on the safe side, I want you to give me your key.'

350

'Ross, that's mine by right as Factory Manager.'

'And *it's my right* to demand it as Production Director!' Ross shouted to make the point. Sullenly, Plunkett handed over the key.

They went back to the programming room. No further progress had been made. Plunkett made the suggestion that Ross perhaps should visit Mother Ryan, to see if she could help. Initially, Ross was reluctant, but as the day dragged on the thought of explaining to Bain the halt in production increasingly weighed on his mind. Finally at five o'clock he jumped in the car and headed for the travellers' camp. It was about fifteen minutes away down a country lane. The lane petered out into an uneven track. Ross was forced to stop for fear the car would get stuck in a pothole. When he open the door he guessed he was on the right track by the foul smell which hit him, a mixture of rubbish and sweat. It took five minutes on foot to reach the camp. A girl pointed out Mother Ryan's caravan to him. As he approached he saw a large, fat woman with white hair waiting outside for him.

'Are you Mother Ryan?'

'And who else should I be?'

'Can I come in?'

'Certainly not, and you with the smell of a corpse about you. Do you think I'm an *ijeet*, to let you bring those black things with you into my house?'

'What black things?' Ross had not told anybody about the dreams.

'*Avic*, O my son, the two black shadows of the *Lianhan Sidhe* which follow you. You have stirred up an ancient evil, which must be appeased.'

'How do I get rid of them?'

'Sure it can't be a question of getting rid of them. In the old days, to be sure, the Druids put them to sleep with a wicker man, it was a giant statue of a man made in wicker. They put a criminal inside, then they burned it. That put the black shadows to sleep, but that is not possible now.'

'Well, what can I do?'

'My son, I can tell you that the shadows cannot cross deep water. You are English. Go back home, safe you will be there. But hurry, the shadows darken. *Go mbeire Dia slan abhaile thu* – may God bring you safe home, as the prayer is in the old tongue. Now go, and leave an old woman in peace.'

Mother Ryan refused the money he offered her. Ross wandered back in a daze. What should he do? All his life he had never questioned his ability to achieve what he wanted, but now the earth seemed to be slipping away from under his feet. Bain would never forgive him if he gave up halfway through. Ross felt a wave of determination run through him, and the way forward became clear. He drove into the centre of Limerick, and bought a large basket. Next on the list was a visit to a hardware shop where various items were bought. On the way back he dropped into the factory and came out carrying a large cardboard box. The security guard stopped him, but backed off when Ross pointed out who he was.

That night he slept with the lights on, tossing and turning. He woke up early, got dressed, and went into the garden to carry out the ritual he'd planned. 'I'm going to get you,' he told himself. The bones were tipped into the wicker basket, and then placed into the incinerator he had bought in town. He danced and sang to himself as the petrol was poured on top. It took about an hour for the flames to die down. The *torque* had been turned into a shapeless lump of metal. Ross was disappointed that the bones, while fragmented, had not totally turned into ash. Nevertheless, he carefully scooped everything up into the cardboard box, and drove to the coast where he threw it all into the sea. It was still only seven o'clock in the morning. He drove back home and lay on top of the bed. He had been asleep about half an hour when the phone rang.

'Mr Ross, it's me, Plunkett! Come to the factory at once! It's urgent!' The voice sounded oddly distant, as if ringing from long distance on a poor line.

'Why, what is it?' But the line went dead. He immediately rang Plunkett's direct line, but there was no reply. Cursing, Ross got into the car and drove to the plant. He got there at about ten to eight. The place looked deserted ahead of the first shift. The security guard seemed to be the only person about.

'I'm looking for Jim Plunkett. Where is he?'

'I don't think he's here yet, sir. He doesn't normally start work until eight o'clock.'

'Well, I think he's here today. As soon as you see him, tell him to come up to my office at once.'

Ross got into the lift, planning to have a strong word with Plunkett. Managers needed to get into work early, and set an example to the other workers. He wondered what the hell had got into the man to summon him to the factory, and then wander off. Maybe he ought to pass his doubts over Plunkett on to Bain. As the lift ascended he was struck by the woodcarving. Normally he ignored it, but today it seemed to be much brighter than usual. With a shudder he realised how closely the whirling pattern of the wood resembled that of the *torque*. The lift had gone past the second floor when it stopped with an abrupt jerk. Ross pressed the 'door open' button, but nothing happened. Suddenly the lights went out. Cursing, he reached for the matches in his pocket.

From the *West of Ireland Observer*, 27 July 1998

NEW FACTORY OPENS NEAR LIMERICK

Mr Milton Bain, Managing Director of Communicom Inc., yesterday formally opened the company's new computer factory based at Boolebeg, near Limerick. Mr Bain stood at the end of the production line as the first new computer came off. He said how pleased he was to donate the machine to the local Marian Sisters junior school. Mr Bain then paid tribute to the achievement of staff, and in particular the Production Director, in getting the plant operating on time. He said that this would enable the factory to generate significant jobs and income for the west of

Ireland for years to come, and he particularly praised Mr James Plunkett for taking over the job of Production Director under such difficult circumstances.

Editor's note: Mr Bain was referring to the tragic death by fire of Mr John Ross, as reported in the Observer *on 15 April. Mr Ross was found burned to death in a lift in the factory. The inquest returned an open verdict. While Ross's clothes had traces of petrol on them, and there were reports that he had been behaving oddly shortly before his death, the coroner stated that it was not clear what had started the fire, which had quickly taken hold in the wicker panelling of the lift. He warned against the use of this inflammable material in future.*